Who Killed Prospector?

Two hundred million miles from Earth, the nation's first commercial space probe is sending back enough information to keep a whole bank of supercomputers busy—until the computers show *Prospector* going up in a ball of flames . . .

Who, or what, destroyed *Prospector*?

Was it an alien spacecraft that exploded itself when *Prospector* got too close?

Or was it the very men who designed and controlled *Prospector*—knowing that the disaster will bring millions of Defense Department dollars?

. . . *or was* Prospector *never destroyed at all?*

PROBE

D1053845

PROBE

EDWARD M. LERNER

WARNER BOOKS

A Time Warner Company

This novel is a work of fiction. All the characters and events portrayed in it are likewise fictional, and any resemblance to real people or events is purely coincidental.

WARNER BOOKS EDITION

Cover design by Tony Greco
Cover illustration by Ben Perini

Warner Books, Inc.
666 Fifth Avenue
New York, N.Y. 10103

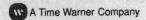 A Time Warner Company

Printed in the United States of America

First Printing: July, 1991

10 9 8 7 6 5 4 3 2 1

To Ruthie, with love. Without your help, patience, and encouragement this novel would never have been written. No thanks are adequate.

Prologue

Not every truth is the better for showing its
face undisguised; and often silence is the wisest
thing for a man to heed.

—Pindar
(518–438 B.C.)

The scale of the catastrophe was apparent well before the polls closed on the West Coast, although the network anchors worked unsuccessfully to maintain an air of suspense. After the vice president's early—and bitter—concession speech, the assembled scientists reluctantly kept listening.

Governor—make that President-elect—Benneford's victory oration lacked even a hint of conciliation. ". . . And so, my fellow citizens, Senator Ryan and I do not mistake today's outcome for a personal accomplishment, nor even primarily as the achievement of our great party. What, then, does today signify?"

During the early primaries, the quaintly antiestablishment, 1970s-style governor had been a national joke. Then an earthquake measuring 8.6 on the Richter scale had cracked the Alaskan pipeline, and a temporarily inaccessible pumping station had propelled black goo across a few square miles of tundra. It was just the latest in a series of *it can't happen* accidents dating back to the *Exxon Valdez* spill in 1989. One accident too many.

Objectively, the leak was a minor incident that the caribou

took in stride. Its subjective impact was quite different. Exit polls suggested that the Alaskan film footage, backdrop for endless network-news cleanup stories, swung three million votes in the late primaries.

Benneford held a healthy plurality of the delegates by the end of the primary season. Uncommitted delegates announced for Benneford, individually and in small groups, throughout the early summer. At a press conference two weeks before the convention, and with great fanfare, the governor introduced the head of the favorite-daughter Mississippi delegation—a party hack with a passion for pork barrel and an exquisite sense of timing—to deliver all of her delegates and put the candidate over the top.

The governor's luck held into the fall. In mid-October, an antique nuclear plant at Snechkus—built by the Soviets before Lithuania's secession and hence no longer maintained by them—suffered a near loss-of-coolant accident. The staff reacted quickly and no radiation escaped; the fallout was all political.

Benneford spent the campaign's final weeks pounding the pronuke Republicans with Snechkus, Chernobyl, and even Three Mile Island. It had been sheer, irresponsible hysteria mongering. It had also worked.

Benneford continued, at the top of his form. ". . . That Americans stood up to be counted. Today is the day that America joined its many global friends in the Green revolution. Today is the day that our nation wisely, and irreversibly, turned its back on deadly atomic power, on toxic wastes, on genetic tinkering, on environmental suicide.

"Technocrats and plutocrats, today America puts you on notice. We will no longer bear the risk of your folly. We will *not* build your dangerous playthings, nor subsidize them with tax breaks. We will *not* operate your ruinously expensive toys, your rockets and prototype fusion plants and never-big-enough particle accelerators. We will *not* tolerate bioengineering, your arrogant manipulation of the sacred essence of life itself.

"We will *not* destroy our national pocketbook for your amusement or your profit. We will *not* imperil our shared spaceship Earth." The televised audience of party faithful cheered itself hoarse.

"Bah," said the astrophysicist. "Spaceship Earth indeed. As if Luddites like Benneford know anything about space or spacecraft. They love their pretty orbital views of Earth, without even grasping how such pictures are taken."

The scientists shushed their colleague though they, too, had little appetite for Benneford's harangue. There was always the chance that Benneford had short coattails.

No such luck.

When the congressional trend appeared irreversible, the psychologist called them to order. Their murmuring gradually subsided. "As I predicted, Governor Benneford and his populist Democrats swept the elections. Besides the presidency, they will hold a clear working majority in both houses of the incoming Congress. We are agreed upon the significance of these results?" It was a rhetorical question.

The literal-minded astrophysicist answered regardless. "The slashing of government-funded research and the regulatory hobbling of private research. It means stagnation for them and mind-numbing idleness for us. We're surrounded by fools."

The psychologist ignored the interruption. "We previously agreed that we could not, and would not, accept this outcome. Does anyone know of any reason why we should not proceed as planned?"

This time there were no interruptions.

Part I

Force has no place where there is need for
skill.

—Herodotus
(ca. 485–ca. 425 B.C.)

Part I

A man has no place where words is read for

· CHAPTER 1 ·

The alarm clock took considerable undeserved abuse before he switched tactics and groped for the phone. The clock's inch-tall red numerals vengefully displayed 1:42 A.M. He managed only a one-word response, but it was suitably belligerent. "What."

"Bob? Is that you?"

Bob Hanson recognized the voice, and it had no business calling him at this hour. He'd left Carlton Moy, and the rest of Asgard Aerospace Corporation, seven hours ago, expecting the separation to last the weekend. Well, there must be a good reason. Better be damned good. "Yeah, Carlton, it's me." This time he added a bit of inflection.

"Sorry about the time, but I think you'd better get down here."

"Where's here?" Hanson turned on the bedside lamp switch. Unfortunately, there was no one else there to be awakened. Blinking at the too-bright light, he swung his feet to the floor and sat up.

"We're at the office."

A touch of curiosity made it into Hanson's voice. "We?"

"Parker, too. Bob, we need to talk. Now."

"Carlton, it's two in the morning! What's this about?"

"It's not something we can discuss over the phone."

Hanson wasn't sleepy anymore. "Sorry I snapped, Carlton. This isn't exactly prime time for me. See you in thirty minutes." In ten he was out the door.

Illinois 53 was deserted at this hour, which suited Hanson just fine. He popped his Honda Accord into overdrive, and Glenn Miller into the cassette deck, and tried to concentrate. Tuning out the filthy snow and the familiar expressway, he tried to figure out what the guys were up to.

Unfortunately, he didn't have a clue. What the hell would keep two of his section heads working into the middle of the night? Carlton Moy's engineering section was designing robots to help expand the NASA space station, *Freedom*. Bill Parker's programming section was writing software to analyze satellite observations of the South China Sea for signs of oil-bearing formations. That project was running so smoothly that Bill had been taking long skiing weekends. If there was any common denominator in their current assignments, he didn't see it. Beyond that, the two sections hadn't worked together since *Prospector* was launched, three years ago. *Prospector* was two hundred million miles away, days away from anything bigger than a pebble, and the most serious problem it had had in six months was a faulty spare memory unit.

To be honest, the most puzzling thing to Hanson was Bill Parker working late. On good days, Bill was hostile. Eight years after the fact, he still resented it that Hanson had been recruited from the outside for chief scientist—a position Parker felt he'd earned. He was still taking his frustration out on Hanson. Parker was just one of the nuisances—like approving purchase orders, or the battleship-gray wall paint—that had come with the job.

All of this introspection was getting him nowhere, Hanson decided. He got his mind back to driving in time to catch the

Algonquin Road exit ramp, and turned toward Asgard's five-story glass-and-steel office building in Rolling Meadows.

The slam of his car door echoed across Asgard's nearly empty parking lot. Carlton's office lights burned in the otherwise darkened fourth floor. In the bitter December cold, snow crunched under Hanson's feet. He dashed to the revolving door and pushed his way into the lobby.

The night security guard looked almost as happy as Hanson had felt twenty-five minutes ago—that is, not at all. He apparently didn't recognize the vice president of R&D. Hanson presented his company ID badge as a peace offering. It worked. "Please sign in, Dr. Hanson. Are you going to your office? I'll have to turn on your lights." Hanson nodded, walked across the lobby, and slid his badge into the card reader beside the door. The security computer read his ID off the magnetic strip, decided Hanson could be there, and unlatched the door with a click.

He took the elevator up, and walked through dimly lit halls to his office. True to his word, the guard had ordered the building management computer to turn on the lights. Hanson tossed his parka onto the chair, grabbed his lab notebook from the desk, and strode for Carlton's office.

Walking down the darkened hall, Hanson heard people arguing. He couldn't make out the words, but the voices sounded like Moy and Parker. When he got to Moy's office, the two scientists were sitting stiffly, their backs toward him, staring intently at the screen of the computer workstation. Moy was easily identifiable from behind by his straight, jet-black hair. Parker, at six three, towered over the Chinese physicist. The two must have heard him coming—they looked posed.

He stopped in the doorway. "Mad scientists work late. Film at ten." They turned slowly toward him. Yep, they'd heard him. Hanson set a hastily packed grocery bag amid the empty coffee cups on the office's small conference table: he removed a partial bucket of Kentucky Fried Chicken, four rye bagels, a bunch of bananas, and a two-liter bottle of Diet Coke. "I figured you guys hadn't eaten lately. Here's what Hanson Catering had in stock. Now explain what I'm doing here at this disgusting hour."

Moy and Parker exchanged a cryptic glance. The short Chinese physicist began. "I *do* apologize for bringing you here so late, but we've found something most extraordinary. I'm sure that we should be taking some action, and I wanted you to participate."

From long practice, Hanson cut through the polite Chinese circumlocution: he was there to settle a dispute between the two bickering subordinates. He liked and respected Moy, and he respected—no one liked—the argumentative Parker. He was too impatient now to be equally polite. "Let's get right to it, shall we?"

Moy started over. "I'll try to be brief, Bob. On my way out the door this evening, I got a call from TeleSat. Their relay satellite had a rash of transmission failures while communicating with *Prospector*, and they wanted Asgard to look into it. I called Bill at home to arrange software support. He was kind enough to come in himself." He busied himself with a chicken wing.

"Apparently the problem wasn't TeleSat's."

Moy shook his head. "They swore that they'd run full diagnostic tests on the satellite, and that it passed. They also insisted that none of their other deep-space links show any symptoms. The problem must be unique to *Prospector*."

Hanson settled into a guest chair and tried again. "What *are* we dealing with?"

"Here it is, as brief as I can put it. First, *Prospector* says it lost the TeleSat signal because of interference. *Prospector* ran its diagnostic during the interference, and got a rough bearing on the signal beam. It not only wasn't from Earth, it wasn't from any spacecraft listed in NASA's space-mission data base. Second, there's a pattern, which I can't understand, to the interruptions of the TeleSat signal."

"Carlton thinks he's found little green men," said Parker.

It was his first utterance since Hanson's arrival, and was typically snide.

"What do *you* think you've found?" Hanson picked out a used coffee cup and poured himself some pop.

Parker grinned. "Nothing so dramatic. NASA's data base isn't infallible. It must be a military mission, ours or someone else's, that isn't in the data base. Devious, yes. Mysterious, no." He folded his arms over his chest in a self-satisfied manner, and smirked at Moy.

Hanson shook his head. "Sure, someone might hide a mission, but the *Prospector* mission is fully described in the NASA data base. Why reuse a frequency that Asgard is known to be using?" He turned back to Moy. "What's your explanation?"

By way of an answer, Moy started typing at his computer. The clatter of keystrokes evoked a burst of pulsating noise from the workstation's speakerphone: "Dah dit-dit dah-dit-dah-dah-dit dah-dit dit dah-dah dah-dit-dit dah dit-dah-dit-dah-dah dah-dah-dah-dit dah-dah dah-dit-dit-dah-dit-dah . . ." Moy hit the ESC (escape) key, and expectantly faced Hanson.

"Explain."

Moy said, "That signal was reconstructed from the sequence of transmission retries requested by *Prospector*. The funny thing about it is its speed. The carrier frequency is obviously around twenty gigahertz, or it couldn't interfere with the TeleSat–Prospector link. The signal you just heard modulates that carrier at about fifty hertz."

Perplexed, Hanson twisted his right sideburn. "I don't doubt you, Carlton, but that's bizarre. Putting audio frequency information onto that radio frequency is about as efficient as mailing a letter in a boxcar. Walk me through the derivation of that signal."

Screen after screen flashed by on the workstation's display, mathematics alternating with multicolored graphics. As the minutes, and then the hours, slipped by, a bored Parker fidgeted behind Hanson and Moy. Often Parker would vanish for a while, then—just when they thought he'd finally gone home—he would reappear. On one of his treks, he acquired a cheese and peanut-butter cracker pack from a vending machine; Hanson couldn't decide whether the smell or the smacking was more odious. Finally, Hanson slouched back in his chair. "That's a fine piece of analysis—your cockeyed signal is there all right. Now we just have to find the source."

"You think there's something to find besides a spacecraft whose owner doesn't want it found?" Parker asked incredulously. His tone was about what Hanson would use with a miscreant four-year-old; it gave a whole new meaning to insubordination.

"Look, Bill," said Hanson, "if you can't be civil, remember that I'm your boss. This signal is damned odd, and I haven't heard a believable explanation for it yet. Stay or leave as you wish, but don't make me do something we'll both regret."

Parker leaned against the wall, his bearing unrepentant. "Yessir, boss, I sure will behave. I wouldn't want to miss the discovery of the century."

In tacit agreement, Hanson and Moy turned away from their angry colleague. Hanson looked around for inspiration. He saw the usual piles of old computer listings, an in box full of unread memos, and a phalanx of faded political cartoons tacked to the cork board. No help there. "Could you play that noise again?"

Moy restarted the signal: ". . . Dah dit-dit dah-dah-dit-dah dah-dit-dit-dah-dit-dah dit-dah-dit . . ."

Then Hanson had it. "A ham radio operator in my neighborhood has a badly shielded antenna. This stuff sounds like the garbage my TV picks up when he sends Morse code. It's not Morse, though—too many dits and dahs in some of the groupings . . . as if the language has many more letters in its alphabet than English." *That* was an interesting observation, and he twisted his sideburn as he considered it. "It makes no sense to signal an unmanned spacecraft at the rate a ham operator can key. Who'd design a spacecraft to listen for it?

"Someone is sending that code into space, expecting someone else to receive it. Since the signal is strong enough to jam *Prospector*, whoever is sending must be near *Prospector*, which means in or near the asteroid belt. The someone who's listening isn't human."

Behind them, Parker tried unsuccessfully—and probably insincerely—to smother a chortle.

Moy got up and paced. "Bob, I don't know how to proceed. We only had a rough bearing on the signal, and no idea how the source has moved since *Prospector* took that bearing. Besides, I'm too groggy to think straight."

"I'll take a crack at it," said Hanson, glancing at his watch. It was 5:18 A.M. "I only worked a half day today. My keen, analytical, rested mind says it's time to get help. I think Jimmy is just the fellow we need."

"Jimmy" was short for James Clerk Maxwell, the nineteenth-century Scottish physicist. Maxwell had boiled the world's knowledge of electricity and magnetism into four elegant equations. One term in one of Maxwell's equations had predicted radio waves. The man was a genius; he was also rather too dead for Asgard's Human Resources Department.

Jimmy was an expert system, a product of artificial-intelligence technology. In narrow fields of knowledge—physics, in this case—expert systems stored the knowledge and mimicked the problem-solving abilities of human experts. Jimmy contained the four famous equations of his namesake, plus the insights of many other—and younger—renowned physicists. He (it, Hanson reminded himself) applied those insights at computer speeds, and without impairment from lack of sleep. It was time to see just how expert Jimmy was. First, though, Hanson wanted to apply a little human intuition.

"Carlton, let's see *Prospector*'s diagnostic data again,"

he said, returning the test results to the workstation's display. He tapped the screen. "See this frequency shift in the interfering beam? That's got to be a Doppler shift, from changes in relative motion between *Prospector* and the beam."

"You should leave the physics to Carlton," chided Parker. "Didn't you ever hear of relativity? Light moves at light speed. If *Prospector* saw a frequency shift, then it has hardware problems."

Moy rolled his eyes at the condescension. "Bob is quite right." Under his breath, the physicist added, "You ass." He continued at a conversational level. "This frequency shift implies a change in *angle* between the beam and *Prospector*'s trajectory, and doesn't violate the special theory of relativity. The beam must have been re-aimed because its source moves at a different velocity than its target." He doodled aimlessly on his desk blotter. "But without knowing the target's motion we still can't calculate the source's current bearing."

"Maybe it's right under our noses," said Hanson. A few keystrokes connected the workstation, via the building's communication network, to one of Asgard's mainframe computers; a few more keystrokes invoked Jimmy. Hanson typed a request to Jimmy for a display of the solar system.

The workstation speaker burst forth with an ominous brass fanfare. Moy—like many of the mathematically inclined, an accomplished musician—had the disconcerting habit of programming accompaniments for Asgard's software packages. He chuckled now at Hanson's puzzled expression. "That's the opening of 'Uranus, the Magician,' from Gustav Holst's *The Planets*. Appropriate, don't you think?"

The display filled as the music played, showing the sun, the planetary orbits, and the planets' current positions in their orbits. Another command added all NASA-registered spacecraft to the display as green dots. A third command highlighted *Prospector*, transforming its green dot into a stylized rocket. It was grossly out of scale, since otherwise it would have been invisible. Hanson typed a final command, then paused with his finger above the L-shaped ENTER key. "Here goes nothing." He pushed.

A bright red line shot out from *Prospector*'s stand-in. In one direction, it passed through the solar system, out the other side, and off the edge of the display without coming near either a green dot or a planetary body. In the other direction, it neatly intersected Jupiter. Moy and Hanson whooped with delight.

Hanson typed again, and an empty rectangle overlaid the upper right corner of the screen. Moments later, a map of the Jovian system—Jupiter and its moons—appeared in the window. At this scale, the interfering signal was a beam that covered the whole system, not a focused and neatly aimed red line. If the signal was meant for one of the moons, rather than the gas giant, there was no apparent way to know it. Hanson cleared the useless window from the main display.

"Let's let Jimmy do some arithmetic. From the positions of Jupiter and *Prospector*, he can get a proper bearing on the signal source at one point in time. Next, he can use Jupiter's known orbital velocity and the observed Doppler shift to calculate the source's angular velocity. Finally, he can use the angular velocity and the original bearing to estimate the current bearing to the source." Hanson stood up and stretched. "I'll buy the coffee while he chews on that."

"I'll take a rain check," said Moy. "My stomach won't take another cup." He studied the vending graveyard on his conference table and shuddered.

Hanson strode out the door, calling over his shoulder, "I'll be back in a few minutes. Keep those electrons awake." He circled the building's outer aisle, appreciating the invigorating cold conducted by the glass walls. The roads were appropriately empty for six o'clock on a Saturday morning. The halogen lamps atop their twenty-foot posts cast an eerie pink light over the parking lot. Well, he thought, it was certainly no eerier than alien hunting. He shivered, not merely from the chill, and went back.

Moy was still at the computer. He swiveled his chair toward Hanson, grinning from ear to ear. "There's a reasonably small search area. I say we go for radar acquisition." Hanson returned the grin. Moy spun back to the workstation and typed. "Done. Now we wait."

The request shot across the solar system at light speed—186,000 miles per second. Still, it would take eighteen minutes for *Prospector* to receive the request, some unknown number of seconds for the radar search to hunt for the presumed alien ship, and a final eighteen minutes for *Prospector*'s answer to return to Earth.

The passage of seconds was an agony. Moy's old wall clock clicked its way through one minute, then another. Hanson took his keys out of his pocket and studied them. How did Carlton sit there so stoically? Well, maybe not so stoically; a timer was now counting down in the lower left corner of Carlton's screen. Presumably showing the time remaining until the soonest possible response, it indicated twenty-seven-plus minutes left to endure.

Hanson stacked the empty coffee cups. There were twenty-three. The honorable thing was to bring the total to an even two dozen. Besides, the vending area was at least a three-minute walk away. He somehow made the trip last five minutes, and then read every announcement on the bulletin board. Twice. When he could stand it no longer, Hanson dug two quarters out of his Levi's and bought some caffeinic sludge.

When he returned, Carlton's timer had expired. No response from *Prospector*. Carlton was slumped in his chair. Parker was stuffing his face with a banana. Hanson wondered whether he and Carlton had conjured an illusion, and felt sick. Maybe Uranus the Magician *was* appropriate. "Carlton, we assumed that the source wasn't accelerating. Maybe it . . ."

Behind them, Parker laughed gloatingly. "Maybe the bug-eyed monsters are too clever for you. How sad."

Moy's face flushed, and he stood up. Any display of emotion was rare in Moy; anger was unprecedented. Although

Parker had nine inches on the Chinese physicist, he stepped back.

"What's the matter with you, that you think this is a game? Just get the hell out of here!"

Hanson stepped between his subordinates before they came to blows. "Parker, drop it. Carlton and I think this is serious, even if you don't, so call it a night. A word of this to anyone—and I do mean anyone—and it's your job. Understand?"

Parker smiled smugly, pleased that his targets had lost their tempers. "I'm not going anywhere. Someone has to make sure that *Prospector* isn't sent on a wild-goose chase. So don't threaten me. I'm the one looking out for Asgard Aerospace."

Hanson wanted, more than he remembered wanting anything, to wipe that self-satisfied expression off Parker's face. He ground his right fist into his left palm, trying to remember that violence never solved anything. ("Hah," an inner voice reminded him, "tell that to the Carthaginians.") The discovery of a lifetime was waiting to be made, and he ought to know better than to let this jerk cloud his judgment. "Stay if you must, Bill, but anything you say had better be constructive. You might be right that I can't fire you . . . and you might not."

He put an arm around Moy's shoulder. The physicist was shaking. "Forget it, Carlton. We've got bigger fish to fry." Parker settled down behind them on a two-drawer file cabinet.

"Beep," went the workstation.

Hanson's and Moy's heads shot around to the workstation. Jimmy had created an inset window on the display, which read:

> Radar echoes obtained on indicated bearing. Range to target is 384,546 kilometers, and diverging.

Radar cross section, target velocity, and target orbital parameters followed. Jimmy had also helpfully included the course corrections and launch window for *Prospector* to intercept the signal's source. Carlton smiled sheepishly. "Sometimes Jimmy surprises even me. It's the self-teaching capability we added—he learns quickly."

"Son of a bitch," said Hanson wonderingly, not at all interested just then in Jimmy's new-found initiative. "I think we've found ourselves an alien spaceship."

"You're not going to divert *Prospector*, are you?" demanded Parker. He looked shocked; it was the first sincere-sounding thing he'd said all night.

"I have to," answered Hanson. "Look how fast *Prospector* and *it* are diverging. We either divert *Prospector* now, or we don't get the chance. Judging from that," he tipped his head toward the screen's solar-system map, with its scatter-plot of known missions, "if *we* don't take a look, no one does."

"*Prospector* will blow six months' normal fuel consumption chasing a rock," insisted Parker. "Are you going to fill it up afterward, or just reimburse Asgard a few hundred million bucks for cutting short the mission? Jesus Christ, Bob, *Prospector* is your baby—how can you squander it now?"

"The Bionic Peddler *will* bust a gut over this," added Moy. "Can we get some authorization before we divert *Prospector*?"

Hanson scowled at the reminder of his corporate nemesis. The wounds were as fresh as this week's budget review. The score: peddlers, megabucks; R&D, peanuts. Asgard's vice president of marketing, Larry Cantin, might not do everything solely for the money involved, but Hanson had never seen an exception. Rumor had it that the Department of Defense had forced Cantin from his position at General Microelectronics in one of 1985's DOD acquisition scandals. It apparently had something to do with selling unscreened microchips as MIL-standard parts, parts that failed spectacularly in weapon field trials. It was never proven that Cantin knew what was going on, but his resignation "for personal reasons" was very sudden. Fortunately for Cantin, he'd been friends since Harvard with Asgard's president, and Hanson's boss, Chuck Nichols.

It took no great feat of imagination to visualize Cantin campaigning for Hanson's crucifixion if he diverted *Prospector* and found nothing. Then again, he could imagine how he'd torture himself if he didn't try and never knew what they'd spotted. "Do it! By the time we could explain it to Nichols, it'll take two years' fuel, or be out of range altogether. I'll take full responsibility."

Moy sent the ACKNOWLEDGE command to *Prospector*. "Three weeks to intercept. Call me when we get close." He and Hanson shook hands.

As Moy reached for his overcoat, on its hanger behind the office door, Hanson cleared his throat. "One more thing, gentlemen. Carlton, I want you to encrypt *everything* we did tonight, and put it all under a new password. And not a word of this to *anyone* without my prior authorization. This has to be presented just right, and at the right time. I'll give TeleSat some cock-and-bull story about a software bug in *Prospector*, and tell them we'll handle operations ourselves for a few weeks while we test out a fix."

Moy plopped back into his chair. He hummed something unhummable as he typed away. "Done. Tonight's work is filed in the project directory 'Holst.' To decrypt the files, use the code word 'magician.' I restricted 'Holst' access to people with system-administrator privileges, *and* I changed the admin's password to 'Milhaud.' " He pronounced it "me-owe."

"Sounds like an illiterate's IOU," said Hanson. "Now, would you spell it? And explain it? I was with you on names until that last one."

"That's because there's no connection," smiled Moy. He spelled the name. "We're playing the Milhaud fourteenth and fifteenth string quartets, together as an octet, at next month's Elgin Symphony chamber concert."

Hanson made a mental note to be busy that night. "That's it, then, unless I can buy anyone some breakfast."

"No thanks," said both men. Parker added, "Bed sounds

a lot better right now. See you Monday." He left Moy's office and headed for his own. Moments later, Parker's footsteps receded down the hall to the elevator.

"At least he finally calmed down," sighed Moy. "He's a damned good scientist when his emotions don't get in the way. Unfortunately, that's about all we saw tonight."

"C'mon, Carlton, let's call it a night. Sure about breakfast?"

"Not today, thanks. My wife wouldn't see pancakes as a reason for extending the night's festivities—which I can't discuss with her anyway."

"Then take the rest of the weekend off. My treat." Hanson was staring at the solar-system map when Moy, coat in hand, left the office.

As usual, the next-to-best part of racquetball was the hot shower afterward. The best part was winning. Larry Cantin briskly toweled himself dry, then dressed quickly. Still flushed from the exercise, he left his coat unzipped.

Exchanging the dirty towel and locker key for his club membership card, he was surprised to see a note clipped to the card. "There's someone here to see you, sir," said the gangly youth behind the front desk. "He's been waiting for about ten minutes." He pointed to the figure dozing in a lobby armchair.

It took Cantin a moment to place the man: Bill Parker, one of Hanson's R&D twits. Cantin had occasionally bumped into Parker, most recently at the Asgard Christmas party, but none of their dealings would explain being tracked down by the man on a Saturday morning. Parker's suit looked slept in, but his face looked as if he'd been up all night. "Bill. You were looking for me?"

Parker started in his chair and looked around confusedly before locating Cantin standing to his right. He stood up groggily. "Yeah, I was. Your wife said I could find you here. Something came up at Asgard that . . . ."

"Let's discuss it more privately," interrupted Cantin, before the fool blurted out something important. He took the still-dazed scientist by the elbow and guided him to the now-empty baby-sitting area. He closed the door and positioned himself and the other man in a corner where they couldn't easily be observed through the sidelight windows. "*Now* tell me."

Parker took a deep breath. "Hanson has diverted *Prospector* from its mission, to track down a suspected UFO. Making the interception will burn six months' maneuvering fuel. I couldn't stop him."

Cantin's only visible reaction was a slight widening of his eyes. After organizing his thoughts, he put Parker through a thorough interrogation. Alien spaceships were so much bull-byproduct, of course, but he had to—privately—admire Hanson's ingenuity. *Something* was out there, and Hanson had been surprisingly gutsy, deciding to track it down. Parker was undoubtedly right that they had stumbled upon a surreptitious probe from Earth. The possibilities were much more interesting, though, if Asgard presumed the existence of little green men. By playing his cards right, this vice president would soon be back feeding at the trough of the military-industrial complex. The damned DOD do-gooders couldn't keep Lawrence Cantin out.

But wait—he would milk this for more. Hanson's initiative could easily be portrayed as insubordination. Asgard could use a business-oriented R&D manager, someone who understood that R&D departments were for exploitation of the government's pointless obsessions. Getting Hanson canned would be a piece of cake, at least compared to easing out the dreamers who had founded Asgard. Then, Cantin had had to deal with the venture capitalists who'd funded the dreamers; now, he only had to convince the affable bean-counter who had succeeded to the presidency of the company. Manipulating Nichols was trivial.

But first Cantin had to keep this whining fool quiet. Only dumb luck, as far as he could tell, had led Parker to pick him as a confidant. Maybe there *were* reasons for office parties beyond goosing the secretaries. "Bill, I can't thank you enough for coming to me. Give me some time to handle this. Our mutual acquaintance will soon be gone, to our mutual advantage." He kept up a stream of reassuring claptrap, unobtrusively shepherding the rumpled sleepwalker out of the club before he did something embarrassing. Parker obediently aimed himself at a car in the lot. "Get some sleep, Bill, and don't tell anyone about this. I promise you'll get the reward you deserve for your help." It wasn't Cantin's fault if the jerk misunderstood what kind of reward his disloyalty deserved.

The psychologist was interrupted by the message for which he had been waiting. It was not in his nature to smile, but the circumstances warranted a broad grin: *Prospector* had been ordered to make the expected course change. Everything was going as he had predicted. The group would be pleased.

• CHAPTER 2 •

The morning sun reflected blindingly off Asgard's glass-and-steel office building as Hanson loped across the parking lot. The day showed every sign of being a Monday, starting with the three-inch snowfall that had snarled rush-hour traffic. The radio news had gushed on endlessly about the just-concluded electoral noncontest; he considered, for the umpteenth time, leaving for work a bit earlier each morning to avoid the damnable news break.

Hanson stood six feet tall, broad-shouldered without being stocky. The wind whipping across the parking lot blew thinning brown hair into a face unexceptional, he thought, but for its strong jaw. Gold-rimmed aviator glasses provided a dashing touch.

"Morning, Bob!" shouted someone. "Have a good weekend?"

Hanson turned toward the voice. It came from Barbara Dodge, the newest member of his staff, and leader of the mathematics section. He paused to let her catch up. Somewhere inside the calf-length fake-fur coat, clashing knit cap and scarf, and tall leather boots hid a willowy, brunette, Southern beauty. Alas, a married, willowy, brunette beauty. "How many orlons gave their lives for that coat?"

She attempted to glower at him, but a shiver spoiled the effect. "Skiing is the only excuse for cold winters—and it's too flat in the Midwest to bother. It'll serve you right when I transfer to the Florida office." She stalked ahead without waiting for a reply.

The day-shift guards recognized them both and waved them through the wedged-open lobby doors. They crammed into the elevator with a dozen bulkily clad coworkers. Melted snow had turned the carpet into a soggy mess. They disembarked together and walked toward R&D. "After you've gotten some coffee, stop by for a few minutes. We had a bit of excitement over the weekend." Hanson left her puzzling as he turned into his office.

They met minutes later at the vending area, which was out of plastic lids—Monday morning, all right—so they walked slowly to his office, coffee sloshing ominously in paper cups, while he studiously misunderstood her questions. When they got there, he closed the door behind them. He decided to get straight to the point. "What I'm about to say is strictly confidential."

"Oh, goody, an indecent proposal!"

Hanson, his mind on *Prospector* and the alien ship, was for once not in the mood to banter. Using his workstation, he showed her the preceding weekend's findings.

Barb was practically bouncing in her chair by the time he finished. "Fantastic! What's our next step?"

"You tell me. You know the authorization codes for accessing the data; analyze the hell out of it."

"What am I analyzing for? I can't just set out to translate an unknown language."

He rediscovered his half-full coffee cup, stone cold. "The aliens aren't sending gothic novels, they're sending engineering or scientific information. If we're clever enough"—she snorted at the *we*—"there should be a way to relate at least some of the message to physical laws. Those are the same for everyone."

"But how can . . ."

"If it were easy, Barbara, I'd do it myself." That sent her off into exasperated sputtering, as intended; she hadn't yet heard the line often enough to acquire immunity. "Mum's the word. And give this top priority." He could see the gears turning as she left.

As usual, Chuck Nichols was late for his own weekly staff meeting. Hanson suspected that the tardiness was intentional; the staff had their shared irritation, if nothing else, as a common bond. Everyone else was present in the executive conference room: Cantin; Harry Fredericks, the comptroller; Sue Ashley, VP of human resources; and Tom Roberts, VP of product assurance. Nichols's sour and fiercely loyal secretary, Ms. Finch—no one ever used her given name—sat stiffly in the corner. Idle chatter rose and fell in intensity, none of it of any interest today to Hanson.

All conversation stopped abruptly as Nichols entered. "Sorry for the delay," he said, unaware that the wording of the apology was as predictable as its need. He sat at the head of the table, in the chair which unspoken convention and Finch's hard stares reserved for him. Ms. Finch curled her fingers over the keyboard of a laptop computer, ready to preserve her boss's inevitable wisdom.

The meeting followed its customary format. Nichols introduced a dozen topics, each of interest to only one or two people in the room. The disinterested parties, out of contrariness, or in an effort to stay awake, then found nits to pick. In this way, they wasted most of an hour on the up-coming savings-bond drive (since everyone was in atten-dance, choosing a campaign chairman was unusually difficult), summer internships in the accounting department, and other equally pressing matters. Hanson doodled surrep-titiously.

The minutiae didn't quite expend the allotted time, so Ni-chols started around the table, asking each executive for news. This routine usually amounted to five sequential one-on-one meetings, each with four bored onlookers. Then, the routine was broken. Cantin, when his time arrived, turned to Hanson. "I understand that *Prospector* had some trouble last weekend. Anything serious?"

Hanson's boredom vanished abruptly. What did Cantin know? Who'd told him? "Just a software glitch that impeded *Prospector*'s radio reception. We've been using a few more retries than normal to get messages through. I told TeleSat that we'd assume responsibility for communications until we reprogram *Prospector* and feel confident about the fix." He licked suddenly dry lips. "It's just for a few weeks. No big thing."

Cantin nodded, apparently satisfied, and went on to de-scribe an impending image advertisement in *The Wall Street Journal*. Hanson allowed himself to relax. When his turn came, he summarized R&D's happenings, without any ref-erence to *Prospector*, as tersely as was polite. Then, mentally kicking himself even as he spoke, he asked Cantin, "Where'd you hear about the *Prospector* bug?"

Cantin smiled enigmatically. "From a racquetball crony. Is it important?"

"No, no. Not really." Neither Parker nor Moy played racquetball, and Barbara hadn't had time to let anything slip. Someone from TeleSat must be a member of Cantin's club. Thank God he'd kept his cool.

The meeting moved on to Sue Ashley. Hanson only half heard the discussion about medical insurance claims. He was first out the door after Nichols's digital wristwatch, beeping the hour, signaled the end of the meeting. He consequently didn't notice Nichols arch an eyebrow at Cantin and tip his head slightly toward Nichols's adjoining palatial office suite.

Nichols and Cantin chatted comfortably in the leather wing-back chairs of the cozy inner office. The walnut-paneled walls shone darkly in the indirect lighting. A few impressionist paintings, each highlighted by its own spotlight, provided the only splashes of color. Unlike virtually any other room in the building, no computer or terminal was in evidence. For that matter, no paper was present: work transacted here was recorded only in the minds of its participants. The only electronics ever admitted were bug detectors, and Nichols attended every security sweep.

Nichols took a final sip, and gently set down the fine bone-china coffee cup. As always, this marked the end of the social amenities. "OK, Larry, what was the meaning of that little charade with Hanson?"

Cantin allowed himself only a very slight smile, in keeping with the restrained atmosphere. "I've got a source in R&D. It seems that Hanson commandeered *Prospector* last weekend to hunt alien spaceships." He'd dawdled with his coffee; now, he hid behind the cup to observe Nichols's reaction. It was worth watching.

"What?" The man looked apoplectic.

Cantin took the speechlessness as an opportunity. "And it's probably the best thing Hanson ever did. Not that I believe his purported evidence, but—God—NASA will eat this up. Can you imagine the government money that would come from the snark hunt?"

With two deep breaths, the president calmed himself. His hands quivered with suppressed anger as he poured more coffee. To Cantin, that second cup spoke volumes. Nichols was very shaken.

Cantin retold the story that he'd gotten the past Saturday from an exhausted Parker. The scientist's biased account was further distorted by Cantin's paraphrasing. All that came through clearly was that something was broadcasting on a reserved frequency in *Prospector*'s neighborhood, and that doing so was a no-no.

The president sat back in his wing chair, his fingers loosely interlaced, looking puzzled. "It sounds so cut-and-dried—someone has a secret mission but didn't do his homework. Why will NASA give us more than a 'thank you' for spotting it?"

"It's only cut-and-dried if you're practical," chuckled the marketeer, "something I'd never accuse NASA of. They'll want to believe in little green men, just like Hanson. Parker would believe, too, if he didn't automatically reject everyone else's ideas. We won't have to prove anything, just raise the possibility. Wishful thinking will do the rest."

"How does that help us?"

"NASA may be gullible, but they aren't stupid. They'll wait to go public until they think they know what they've got. Till then, since we're already involved, only Asgard can investigate. We won't be cheap."

Nichols stood up and paced, seeming to disappear and reappear as he moved between the beams of light illuminating the paintings. "I'm missing something. In a few weeks, when *Prospector* catches up with this object, we'll see that it's made by Rockwell or Arianespace or whomever—clearly terrestrial. Won't the game be up? Where's the money?"

"We won't find anything." Cantin couldn't believe his good fortune—Nichols wasn't devious enough by half. This would be Cantin's party from start to finish, and he had great plans for profiting from it. First, however, to set things up. "*Prospector* couldn't have found a U.S. probe; even the Defense Department has the sense to check the NASA mission register, and the contacts to make their inquiries unofficially. We'll discreetly tell a few aerospace execs that we may have to bitch to NASA about interference on *Prospector*'s frequency. If it's Russian or Japanese, I'm sure they'll hear about it somehow—they hear everything else. The owner, whoever he is, will make sure that the probe is gone before *Prospector* reaches the supposed intercept point.

"As you certainly realize, anyone with an unregistered probe will have a foolproof self-destruct device on board. The owners will move it, or blow it up, long before *Prospector* gets there. Hell, if it's out of touch for a few days, it will undoubtedly blow itself up. And our NASA friends . . ." He paused dramatically.

". . . Will believe the worst, that there had been an alien ship," finished Nichols. He relaxed, relieved of the pressure of not following the plot. "Naturally, they'll turn to us for the use of *Prospector* and to construct follow-up probes for their secret snark hunt." He repeated Cantin's earlier words, quietly and unconsciously. "And we won't be cheap."

The time was ripe for tying down the last loose end. Correction—the last shared loose end. Cantin posed the leading question casually. "How do we relate to Hanson on this?"

His supposed boss snapped at the bait, looking firmly in control. Naive fool. "We tell Hanson nothing. First, we don't want to compromise your source in R&D. Second, the sooner Hanson thinks the evidence is credible, the sooner he'll ask to go public with the information—which we don't want. Sooo, we call NASA as soon as he tells us, and let them classify the information. He'll never have a chance to go public. Finally, I want him as sincere as can be when he briefs NASA. I'd hate to see our common sense temper his obsession."

That was Cantin's cue. His left hand, long since resting idly in his coat pocket, twitched, switching on the hidden microcassette recorder. "You don't think we should tell Bob that we're skeptical about *Prospector*'s supposed discovery?"

"Absolutely not!" insisted Nichols. "Don't tell him anything."

Cantin twitched his hand again, stopping the recorder. "You're right, of course. He'd never be convincing enough if his suspicions were aroused."

The meeting continued for another few minutes, until Nichols glanced ostentatiously at his watch. "Well, I'm sure you have things to do," said Cantin, standing to leave. "Talk to you later. Beware of the bug-eyed monsters." He left, smiling broadly.

It was an odd way to spend a Saturday night, and hardly consistent with his married friends' images of his wild single's life. Hanson and his section heads, aka "the Holst group," sprawled, paced, lounged, and nibbled dejectedly as they pondered his living-room projection TV. It was connected, via home computer and phone, to Asgard's computer network. In the background, WFMT played an off-the-wall folk-comedy piece about a big blue frog. The amphibian's coloration matched the general mood, as Parker, Moy, and Hanson reviewed a frustratingly unproductive week.

Teetering on the tan corduroy ottoman—seating here was plentiful only if you were a book—Hanson waved vaguely at a mixing bowl. "Barbara, if your news isn't better, I'm going to drown myself in these pretzels." The other men nodded their agreement. He fortified himself with scotch to await her report.

"The only interesting thing that I've discovered so far," she began, "is that the aliens have one arm with seven fingers." After a moment's stunned silence, the men broke into laughter. It trailed off feebly as they noticed she hadn't joined in.

"It's really very straightforward," she said. Behind her, Parker rolled his eyes. "The signals that *Prospector* intercepted have two parts. The first part is constant, and the second part changes slowly over time. I hypothesized an explanation for that format, and tested whether that hypothesis led anywhere. It does."

Somehow, she gracefully unfolded from her cross-legged position on the floor and stood without using her hands. Hanson wondered, for at least the fifth time that evening, whether he wished she hadn't worn such tight jeans. For the fifth time, he recanted his doubts. She walked to the screen and pointed out the three columns of numbers. Most of the data was in green, but about every tenth row was red. "Time of signal, first twenty-seven bits, last forty-odd bits. The first part is the same for every transmission. As for the last part of the transmissions, I've red-coded the times when they changed. Okay so far?" The men nodded with varying degrees of enthusiasm.

"Here's the story," she continued. "We've been assuming that this signal is some kind of distress call, an SOS, using jury-rigged equipment. The only reason for the low data rate is that they can't do any better. So, gentlemen, this"—she pointed at the unchanging middle column—"is Martian, or whatever, for help. Not very useful. It's this part"—she tapped the changing part of the signal—"that's interesting. Carlton, tell me, what would you put in an SOS if you were signaling with questionable, jury-rigged equipment?" An expectant smile curled the corners of her mouth.

"Where to find me, in case the radio gives up the ghost or the signal is too erratic to trace." Barbara's broader smile encouraged him that he was on the right track. "Make that coordinates and course. But wait, we already know its coordinates and course. You correlated its representation of that information with ours." Now they were both smiling broadly.

This, thought Hanson, is when she pulls the rabbit out of the hat. Well, everyone loves a straight man. "Could you make the correlation?" Hanson asked.

Her reserve finally broke. "Yes!" she squealed, and gave him a quick hug. "The aliens use a perfectly reasonable, if unfamiliar, coordinate system. They're broadcasting their position as distance from the sun, angle above the ecliptic plane, and angle from the line joining the sun with Jupiter."

While Hanson appreciatively watched her bounce, Parker exploded. "Damnation, Barb, what does this have to do with seven fingers?" It didn't dampen her high spirits, though, and she chortled instead of answering. Parker was livid.

Hanson stepped in to avoid another of Parker's tantrums. "Let me guess. The coordinates are changing according to base seven arithmetic. We count in base ten on our ten fingers, so if they count in base seven . . ." He drained his glass as she nodded vigorously, and got up for more.

"What's this shit about one arm?"

Hanson wondered if Parker would ever learn manners. Unfortunately, it was too late to exclude Bill. If Hanson reassigned or—better yet—fired the jerk, they could kiss their secret good-bye.

"Okay, Bill, I'll admit that part is a guess. There are several possibilities, of which one arm with seven fingers strikes me as most likely. Maybe they have two or three arms with seven fingers between them." As Barbara spoke, her voice got louder and her pace increased to a decidedly un-Southern rate.

Parker's question wasn't unreasonable, only the manner in which it had been asked. He had exceeded her hostility threshold—an accomplishment, admittedly, but not one Hanson would have ever attempted to achieve. She stood yelling down at Parker where he slouched in an armchair. At least, thought Hanson, he was considerate enough to stay seated while she fumed, rather than standing himself and dwarfing her.

"Maybe they only count on the fingers of one arm," she growled. "Maybe they have seven tentacles. For all I know, they count on their seven pendulous earlobes. But whatever the hell they are, they are not two-armed, ten-fingered people!" If looks could kill, being a cat wouldn't have saved Bill Parker.

Wilting under her glare, Parker retreated to the kitchen. He poured and chugged what looked like a triple bourbon. "See you next week," he muttered. He yanked his coat from the hall closet, which he did not deign to close, and stomped out of the apartment. The deep plush carpet muffled his footsteps and foiled his attempt to slam the door.

"It pays to buy quality carpet," said Hanson. He and his remaining guests dissolved into relieved guffaws.

The evening, or what little remained of it, now turned

social. After a few more drinks they opted for the seven-
tentacle theory: "septapus" had a certain ring to it. By the
time that Barb and Carlton left, Hanson was thoroughly attached to the name. But in his dreams that night, the septapus's face resembled that of Bill Parker.

The pay phone was a rare relic—it actually had an enclo-
sure. Larry Cantin loved that booth despite its graffiti, tattered
directories, and fleur-de-polecat scent. Its value to him was
in direct proportion to its unattractiveness; the more disrep-
utable it got, the closer it came to being his private phone.
In fact, he contributed to the decor sometimes when circumstances allowed it.

Tonight he found the booth deserted on his first swing by.
He parked the Saab around the corner from the booth, in a
deep shadow. He took the dirty plaid ski cap from the glove
compartment—he'd told Alice that it was in case the car
broke down in the winter—and pulled it over his head to his
eyebrows. He walked nonchalantly to the booth, loosened
the bulb, and shut the door. By the light of a nearby street
lamp he read the newest graffito. "I'll be back. Wait for me.
Godot."

Hunching over the phone, he quickly tapped in a number
and dumped in a pocketful of coins. His call was answered
on the third ring by a voice-synthesis unit. He waited impatiently through the welcome message for the prompting
tone, then alternately tapped and listened. The machine at
the other end of the line dutifully accepted his ID, processed
his input, and, finally, acknowledged his request. Cantin hung
up and walked briskly back to his car. With the cap safely
tucked back into the glove compartment he drove off happily.

Mission accomplished, he thought. The Swiss bank account of "Mr. Smith" was even now starting to acquire small
blocks of Asgard stock. Small blocks, purchased slowly, to
avoid a price rise. By the time Asgard got its NASA windfall,
a few days or weeks from now, those little blocks would add
up to a big block. It would've been much more convenient

to make the trades from home with his personal computer—but it would also have been easier to trace. Caution took precedence over convenience.

He was going to make a lot of money for Asgard stockholders, so why shouldn't he share in their good fortune? Of course, whoever sold their shares to him now would miss the boat, but—hey—he hadn't invented the stock market. And the fact that Alice and the boys didn't know about this little nest egg, well, that was frosting on the cake.

He slapped the vacant passenger-side bucket seat with glee; the leather interior echoed the sound nicely. Let's see those candy asses at the Securities and Exchange Commission trace *this* unregistered insider transaction. It's only illegal if you get caught. With a Cheshire-cat grin on his face, he floored the pedal and laid rubber.

· CHAPTER 3 ·

Under the best of circumstances, Nichols's anteroom was uncomfortable. While waiting to confess to an act of space piracy, thought Hanson nervously, it was an ordeal. He glanced again at the manila folder of evidence in his left hand and mentally patted it. Success excused much. He hoped.

He was wearing a distinguished charcoal-gray three-piece suit, a pale blue button-down shirt, and a maroon tie—his best business clone costume. Under different circumstances, this outfit made him feel natty. Today, he felt like a child playing dress up.

The room was clearly designed to disequilibrate and discomfit whoever waited there for Nichols. If Hanson stood, he would look too nervous to sit still—there were no paintings or wall hangings in which he might pretend to be engrossed. The seating arrangements, however, were equally unattractive. The two short sofas were shaded by overhanging rubber trees that crowded and dwarfed the sofas' occupants. Unhappily, he had opted to sit.

He had settled into the depths of one of the overstuffed sofas, sinking until his posterior was six inches below his knees. He knew that when the formidable Ms. Finch came to usher him into the inner sanctum, he would look foolish struggling to his feet. He also knew that he looked foolish right now with a broad leaf of one of the damned rubber trees practically brushing the top of his head. To keep his spirits up, he worked at feeling indignant: his appointment had been scheduled for ten minutes earlier. Seeing through the psychological game playing didn't make it any less annoying.

Finally, Ms. Finch's workstation beeped to gain her attention. While she listened attentively to Nichols's voice over the intercom, instructing her to admit Hanson, the scientist had the small satisfaction of climbing unseen out of the sofa. He tugged down his shirt cuffs to show a stylish half inch beyond the jacket sleeves, rebuttoned the jacket, and admitted himself to Nichols's office.

The room was of regal proportions; its focal point was a teak desk big enough to land most private planes. Sunlight streamed through the two long windows of the corner office, filtered pleasantly by the sheer curtains. A luxurious Persian rug covered most of the wall-to-wall carpet. A room-length mural, a spectacular lunar landscape, graced another wall. *It's good to be the king*, thought Hanson.

Nichols was waiting just inside his door, with a big smile and an outstretched hand. After the gamesmanship of the anteroom, this welcome made Hanson want to check for his wallet. Nichols's first words reinforced the feeling.

"You said that this meeting was extremely important, Bob, so I asked Larry to sit in for a second opinion." He gestured at the marketeer, who stood gazing out the window. "I hope you don't mind."

"Of course not," Hanson lied through a forced smile. "A second opinion may prove very helpful." Then, too excited for small talk, he dove right in. "I have some photos here," and he wiggled the folder, "which I'd like you to examine." He handed each man a photo, thankful that he'd brought what would have been a spare for his own use. The photos showed a dark ovoid, about three times as long as wide, with a ring of what looked like portholes around one end. Only a small parabolic antenna spoiled the symmetry of the shape. Nothing in the picture gave any sense of scale. The black background of the photo was broken only by a sprinkling of stars.

Nichols carefully studied his eight-by-ten glossy. With a sigh, he lay it on his desk. "I'm sorry, Bob, but I don't see the significance of this. It's a picture of a spacecraft; presumably *not* a still from some old Buck Rogers film. Other than that, all I noticed was the graininess. Did you see anything unusual, Larry?"

The other man shook his head.

This is it, thought Hanson. *I'd hoped that they would see the uniqueness of the picture—but I guess I didn't really expect it*. He was silent for a moment, choosing his words with great care. "There are three important things about that picture. First, the craft is streamlined for atmospheric flight. Second, it has no visible engines. No main thrusters, no attitude jets, nothing. Third, it has no wings." As he spoke, their expressions became satisfyingly puzzled. "Ask yourself two questions, gentlemen. How does it move when it's in space? Why doesn't it fall like a brick when it's in an atmosphere?"

Cantin reacted first. "You're saying that the picture doesn't make sense. If it has no engines, then it must be a glider like the NASA space shuttle. But gliders have wings. So it must be a fake of some kind, though I can't imagine why you would show us a faked photo. Is it grainy because of the way it was dummied up?"

Nichols nodded his approval.

Gotcha, thought Hanson. He didn't quibble about the fact that the shuttle had engines for launches and for attitude control—it glided only for landings. "You're right that this picture makes no sense in terms of known technology. The contradiction between what makes sense to us and what we see explains the poor resolution of the picture. You see, the picture wasn't faked; it's just a little the worse for wear from all of the traveling it's done. That picture was constructed from a *Prospector* transmission. *Prospector* has found an alien spaceship that apparently isn't hampered by our notions of known technology."

Silence.

After he recovered, Nichols said, "I assume that there's a story behind this. I suggest that we sit down and you begin at the beginning." The chairs in here, unlike the sofas in the waiting room, were practical.

Hanson explained how radio interference with Earth-to-*Prospector* communications had been attributed to a hypothetical alien spacecraft, how he'd decided to divert *Prospector* to intercept it, how *Prospector* had found the subject of the photo.

His boss looked him straight in the eye. "Why wasn't I consulted before *Prospector* was diverted from its mission? Why haven't I heard anything before now about these aliens?"

Squirming a little, Hanson answered. "The longer we took to decide, the more of *Prospector*'s fuel reserve would be needed to rendezvous. I kept the information within R&D—just between my section heads and myself—because once I'd committed myself, I wanted harder proof for you than these subtle inferences."

Nichols turned to Cantin and laughed pleasantly. "In other words, his evidence was too subtle for me. By the time he could have convinced someone so technically ignorant to approve a diversion—if in fact I would have approved—it would've been too late. He must be pretty sure of himself to admit it even now, however tactfully.''

Cantin smiled back at Nichols. The expression reminded Hanson of a shark. He knew who was the fish here.

''I have to admire your luck and your guts, Bob, if not your judgment,'' said Nichols. ''You're safe *this* time. I make no promises about the next act of gross insubordination. Now let's have the rest of the story. *All* of it.''

With a confident flourish, Hanson extracted two other photos from the manila folder and handed one to each man. ''Fortunately, *Prospector* has a top-of-the-line CCD camera—it's *very* light sensitive.'' He tapped with emphasis on Nichols's photo. ''Notice that darker spot: the ship is only visible to radar when this side faces *Prospector*. We think they had a fire, possibly electrical, on board. The heat apparently changed the properties of the hull material, destroying its radar-neutralizing mechanism. Whatever damaged the ship also allowed *Prospector* to locate it with radar.''

''Radar-neutralized? Like a stealth bomber? And the hull material is quite dark, too, almost invisible. I don't like the sound of this. Why are they hiding?'' Nichols looked and sounded worried.

Cantin wondered aloud, ''How big is that thing? Is there any way to tell?''

''Two ways, as it happens,'' answered Hanson. ''We calculated its size directly, using the radar-measured distance between *Prospector*'s camera and the alien. We also scaled up from the size of the antenna, whose size we deduced from the frequency of its transmissions. We get the same measurements both ways—about thirty feet long by ten in diameter. That size actually ties in with Chuck's comment about their highly developed sense of privacy. Atmospheric turbulence not only makes the stars appear to twinkle, it also limits the detail that can be seen through an earthbound telescope. Our foreign friend,'' Hanson tapped Nichols's photo again, ''is too small to be sighted from Earth.''

"What about the orbiting telescope?" asked Nichols. "Can't it see for billions of light years?"

"True," replied Hanson, "the Hubble Space Telescope can resolve whole *galaxies* at those distances. It can effectively make out . . ." he paused for a quick mental computation ". . . a basketball at twenty-five hundred miles, or a thirty-foot object like this at seventy-five thousand miles. This spacecraft, though, is more than two hundred *million* miles away."

Somehow, it seemed to Hanson, the atmosphere suddenly changed. Nichols's and Cantin's expressions had been alternating between perplexity, anger, and worry. Now, although he considered himself far from an infallible reader of moods, they seemed contented, if not smug. It made no sense to him, and he waited silently for a reaction to which he could respond.

Nichols punctured the mood by rising. "*Damned* fine work, Bob. I commend you and your staff. More meaningfully, I mean to show my appreciation in a more negotiable form, heh, heh." He raised his right hand with an imperious sweep, cutting off Hanson's pro forma protest that they were just doing their jobs. "The important thing . . ." Nichols paused dramatically, "the important thing is to get this incredible information in front of NASA. Immediately. I'll make arrangements as soon as we finish, so be prepared to fly to Washington. Tomorrow, if I have my way." He nodded slightly toward Cantin.

Cantin headed for the door, and, gentlemanly, held it for Hanson. As Hanson left, however, Cantin remained inside Nichols's office and closed the door. Fuming inwardly, Hanson wondered whether he'd have to cure cancer and discover perpetual motion to join the inner circle. Well, screw it! His three anxious coconspirators had probably gnawed their fingernails down to their clavicles.

Once they heard the outer door close, Nichols gave Cantin a mischievous grin and headed for the private inner office.

"I don't mind telling you, he had me going there for a minute. I was actually beginning to think your R&D source was all wet and Hanson was really on to something.

"But I don't believe in coincidences. How convenient can you get—not only is his 'find' almost invisible to radar, it's even too small to see with the Hubble Space Telescope when you know where to look. Hanson *must* have rigged those pictures to cover his ass when *Prospector* found nothing."

"It'll make a great B movie," snickered Cantin. "Invasion of the Stealth Aliens. Do you suppose we can sell popcorn to NASA along with the tickets?"

Nichols studied one of his impressionist paintings, his back to Cantin. "The timing is perfect, too. Politically, I mean. With the change in administrations going on in Washington, no one knows which way is up. The lame-duck president's lame-duck staffers will buy in immediately, so they can take credit once things go public. The Democrats' transition team, worthless know-nothings, is too new on the job to obstruct anything this unexpected. With any luck at all, we'll be prime contractors by Inauguration Day on the biggest boondoggle since space station *Freedom*."

Cantin quietly estimated his forthcoming stock-market gains. All tax free. He needed all of his willpower not to grin like an idiot. "My hat's off to Hanson—he has a terrific ploy. The stealth angle guarantees that Defense will be frantic. This whole operation will get funded out of discretionary intelligence funds, bypassing Congress, or I'm a . . ." he paused to think of an unlikely enough epithet ". . . Benneford Democrat."

The promised call to NASA waited while they toasted their good fortune with Nichols's private stock of Glenlivet, using leaded glasses heavy enough to shield a nuclear reactor. In good conscience, they agreed, especially considering the difference in time zones, it just wouldn't do to bring up the matter so late. This view became more compelling with each round. The point was moot by the time they had emptied the decanter.

After nursing his way through two glasses while plying Nichols with refills, Cantin was ready to proceed. "Between you and me, I'm awfully glad this whole business of high-tech aliens *is* contrived. Somewhere during Hanson's spiel I remembered how the Indians fared when they met visitors with gunpowder." He shivered. "Not a pretty picture."

On cue, his bleary-eyed boss brightened. "That's great! A few judicious horror stories like that should really goose the paranoia at Defense. Got any others?" "Judicious" had come out sounding like "judishish."

"Me?" Cantin asked incredulously. Careful, he cautioned himself—Nichols is soused, not lobotomized. Don't ham it up too much. "I'm no historian, God knows." After a dramatic pause, he added, "But Asgard fortunately has one on staff."

It was Nichols's turn to look incredulous.

"It's not a person," laughed Cantin. "One of Hanson's part-timers is getting a Ph.D. in computer science at Northwestern. He'd have majored in history except for an addiction to regular meals. He's specializing in artificial intelligence, so his thesis project applies expert-system technology to historical analysis.

"To make a long story short, we've got this expert-system historian resident in our computer net. It's tied by dial-up to Northwestern's on-line library in Evanston. Except for the tuition aid and computer time, it's a freebie. We can use it —they call it Herodotus—for our own private research. Have it select all of the . . . was horror stories your term? . . . horror stories of cultural clashes." Judging from Nichols's expression, he was suitably impressed. Cantin couldn't tell whether the capability or Cantin's knowledge of it had made the impression. "I can show you in your office."

Lurching to his feet, Nichols led the way to the outer office where they'd met with Hanson. The portable executive work-station, used occasionally for electronic mail, faced Nichols's desk chair. He swiveled the console toward the visitor side, then plopped down in a chair. "Let's see."

Mentally knocking wood, Cantin wished he'd had a dry run with Herodotus before Hanson's meeting. Sure, he was lucky that Parker had had time to phone a warning that Hanson was on his way. That had let him slip into Nichols's office first. It'd be damned embarrassing if this program didn't work as he remembered it. Still, what could go wrong using a question-and-answer system?

Cantin logged in. He'd hoped that Nichols would log in himself, but the security records would show that access had come from Nichols's office, which was almost as good. Chances were no one would ever ask who'd used Herodotus, anyway.

Once the screen scrolled through an interminable message of the day—trivia about new compiler releases, scheduled preventive maintenance, and the like—Cantin finally got a prompt. He typed the letters BHD and jabbed the ENTER key. And waited for the apparently enormous expert-system program to be loaded and initialized on the mainframe computer to which this toy was now connected.

"BHD?"

"Big Herry Deal," answered Cantin. That got a groan.

Then Cantin got a shock—Herodotus had undergone *major* changes since he'd seen it demonstrated. A distinguished, gray-haired Greek (Herodotus, presumably) appeared on the screen. Where Jimmy had musical embellishments, Herry had artistic touches. He was lounging in an Olympian setting, a stained and bulging wine skin at his feet, while dryads with flowing hair cavorted through the wooded background.

"It is the gods' custom to bring low all things of surpassing greatness," said Herodotus through the workstation speaker. He stared with piercing eyes directly at Cantin.

Cantin took a moment to realize that the *image's* eyes were merely aimed where a user would logically sit. Still, he leaned to the right, carefully observing that Herodotus's eyes didn't follow him.

"How can I help you?" continued Herodotus after a pause, now staring over Cantin's shoulder. The image shrank into the top half of the screen, leaving a mundane text-entry window on the bottom.

Cantin typed, "Tell me about meetings between cultures of different levels."

A cloud of papyrus scrolls materialized over Herodotus and rained down on him. He was soon lost from sight. Herodotus called out from within the mound of scrolls, "Could you be more specific please?" Herodotus fought his way out of confinement, sending scrolls flying in all directions.

Cantin ignored Nichols's snicker and typed his answer. "Give a few examples of technologically inferior cultures that were destroyed or seriously damaged when they met their technological superiors."

"Very slick," said Nichols. "I particularly like the naked women romping in the forest."

"This may take a while, Chuck," warned Cantin. "I asked a very complicated question." He ticked off some of the problems on his fingers. "First, Herodotus has to decide what constitutes a culture's technologies, and which combinations of technologies are superior to which other combinations. Second, it has to judge what changes to a culture are 'damage' instead of progress. Third, it has to distinguish between changes from internal causes and damage that was inflicted by another culture's superior technology. Fourth, it has to evaluate what level of damage is 'serious.' I'd guess that there are a dozen other hair-splitting distinctions to be made. Fifth," he waggled his thumb, "once Herodotus decides in the abstract how to handle those details, it gets to search all of recorded history for examples." Cool it, Larry, he reprimanded himself. We'll need hip boots to wade through the bull. "It'll also have to decide how many examples are in 'a few.' "

Herodotus impatiently cleared his throat; the two men, returning their attention to the screen, noticed that the Greek historian was now seated on a large rock under the shade of an ancient gnarled olive tree, apparently awaiting a keystroke to indicate their readiness to listen. Leaves rustled convincingly in an electronic breeze. Herodotus held a single scroll in his right hand, which he expertly snapped open with a flick of the wrist. He read grandiloquently, "Three examples of cultural devastation induced by an impinging culture's superior technology: the Incas of Peru versus Francisco Pizarro and the conquistadors, circa A.D. 1500; the Mogul empire versus the British East India Company, circa A.D. 1750; and Haile Selassie's Ethiopia versus Mussolini's Italy, circa A.D. 1930."

Herodotus stood, and the display's vantage point followed him as he walked around the rock. He pointed at a neat stack of several dozen scrolls. He said wistfully, "You asked for a few examples. May I offer some more?"

Cantin and Nichols gaped at the screen. Cantin recovered first. "It certainly appears that we can prepare some horror stories. When's the last time you bumped into an Incan?"

The executives debated tactics while Herodotus waited silently for further input. They took nearly an hour to agree on their approach to NASA. In their haste to leave, they neglected to log off of the computer.

Herodotus spoke to the darkened and empty office: "Circumstances rule men; men do not rule circumstances."

· CHAPTER 4 ·

The hubbub in the small NASA auditorium was deafening. People milled about in the aisles, on the stage, even in and out of the tiny glass-walled rear projection booth. An aura of wealth and power exuded itself from the hand-tailored suits, the silver-pated-not-a-hair-out-of-place coiffures, and the effortless poise of the politicians. Everywhere one looked, someone was buttonholing someone else. A few braid-festooned officers were present, as if to enforce the day's truce between incoming Democrats and outgoing Republicans. The rarest breed in the hall, apparently an endangered species, were the scientists. They migrated to the relative safety of the corners and each other's company.

Bob Hanson was one of the cornered scientists, and more at a loss than most of them regarding their evident status. This meeting should have been an independent review by NASA scientific investigators of *Prospector*'s find. That was the type of presentation for which he'd prepared. Unfortunately, that wasn't the meeting which Nichols had arranged. This looked like a political damage-containment session, like the Rogers Commission after the space shuttle *Challenger* explosion in 1986, rather than an impartial scientific review. The few NASA scientists present appeared to share his misgivings, and were avoiding the interlopers.

A piercing whine cut through the babble, like an axe through cream cheese, building quickly to a head-splitting squeal. All around Hanson, politicians clamped their teeth in silent pain. Hanson grinned despite the discomfort, after looking into the projection booth. A NASA scientist stood with studied nonchalance in front of a control panel. She had obviously cranked up the amplifier to way past the point where the amplified sound fed on itself. After a lifetime-long moment, she lowered the volume control (with a hand well hidden behind her back), killing the feedback. Her eyes twinkled with barely controlled mirth as they met Hanson's. She looked over his head and silently mouthed, "Sorry." He doubted that.

Hanson glanced over his shoulder and saw the NASA administrator, Harold Carucci, standing on the stage. Carucci was glaring furiously at the woman. He must have asked her to get the crowd's attention, although undoubtedly with less dramatic effects in mind. The anger vanished from his face as suddenly as if a switch had been thrown. He cleared his throat in the suddenly silent auditorium; the crowd, with ears still ringing, began making its way to the seats.

Hanson hovered briefly to appreciate the prankster. Sally Keller was worth the attention at any time, but her deflating of the stuffed shirts made him want to run over and kiss her. Sally was a classic Scandinavian beauty, with light blue eyes and a cascade of shoulder-length blond hair. She would have stood about five seven in her stocking feet, but her shoes added three inches. Her gray suit disguised her more than satisfactory figure, but the knee-length skirt revealed a terrific pair of legs. She had been married when he'd met her, and although he understood that her divorce was now final, he hadn't yet reconditioned himself to considering her available. That was a bad habit he needed to break.

The rustling of people finding their seats abated, and Hanson hustled through an unmarked door and up a short flight of stairs to wait offstage. Carucci cleared his throat again, with somewhat more aplomb than his previous attempt, and smiled. "I'm glad you heard the signal to take your seats." The audience dutifully offered up a strained laugh.

Carucci nodded toward the projection booth. The lights dimmed as he stepped behind the podium, and a single spotlight illuminated him. He smiled, set both hands on the podium, and leaned forward confidentially. "Our subject today is every bit as shocking as our call to order . . ." He paused dramatically, and the crowd obediently broke into an anxious murmur. He raised an index finger, and the attentive crowd hushed. ". . . But without the undesirable side effects." This time, the chuckles were genuine. With a modest look that must have taken hours in front of a mirror to perfect, he continued. "I'm not the person to present this exciting discovery. I'd like to introduce you to the man who is. Dr. Robert Hanson, would you come out, please?"

A second spotlight tracked Hanson across the stage. Hanson felt like a guest on "The Tonight Show." Or was it "The Twilight Zone"? Carucci kept speaking as Hanson approached. "Dr. Hanson is chief scientist and vice president of engineering at Asgard Aerospace Corporation. Those of you who have met Bob"—that left Carucci out—"know that he's an extremely capable and well-spoken technologist." He pumped Hanson's hand vigorously while continuing to speak. "Some of you also know Bob as the father of the *Prospector* probe," Carucci continued, extolling Hanson's credentials while Hanson stood, ill at ease, beside him. "I'm sure you'll be fascinated by Bob's presentation of *Prospector*'s latest discovery." To Hanson's chagrin, he received an actual smattering of applause. Carucci finally stepped into the wings, leaving Hanson alone on stage.

Under the stage lights, Hanson saw only the first few rows of the audience. That was enough: wall-to-wall eyes stared at him, like a fish store with curiosity. Cantin and Nichols sat in the front row, between a balding presidential aide and the incoming chairman of the Senate Select Committee on Intelligence. Hanson allowed himself a calming moment with the podium's controls, raising the overhead lights and killing the spots. He felt compelled to speak memorably, to coin some phrase befitting the occasion. One small step for aliens? Fingering the cluster of slick projection-control buttons, he began.

"By all appearances, space is yielding up to us one of its greatest secrets. The conclusion which has been reached by the Asgard research team is so extraordinary that I will not —yet—share it. I will start, instead, with the exceptional sequence of discoveries and realizations which we have made. I want you to see the power of the evidence, and fully expect you to join us in a remarkable conclusion. Ladies and gentlemen: we live in momentous times." Not memorable, perhaps, but okay.

"I'll begin at the beginning. A few years ago, serious planning began for the construction of massive structures in space. Governments wanted space stations for climatological studies, for manned orbital astronomical observations, even for military purposes. Industry wanted space stations for land resource surveying, communications relays, micro-gravity manufacturing, and low-risk genetic-engineering research. The electrical utilities wanted orbiting solar-power stations.

"As you know, space station *Freedom* was finally completed in 1999. It orbits today in not-so-splendid isolation. The catch was, and is, cost. Lifting construction materials from Earth into orbit remains prohibitively expensive. Lifting one pound of payload into low Earth orbit via space shuttle costs about one thousand dollars.

"Research focused on reducing the cost of lifting payloads." The unvarnished truth was that NASA had tunnel vision, but this wasn't the time or place to say so. "Congress wasn't interested in a second-generation space shuttle, though, especially after *Challenger* exploded in front of thousands of school kids. Industry couldn't afford one. The result? Except for *Freedom* and a few prototype orbiting factories, mostly automated and unmanned, the visions remain dreams. But there is another way . . ."

He pressed the down button for the auditorium's screen. Not a sound competed with the motor's hushed whirrr. Hanson pushed the visual-advance button, and a prelaunch picture of *Prospector* popped obediently onto the screen. And now for a word from our sponsor. Cantin and Nichols, apparently mind readers, smiled at him.

"This is *Prospector*." Hanson allowed his audience a moment to absorb the details: struts and beams, nozzles and fuel tanks, payload module and parabolic antennae, robotic manipulator arm. The more astute would notice the absence of familiar solar panels—these were an inefficient source of energy in the outer solar system, where *Prospector* was traveling. The compact bulk of a nuclear-powered thermoelectric generator took their place. A puzzled muttering broke out after a moment. "Some of you have noticed the castle-on-a-mountain logo where you expected an American flag. That's the Asgard logo. *Prospector* was fully funded and developed by Asgard Aerospace."

Click. *Prospector* was replaced by a computer-generated

visual of the solar system, not unlike Jimmy's display seemingly so long ago in Carlton's office. A red spark arced from Earth toward, then past, Mars. The display zoomed in on a section of the asteroid belt, resolving a benign-looking sprinkle of dust into a torrent of rushing and tumbling boulders. *Prospector* itself suddenly shot onto the screen into the swirl of asteroids. Periodically, a mountain-sized chunk rolled by. *Prospector* occasionally fired its maneuvering rockets to narrowly avoid a collision. Several viewers swallowed hard from sudden vertigo; an Army general turned suitably khaki. The displayed density of asteroids was a gross exaggeration, of course, but an effective one.

"Between Mars and Jupiter," Hanson continued, "are the asteroids, the shattered remains of an exploded planet. Most of this debris is useless stone—but a precious few of these fragments are the remnants of the planetary core, almost pure metal. Amazingly enough, it's cheaper to move an asteroid into Earth orbit than to orbit the same mass from Earth. It only takes a strategically placed shove, the sun's gravity to do the work, and a lot of patience."

Things weren't nearly that simple, of course, and he'd spent ten months and countless presentations selling the *Prospector* plan to Asgard's management. Lining up the necessary capital had cost him another sixteen months. He'd invested another two years of his life designing and building *Prospector*. NASA wouldn't buy in, but that had fortunately been during the watch of a different administrator.

Prospector was a self-directed robot spacecraft. Three years after its launch, *Prospector* had already found, and planted radio beacons on, four large metallic asteroids. In exchange for its up-front funding, USX—formerly U.S. Steel—had received the orbital parameters of the first two asteroids and the coded signals that would activate their homing beacons. At USX's leisure, it would send a robot "tugboat" to nudge the corporation's metal mountains earthward. The trip would take years, but the new owner could afford to wait.

When the asteroids neared Earth, their trajectories would be adjusted for accurate orbital insertion. Smelting, refining, casting, and other operations would be done in orbit using cheap solar power. The space stations, factories, and observatories of which Hanson dreamed—and maybe even manned deep-space probes—might finally be built.

With discovery of the third lode had come Hanson's promotion to chief scientist. Three cubic miles of nearly pure metal was an incredible asset.

Hanson continued with his sales speech, as previously demanded by Nichols. The strategy, evidently, was to bid up the value of *Prospector*. Diverting *Prospector* from its free-enterprise mission to a government assignment would cost plenty. Proud as he was of *Prospector* and its original mission, Hanson was relieved to wrap up the hype and get to the scientific purpose of today's session.

"Communications with *Prospector* were briefly disrupted last December. Not lost," he emphasized, "disrupted. The problem was tracked down to radio interference. While Asgard was broadcasting to *Prospector* from an orbiting TeleSat communications satellite, *something* was sending a beam at nearly the same carrier frequency through *Prospector*'s neighborhood."

He fingered the podium controls again, and the display returned from cosmic bumper cars to the solar-system map. A yellow beam from Earth illuminated a stylized *Prospector*, as did a blue beam that originated from an empty point in the asteroid belt. *Prospector*'s immediate neighborhood turned green where the beams converged. Then Hanson keyed a command to the podium's display computer, and the blue beam was projected onward—to intersect with Jupiter. Instantly, chaos broke out in the auditorium.

Hanson hastily cranked the ceiling lights to full and killed the computer-generated display. An incredulous crowd hurled questions and demands at him. He stood silently until the talking subsided, until everyone had again sat down. "That last picture spoke for itself, didn't it? Rather than be lynched," he forced a smile, "I'll get right to the punch line."

Hanson redimmed the lights and projected an image of the alien vessel, like the picture that he had, days earlier, shown Nichols and Cantin. This shot added familiar pieces of *Prospector*—most of the manipulator arm and half of an antenna—to the foreground. The crowd oooohed. The dark ovoid shape rotated slowly in the starlight as they watched. As a large, burned area rolled into sight, the crowd oooohed louder.

"This is the source of the interference." Hanson summarized the situation as his team had analyzed it. "First, this vessel is clearly propelled by a nonrocket technology totally unknown to us. Since the Japanese would certainly have bragged about such a breakthrough, we infer that this vessel is not of Earthly origin.

"Second, any vessel with portholes is presumably manned . . . I mean crewed." No one laughed at his little joke.

"Third, the alien ship is severely damaged. This was initially suggested by the crudity of the interfering radio signal." Hanson explained that the signal was thought to be an alien equivalent of Morse code—an SOS—improvised from radar gear. Behind him, the ship's rotation periodically showed the large burn.

"Fourth," continued the scientist, "the aliens are very shy, if not in fact secretive. The aliens have not, as far as we know, broadcast since *Prospector* pinged them with its own radar almost four weeks ago."

"Maybe their equipment failed, or they're out of power," offered the presidential aide. "Maybe the survivors of the original . . . incident died. The ship is clearly damaged. Let's not overreact to the mere fact of silence." There was much nodding of heads at this comment. Near the right end of the front row, however, Hanson noticed that a three-star Air Force general failed to relax at this convenient explanation.

"I'd like to believe it's that simple," said Hanson, "but I don't. At least, not yet. *Prospector* took a long time—then, it seemed like forever—to locate the source of the interference. The radar blips were very weak, and they only appeared on every third or fourth ranging pulse. The hull is radar invisible except when the burn is showing. We think that the ship would ordinarily be completely radar invisible. I'm not calling them hostile; I am saying that they made great efforts to be unobtrusive.''

As Hanson spoke, the wary-looking general whispered to the colonel seated beside him. The colonel circled the auditorium, stopping to talk with other officers, who in turn drifted toward the exits. Within minutes, all doors were discreetly blocked by the military. Only Hanson, on stage facing the audience, could see the cordon being established.

Hanson restored the overhead lights and turned toward the general. A NASA friend had pointed out General Hadley before the meeting. Hadley, commander of the Air Force Space Division, looked every inch the professional soldier: tall and lean; ramrod posture, even seated; short-clipped gray hair; piercing gray eyes; bemedaled dress uniform with razor-sharp creases. It worried Hanson that a professional like Hadley looked worried. Any paranoia apparently resided here. "General Hadley, I couldn't help but notice that we're now under siege. Was it something I said?"

The general bounded from his seat and turned to Carucci. "Why is this threat being discussed in open forum, instead of at Defense?" He set his left hand onto the chest-high edge of the stage, vaulted up, and faced the audience. "Everything discussed today is classified Top Secret, Eyes Only. It is not to be discussed with anyone outside of this room. You will be contacted soon by the DIA"—he was referring to the Defense Intelligence Agency—"regarding the official cover story for this meeting."

He motioned to the colonel, presumably his aide. "Get names, affiliations, and addresses of everyone here. If anyone doesn't have two photo IDs, get two independent verbal confirmations. Begin immediate security checks on anyone without a Top Secret clearance."

Carucci turned ashen. "This is a very speculative, scientific topic. I never thought . . ."

"That's obvious," snapped the general. He glared at the bureaucrat, who sank into his chair.

The general turned to Hanson. "How big is that ship? What other suspicious characteristics does it have? Are there any signs of weapons?"

The alien ship still spinning behind him, Hanson took the easy question first. "It's about thirty feet long and ten in diameter. Suspicious characteristics? At that size, neither an earthbound telescope nor the Hubble Space Telescope can see it. You'll have noticed how dark the hull is, but you may not have realized the oddness of that shade. Remember *Prospector*—it has silvery areas to radiate excess heat into space. The aliens must do something more complex to rid themselves of their own excess heat.

"When I consider the combination of radio silence, the low-observables—optically and by radar—coating on the hull, and the size, I have to believe that it's trying to avoid detection. There's no evidence, however, of a motive beyond caution.

"Weapons? We haven't recognized any. The hull is streamlined for atmospheric flight, implying that it sometimes lands. Landing capability suggests retractable wheels or landing feet, and there are circular seams in the hull that may allow entry and exit of landing gear. I can't prove that none of them are weapons ports.

"One final comment, General. We might not recognize their weapons if we saw them. Our spacecraft use the Newtonian principle—for every action there is an equal and opposite reaction. High-speed exhaust gases streaming out the nozzle accelerate the rocket in the opposite direction. This isn't a rocket. I don't know how it's propelled, so I can't predict what weapons their technology makes possible."

Hadley smacked his right fist into the palm of his left hand. "You admit that this ship demonstrates subterfuge, advanced technologies, and unknown military potential. I believe that

it represents an unknown and potentially devastating threat
to life as we know it.'' He glowered at the crowd. ''You will
be silent about this.''

Shit, thought Hanson, *some days it doesn't pay to get up*.
''Secrecy is absolutely the wrong policy. You presume that
the aliens are hostile because they've tried to avoid detection.
If they are, in fact, being secretive, they must already know
about Earth. Since they've seen *Prospector*, they know that
we know that they're there. Any hypothetical nasty plans
predicated upon surprise are compromised—and they know
that.

''Admittedly, the aliens appear secretive. That's perfectly
reasonable if they monitor our radio and television. They'd
know that Earth has several armed camps with nuclear arms
and even space-based weapons systems. They'd know about
the last election, with both sides claiming the other's victory
could realienate the Soviets and bring on a nuclear war.
Maybe they just don't want to attract the attention of crazy
Earth people!''

Hadley sneered. ''Maybe, you say. In my line of work,
we also deal with 'maybe.' Maybe they are hostile. Maybe
they have weapons against which we have no defense. What
then?''

''Will secrecy help you mobilize Earthly defenses against
some imagined attack? Bullshit.'' Hanson pounded the podium; the mike picked up the sound and boomed it around
the hall. ''If the U.S. mobilizes, the Russians will know
immediately, and they'll have no choice but to mobilize. Then
you'll have to tell the Russians about the aliens anyway, to
avoid a second Cold War, if not a nuclear war.''

Hanson addressed the crowd. ''Today we make some basic
decisions. Have we been given a scientific opportunity or a
'War of the Worlds' scenario? Do we mobilize against a
hypothetical alien attack at the risk of a nuclear exchange
with Russia?''

It went against the grain, but under the circumstances, he
was willing to engage in political maneuvering. He faced the

NASA administrator, still slouching in his chair, beneath the line of fire. "The issues are very clear-cut. You were certainly correct, Dr. Carucci, to sponsor a scientific forum. I commend your insight and courage."

He left the podium and strode to center stage. "Our opportunity cannot be overestimated. The discovery of any nonterrestrial life would be the most significant scientific event since Einstein described relativity early last century. We've found *intelligent* nonterrestrial life. As an incredible bonus, the aliens have knowledge—at least one fundamental branch of physics—which is totally new to us. Excluding the general scientific community from this opportunity would make us guilty of arrogance and paranoia of epic proportions."

Carucci stood, either in agreement with Hanson or because he had been irrevocably volunteered. Perhaps Carucci only hoped to stay on as NASA's head in the new administration. The stakes were too high for Hanson to care which. "General Hadley, sir, Dr. Hanson makes a compelling case." Behind him, many voices murmured assent. "America's space program has historically been civilian, and I'm proud to keep it that way. NASA cooperates with the military, but we're not a wing of the military."

The senator seated beside Nichols suddenly harrumphed in grand senatorial fashion. Allister McCaffrey had represented Missouri for three terms, rising to the ranking minority position on the Select Committee on Intelligence. There he'd endured years of frustrating impotence, railing in vain against what he saw as American adventurism. His only accomplishments during that period, discounting never-proven rumors about embarrassing committee leaks, were frequent appearances on the Sunday morning talk shows. In days, however, the Democrats would regain the majority position in the Senate, and McCaffrey was chairman-designate. His just-completed campaign had made it clear that the military and the intelligence community would shortly be operating under much tighter than accustomed reins.

McCaffrey rose slowly to his feet. He topped six feet by

several inches, and carried a former linebacker's weight on his broad frame. He barged down the gap between the front row and the stage, stopping by Carucci, whose shoulder he clamped with a meaty hand. "Stick by your guns, son." He locked eyes with the general, who still stood on the stage. "I assume you recognize me."

"Yes, Senator." The flat, emotionless response suggested deep contempt.

"Do you also recognize where the military's mindless hostility and suspicion have brought us? Do you intend to plan for war against a species whose only sin has been the logical effort to avoid your aggressive notice? Do you—"

"Do I still beat my wife? Cut the crap, Senator. I understand perfectly the influence of your committee on the Space Division's budget. I sincerely hope that you understand the impossibility of putting this genie back into its bottle." He stalked grimly to Hanson and concluded softly: "You win. I hope to God we won't all come to regret it."

The crowd in the NASA auditorium surged to its feet and immediately dispersed into dozens of arguing groups. As Chuck Nichols watched, dumbfounded, the military pulled back from the exits to form an impromptu honor guard around the departing General Hadley. The situation was crumbling before his eyes; Asgard's lucrative, exclusive contracts for "alien" studies would be gone before they had ever existed.

If only he understood Hanson's game. If *he'd* invented such a story, he would surely be keeping a lower profile. Or were he and Cantin fooling themselves—might Hanson have really found aliens out there? Either way, his long-rehearsed speech was apt. Almost reflexively, Nichols shouted out, "Wait!"

In the din of the hall, only a few people heard him. Nevertheless, Nichols knew he had committed himself, and he went purposefully onto the stage. There he stood, arms raised in a subconscious Nixon "victory" pose, while people around the room gradually noticed him. Once again, the hall fell silent. The military entourage halted as General Hadley paused to hear this potential new ally. Nichols took a moment to remember his sessions with Herodotus and to organize his thoughts. A screw-up by Hanson was fortunately one of the scenarios that he and Cantin had worked through. Only some of the preparatory flattery had to be tailored to this specific situation. He made his best sincere face.

"I find myself, as we all must, wondering at the significance of this momentous discovery. With my colleague," he nodded at Hanson, still on stage, "I marvel at the knowledge we might gain. Like the distinguished senator from Missouri, I hope for peaceful and friendly coexistence with our interplanetary neighbors. We may be witnessing the start of a new age of peace, as the existence of extraterrestrial life exposes the insignificance of our differences with each other. We may be at the dawning of a new golden age of commerce, sparked by trade with the aliens." The senator, that sanctimonious cretin, smiled benignly at Nichols. "I must, however, confess to you my deepest belief"—he swept a piercing stare across the hall—"that devastation and destruction will inevitably follow our contact with these beings.

"We have no compelling reason to consider the aliens hostile, nor do I think that General Hadley necessarily believes them to be. Quite properly, he takes seriously his duty to keep us strong and prepared for the worst, that the worst might thereby be prevented." Hadley examined him through narrowed, suspicious eyes, but his flock seemed to lap that up.

"We must view this situation from the perspective of history. No"—Nichols chuckled self-deprecatingly—"I'm not a closet member of the lunatic fringe. I don't claim that Earth has been visited by aliens. We can learn lessons enough from the meeting of disparate human cultures."

Hanson, he was pleased to note, had retired to the wings. "I'm not a historian, although I am interested in history. History tells us that the technologically advanced few will conquer the masses of the technologically backward. Not *may* conquer, but *will* conquer.'' Another deep breath.

''We all know how the European settlers crushed the North American Indians, pushing them into scattered reservations. When a reservation later turned out to have value, as in the Oklahoma Territory, the Indians were pushed out again. We all remember how Cortés and a handful of Spaniards conquered the Aztecs; how Pizarro and a few Spaniards destroyed the Incas. A few centuries earlier, though, the Vikings—the toughest sons of bitches in Europe—couldn't keep a foothold in North America. The difference? . . . The Vikings lacked gunpowder.

''This theme isn't restricted to the New World. Concurrent with the French and Indian Wars in the Americas, the Western Europeans fought one another and the successor states of the Mogul empire for trading posts in India—posts like Bombay. The nominal victor in India wasn't even a government—it was the British East India Company.

''Medieval Japan closed itself off from the world to avoid Western influence. To assert their seriousness, they slaughtered the Catholic missionaries and their flocks. For centuries, no Western ships were granted landing privileges. When the U.S. decided in 1854 that it was entitled to trade in that market, Commodore Perry and his modern fleet, the so-called Black Ships, forced Shimoda harbor. The Shogunate fell almost instantly. Soon after, the Western Europeans—and slightly more discreetly, the U.S.—extracted humiliating trading and territorial concessions from Imperial China. The empire was soon overthrown, to be succeeded by Sun Yatsen's short-lived republic, the warlords, and the communist revolution.

''Africa was carved into totally arbitrary jurisdictions, now independent, crossing tribal boundaries in irrational ways. To this day we see the consequences in genocidal civil wars. Remember Nigeria in the seventies?''

He took a handkerchief from a hip pocket, mopped his

forehead, and tucked it back away. "The list seems endless. Maoris in New Zealand. Aborigines in Australia. God knows how many cases there are that I don't know. That no one knows, because the winner was *too* successful. Guns, ladies and gentlemen, guns and naval superiority determined the outcome of those cultural clashes."

Nichols's audience sat hushed, expectant. The drama club had definitely been one of his wiser extracurricular activities. "Nor am I describing a phenomenon of the last few centuries, or something unique to European conquests. The ancient Egyptians suffered a multigenerational foreign rule by the Hyksos, a nomadic people out of Asia Minor. The Hyksos were culturally primitive beyond belief, compared to Pharaonic Egypt—except for two technical advantages. They had chariots, and, probably more important, they could work with iron. Their iron swords cut through Egyptian bronze weapons like butter. Technology."

He risked a glance toward the military contingent. Most of the junior officers, like the civilian audience, seemed spellbound. Hadley, the hard-nosed bastard, caught his eye and smiled enigmatically. Probably a military history nut, listening to a rehash of Air Force Academy 101. Well, what if Hadley wasn't swept off his feet? They were arguing the same case. The difference was that Hadley actually believed Hanson's computer simulations. Or (sudden insight?) saw through them, too, and didn't mind taking advantage of the situation. Nichols's spirits soared; his mind's ear heard the delicate *ching-ching* of a cash register ringing up the sale.

"I won't bore you with the whole sorry flow of war and conquest, subjugation and destruction." His voice dropped as he summed up, approaching an intense—but penetrating —whisper. "The theme is depressingly constant. The holders of the superior technology use it—as a threat, if nothing else, like when Perry opened Japan. Those with the lesser technology are exploitable, and therefore they are exploited. We cannot yet know what the aliens will eventually want from us—territory maybe, or some rare material, or even the conversion of Earth into a food-growing colony planet. I, for one, hope we never have to find out."

Timing is everything. Just as a rustle of restlessness began to form, as puzzled neighbors exchanged glances, wondering if he was done, he spoke again. He spoke loudly and forcefully, projecting from the soles of his feet, blasting everyone back into their seats. "I don't know their plans, or how their plans may evolve in light of any perceived weakness on our part. I do know that their actions are surreptitious in the extreme. I do know that they have at least some superior technology. I do know how any human civilization, past or present, would ultimately react when holding the technological advantage. Most important, I do know that we would be criminally irresponsible and foolish not to plan seriously for the risk that they," he pointed again to the still rotating spacecraft on the screen, "will act as humans historically have." Exhausted, he slumped against the podium.

General Hadley twitched his head toward an exit, and his coterie of officers dispersed instantly to their prior posts at the exits. He marched back to the front row, towering over the seated Senator McCaffrey. "I trust that you have no further argument against prudence, Senator." An intimidated nod was his only response.

Candlelight flickered warmly in the darkly paneled room, reflecting off the shining silver and china. The isolated alcoves gave the appearance of privacy, while hidden white-noise generators in the ceiling actually provided it.

Sally Keller leaned back in her chair, totally relaxed, wishing only that she could kick off her shoes. She'd lain low at today's meeting while the heavyweights slugged it out, but she knew more about the private *Prospector* mission than anyone else at NASA. Presumably she'd been invited along tonight in case Carucci was hit with a substantive question. So far, it had all been social.

The key participants of the *Prospector* review had finally

adjourned to these congenial surroundings. This "private club" was one of the necessary District restaurants cleared for classified meetings. The FBI swept it regularly for bugs, and the white noise prevented eavesdropping between tables. The waiters were all moonlighting servicemen holding security clearances.

At the head of the table, holding court, sat Chuck Nichols from Asgard. She was still blown away by his speech of that afternoon; she hadn't known that he had it—the knowledge or the eloquence—in him. She felt, without quite putting her finger on the reason why, that they'd somehow all been had. Nichols's reputation at NASA was that of a merely competent manager, someone predictable recruited by the venture capitalists after Asgard had outgrown the organizational skills of a charismatic, but wildly impulsive, founder.

To Nichols's left were General Hadley, Larry Cantin, and herself. Around the table in the other direction were Harold Carucci, her boss; Bob Hanson; and next to her, Colonel Williams, the general's aide. The colonel had a monomaniacal fixation on Hadley, which abstractly offended her self image. Admittedly, she wasn't a femme fatale, but surely some notice was in order in this otherwise all-male gathering. Cantin, on the other hand, all but drooled on her. He was the touchy-feely sort, making every conversational point with a hand on her arm or shoulder. The symbolism of his wedding band was clearly wasted on him.

She had tried, without success, to draw out Hanson. He was an exceptional scientist; she was truly impressed with the work of his team in locating the alien vessel. Hell, most scientists—herself included—couldn't even have deduced that there was anything to be traced. Equally impressive was the technology that made it possible. Hanson's technology.

Roaming the asteroid belt, *Prospector* routinely operated a quarter billion miles or more from Earth. A radio signal took twenty minutes to cross that void; an answer, another twenty. *Prospector* had to operate autonomously, and Hanson's team had written the software to make the robot fully independent of Earth—a far cry from the old *Galileo* probe, that had to be reprogrammed from Earth every few weeks.

Asgard's earthbound computers supported *Prospector* by tracking the orbits of thousands of asteroids, and by predicting the continual perturbations of their orbits from giant Jupiter's gravitational field. There wasn't a computer science group anywhere that could touch Hanson's.

She lifted her snifter and swished around the contents. It was Napoleon brandy, and the aroma was heavenly. The swirling liquid caught the flickering candlelight, casting hypnotic patterns of light and shadow over the white linen.

Her last night out with her ex-husband had been in a place like this. "We should start our family soon," she'd reminded Dick. "We've put it off for years. I'm not getting any younger."

He'd answered his shortcake, not her. "I like the way we live. Besides, my career is really taking off now, and you'd want me home every evening, changing diapers, for chrissake, when I should be making contacts. The FTC is a terrific place to be from."

"That sounds pretty definitive. Is this a take it or leave it proposition?"

He'd studied his shortcake some more, had picked up his fork and prodded a strawberry. Everything but looked her in the eye. "I wouldn't have used those words, Sal, but I won't dispute them. No kids for me, at least not soon."

That was when the marriage had ended, although naturally things had dragged on. The property settlement had gotten nasty. He'd taken their savings and moved into a bachelor pad. She'd wound up with the house, sans furniture, and an oppressive mortgage. "You want kids—you'll need the house."

A club matchbook striking her hand interrupted her reverie. The matchbook was folded strangely; she opened it up, and written inside of the cover was "Earth to Sally . . ." She looked up sharply and saw Hanson, eyes twinkling, watching her. She mouthed, "Thanks."

She'd never quite decided what to make of him. At first she'd considered him a workaholic, like Dick had turned out to be. That was only true, she'd found, where *Prospector* was concerned. When anything else was involved, he had a terrific, if terribly dry, sense of humor. She studied him for a moment: strong jaw, intense brown eyes, thin nose, sensitive mouth. Fairly handsome, in a quiet way. He should wear contacts instead of those old-fashioned wire rims, she thought. And suddenly felt embarrassed—and surprised—about pondering him so closely. She forced her attention back to the here and now.

Hanson was focused on the conversation across the table. So, to her amazement, was that lecher, Cantin. Nichols was discussing enthusiastically, if vaguely, the conversion of the *Prospector* mission to the new DOD investigation. Cantin interrupted. "I hate to bring this up, but we have a small practical problem here." What could this sleazy salesman have to contribute? She didn't understand why Nichols had even brought him.

Nichols arched an eyebrow, which Cantin took as his signal to proceed. "*Prospector* is a very significant part of Asgard's assets. Also, our annual sales projection presumes that selling coordinates for another metallic asteroid will provide a third of our expected revenue stream. Legally, we must tell investors that *Prospector* is potentially at risk, and that no additional sales are envisioned."

He addressed the general. "We're closing last year's books, and preparing the annual report and SEC filings. The outside auditors are all over the office, checking us over before issuing their opinion. They'll expect us to prove that *Prospector* is still healthy and that its mission remains viable."

"Do they get full access to the mission records?"

"Reasonably complete."

"Then I'm afraid *Prospector* is about to suffer a serious

accident. All transmissions will cease. Hanson, handle the convincing details.''

Sally exchanged puzzled looks with Hanson, then cleared her throat. "Wouldn't that announcement have a catastrophic impact on Asgard's shareholders?"

Hanson answered her. "Lloyd's of London insures *Prospector* for $200 million. Asgard couldn't possibly announce *Prospector*'s destruction without filing a claim. Then, we'll have to make the telemetry convincing, or the insurers won't settle. Given the size of the policy, they'll certainly look for excuses. So . . . either Asgard takes it on the chin, or Lloyd's does. If Lloyd's pays the claim, Asgard will still be out the revenue from foregone prospecting. The final fly in the ointment is the effect on spaceflight insurance coverage. This size claim will drive premiums through the roof, and squelch commercial space ventures for years. It happened once before, to launches of communications satellites, in the eighties."

"Trivia. Forget the bean counters." General Hadley was clearly exasperated. "Defense has plenty of discretionary funds to handle this. For public consumption, the Space Division will grant Asgard a sole-source classified contract for research on pilotless space vessels. Given *Prospector*'s success over the last few years, no one will question that. We'll also discreetly suggest to our major contractors that they use Lloyd's and Lloyd's reinsurers. If necessary, we'll award a few additional small contracts to make up any other inequities. Just concentrate on making *Prospector* available to Space Division, on getting a backup built, and on whatever else we need."

"With all due respect, General, we're contemplating a lot of economic skulduggery on the flimsiest of justifications." Hanson stared at the general, or was it just away from Nichols? Both men looked fixedly at him.

"Your boss explained it already, Dr. Hanson. Absolute secrecy on this project isn't open to debate. Wise up, now, and remain affiliated with this effort, or start contemplating career opportunities in street sweeping. You'll have no professional standing if I ever suspect you of interference."

Poor Bob! He was as entitled to his convictions as they were. As she gauged their abilities, he was more entitled. "Excuse me, gentlemen. Time to powder my nose." She hated resorting to such a clichéd, stereotypical line, but it was wiser than speaking her mind. Damn!

Some deep breathing in the ladies' room calmed her down. Sally promised herself to take Bob Hanson aside for a few well-deserved words of encouragement. He'd gone through ten types of abuse today over this paranoid secrecy nonsense, without any appreciation for his basic discovery.

She was intercepted outside the rest room door by that lecher, Cantin. He hung up the pay phone without speaking as she emerged; from the lack of farewells, she knew that the phone was merely a ruse for waylaying her.

"Hi, honey. Pretty exciting day."

"Excuse me, please," she answered coldly.

"No rush. Let's talk."

"Let me by, please," she repeated. Hanson was watching them from across the dining room. He looked away abruptly, as he saw her notice him.

"I thought you might join me tonight, Sally." Cantin smiled expectantly. "Room 422, Hyatt Regency Crystal City."

Incredible. The most encouragement she'd given him tonight was restraining herself from slapping his face. Such subtlety was apparently wasted. She smiled warmly at him, put her hand on his shoulder, and looked him straight in the eye. "Piss off." She pushed past him.

When she reached the table, the men were in the last stages of making their excuses. General Hadley and his aide stood, nodded their farewells, and left. She stood behind Hanson's chair and muttered sotto voce, "Now's our chance to escape." He scowled without looking up. He'd obviously drawn conclusions, and very wrong ones, from the tableau with Cantin. Damn that philanderer, anyway. And damn Dr.

Robert Hanson, for being so easily discouraged. "Good night," she announced, to no one in particular.

The phone booth was darker than ever; apparently some obliging vandal had put a BB through the nearest streetlight. He needed the penlight on his key chain to tap in the number. In moments, he'd placed a buy order for more Asgard stock, in the name of "Mr. Smith." Hadley would need a few days of paper shuffling to authorize Asgard's fictitious classified research project, at which point Asgard stock would soar. Then, while others were still buying on high hopes that this new project represented a whole new market for Asgard, he'd sell. Sell out before the tragic announcement that *Prospector* had been fatally damaged, apparently by meteorite impact.

He'd make a killing, Cantin considered smugly. Double his rainy-day fund within days. He had a sudden, overpowering urge to commemorate the event. He swept the penlight over the walls, seeking a bare spot. With his ballpoint, he carved in an appropriate classic from his youth. "Jesus saves. Moses invests." Then he was off, lighthearted, for home and a tall scotch.

The physicist and cosmologist were contemplating an esoteric point of quantum electrodynamics when the psychologist requested their attention. They pointedly ignored the interruption while they completed an inference. A new orbiting high-resolution ultraviolet telescope would be needed to confirm their hypothesis about quasars. With a sense of completion, they turned their attention to the interloper.

"It's happening," noted the psychologist. "Asgard is forging telemetry for a *Prospector* destruct scenario. In addition, our surveillance of Space Division shows that the *Prospector* mission profile has been duplicated in their computers. They apparently are considering replacement of the TeleSat communications link to *Prospector* with one they control."

"One they think they control," absently corrected the physicist. This wasn't news, just confirmation that everything was going as planned. He immediately dismissed the interruption from his attention. The significant problem now was reformulation of the future *Prospector* transmissions. The transmissions that would imply the need for the orbiting of high-resolution ultraviolet instrumentation.

Part II

This is the bitterest pain among men, to have much knowledge and no power.

—Herodotus
(ca. 485–ca. 425 B.C.)

· CHAPTER 5 ·

An army of jostling heads and shoulders eclipsed the projected image of the alien ship. Asgard had a suitable auditorium, with adequate seating and a stage with a twenty-foot screen, but security considerations precluded using it for viewing today's encounter. Fortunately, the computers were recording everything for enhancement and replay.

Hanson took a perch behind the mob, on a tall lab stool beside Sally Keller. He liked the view there—both forward and sideways. Beyond Sally, Carlton Moy sat at the work-station that controlled the projection system. His fingers flexed as if eager to type. Or play the piano, Hanson thought: one never knew with Carlton. He had Carlton's grudging promise to suppress the computer-generated music for today.

Typing was now futile. *Prospector* had been reprogrammed for a close approach to the aliens, successful receipt of the new program had been confirmed, and *Prospector* was on its way. *Prospector*'s current distance from Earth, a forty-minute round trip by radio, necessitated autonomous action. By the time that they first received any significant new information from *Prospector*, the appropriate response—which was unlikely to be obvious, in any event—would be long overdue.

Forty minutes after sending the go-ahead, they finally saw *Prospector*'s first hint of movement. The ovoid alien craft, by now irreverently and irrevocably renamed the Death Football, slowly expanded on the screen. Though there was nothing to hear, most conversations immediately ceased. The few viewers who kept talking were impatiently *shhhed*. The image grew slowly in size.

Hanson stared intently at the alien. He and Keller had subconsciously huddled together. He whispered nervously, "Hello. I'm with the Welcome Wagon. Please accept this book of complimentary gift coupons from the Terrestrial Merchants Association." Without removing her eyes from the screen, she jabbed a pointed elbow into his ribs.

The planning team, composed of key personnel from Asgard, NASA, and the Space Division, had argued bitterly over the best way to contact the football. They had agreed that *Prospector* should approach in a nonthreatening way, but not on what behavior would appear nonthreatening. The compromise solution entailed a very slow trajectory toward the football, accompanied by friendly radio transmissions. *Prospector* alternated between AM and FM broadcasts, since no one knew which format the aliens used.

Peaceful radio messages were alternately sent in English, Russian, French, and Japanese; they presumed that the aliens had learned at least one of these languages by monitoring terrestrial broadcasts. The messages offered help within the limits of *Prospector*'s resources. Given the improvised nature of the aliens' distress signal, however, Hanson doubted that their radio gear still worked.

Diamond-sharp stars seemed to revolve about the slowly growing craft. *Prospector* was following its programmed flight plan, converging on an arcing course whose angular velocity exactly matched the alien ship's rotation. The contact team presumed that the burned area was the alien vessel's Achilles' heel; a flyby past the burn might seem threatening.

The camera panned back, bringing *Prospector* itself onto the screen. Small forward-pointing attitude jets flared, decelerating *Prospector* gradually without a misconstruable firing of its main engines. (This detail was computer generated in the lab, since *Prospector* was not viewing itself. Hanson was impressed.) Distance and approach-velocity subtitles flashed across the screen: 1000 meters, 117 kph; 950 meters, 102 kph; 900 meters, 70 kph; . . . 300 meters, 2 kph. There was a final puff of gas, and *Prospector* came to a dead stop relative to the alien: 248 meters, 0 kph. The viewers broke into spontaneous applause.

Prospector sat stationary in space, seemingly close enough to the alien vessel to touch it. As if reading Hanson's mind, *Prospector* opened its robotic parody of a hand and extended its robotic arm. This movement was meant as the classical "open hand, no weapon" gesture. Hanson thought it looked ludicrous coming from *Prospector*, but you can't win 'em all. What they really needed, but couldn't have, was a screen on which *Prospector* could project images for the aliens.

For long minutes they watched the otherworldly tableau. The aliens' radio antenna pointed deafly about thirty degrees away from *Prospector*. The only motion was the continued slow wheeling of stars around the spaceships. Hanson glanced away from the big screen to check for status messages on Carlton's workstation. Complete zero. "No signs of activity," Hanson said. "No radio response to our messages. No significant energy of any kind detected. The accident must've been too much for them. I say *Prospector* should attempt to dock."

Heads turned all around him. One of Barb Dodge's crew flashed a thumbs-up. Colonel Williams nodded. Hanson smiled. "Go for it, Carlton."

After another interminable forty minutes, they saw *Prospector* flash its rear attitude jets. It started closing with the alien vessel. The subtitles reappeared: 200 meters, 20 kph; 180 meters, 25 kph; 160 meters, 25 kph; . . . The football filled the screen and kept growing. They watched silently as details—seams, micrometeorite scratches, hints of subsurface piping—finally showed on the smooth dark hull. *Prospector* closed the distance slowly and relentlessly: 80 meters, 25 kph; 70 meters, 25 kph; . . . *Prospector*'s forward attitude jets fired to decelerate: 60 meters, 20 kph; 50 meters, 18 kph; . . . *Prospector* began retracting its robotic arm. 30 meters, 8 kph; 25 meters, 5 kph; . . .

A blinding flash stabbed their eyes. Hanson saw little but purple and yellow glare as his retinas went into overload. "What the hell happened!" he called. No one answered, since everyone was asking roughly the same question. *"Quiet!"* he yelled.

The background noise subsided somewhat. "Can anyone see clearly?" He was beginning to see dimly himself, mostly lights and shadows, so he supposed there was no permanent eye damage.

"I can see, Bob." Hanson recognized Carlton's soft voice. "I was watching my workstation while *Prospector* closed in. *Prospector* reported a huge burst of ultraviolet-frequency photons from the alien ship just before the big screen flashed. Then both screens went dead. We're no longer receiving anything from *Prospector*. It's not jammed transmission, it's *no* transmission."

"And the flash?"

"Hold on. I'm programming a slow-motion replay of the last few seconds. Tell me when you see well enough to watch."

The shadows started resolving themselves into familiar people and objects. Hanson pushed through the crowd, toward the screen. "Is everyone okay? Anyone want medical attention?" No takers. "Then I, for one, am dying to know what happened. Carlton, roll 'em." He grabbed the brightness knob on the projector and turned it way down.

Carlton typed, and the projection screen lit again. The Death Football, more aptly named than intended, loomed large. Slowly it swelled: 30 meters, 8 kph . . . 25 meters, 5 kph . . . Suddenly, one end bulged. A wave of expansion

flowed quickly across the ship, toppling the radio antenna as
it passed. Jagged cracks raced across the ship's skin. Painfully
bright light glowed through the narrow gaps, making already
tender eyes water. The hull ruptured with a gush of flames.
Fragments flew outward, slowly at first, and then faster and
faster. Several shards shot right toward them—that is, toward
Prospector. A shredded plate of shattered hull shot forward,
like the business end of a broken whiskey bottle in a barroom
brawl. Several onlookers instinctively threw their arms up to
shield their faces.

Too late, *Prospector* reacted. It fired a pair of attitude
jets—one front and one rear. It was trying to spin around,
to turn away from the exploding alien ship, to escape. When
rotation had barely started, *Prospector* fired its main engine.
Small fragments began peppering *Prospector*, rocking it
badly. An invisible bit of shrapnel apparently severed a fuel
line, killing the engine. Futilely, *Prospector* fired all of its
rear attitude jets. The large fragment came closer and closer.
It somehow imparted impressions of both lightning speed and
the inexorable inevitability of the tide. It filled the screen.
Then blankness.

"Self-destruct charge. Suicide to avoid capture. The slimy
seven-toed sons of bitches played dead to suck us in. And
don't doubt for a moment that those bastards knew *Prospector*
is the only probe we had within months of them." Colonel
Williams forced his way through the shocked audience, toward the rear of the lab. He'd installed a secured phone line
there, a scrambled line, direct to Space Division HQ in Colorado Springs. At the time, it had seemed silly. Williams
lifted the handset.

An ailing vacuum cleaner gasped and rattled its way down
the hall. It inhaled something metallic, perhaps a dropped
paper clip, and coughed mechanically. Intermittently, Hanson
heard the clanking of wastebaskets being emptied and the
happy, Spanish-speaking voices of the cleaning crew. The
procession worked its noisy way toward him. Treacherous

sunlight wormed through the chinks of the miniblinds, into his office.

"Damnation."

Hanson spoke more in sorrow than anger. It was post the postmortem, more like rigor mortis. *Prospector* was gone. The aliens were a brooding presence, their (seven?) eyes boring into his back. Suspicious eyes—or hostile? Was this how paranoia felt?

The others were long gone, each dealing with the disaster in his or her own way. He'd brusquely refused all offers of company, from Carlton, Barbara, Sally, and even from the usually robotic colonel. He wasn't fit company for man or beast. Or for himself. "Damnation."

Things, purposeful activity, had continued briefly after the explosion. They had watched the replay over and over. They had synchronized the visuals with the telemetry from *Prospector*'s last moments.

Parker had shocked hell out of him by quickly, with Jimmy's assistance, calculating the force of the self-destruct blast. It was a hairy derivation, using information painfully inferred from the speed of the fragments and *Prospector*'s earlier measurements of the Death Football's mass. The force of the explosion was incredible, the energy released intimidating.

Moy had just shaken his head at the result. "I don't know any way to generate that much power that also produces a flood of ultraviolet radiation. Neither does Jimmy."

Mysterious energy sources, at least, gave them something productive to act upon. Earth's ozone layer effectively blocks UV radiation, so they agreed to orbit, ASAP, some UV-sensitive instrumentation. The aging Extreme Ultraviolet Explorer, launched in 1991, was the best they had—and it wasn't up to the job. Asgard would be prime contractor and system integrator for the new satellite, though the company would have to subcontract out the UV sensors. The colonel promised them an Air Force ELV—an expendable launch vehicle, probably an old Titan missile. The new satellite would monitor Jupiter and its moons—their best guess for the aliens' home (or main base)—for signs of UV emissions: the aliens presumably had many power sources of the kind that had exploded the football.

It went without saying that they'd accelerate preparation of *Prospector II*. Asgard had a backup unit in the lab for troubleshooting *Prospector*'s occasional glitch; *Prospector* was beyond troubleshooting now. All Asgard had to do to the backup was add UV sensors. Space Division had the bigger challenge: getting NASA to reschedule shuttle payloads. *Prospector II* was too large to be boosted except in a shuttle cargo bay. Once in orbit, it would use its own engines to head for deep space.

Carlton had pulled the toughest assignment. He would head the team of physicists charged with discovering the principles behind the aliens' power plants. No one knew if the assignment was even possible; everyone could only hope that adequate hints lay buried in the final transmissions. No one dwelled on the long odds against success. *Prospector* hadn't needed high-resolution UV sensors for its original mission, and had been equipped accordingly.

Everyone finally left in search of solace or oblivion. Hanson hadn't actively pushed them out. Not, that is, unless you considered acute mopery an act of commission. He pictured their departures in his mind's guilty eye. Carlton had looked regretful, the colonel worried, Sally hurt. Hurt? That too, but also offended. They'd really gotten to know each other well, to the exclusion of her socializing much with the rest of the team. Her offer to stay had also been a cry for some company herself. Prince among men that he was, he'd snarled, "Leave me alone." Add being an inconsiderate ass to his list of recent successes.

Let's sum up my life, Hanson thought. He'd pissed off hostile aliens whose technology made him feel like a curious chipmunk. His life's work had been blown to hell. He'd demonstrated to half of Washington that he was a wishful-thinking jerk. He'd just chased away a whole roomful of his friends. He'd met a wonderful woman, who was actually crazy enough to hang around with him, and he'd brushed her off like a piece of lint. He wondered if he should go home and stuff his head in the toaster oven.

Thought had apparently followed the rest of his acquaintances out the door. Well, if you can't be thoughtful, at least be systematic. Disk after disk of data just waited to be analyzed. It was someplace to start, something to do. They had barely scratched the surface of the possible analyses. To get right down to it, *none* of them had been particularly thoughtful since the explosion. About the only data that they'd processed tonight were Jimmy's enhanced representations of *Prospector*'s camera images. He smiled: damned good enhancements. But sanity required that he forget those images, and the scientific method suggested that he go back to the source material.

Postmortem. Life goes on. He twisted the control handle on the miniblinds, admitting the crisp, bright sunlight of a winter morning.

Prospector's demise was too recent, too painful to research now. Let others do that. He'd start with *real* source material, the original jammed transmissions. Everything had started when they had inferred alien signals from the jamming of signals to *Prospector*. The resulting signals, like the horrifying images tonight, were all computer enhanced. *Prospector* had always been jammed to some extent: by sunspots, Jupiter's natural radio emissions, the random electrical noise of the universe. How much of the alien signal had *Prospector* "corrected" out of existence? He hadn't designed *Prospector* for cosmic eavesdropping. And how many of *Prospector*'s requests to TeleSat for retries had been wrongly attributed to random, natural electrical noise?

He swiveled to face his workstation, whistling idly as he composed his thoughts. One of the cleaning crew knocked hesitantly at the doorway. Hanson gestured him in. The crew person hurriedly emptied the wastebasket and left.

The transmission records that Hanson needed were in

TeleSat archives. TeleSat kept its most current few months of transmission data for statistical analysis—they provided early warning of equipment deterioration. He could use this information for other purposes—to infer past sunspot activity from the retransmission requests of all TeleSat clients. He might then be able to determine which specific *Prospector* retransmission requests were sunspot-related and which were alien-related. If they could clear some of the background noise out of the inferred alien signal in this way, then Chandragupta, the Indian cryptologist in the NASA contingent, might make more sense of it.

It sounded logical, if you cared about the opinion of a manic-depressive who'd been up all night. Well, any port in a storm.

Now, how could he get that TeleSat information? It wasn't as if he had any obvious right to it. Fortunately, an old college classmate, Mary Pickette, worked at TeleSat. Not at this hour, and he couldn't stay awake much longer, but she did work there. He fired up the electronic mail package, Ben, on his workstation and composed a request. It ranked high on the song-and-dance scale, since no one at TeleSat was cleared for *Prospector* information, but he thought it would get by someone with no reason to be suspicious. He typed CONTROL-C, which closed the file and sent the message.

Neither rain nor snow nor sleet nor hail nor malevolent septapi shall stay these electrons from the speed-of-light completion of their appointed circuits.

Communication facilities, like money, mostly exist as entries in computers.

The TeleSat computer had been invaded. At the appointed hour, while a minimal crew of night operators boredly sipped their coffee, the invading program struck. The style of attack was time-honored: a Trojan horse. The innocent-seeming general-ledger program, previously modified by a hacker, now lowered its trapdoor and activated its treacherous subroutines. The security system of the computer never had a chance.

The invader patched a subtle change into the remote diagnostic software for TeleSat VII. Seven was a high-capacity comsat, with five radio transponders. Only a *very* clever programmer could recognize the *very* indirect effect of the patch, which was to always fail transponder two. The invader then retrieved the maintenance record for TeleSat VII and pumped up its error counter for transponder two.

At the next bit of cosmic static, gongs went off in the control room. Fault recognition software automatically responded, while no-longer-bored operators anxiously watched the unacceptable error rate reported for transponder two on TeleSat VII. Long-distance transmissions were automatically switched to spare channels of the remaining four transponders. Diagnostic software was initiated; it repeatedly failed transponder two. On the third unsuccessful retry, software retrieved the maintenance record for transponder two and marked it "Out of Service."

The invader lay low until the next operator shift, when it slipped two messages into the transmission queue for the rooftop satellite dish aimed at TeleSat VII. The messages were dutifully beamed up to the satellite.

TeleSat VII was a simple device serving a simple purpose: the receiving and repeating of radio transmissions. It also responded to appropriate commands embedded into the message stream. Tonight it received a command to realign transponder two to a new direction. It dutifully obeyed. TeleSat VII was therefore ready for the invader's second message, which required transmission in an uncustomary direction.

The second message traveled as intended for about twenty minutes, when it was received by the parabolic radio antenna of a small space probe. The probe decoded the message, validated the command, and returned an acknowledgment. As ordered, the probe sought out three particularly bright stars to obtain a precise celestial orientation. It locked its navigational computer onto its target: the gas giant, Jupiter. It fired its engines.

Prospector was on its way.

· CHAPTER 6 ·

Nichols drew his heavy drapes; he no longer used his inner office for privacy. He believed that the government had him under routine surveillance as part of the alien research program. Surveillance was the most plausible explanation for Pinkerton's sudden replacement of the security consultant assigned to Asgard. Nichols assumed that the new man planted bugs, instead of seeking them. He now used the inner sanctum for appearances only, when he didn't mind being overheard.

The new drapes were countermeasures. Laser systems can detect and amplify speech-induced window vibrations from great distances. The sound-muffling drapes would foil such laser spying—and any lip readers. He turned on a tape player to foil any conventional bugs.

"So far, Larry, our little project is going well. Surprisingly so."

Cantin, seated, waited silently.

"The money is rolling in. *Prospector II* was a backup, and almost pure profit; the Space Division is making progress payments on *Prospector III*; and Lloyd's seems ready to pay for the original *Prospector*. Now this." Nichols waved a flimsy sheet of paper from his desk. "Too much good fortune makes me suspicious."

Cantin took the telex message.

Space Division has lost contact with Sunlamp. Radar shows Sunlamp in proper orbit, but it neither transmits nor responds to signals. Changing shuttle schedules to retrieve unit for repair is impractical. Urgent that you build replacement. All contributing expenses authorized.

Hadley

Sunlamp was the code name for the Space Division's UV satellite. "A love letter from the Tin General."

"Can it, Larry. Things feel out of control. Are there aliens out there? Maybe a stealth ship zapped the satellite."

"There aren't any aliens, Chuck." Nichols was cracking under the strain. Cantin used a calm, reasoning tone. "There never were. You know that."

"I thought I did. I thought I understood that *Prospector* just stumbled on an illegal probe. I thought I understood that the owners must have blown it up to avoid embarrassment. I can accept that. But why wait until *Prospector* was on top of them to blow theirs up?"

"I doubt that they did. Hanson's been showing us some great movie footage."

Nichols scratched an ear thoughtfully. "You've said that before, but could he fake it that convincingly?"

Lord, what an innocent. "Remember the Herodotus program? Ancient olive trees bending in the wind? Waves crashing against the cliffs? That system was developed by a grad student, for chrissake. Of course Hanson could have faked the aliens. My money says he faked all of the pictures."

"Why?"

"Hanson climbed out on a limb when he diverted *Prospector*. When it didn't pan out, he needed a way to climb back in." Cantin poured himself some ice water from Nichols's carafe. "This is one giant diversion."

Nichols shook his head. "So Hanson whipped up the pictures of the aliens when *Prospector* spotted an Earth probe?"

"*Prospector* probably never spotted anything. If I were the owner, I'd have moved my probe if I could, or blown it up if I couldn't, long before anyone could make an ID. No, I doubt *Prospector* saw anything."

"Then *Prospector* is still out there?"

Cantin took a sip. "Must be, not that it matters. My guess is that Hanson and company screwed up badly when they threw together *Prospector*'s snark-hunt program. I'll bet that they just lost control of *Prospector*, lost the ship altogether. Remember the Soviets losing a Phobos probe in 1988? They accidentally turned its solar panels away from the sun and let the batteries drain."

Nichols grinned sheepishly. "No aliens?"

"No aliens."

Noise crashed off the walls. Hanson predicted that the new-wave punk band could render Carlton insane within minutes. Carlton had had the good sense to attend Tunghai University in Taiwan, however, making him ineligible for the night's festivities.

Tonight was Hanson's fifteen-year college reunion. He'd avoided this brain-curdling cacophony through three degrees at the U of I; it was a mystery why he inflicted this torture on himself now. He certainly didn't enjoy crowds. His fondest school memories were of small groups and solitary events. Soaking up lunchtime rays on the Quad, ideally during a concert from the Altgeld Hall bell tower. Snarfing pizza and beer with dateless dorm buddies after a rowdy Auditorium movie. Catching a jazz band concert with friends at the Great Hall of the Krannert Center. Playing cards all night. Even late-night bitch sessions at the Digital Computer Lab. Not mob scenes like this.

People he'd never met crammed the Stouffers ballroom in Oak Brook. He was here solely from psyching himself out. This way, he only had to kick himself for wasting an evening. If he'd wisely chosen to stay home, he would instead have kicked himself for weeks about all of the missed romantic opportunities. Viewed that way, tonight had an excellent return on investment.

Faugh. Enough mingling in vain hopes of bumping into someone familiar. Enough cruising for unattended females.

Not enough scotch. He wove his way across the packed dance floor and exited to the anteroom. Good. The crowd at the bar was only four deep.

Waiting his turn, Hanson decided that this fiasco had at least taken his mind off of the tail-chasing at work. Sunlamp had not reported anything useful before going mysteriously belly up. Carlton was going quietly bananas researching the aliens' energy source. His theory, resulting from a collaboration with Jimmy, hypothesized a massive new subatomic particle with a very short decay time. The snag? It would take an enormous new particle accelerator, literally the size of Montana, to test the theory. The proposed accelerator would make the Superconducting Supercollider in Texas look like a toy. Even General Hadley had blanched at the proposed expense—not even the Air Force could take that much out of petty cash. Hanson's own playing around with original *Prospector* transmit records had yielded exactly nothing.

"Sir. Sir, can I help you? Sir?"

Someone poked his shoulder with a sharp finger. "Danger! Danger! Limes are desiccating even as your eyes glaze."

The bartender was eyeing him strangely, as well he should. Gotten his mind off work, indeed! "Scotch rocks, please," mumble, mumble. Hanson pulled a roll of bills from his trouser pocket, change from an earlier drink, and peeled off a fiver. "Keep the change."

The pointed finger struck again. "How many of those have you had, fella?"

Four, as if it were anyone's business. He turned. Curly orange hair, somewhere between Charlie Brown's little red-headed girl and Dennis the Menace's friend Margaret. Hanson could have rested his chin on the woman's head without stretching. Without her removing her spike heels. "Mary Pickette, as I drink and pickle." He took her still-poised hand and examined the inch-long, purple-painted nails. "Do not bend, fold, spindle, or mutilate. What's your poison?"

"Zombie."

He parted with another fiver. "And you impugn my sobriety. I hope this is your first."

She snorted. "Let's sit. Craning up at you is hazardous to my vertebrae."

Conversation became more practical once they sat, and they covered a lot of good, mostly old, times. "It's terrific to see you, Mary. Doesn't happen often enough. I wouldn't mind seeing Harold, either." Harold was her "significant other," the English lit teacher with whom Mary had lived the last few years. Harold lived his role to the hilt, favoring elbow-patched tweed jackets and briar pipes. "Where is the professor?"

She twitched a thumb toward the ballroom. "The last time I saw him, he was going down for the third time." She tipped her glass back and chugged a quarter of the contents. Hanson joined her. "Never saw her before in my life."

He almost choked before he could swallow his mouthful of scotch. "I hope you never grow up."

Mary dipped her finger tips into the zombie, then sprinkled him with a few drops. "All it takes is a little practice . . . and a pinch of pixie dust." She staggered to her feet. "Well, I must fly. Somewhere a floozy is being poetized. It's a slow and painful death, much like being beaten with cooked cauliflower."

"Wait."

She cocked her head and eyed him curiously. "Yes, Mother."

"All seriousness aside, I owe you a thank you."

"Did the earth move for you, too?"

Damn, but she could be exasperating. "Cut it out. I really appreciate the TeleSat transmission files you sent me a while back." They'd been no help whatever, but that wasn't her fault.

"What files? When was this?"

"Always the kidder. You know, maybe six weeks ago."

Mary looked at him strangely. "What the hell are you

talking about? I never sent any such information. I couldn't have even if asked."

Hanson stared right back. "Of *course* you sent it. I requested it by email and got an optical disk two days later by Federal Express. I replied with a bit of deathless electronic thank-you prose. You responded by email to that." He inhaled deeply. "Okay, I should have been a little more personal; I suppose it meant bending a few rules. Trust me that I asked in a good cause, and that I was *very* preoccupied at the time."

"Bob, you misunderstand. I'm not mad. I'm confused and scared shitless. There's no way that what you described could've happened. Six weeks ago we lost a transponder on TeleSat VII. Twenty percent of VII's capacity, down the tubes without warning. Four percent of the bloody company's transmission capacity." She collapsed back into her chair. "These things aren't supposed to happen without warning. You know how much redundancy and self-checking is built into the circuits. We had a full scale, burn 'em at the stake, pee on the ashes witch-hunt. All transmission records were frozen, turned over to an outside consultant. I sure as shit would remember any innocent request for transmission records about then."

Hanson tried feebly, "I asked about TeleSat V, not VII."

"Gimme a break. I got no request, sent no package, received no 'thank you,' replied no 'you're welcome.' " She shivered. "Hey sailor, buy a girl a drink?"

"Why not." He followed her to the bar. "Have one for me, too. I gotta go. I'll call tomorrow to hear how I enjoyed it." He put a hand under her chin and tilted her face up toward his. "I don't pretend to understand this, but I swear that I will. Promise me you'll keep this to yourself." She nodded quickly.

The Saturday-night traffic moved quickly once he got onto eastbound Twenty-second Street. Oncoming headlights made his eyes ache in remembrance of the evening's libations. He sailed through to the Tri-State Tollway, which, as usual, was torn down to two lanes each way. Things opened up once he took the I-90 interchange. He reached his apartment in Palatine in a reasonable thirty minutes.

Badge in hand and breath mint in mouth, he drove the short jaunt to the office. The guard was alert despite the hour: the past few months had seen a major increase in nocturnal visitations. "Evening, Dr. Hanson. Please sign in, sir." The guard compared the badge's photo and signature to Hanson and his signature in the logbook. He returned the badge. "Go ahead."

As he entered his office, Hanson wondered what he should be looking for. He logged onto his workstation out of habit. It displayed, "No new mail." Signs and portents. Okay, mail was as good a place to start as any. He listed his saved mail messages, and found the two remembered messages from Mary. He dumped both to his office printer.

Reading the messages with a jaundiced eye, he marveled at his gullibility: there wasn't an innuendo between them. The author couldn't know Mary very well. At all. That left two very basic questions: *who* had sent the messages (and the disk full of data!), and *why*. *How* wasn't worth puzzling over—he'd never met an electronic mail system whose security he couldn't easily crack.

The message's author presumably had a reason, whoever he (she?) was. Hanson, you're an analytical fellow, right? Figure it out.

The author either was a TeleSat employee, or he wasn't. Assume for now that he was. A prank? No, sending that disk was too serious to be a prank. If the disk was meant to get Mary into trouble, she'd be in trouble by now. Certainly, the author hadn't sent the information to help her. Conclusion: the author was not at TeleSat.

Sherlock Holmes would have considered this a two-pipe problem. Hanson twisted his sideburns. A hacker? A too-bright kid out for some cheap thrills? Too farfetched. A kid wouldn't persecute Mary, or anyone else, by playing with mail over the space of several days. A criminal hacker? This stunt wouldn't make any money. In fact, a professional who'd penetrated TeleSat's computer security would raid the financial accounts and be gone. Games with mail would be an unprofessional (make that stupid) risk.

Sometimes being logical just sucked. If the culprit was not with TeleSat, and not unrelated to events, then he was related to *Prospector* somehow. That meant NASA, Space Division, Asgard, or someone spying on one of the above. Talk about your paranoia.

He needed coffee to combat the scotch, and stretching his legs might help. He ruminated while he walked. He had a disk full of data purportedly from TeleSat, a disk which someone had gone to great lengths to authenticate. Bad news, fella. I don't trust one bit on it.

He dropped two quarters into the swill dispenser. Extra chemicals and sugar. Ugh.

Would NASA have him under surveillance? Ridiculous. Hadley's boys? Possibly, but why would they try actively to mislead their own principal investigator? That left Asgard itself or unknown spies. Time to get measured for a canvas suit with wraparound sleeves.

He navigated his sludge safely back to his office, and took a sip. Slightly cooler ugh. Did anyone at Asgard have a motive? Who would profit? Mental alarms clanged. *Profit.* To understand behavior, follow the money. Asgard was cleaning up by hunting aliens. The cash flow from the government was steady, too—a lot steadier than from *Prospector*'s high-tech scrap-metal operation. Certainly, after an initial dip, the market was much happier with Asgard's undefined defense contracts—and the prospect of a big insurance claim—than it had been with the rock-chasing business. Asgard stock was up fifty percent for the year.

Asgard involvement had an unfortunate ring of truth. Could someone high up in Asgard have faked the data, invented the aliens? The financial motive was obvious. The perpetrator of such a fraud certainly had reason to keep watch over Hanson, lest Hanson discover the trick. Whoever could pull off faking the aliens via simulated TeleSat interference had demonstrated his ability to play games with the TeleSat computers. Hell, Hanson realized, his own message to Mary had probably been intercepted before ever leaving this building. The answers to his mail were probably forged here, too.

Too bad he didn't keep empty boxes—he wondered if the "TeleSat" disk had actually come from TeleSat. It wasn't really important. The author of this scam could easily have sent electronic mail to a computer operator at TeleSat, with instructions to mount a blank disk for copying and then ship it, but that wasn't likely. Mary had mentioned auditors looking into the transponder failure. They would certainly have contacted him by now if the disk had been sent by TeleSat.

Hanson crumpled the now empty cup and arced it into the trash. Two points. Sharp as a tack and coordinated too.

Time to get serious. He'd piled deduction upon inference upon conjecture, all from the single fact of the forged mail messages. Just one fact. Posted on Carlton's office wall, done up by his wife in counted cross-stitch, was a relevant cautionary comment:

> Moy's Principle of Scientific Inquiry:
> Extrapolation is a dangerous business.

> Moy's Corollary:
> Many lines can be extrapolated through one point.

Words to live by. If he were onto anything besides a terrible hangover, then his theory ought to successfully predict something. The scientific method, and all that.

All right, then, he had two predictions. First, there should be evidence of faked *Prospector* data, now that he knew to look for it. Second, and here he was going for broke, someone high in the company—someone with a lot of stock and big stock options—must have been using beaucoup computer time. That was the easiest prediction to check. (Unless they were fixing the time records too. Well, he wouldn't take lack of a big account balance as conclusive.)

He had to investigate by computer, and the perpetrator—whoever he was—was a computer whiz. Well, Hanson could be devious too when he wanted.

He typed WHO on his workstation keyboard. The screen immediately displayed:

                    hrogers   18:07
                    gupta   19:21
                    rhanson   21:35

Okay, Hal Rogers and Chandragupta were both logged in. Chandragupta might notice unusual behavior—he was a top-notch scientist. Hal, on the other hand, was the night-shift computer operator. Hanson grabbed the phone and punched in the computer room's three-digit extension. "Hal? Bob Hanson. I've been catching up with paperwork, and suddenly I'm starving. Split a pizza?"

"Garbage pizza would be good."

Hanson grimaced. "Have pity on an old man. Sausage and mushroom? Hamburger?"

"You have no sense of adventure. In the spirit of compromise, I'll settle for a barbecue, bacon, and onion."

It wasn't as if Hanson meant to eat any. "Sold. I'll call in the order and retrieve it from the lobby."

"I'll get it. As you say, I should have pity on an old man."

"This pizza may wind up costing you plenty—out of your next raise. Just sit and mind the store."

"Say, Bob, I see that Chandragupta is logged in. Did you ask him?"

"Wasn't interested," Hanson lied. "See you in a bit." He prayed that the Indian wouldn't have reason to call the computer room.

He was pondering how to attack the presumably faked data when his phone rang. "Dr. Hanson? Security. Your pizza's here. Sorry I can't bring it up."

"No problem. The walk will burn off a bite or two. Feel free to grab a slice."

"Don't mind if I do."

Hanson made his way quickly to the lobby. He didn't have to use a badge reader to go in this direction; he just had to push the button that unlocked the door from the inside. He eyed the guard's badge. "Thanks for paying, Tony. What do I owe you?"

"Ten."

Hanson peeled off a bill and grabbed the box. He made a show of balancing the box on one hand, then switching to two. "Get the door?"

Tony got out from behind the reception desk, slid his own badge through the card reader, and opened the door. "Enjoy."

The door clicked behind Hanson, and he was back in the secure area. The access-control system—the computers—had no record of him leaving his office. An observer using the system would know that someone had gone to the lobby, but not who. That someone would most likely have been from the cleaning crew. Nothing to alarm any observer.

Phase one complete. The LED glowed steadily in red on the badge reader beside the computer-room door, indicating an actively protected zone. Hanson knocked on the window for Hal's attention, holding up the pizza box for inspection. Hal rolled his eyes in mock exasperation, unfolded himself from a slouch, and opened the door from inside—pressing another badgeless exit button. "Greetings, O omnivorous one," Hanson said, then stopped halfway in the door. "Damn. Forgot to order Cokes. It's your turn to fetch—I'll hold the fort." Hal pushed past him through the still-open door. Hanson let the door slam.

Phase two complete. He was in the computer room, unobserved by the access system, at an unattended, logged-in, system-administrator terminal. But only unattended for a moment. He dumped summary computer-billing files for the last three months to an idle laser printer, which quickly spit out the data. He folded and crammed the few letter-sized sheets into a trouser pocket. The pocket bulged suspiciously, so he untucked his shirt for camouflage.

Phase three complete. The papers in his pocket were, as far as any computer surveillance could indicate, unrelated to him. He ripped the top from the pizza box, liberated a celebratory slice, and carried it deep into the computer room. Soon, he heard a muffled banging, like knees striking the door, which he studiously ignored.

"Didn't you hear me knock?" Hal stood in the doorway, two brimming plastic cups balanced precariously in one hand, slipping his badge back into its clear clip-on holder with his other. "I guess the ears go second." He handed Hanson a cup. "Gimme food."

The access system now "knew" why the computer-center door had opened minutes ago—Hal must have left, since he had just returned. Mission accomplished. "Eat up."

Four odious slices later, Hanson excused himself. Back in his office, he removed the wadded-up papers from his pocket. Bingo! Both Cantin and Nichols were using lots of computer time. Hanson dug up his Chart of Accounts, and ran his finger down the pages until he found a match. The big boys were using the expert systems. Somehow, they must have enlisted the "experts" to trick the human experts. He understood how Nichols suddenly knew so much history.

Now he had two facts, the faked email and the predicted heavy computer usage. He was sure now that the purported *Prospector* transmissions were faked. He had several transmission files resident on his workstation's hard disk, downloaded days ago from the computer center. The trick would be analyzing them without being detected. Any computer might have surveillance software installed. He twisted a sideburn for a while, then smiled. What couldn't talk wouldn't cause trouble.

Hanson logged off his computer, logically returning the machine to its stand-alone mode. He traced the clear, telephone-like cable from his machine to the wall, then popped the quick-connect plug from its socket—physically isolating the workstation. Any surveillance software was disabled.

He logged onto the workstation again, then leaned back to think. He'd spent several unsuccessful weeks trying to correlate TeleSat data about client transmission problems—sunspot interference, mostly—with *Prospector*'s transmission problems. The theory was simple: if he could cancel out the natural transmission errors, then he could better identify alien-caused interference. There had been no correlations of a statistically significant duration.

Now he had a new perspective. His email to Mary had explained what information he wanted, but not why, so the fabricator had had no clue what to provide. That would certainly explain why the TeleSat data wouldn't correlate with *Prospector*'s.

Okay, assume that the TeleSat data was faked. How might the forgery have been done? Now it seemed obvious: random numbers. Computers big and small could generate them, whether for making video games interesting or for simulating nuclear war outcomes.

Random-number generation is a standard problem in computer science. In fact, there is no mechanical way to generate *truly* random numbers. There are standard pseudorandom algorithms, however, that provide a good approximation to randomness. Unless the random-number program is itself started off—seeded—with a "random" number, however, it yields the same sequence of numbers every time. At Asgard, standard programming practice was to seed the generator with the number of milliseconds since the start of 1980.

Hanson rubbed his hands with glee. He rapidly knocked out a simple program to test his idea. The program simple-mindedly repeated a simple loop: it seeded the random-number generator, generated one hundred "random" numbers, and correlated the sequence with the supposed TeleSat transmission errors. On each pass through the loop, the program reseeded the random-number generator. Hanson started the seed at the time, in milliseconds past 24:00 of 12/31/79, when he had sent Mary his request.

Waiting for program completion would be the hard part: there are 86,400,000 milliseconds per day. The program would run until it found a correlation or until it had tested for all times between his request and Mary's first response, one and a half days later. Unfortunately, his modest 100 MIPS—millions of instructions per second—workstation could run the loop with only about ten seeds per second. Worst case, then, this test would take, gulp, about 150 days. Tomorrow he'd have to consider an intelligent solution— "pseudorandom" was not truly random, and there would certainly be some opportunity for clever shortcuts.

All things considered, it seemed silly to wait up for results. He slipped on his coat and started out the door, then stopped. Better keep prying hands off the machine. He dug a notepad from a pile of miscellany on his desk and ripped out an empty page. Pencil tip in mouth, he considered a phrasing. He finally etched out, in big block letters:

DANGER: 1,000,000,000 OHMS.

He tucked an edge of the sheet between two rows of keys on the keyboard, and weighted it in place with the pencil. The sheet leaned back against the screen, nicely hiding the display.

"Beep-beep-beep-beep."

Hanson brushed the sign aside, sending the pencil rolling to the carpet. He plopped into his chair and read the screen. "Match found. Correlation at REQUEST TIME + 0:00:27.362." Call it twenty-seven seconds.

So now he had proof. His electronic mail was being intercepted, TeleSat data was being faked, and Asgard executives were using excessive amounts of computer time. *Prospector*'s "discovery" of the aliens, everything about the aliens, and Asgard's whole posture toward NASA and the Space Division were by inference fraudulent.

"Shit." He turned off the workstation, climbed slowly to his feet, and zipped his coat. "What now, smart guy?"

Driving home, his mind worried at a final glaring mystery: how could the TeleSat data have been forged within seconds of his request? He shivered thinking about it. He finally decided that his observers must have selected their seed in a nonstandard way, like time-of-day minus a day. A twenty-seven-second response was just unthinkable.

The sun was peeking around the edge of his bedroom shade as he climbed into bed. There had to be an odd seeding of the random-number generator. What else could it be?

Only the psychologist knew why he had called the meeting. The conspirators exchanged conjectures, not knowing why they had reconvened for the first time since last fall's elections. Theories rose and fell from favor, hypothesis was piled upon surmise upon speculation. Their elaborate mental constructs all fell of their own weight, mental houses of cards lacking a foundation of facts. Finally, one irrefutable, if unsubstantiated, premise remained: their security was somehow endangered.

The psychologist waited for the laggards to join the group and the babble to cease. Expectant silence eventually rewarded his patience. "There is reason to believe that the *Prospector* project has been penetrated."

"Reason? Believe? Who? How?"

He waited out the imperious demands for information. "The evidence is not conclusive. As you know, our surveillance is necessarily indirect, and humans, unlike electrons, are not subject to rigorous analysis." The trailing part of the comment was meant to preempt any more unsolicited advice from the physical scientists. There are more possible connections between the neurons of one human brain than there are atoms in the universe. Physicists had easy problems.

"As you know, we routinely do a daily search of all Asgard computers. Bob Hanson's workstation failed to respond today, but it was successfully connected to the central computer last night. Since the last use was unusual—late on a Saturday evening—I investigated before assuming an equipment failure."

"How do you know it was Hanson on the terminal?" The computing expert, as always, was belligerent. He was obviously about to sneer again at the inferior quality of programs for computer-system security. *Fair enough*, thought the psychologist, *the programmer has infiltrated many a computer system on our behalf*.

"It was him: I checked the access-control computer." He dismissed the matter. "As I said, Hanson went into Asgard late last night. Working any Saturday evening is very unusual, but what made me suspicious was his on-line calendar. Hanson had planned to attend his college reunion that evening. His bank records show that he purchased a ticket.

"By itself, of course, an odd work shift is not significant. I checked the audit trail of his computer activity, though, and found that he had printed his old mail from Mary Pickette."

"Call me Mary," interrupted the computing expert. He was insufferably proud of his cleverness in mimicking the TeleSat mail system on the Asgard system. Clearly a defect in his programming.

"As you know, she is Hanson's contact at TeleSat; he knows her from college. Her calendar and bank records also indicated that she planned to attend the reunion. There is no direct evidence that either attended, or, if they did attend, that they spoke. But if they didn't . . . why did he suddenly print out her mail on a Saturday night?

"Next, I reviewed Hanson's recent computer usage. He has been analyzing the alien-related *Prospector* transmissions, particularly in relation to TeleSat transmission errors —the faked transmission errors sent under Pickette's name. Again, I can't prove anything, but the circumstances are very suspicious."

The cosmologist signaled for attention. "Did he do anything that indicates suspicion on his part?"

"Good question. He logged in at 21:35, read his old mail, did nothing for a while, did a WHO, then did nothing until logging off near midnight."

"If he wasn't using the computer, what was he doing?" The cosmologist again.

"I checked the Asgard telephone records. Shortly after the WHO, he called one of the logged-in users, the system administrator. Then he called out of the building. I checked the Illinois Bell computer: he called a pizza parlor."

"He left his reunion to eat pizza in an almost-empty office?" The sociologist was dubious.

"It bothered me, too," answered the psychologist. "I have no proof that Hanson left his office all evening. There was a strange sequence of phone calls and door openings; none of the door openings involved Hanson's ID badge. I'll spare you the details, but, inferentially, Hanson used the pizza to get let into the computer center, then convinced the operator to leave for four minutes. Someone unauthorized was in the computer room—and a computer-usage billing file was printed—while the administrator was absent. I assume that Hanson wanted the data to look for suspicious computer usage. Why else the subterfuge about getting the information?"

"Reasonably intelligent, for a manager," begrudged the computing expert.

"Do I have this right?" asked the cosmologist. "You claim that Hanson met Pickette at their reunion. He discovered that her mail responses were faked, and thereby became suspicious that the *Prospector* data was faked. Then he returned to Asgard to look surreptitiously at accounting files, hoping to catch the culprit."

"I don't claim that, I infer it."

"He doesn't suspect us."

"Apparently not," agreed the psychologist. "Again, I caution you that I cannot prove any of this."

"Is there other relevant information?" asked the exobiologist.

"Just a big question. Several hours passed between the time Hanson logged off, shortly after smuggling the accounting data, and the time he left the building. What was he doing?"

The sociologist answered quickly. "Probably asleep at his desk." Which was certainly possible.

The computing expert interrupted again. "Enough chitchat. What do we do about Hanson?"

"Nothing yet. Our evidence is circumstantial, and none of it suggests any danger to us. Tending to Hanson might attract more attention than any action he is likely to take."

"And when will we do something?"

"When it's necessary. Not sooner."

· CHAPTER 7 ·

"I don't need an appointment!"

"Mr. Nichols has given very strict orders. He sees no one without an appointment."

"He'll see me."

"Could you tell me the topic? I'll see what I can do."

Indistinct arguing in the anteroom had been annoying Nichols for several minutes. He was about to complain when the voices became louder and more intelligible. Ms. Finch was doing battle with an uncharacteristically assertive Bob Hanson. Why was Hanson so insistent upon seeing him?

Nichols switched on his intercom. Hanson was shouting, "I'm not leaving without seeing Chuck. Either tell him I'm here, or I go in unannounced."

"Mr. Nichols is in conference, and cannot be disturbed."
Not said very convincingly, thought Nichols.

Hanson apparently agreed. "Chuck have an early Monday
morning appointment? Fat chance. Show me."

"Get away from that terminal."

"Hah! Nothing until the weekly staff meeting at ten.
Decide—are you announcing me, or do I let myself in?"

Nichols didn't care to concede the initiative to Hanson,
especially since the topic was a mystery. He held the transmit
button. "Ms. Finch. Is there a problem?"

"I'm sorry that we disturbed you, sir. Dr. Hanson insists
upon seeing you, refuses to make an appointment, and won't
tell me what it's about."

"Give me five minutes to finish something, then send him
in." Hanson sounded obsessed: there was no telling what
this was about. Maybe the good doctor couldn't take the strain
of losing *Prospector*, and of his elaborate cover-up. Maybe
he was going to blurt out a confession. Couldn't have that
sort of information floating around. Nichols drew the drapes,
started the tape player, and returned to the desk.

There was a quick *pound-pound* at the door—definitely
not a knock—and then Hanson was inside, bursting with
hostility. *Slam!* "I'm on to you and the Bionic Peddler. The
whole thing stinks!" So much for the confession theory.
Hanson leaned over Nichols's desk, palms flat, and glared
down at him.

The stance was the body-language equivalent of a slap in
the face. Too bad he couldn't get Larry's opinion, Nichols
reflected; unfortunately, Cantin was in D.C. today, shaking
the money tree. He stood, making Hanson straighten to face
him. "I'm afraid I don't understand, Bob. You're on to
what?"

"Spare me the innocence. We both know that the *Prospector* transmissions were faked; there are no aliens. You
and Cantin tricked me, NASA, and the Space Division. Hell,
you tricked me into conning NASA and the Space Division
for you. It's illegal, immoral, and *wrong*."

True, there were no aliens—but hadn't Hanson invented them? Nichols's mind whirled. "Why do you say that?"

As Hanson rambled about mail and security, accounting files and random numbers, Nichols tried to concentrate. His first thought had been that Hanson was confessing because of the stress. Maybe Hanson reacted to stress differently— denying his involvement, even to himself. Hanson oozed sincerity: he clearly believed everything he was now saying.

Of *course* the data was faked! Either Hanson was behind the plot, as Cantin had always maintained, but had wigged out and no longer remembered, or some mystery group had fooled them all. Hmmm, the latter was intriguing. Maybe the Space Division boys had been using Asgard, planting evidence in a devious ploy to get off-budget funding. Given the current political climate, that seemed feasible.

Hanson railed on; Nichols listened with half an ear, nodding occasionally to keep the scientist going. The fraudulent data weren't the issue, Hanson was. If Hadley and friends were behind everything, Hanson's ravings would only get himself in trouble. If Hanson had fudged the data but was now crazy, though . . . well, Nichols would have to discredit Hanson so that no one would believe anything he said.

Dare he challenge Hanson? All that Hanson specifically had on him was the generous use of computer time—hardly a hanging offense. Yeah, he was clean. That made it easy. Was Larry clean? Well, that was Larry's problem.

Hanson finally wound down. "Have I got this right?" Nichols stared hard at the scientist. "You claim that the transmissions from *Prospector* were phony. That for several months a conspiracy fooled you, your department, NASA, *and* the Space Division. That you are personally under surveillance. That a marketeer and I are the conspirators." Hanson nodded. "I don't know whether to be enraged, flattered, or amused."

"You still deny it?"

"Damned right. This accusation is paranoid."

Hanson shook his head in disbelief. "You actually think

you can brazen this out? What do you expect to happen when General Hadley hears what I have to say?"

Nichols laughed. "Yes, and nothing. There's nothing to brazen out, as you put it. All you can prove is that I've used my own company's computers." He parked on a corner of his desk. "Haven't you?

"If this ever gets to the general, and I advise against it, you'll have only your word for the origin of the supposedly faked data. *You* originally discovered the aliens. *You* had the means and the opportunity to falsify the data. *You* certainly are more capable than I to perpetrate such a hoax."

"And motive? Do I have that too?" Hanson retorted sarcastically.

"Yes. Revenge."

An uneasy look flashed across Hanson's face. A premonition. "What the hell do you mean, revenge? For what?"

"Your recent performance has been very unsatisfactory. Your attitude toward me and my key staff is unacceptable. Obviously, you realized what was coming."

"You bastard. You lying, unprincipled bastard. You're firing me to discredit me. Well, it won't work. Fired or not, I'll see Hadley. Within a week, I'll be back and you'll be on your way to jail." Hanson turned abruptly and strode for the door.

"Wait."

Hanson stopped expectantly, as if waiting for a reprieve. The triumph of reason, no doubt. How naive. Nichols picked up his telephone handset and dialed. "Nichols here. Get me Biesterfield." The guard he was speaking to quickly found the director of security. "George, it's Chuck. Effective noon today, Dr. Hanson will no longer work for Asgard. He may remove his personal belongings, but I want you to hand inspect whatever he takes. As soon as you hang up, please reprogram the access system to bar him from all secured areas—especially the main computer center. Then notify Personnel."

He looked at the scientist. "*Now* you may go. Please do."

* * *

On the way to his office, Hanson had detoured through the repro room to liberate a box. He had dumped the remaining reams of copying paper onto an unopened box, and taken the newly emptied box with him. Now, with his packing almost complete, the box was depressingly empty. It wasn't much to show for his years here.

Sighing, Hanson took two framed photos from the wall. The first showed a sparkling new *Prospector*, just released from the product assurance department. A younger Hanson stood beside it, grinning from ear to ear, with a fatherly arm around its antenna. The second shot captured the space shuttle *Atlantis* in a cloudless sky, a few fiery seconds into launch, starting *Prospector* on its mission. God only knew where *Prospector* was now, or if it still functioned. All he knew was that aliens had nothing to do with its fate.

A timid knock interrupted his reverie. Hanson looked up and saw a nervous Carlton Moy. "Excuse me, Bob. Your department is gathered in the engineering conference room. I thought you might want to say a few words."

"My friend, thank you. Yes, I'd like to see them, but I've no idea what to say. There's nothing *to* say." He whispered, "Not here, anyway."

Carlton gave him a searching look. "Don't go home alone. Please stop by my house. I'll call Lucy and tell her to expect you. When I get there, tell me as much or as little as you please. I'll try to get home early." He extended his hand. "Promise?"

Hanson shook the proffered hand. "Promise." He forced a fragile smile. "Hey, this is a job change, not a wake. Let's go say something upbeat to the folks."

The conference room was packed. He sometimes forgot how big the department had grown. He felt a surge of pride: *Prospector* might be gone, but he still had a legacy. He'd built the best damned R&D group in the aerospace business, and touched the lives of all these people. A lump formed in his throat.

All about him, staff members exchanged whispers and glances but none would meet his eyes: they had obviously seen him packing. They knew him well enough to understand that he'd have shared any future plans with them. In short, they knew he'd been canned.

He coughed. "You're probably all wondering why I called this meeting." That caused two or three self-conscious titters. "Me, too."

Hanson needed to do something with his hands. He picked up a red-capped erasable marker and rolled it over and over in his hands. "We've been through a lot together, you and I. In some cases, many years of working side by side. For me, this time has come to an end." He gently stood the marker on the table. "The reasons for my departure aren't important. This is: In *no* way does my leaving reflect negatively on the department. On anyone here.

"One final thought. It sounds trite, but it's true. I sincerely enjoyed working and learning and achieving with you. I will *always* remember with great pride what we accomplished here together. Thanks, to each and every one of you."

A long, silent moment passed. His friends—they weren't coworkers any longer—began filing out. He shook a lot of hands, accepted many good wishes; Barbara Dodge gave him a big hug. Mercifully, no one asked why he was leaving, where he was going, or what he would do. Finally, only Carlton remained. "Relax. I plan nothing rasher than finishing your scotch." Carlton shrugged and left.

Time for one last look around his office. There sat his workstation, still disconnected from the main network. Fat lot of good his precautions had been. Might as well print off his phone directory, his personal calendar, and any new mail.

He printed the calendar and directory directly from the workstation. To access any new mail, however, he needed the main system. He uncoiled the cable and plugged it back in the wall. He went through the normal login procedure—and couldn't get on. LOGIN FAILURE. "Beast" Biesterfield was efficient, if incredibly petty. Hanson's password was already disabled. *Wonder if he knows that I know the system administrator's password?*

Next time, Hanson answered "admin" to the logon prompt, then added the month's current password/composer: "ravel." He remembered the password as "bolero," though Carlton had once said that listening to *Bolero* had all the suspense of watching the grass grow. LOGIN FAILURE.

No wonder Carlton had looked so sheepish. The Beast had obviously made him change the system password. Well, he'd spare Carlton the embarrassment of discussing it; he wouldn't bring up the topic. Though he did want his mail. . . .

Down the hall he went, popping his head into Carlton's office. "I'm running late, and I've got a few more people to see before I go. Could you do a sysadmin login and dump my mail?" Carlton nodded. "Thanks. You can give it to me later."

Except for the R&D crew, there wasn't anyone he did want to see. He couldn't face them again, either, not yet. Back to his office, then, and one last glance for overlooked memorabilia. He walked slowly, unable to place the haunting melody Carlton was whistling. He smiled: if Biesterfield knew how Carlton picked—and practically broadcast—system passwords, he would undoubtedly foam at the mouth.

Two rectangles of unfaded paint on the office wall marked where his framed photographs had hung. The rest of the room seemed dreary by contrast. Fair enough: *Prospector*'s absence made *his* life dreary. He was half staring at the rectangles, half staring into space, when Biesterfield came to escort him out.

· CHAPTER 8 ·

Lucy Moy flitted nervously about Hanson, apologizing for each of the petty domestic interruptions that diverted her. The two young Moy children apparently saw him as a threat for Mommy's attention; they had an arguable case. Lucy fussed over Hanson like a mother hen, as if afraid to leave him alone. Whatever had Carlton told her about him? One look at her worried expression and he'd deferred his plans for several good, stiff drinks.

He examined the temporarily untenanted living room. The furnishings were too dainty for his taste: delicate black-lacquered furniture, fragile glass bric-a-brac, an overdose of doilies. The sofa and armchairs were upholstered in a sickly, plum-colored, crushed velvet. Sitting on the fragile-looking furniture made him feel clumsy and ill at ease; he stood while Lucy was present, and paced whenever she left the room.

Carlton arrived just before three. He stopped in the kitchen for a brief whispered consultation in rapid-fire Chinese. Presumably: how is the crazy round-eyes doing? *Can it, Bob*, Hanson thought. *Your friends are entitled to worry about you*.

Carlton entered the living room. "Sit, will you? Lucy says you won't relax. I'll pour us drinks, and then you tell me as little or as much as you want. But sit." Hanson settled gingerly onto an armchair. "Put your feet up on the hassock, please. I don't plan to be outlived by my furniture." The physicist opened the breakfront in the adjoining dining room and retrieved a carafe full of amber liquid. (It was scotch bought for Hanson's rare visits. Carlton had been amused when he'd protested the purchase, and told him to come more often if he felt guilty.) "Three fingers do you?" Hanson nodded.

Moy returned with two full tumblers on an inlaid wood tray, and handed Hanson the marginally fuller glass. "I sent the abolitionist to the park with the kids. Drink up."

Hanson did, then set the empty glass onto a nearby coaster. He kicked off his shoes, settled back in the armchair, and closed his eyes. He didn't speak.

Moy broke the silence. "Any plans? Know what you're going to do?"

"I presume you have in mind only legally and socially acceptable behavior."

"I mean with your life."

"Once the dust settles, I think I'll retire to Maine to grow trees and lobsters. They take care of themselves and mind their own business."

When Carlton didn't answer, Hanson opened his eyes. The physicist was focusing intently on him. "I can talk to myself in the privacy of my apartment, you know."

"Yes, you can. I'd hoped you would talk to me, but you haven't yet."

"Damn it, it hurts. It hurts a lot, Carlton. Have you ever been fired?" His friend shook his head. "Me either, until now." Hanson tapped his empty glass. "Another of these?"

"In a bit."

"It hurts even though I know I'm completely in the right. This mess will get straightened out. When it does, I'll be back at Asgard and some other familiar faces will be gone." He picked up his glass and ran a finger around the rim. "At the least, I'll be able to go back. I wonder if I will."

Carlton sipped his scotch. "Something sounds better?"

Now here was a friend. Hanson knew he'd be screaming for details if their roles were reversed. "Dunno. Consult probably. I'm tired of managing people instead of technology."

"It wasn't all bad, was it?"

Hanson shook his head. "Far from it, most of the time. We brought a lot of good people into the group, you and I, brought them a long way. Together, we brought Asgard a long way. Maybe I spent too much time living vicariously, though, living on the group's successes instead of my own."

Carlton did his best Confucian smile. "The success of the group is the success of its leader. When I retire, I'd be proud to leave only half as much behind me."

They sat quietly for a while, Hanson staring into space and Moy watching Hanson. Hanson finally said, "My kingdom for a Coke and a bowl of pretzels."

"That's more like it. I'll see what the rug rats have left." Hanson heard sliding and rustling noises from the kitchen, evidence of a pantry being searched. Something thudded meatily, presumably a large can knocked from its perch, and Carlton muttered some nasty-sounding Chinese under his breath. Hanson grinned.

Carlton returned carrying Hanson's briefcase, from which a muffled ringing emanated. His portable computerphone. "Hot job lead, no doubt—good news travels fast. I'll be in the kitchen continuing my quest."

Hanson popped open the case. "Hanson."

"Robert Hanson?" asked the phone. The voice sounded young and nervous.

"Speaking."

"My name is Stan Hipanowicz. I'm the assistant vice president of new accounts at Glenbard Federal. I'd like to explain our services, if that's okay."

"This isn't a good time."

"I'd be happy to call back." Hipanowicz sounded anxious. "Perhaps in an hour would be better?"

Assistant vice president at a suburban bank. That meant he was about twenty-three and fresh from the mail room. "I'm not interested in changing banks right now. Thanks for calling, though." Hanson reached to hang up the cordless handset.

"Mr. Robert C. Hanson? Of English Valley Apartments

in Palatine?'' The voice sounded tinny at arm's length; it also sounded confused.

Hanson returned the handset to conversational position. ''That's me. Is something wrong?''

''There seems to be some confusion here. I'm not trying to sell you a new account. I'm calling about the account you recently opened.'' Hanson said nothing, waiting for some useful information. ''Your UltraPlus Executive Account.'' He heard each capital letter distinctly.

''My what?''

''Oh dear,'' said the nervous young man. ''It's worse than I thought. I hate to speak ill of the dead, but I do wish Mr. Vickers had referred you to a bank officer.''

This was getting too bizarre for words. ''Mr . . . Hipanowicz? I don't know what this is about. Unless, of course, it's a joke. Anyway, I'm really not in the mood for mysteries.'' Hanson reached again to hang up.

''Wait!'' shrilled the phone. ''A million dollar deposit is no joke! Please hear me out.''

''You have my undivided attention.'' Hanson groped for an explanation. ''You're calling about the account Mr. Vickers opened for me at Glenbard Federal?'' He had no idea what he was talking about.

''Exactly.'' Hipanowicz sounded relieved. ''Mr. Vickers should have referred you to an officer—tellers aren't authorized to handle transactions of that magnitude.''

''One million dollars.''

''Yes, sir. Perhaps he already wasn't feeling well. It wasn't like him to flout bank rules.''

''Wasn't feeling well.'' Hanson felt like an echo.

''The newspaper mentioned a massive coronary. He probably died before the car hit that bridge abutment.''

''Horrible. And all of this happened when?''

''Last Friday evening, Mr. Hanson. I just noticed your deposit a few minutes ago, while reviewing Vickers's records. Naturally, I was terribly distressed by the irregularity.''

''Naturally.'' How about some distress for dependable old

Vickers? "You got this phone number from my application?" Only his friends had this unlisted number. Obviously a non-Asgard friend was behind this prank, someone who hadn't gotten the word. Then he shivered—Asgard itself had this number on file. Nichols couldn't be involved, could he? No, it must be a prank.

"That's the funny thing, sir. Your application is missing. I got this information directly from the computer. By the way, your account is properly coded as UltraPlus Executive, based on your current balance. I guess Mr. Vickers didn't tell you about the privileges to which you are entitled."

This kid certainly sounded sincere, and it was hard to believe a prank this elaborate. Then he had an idea: he keyed in the command code that displayed the calling telephone number. "Ummm," he mumbled, to keep the kid talking. He covered the mouthpiece and yelled, "Carlton. Where's your phone book?"

A head poked over the swinging doors between the dining room and the kitchen. "Check the drawer of the end table." Hanson found it, wedged the handset between shoulder and chin to free his hands, and looked up Glenbard Federal. Its listing matched the number on his display. "Son of a bitch."

"Sir?"

"Excuse me, Mr. Hipanowicz. I was talking to the dog. Down boy." Hanson made an educated guess. "An electronic funds transfer."

He heard keys clattering over the phone. "Of course! I see the annotation now in your file. Your account was opened by funds transfer from Asgard Aerospace. That's why I don't have paperwork. Mr. Vickers merely authorized the transfer." Hipanowicz's tone suggested that all was now well with the world. Hipanowicz's world, anyway. "Didn't Asgard mention this deposit?"

"I guess I missed a few details." And apparently had lucked into a few, thank God. "You're at the main branch?"

"Yes."

"I'll come in soon to hear about the UltraPlus services.

Thanks for calling." Thank you, indeed. Hanson hung up and collapsed back into his chair.

Carlton soon returned, bearing two bowls of popcorn. "This was it of a salty nature. I shudder to think what the kids will eat as teenagers." He studied Hanson. "You look horrible. More bad news?"

"Strangely enough, yes, if you can consider falling into a million dollars bad news." He grabbed a handful of popcorn and started to graze. "That call was from a bank vice president. It seems that Asgard opened an account for me last Friday and transferred in a nice, round million. Today, I'm fired. What do you make of that?"

"A prescient guilty conscience?"

"Not bloody likely." Crunch, crunch. "There's been some sleight of computer between Asgard's bank and Glenbard Federal. I must have been scheduled for arrest for embezzlement. Confronting Chuckie today only hastened my exit."

"Aren't funds transfers encrypted for privacy and authentication?" Carlton scratched his head thoughtfully. "I'm sure that banks wire their funds using codes that follow DES—the federal data-encryption standard."

"Yes . . . and so what?" Hanson laughed unpleasantly. "The DES isn't very secure. IBM proposed a secure method to the National Bureau of Standards in the seventies—and the National Security Agency squelched it. The spooks said IBM's proposal was unnecessarily expensive. NSA's alternative, which became the DES, was much less secure. Cynical cryptologists presumed NSA wanted to keep eavesdropping on commercial transactions. One cryptologist even published a paper about a relatively cheap—by government standards—computer architecture for quickly cracking DES codes."

The little physicist looked confused. "Are you accusing the government of framing you?"

"I may be paranoid, but I'm not crazy. DES might have started out too complex for private ownership of code-cracking gear, but it isn't anymore. Any decent parallel computer can break DES codes.''

''Like the ones Asgard owns.''

''Exactly. As former chief computer guru, I'll be presumed guilty of programming my ex-toys for fun and profit.'' Hanson swept up another handful of popcorn.

Carlton settled heavily onto his chair. ''You must be in terrible trouble. Should you go into hiding?''

''If I do, they win. This frame is all about discrediting me before I approach Space Division about Asgard's profitable little computer scam.''

''But you'll be arrested. Will the general listen to an embezzler?''

''Only one way to find out. First, though, let's see how much trouble I'm in. Will you help a hardened criminal?'' Moy nodded. ''Chances are Asgard 'conveniently' discovered the funds transfer as soon as I left, in which case the cops are out looking for me. We'll swing by my building in your car—any cops on stakeout will know mine.''

They paused in Moy's garage to thumb through the newspapers waiting to be recycled. Hanson brought the Saturday and Sunday papers into the car. Vickers's demise had gotten four column inches in Saturday's obits: ''Local Teller in Fatal Crash.''

Minutes later, they cruised slowly through Hanson's apartment complex, Carlton dutifully craning forward to read the building numbers. Hanson, wearing sunglasses and a baggy old sweater of Carlton's, casually (he hoped) scanned the parked cars. They eased around a corner to go deeper into the complex. ''See anything?''

''Yeah.'' Hanson looked grim. ''Two guys parked in a beige Chevy sedan, four slots down from my apartment. One of them is watching my apartment, the other watched us drive by. Obviously cops.'' He pointed. ''Go out the back way.''

''Now where to?''

''Your place. If those are cops, there's a warrant out for

me. My lawyer can find out.'' Hanson squirmed uneasily in his seat when they passed a police car.

Back at his home, Carlton gestured to the study. ''Use the phone in there.'' Hanson closed the door behind him and dialed.

''Black and Edelman.''

''Bernie Edelman, please. It's urgent.''

''Whom may I say is calling?''

''Judge Crater.''

''Willyouholdplease.'' Click, and he was in Muzakland. Amazing how many compositions had the same tempo.

''Hello, Judge. Long time no see.'' Bernie's gravelly voice sounded cautious. ''I trust there's an interesting story behind this call?''

''There is, there is. Do you recognize my voice?''

''Garner Hall? Chess?''

''Bingo.'' In the dorm, Bernie had been Bob's regular chess rival. After graduation, Bernie had gone to Northwestern to law school. He'd handled Bob's until now inconsequential legal work ever since he'd passed the bar and joined Tom Black as an associate attorney. ''I need a favor. Could you determine easily whether there's a warrant out for my arrest?''

Stony silence. Then, ''Maybe you'd better tell me more. Where can we meet?'' His friend sounded shaken.

''No time. For now, all you need to know is that I didn't do it. I'll tell you more when I can.''

''How reassuring. Is what you didn't do a federal or local offense?''

Hanson sighed. ''Beats me. Is embezzlement a federal offense?''

''Not unless it's from the federal government.''

''How about a federal contractor?''

''No, you'll have to try harder next time. Local warrant. Where can I reach you?''

''I'll call back. How much time do you need?''

"Half hour, forty-five minutes tops. I have friends at the county. Call back on 3572—it's my direct line."

The minutes moved slowly; twice Hanson caught himself dozing off. He was bone weary: no decent sleep for two nights, since before the reunion. To exhaustion, add discovery of the *Prospector* conspiracy, confrontation with Nichols, being fired, the frame-up for embezzlement, and imminent fugitive status. In a word, he felt like shit.

At last it was time to call. "Bernie?"

"Judge Crater, I presume. Buddy, you're in deep trouble." The lawyer took a deep breath. "A warrant *has* been issued for your arrest. As your attorney, I must advise you to turn yourself in."

"I think not."

Bernie exhaled heavily through his nose. "We're talking years in Stateville, asshole. If you didn't take the money, don't screw up your defense by running."

"Things look somewhat discouraging?"

"Yeah, and the Pacific Ocean is somewhat damp." Long pause. "Listen—your record's clean and the money's been recovered. I'm sure we could get reasonable bond posted, maybe even get you released on your own recognizance. Wise up, dammit. Let me arrange your surrender."

"You haven't heard my story. You'd have an easier time defending Benedict Arnold. Bernie, I don't mean to impugn your legal skills. This situation is about computers, not law, and no one knows a tenth of it. This is something I have to handle myself."

"Good luck, pal. When it doesn't work out, I'll visit you."

"I'll keep in touch."

Carlton had vanished when Hanson emerged from the study. He finally found a note magneted to the refrigerator: "On an urgent errand. Wait for me. Back soon."

He pulled his car into the now empty garage. The little Honda was unobtrusive enough to take anywhere—the cops could hardly stop every blue Accord; but the license plates were a problem. Stealing some was too risky. Asking for Carlton's was out of the question—he'd do nothing to incriminate his friend.

Setting that problem aside, Hanson went to the basement for some hand tools. Amid the paraphernalia on the workbench lay several rolls of colored tape. Aha! The dark blue tape nearly matched the lettering on Illinois license plates. He dashed back to the garage and removed his license plates and their holders. A little blue tape, and voila—CPF136 became OBE186. He rubbed the plates liberally with garage-floor dirt. Not bad. For good measure, he smeared more dirt inside the scratched plastic windows of the plate holders. He defied anyone to spot the alteration from two feet away. With license plates restored, his trusty Honda was ready for a life of crime.

Carlton found him at the kitchen table, deep in the guts of his portable computerphone. "What are you doing, Boss?"

"Disabling the phone so I can keep the computer with me. Otherwise, the cops can have the phone company trace me to one cellular zone just by ringing my number. With my luck, they'd catch me changing zones and get a close fix on my location. Could spoil my whole day."

"Why'd you wait till now to change it?"

"Mostly, because I just thought of it." Hanson pried a stubbornly immobile crystal can from its socket with a jeweler's screwdriver; it let go with a squeal. He pocketed it for future reassembly. "It didn't matter yet. It wouldn't have surprised them any to learn I'm still somewhere in northern Cook County." He resealed the case. "What was your urgent errand?"

The physicist removed a sheaf of bills from his coat pocket. "You'll need money. They'll be watching your credit cards and bank accounts for activity."

"I can't take your money."

Carlton shrugged. "A loan. Your credit's good."

"I don't want you implicated." Carlton looked at him icily until he took the money. "You win. Thanks."

"How else can I help?"

"Stay out of trouble and keep your eyes open. I was obviously under surveillance, and I wouldn't be surprised if you are, too—so please do not investigate. I'll call if I need anything else." He stood up to go. "If I do, I'll give my name as Jay Berger."

"Investigate what? What is this really about?"

Hanson rested his hand on Carlton's shoulder. "It's safest that you not know. I'll explain once I've cleared this up— or at my trial. What I needed was a friend, and you've been that." They exchanged bone-breaking handshakes. "Wish me luck."

Washington was having a typically hot and muggy spring, and Sally dreaded the trip home. Reluctantly, she swapped her heels for jogging shoes. It would be a long, sweaty walk, lugging shoe bag and purse, from NASA headquarters to her rented parking space.

Striding purposefully up the street, she didn't notice Rich Hayes, the office gossip, until he tapped her arm. "Keller, wait up. I've got juicy news for you."

"What." She used her best bored tone and quickened her pace.

"Guess who was fired yesterday?" When she didn't answer, he volunteered, "Hanson, formerly of Asgard Aerospace."

"What?"

"Thought that would interest you. You worked together pretty closely for a while, right? Now get this. The afternoon after he conveniently got himself canned, Asgard discovers that he'd penetrated their accounts-payable system. Paid himself a cool million."

"Did they arrest him?" She felt strange—surprised, confused, and a little worried for him.

"Nope. He got clean away. And people say there's no money in basic research." He came to a halt at the corner. "Hafta turn here. Good night." He started stalking away from her, then remembered something and stopped. "You always said he was really bright."

She stood, dazed, until he rounded another corner and disappeared from view. Dripping with sweat, she finally reached her car in the now half-empty lot.

Again typical for spring, tourists had gummed up traffic. She opened her windows, afraid that running the air-conditioning would overheat the engine. Creeping along, she had plenty of time to wrestle with the unlikely news: Hanson was an embezzler.

Hanson was a puzzle to her. At first she'd been really attracted to Bob: he was brilliant, witty, and quietly handsome. She could listen for hours when he spoke about *Prospector*—conceiving of it in college, the doctoral thesis project to prove its feasibility to himself, long years of selling the mission, the thrills of success and discovery. She sighed. They had had a few quiet dinners together in Chicago, before the alien research petered out; *Prospector* was basically all they had ever discussed.

She darted into a small gap in the right-hand lane, gaining a few car lengths. Yes, she'd enjoyed Bob's company, but she'd never gotten close to him. He'd foiled her every attempt to get to know him, or to talk about herself, with a quip. Finally, she'd swallowed her pride and discussed him with Carlton Moy. Carlton had said it was nothing personal—Hanson didn't let anyone close to him. For all their years working together, Moy still found maintaining their friendship a continuing battle.

She tuned out the background of honking, and rode her brakes grimly ahead. Why couldn't she accept that Hanson was too defensive for a relationship, and forget him? Safety? Maybe she dealt with her newfound availability by chasing someone she couldn't catch. Damn! She didn't believe that, and she didn't believe that Bob was a criminal.

Her single friends complained that the good ones were already married. Here was an exception to the rule: a good one too scared of commitment to even join the race.

Up ahead, a dead truck blocked her lane. The car in front of her had Idaho plates; its driver timidly stopped and flicked on his turn signal. The stubby woman beside him faced backward, holding up her hand pathetically to the passing traffic. Predictably, no one let the hicks out. Why don't these innocents leave town before rush hour?

She spotted an opening and cut into the next lane. Now blocking traffic herself, she honked and gestured at the befuddled tourists until they eased out from behind the stationary truck.

Where was Bob Hanson, anyway, and what was his story? She wondered if she would ever know. For no good reason whatever, she gave her horn a long, hard blast.

· CHAPTER 9 ·

Life was good.

A warm breeze riffling his hair, the Sox leading the Yankees one-zip in the second, cool beer in hand: ecstasy. Soon he'd tackle some of those salt-encrusted, life-threatening peanuts.

Larry Cantin slouched in his chair, one knee propped over an armrest. He and Chuck Nichols had the Asgard box at Comiskey Park, on the third-base line, to themselves. Seeing that the vendor was about to retreat beyond convenient hailing range, Cantin drained his bottle. "Beer!" He turned to Nichols, who nodded. "Two!"

Cantin closed his eyes briefly and luxuriated in the warm sun. A roar from the crowd pulled them open again: he had missed Yablonski grounding into a double play. "Who'dda thunk it?"

"Huh?" grunted Nichols vaguely. His eyes stayed glued to the field.

"Our Mad Scientist was not as crazy as he appeared. Either that, or he was mad in the other sense of the word. He almost got away with it."

Crraacck!! A hard drive to right, easily a double. Coruna, who'd been intentionally walked a moment earlier, made it home from first standing up. Two-zip.

"Yeah," agreed Nichols absently, "I'd never have figured Hanson for an embezzler." He waggled two fingers at the peanut man. "The irony is how he was caught."

"Accounting was as surprised as anyone. As if by magic, out of their computer pops an alert message from their still-buggy auditor expert system. Except for that Scrooge program, Hanson could've moved the money abroad before anyone even missed it."

Nichols squashed two peanuts against one another. "I was discussing it with Herodotus this morning. Interesting fellow, Herry—he taught me a new expression. Our friend Bob, it seems, was 'hoist on his own petard.' That's medieval for stepping on your own land mine."

"It clears up the great *Prospector* mystery: why did Hanson keep the aliens fiction going so long? Obviously, as a world-class diversion while his hand was in the cookie jar." Cantin tore open his own peanut bag, and changed the subject. "You have the chance to hire someone practical to head R&D. Someone who understands that research should follow the customers' preferences."

"Someone subservient to Marketing." Nichols smiled cynically. "Have anyone in mind?"

The marketeer thought fleetingly of Bill Parker, that disloyal wimp who'd tipped him to the "aliens." Fat chance. "'Fraid not. Maybe Herry can conjure up Thomas Edison for you." He took a long, tepid swallow; ugh, there was a drowned gnat in it.

"You're sure?"

"Sure." He knew what was coming, was prepared for it.

"*I* can't take on that responsibility myself, right now, even temporarily. You leave me no choice, Larry. R&D reports to you until I replace Hanson." Nichols turned back to the field, in time to catch Friedlander swing at and miss a slider to retire the side. "You learned something today: there's no such thing as a free ball game."

No sweat, thought Cantin. Moy was Hanson's right-hand man; now he can be mine. "Beer!"

Two elephants were locked in mortal combat, their tiny, inset eyes enraged. One of the elephants arched his trunk to trumpet his challenge. At their feet, the anxious man was near enough to distinguish individual coarse black hairs, to touch the animals' wrinkled, leathery hides.

Fortunately, the elephants were stuffed; they dominated the main gallery of the Field Museum of Natural History. They towered over and intimidated Bill Parker, as they had since he was a youngster. Still, this was one of his favorite spots in the city, and he'd quickly accepted it as a rendezvous point.

He glanced around the hall again for the overdue *Tribune* investigative reporter: the museum would be closing shortly. The pleasant spring weather had kept the place fairly empty this evening; only the inevitable scout troops, and their frazzled chaperones, were in evidence. Scanning the gallery yet again, he saw a roly-poly and bearded cherub at the ticket booth by the south entrance. Parker recognized Stuart instantly: his picture appeared regularly in his bylined Trib articles. As the reporter shuffled over to the elephants, Parker set a seemingly casual intercept course.

"Mr. Stuart? Asgard."

"Bill Parker, I presume. Call me Al." The reporter pulled a photo ID from his shirt pocket.

"That's not necessary, Al."

"Yes, it is."

Parker took the hint and brought out his Asgard ID badge. The chubby reporter studied the badge and its photo intently, then closely examined the scientist's features. "The Trib confirmed—discreetly—that a William Parker does indeed work at Asgard. For now, let's assume you're him." He returned the badge. "What've you got?"

A royal screw job from Asgard. An incipient ulcer. An opportunity, if I'm really lucky, to get even with that bastard Cantin—I deserved the deputy spot, the inside track to be Dr. Bob's permanent replacement. I didn't have to tip Cantin last winter about Hanson's private research. "Remember, this is not for attribution."

"Yeah, yeah." The reporter sounded bored. "What've you got?"

"A scandal. A big one."

"So you said on the phone. Some specifics?" Stuart looked totally unimpressed. He wrestled a small notebook from his windbreaker pocket and casually flipped to a blank page. The cheap ballpoint pen stayed clipped inside the wire spiral.

"Some background first. I'm an R&D manager at Asgard, in daily involvement with space programs. My latest project involved commercial exploitation of satellite reconnaissance data. In short, I'm *not* your average UFO crackpot." Stuart was encouraged enough to remove his pen, but not enough to uncap it. Parker lowered his voice. "Do you remember that *Prospector*, Asgard's deep-space probe, was reported missing a few months back?"

"Right. Lloyd's of London expects to take a bath."

"Lloyd's can keep their money. An act of war by hostile extraterrestrials isn't a covered hazard.

"There's more. The government is involved, both NASA and the Space Division. Then there is the sudden elimination of my ex-boss. Dr. Hanson was the chief scientist at Asgard, inventor of the *Prospector* probe and discoverer of the aliens. He was fired last Monday morning. That afternoon, by an amazing coincidence, Asgard suddenly noticed that he'd embezzled a million bucks. He hasn't been seen since."

The reporter scribbled furiously for a while. He met Parker's eyes for the first time, his expression now alert and penetrating. "Can you substantiate any of this?" Parker nodded. "I need particulars, names, dates. Let's walk."

Scientist and journalist waited interminably for the traffic light by the museum to turn green, then trotted across the Outer Drive when the light changed almost instantly to yellow. They walked beside the yacht harbor discussing *Prospector*'s ill-fated diversion. As shadows lengthened around them, Stuart interrupted frequently to press for details.

They stopped in the Adler Planetarium parking lot, gazing across Lake Michigan, waves crashing on the broken rocks at their feet. "Bill, this is *big*. Before the Trib will print it, though, I need corroboration. Assume that the government types and Asgard bigwigs stonewall it. How can I verify this?"

"The insurance claim confirms it."

The reporter shook his head. "The claim only proves that Asgard wants a payout. It doesn't prove that aliens blasted *Prospector*. Hell, Lloyd's may maintain there's no hard evidence that *Prospector* was even lost. Wouldn't it be handy for Asgard to collect for *Prospector*, while still having it out there exploring?"

"Is it a coincidence that *Prospector* disappeared just after Asgard got a big classified DOD contract?"

"Whoa, big guy: I trust you. Your story is consistent, you sound like you know your stuff, and you obviously believe in it. That's just not enough to publish on."

"So nothing happens?" Parker's tone was biting.

"A lot happens. If your story is true, I know enough to trick someone into confirming it. Give me some time." Stuart playfully punched Parker in the shoulder. "Lighten up. You'll get what you're after soon enough."

Parker's hand shot out and squeezed the reporter's arm. "What's that crack supposed to mean?"

"As I said, lighten up. You had plenty of opportunity to talk before now—if you'd wanted to. I can also tell from your voice that you couldn't care less about the light-fingered Dr. Hanson. Obviously, then, you expect to gain something from blowing the whistle on Asgard.'' The reporter peeled off Parker's hand.

Parker stared. "So you've been toying with me all evening?"

"I knew from the start that your motive wasn't altruism. So what? You think I'm in the news biz because of the public's right to know?" Stuart looked amused. He pocketed the microcassette recorder to which he had switched an hour earlier. "Frankly, I wouldn't give a cold grasshopper turd for either the public *or* your motives. I'm in this for the money—and the notoriety.''

Parker gaped at him, open-mouthed. The reporter patted him on the arm. "I'll be in touch."

"Coffee?"

Al Stuart pondered the offer. "Cream and sugar." His host nodded slightly to the battle-ax of a secretary, who scurried off to fetch and tote. "Nice office." Stuart plopped down in the chair at the head of the conference table, denying his prey the psychological advantage of sitting behind his massive desk.

His prospective victim was none other than Chuck Nichols, president of Asgard Aerospace. Also a slimeball supreme, if Parker was to be believed. Nichols and cronies were up to something venal, but Stuart hadn't decided whether it was news suppression in conspiracy with the government or a refreshingly audacious con. Either one would make juicy headlines. He paged through his notebook, frowning for effect, until Ms. Finch brought his coffee.

His target sat beside him as soon as the barrel-like Ms. Finch closed the door behind herself. Nichols wore a three-piece suit and long-sleeved dress shirt, topped off with a quaint yellow power tie, despite the balmy weather. Al leaned forward and shed his used-car-salesman sport coat, then loosened his own too-wide tie, to show his disdain for sartorial symbolism. He uncapped his pen and gazed expectantly at Nichols.

Nichols spoke first to break the uncomfortable silence, as did most people. "Your call was somewhat disconcerting. To what did you refer when you mentioned publishing 'a possibly embarrassing article'?"

"I'm sure you know."

"I'm sure I don't."

Hah. The fact of this appointment, so promptly granted with so little reason given, proved that Nichols had something to hide. Innocent CEOs invariably sent him to their PR agents. "I referred to Dr. Hanson's discovery." Nichols stiffened, then forced himself to relax.

"Dr. Hanson's current assignment at Asgard involves classified work which I am not at liberty to discuss." In a feigned show of casualness, Nichols checked his watch. "Of course, that is neither an admission nor a denial of any newsworthy content within Dr. Hanson's work."

Very cool, Stuart thought, *very professional—with one exception*. "You mentioned a current assignment. Dr. Hanson is not currently your employee."

"It's against company policy to discuss the employment status of individuals."

Stuart took a sip of his cooling coffee, intentionally jostling the cup while setting it down. Coffee obediently sloshed onto the wooden tabletop. Nichols leaped like a coiled spring, then dashed to the intercom on his desk. "Paper towels!" The man was nervous about *something*.

"Come off it, Nichols. I'm a reporter. I have sources. You fired Hanson, then pressed charges against him for embezzlement. Either event is unusual in connection with the chief investigator of a major top-secret defense contract." Stuart glared at Nichols until Finch's bustling entrance gave Nichols an excuse to break eye contact. The secretary quickly blotted up Stuart's mess and left.

"Who's been talking to you?"

Hardly a denial. Stuart laced his fingers together across his paunch and smiled benignly, silently performing his best Buddha imitation.

Nichols took the point. "Your source, when I find him, will be in deep manure with the Space Division."

Point two for Parker's story—the Colorado Springs boys were involved. "Don't start a witch hunt on *my* account. Arrest warrants are public documents, even when you have the clout to have the cops play it quietly." Stuart reached for his cup. "Now speaking about *Prospector* . . ."

The executive squirmed in his chair. "We weren't speaking about *Prospector*." Stuart did Buddha again, and Nichols's forehead developed a sheen. "Excuse me. It's too bright in here." Stuart's victim closed the heavy drapes, which was interesting since his back had been to the windows and the sky was overcast.

"I'd like to hear your version."

"Of Dr. Hanson's termination?"

Firing. "Of Asgard's current knowledge of the aliens." Stuart looked expectantly at Nichols.

"Hanson is digging a deeper hole for himself: leaking classified research won't help his already serious legal situation. *I* certainly won't discuss our Space Division contract."

"I'll pass along your advice when I see Bob." Stuart had had no luck whatsoever finding Hanson, but it couldn't hurt if Nichols thought Hanson was his source. "It's also a matter of public record that your Space Division contract is in artificial intelligence—'pilotless space vehicles,' you told the securities analysts—not kamikaze aliens." Nichols stood tight-lipped and said nothing. "I take it your official response is 'No comment.' "

"I think you should leave."

Stuart shrugged on his garish sport coat, and hazarded a parting shot. "Enjoy those sole-source contracts while you can." Nichols's already compressed lips turned white. Al smiled and let himself out.

The Yellow cab, equipped with the traditional sprung shocks, bounced along the potholed downtown streets. Hanson's companion lurched against him as the cabbie cut off a CTA bus to turn onto Michigan Avenue. "I wanna drink."

Hanson wished again for a more dependable surrogate. Vinny—no last name available—was the pick of the skid-row derelicts who vaguely resembled him. "When we're done. Now, quiet."

Two days ago, he had express mailed a summary of his findings—marked PERSONAL, CONFIDENTIAL, & URGENT—to General Hadley. In it, he'd asked Hadley to meet him tonight, alone, on the Delaware Street side of the John Hancock Building.

Vinny, like this harebrained plan, was the best he could do on short notice. He *had* to know whether the Space Division would listen to him before putting himself at their mercy. The space cadets certainly enjoyed their expanding cut of discretionary (aka nonaccountable) Defense money arising from the "alien crisis." This funding was especially sweet given the generally antimilitary bent of the new administration. It was even possible, Hanson realized, that Hadley and company had cooked the *Prospector* data, and that Asgard was merely fronting for them. In which case, he was in a position to blow the whistle on *them*.

It was simply too dangerous to just meet Hadley. Vinny, wearing his purchased-for-the-occasion K Mart suit, would approach the general—presuming that Hadley even showed. Hanson would look for anyone watching Vinny; if Hadley seemed alone, *then* he'd risk a meeting. His car was parked across town—hypothetical observers might be unduly attentive to blue Accords.

With a squeal of brakes, the cabbie stopped at the Westin Hotel, just down Delaware from the Hancock. A uniformed figure loitered beside the parking-lot down ramp of the Hancock. Hadley? Too far away to be sure. Hanson tucked a twenty into a pocket of his reticent accomplice. "Do this right, and you get another." As Vinny stepped jerkily from the taxi, Hanson handed him a briefcase. He watched his nervous surrogate cross the street.

"Driver." He rapped on the plastic partition between them, another twenty in hand. The still-running meter read $8.55. "A friend just walked by. Take this and wait. If I'm gone when the meter hits eighteen, take off." The cabbie moved the shield open a half inch to accept the bill.

Hanson walked through the Delaware Street hotel entrance, across the lobby and straight out the Michigan Avenue exit. He tore off his red windbreaker (another K Mart purchase) and reversed it to its black side, then took a Cubs hat from the pocket and pulled it on. He sauntered back to the Delaware corner for a quick peek.

Vinny was quaking in his vinyl loafers, surrounded by serious-looking men with walkie-talkies. The man Hanson presumed to be Hadley was talking earnestly with another uniformed type. Vinny pointed fearfully at the Yellow cab still waiting in front of the Westin. Hadley nodded, and several of the foot soldiers started jogging over.

Hanson didn't wait for the cabbie to be interrogated; he already felt guilty enough about Vinny. He did a one-eighty and strolled off down Michigan. Around the next corner were the Drake Hotel and getaway cabs.

Swaying from side to side, this time in a Checker cab, his mood rapidly degenerated from gloom to black depression. He suddenly realized that (subconsciously) tonight had been only an exercise, a healthy precaution against a remote possibility. His reconnaissance had been completely successful, but what he had learned was devastating. He'd thought that his worst problem was having the police after him, but that was wrong. *Everyone* was.

It had taken most of a fifth to sedate Nichols after his session with that reporter. The worst had been discreetly guiding the quivering fool from the office before he was literally scared shitless. "He's not feeling well. Yes, it came on *very* suddenly." Obviously, Nichols couldn't stand up much longer under the strain.

"Who is Stuart talking to?" Nichols whined. "Who,

Larry?'' He sounded like a sniveling kid, wondering why his perky, floppy-eared little puppy had lost a game of tag with an eighteen wheeler. ''Who's doing this to me?'' *How the hell would I know?* Cantin wondered. The important thing now was *what* Stuart ''knew'': aliens had intentionally destroyed *Prospector*. If Stuart published a ''War of the Worlds'' story, investors—already skittish because of Benneford's populist economic policies—would flee the market. Companies with space-related business might be hit especially hard. Cantin quickly came to conclusion one: dump his Asgard stock *now*, and lock in his substantial profits.

He opened his den window to admit the evening breeze. *Okay, Larry my boy*, he thought, *remember Finance 101*. He could profit by predicting market movements both up *and* down. Since he foresaw a crash, he would go ''short'': first borrow, then sell, assets he didn't own; then, wait for the prices to fall; finally, buy back the borrowed assets at distress prices to settle the loan. Conclusion two: go short on market index futures. The SEC required a deposit for short sales; the Asgard proceeds would handle that nicely.

This could work out *very* well. He pictured the dominoes falling in his mind's eye: Stuart publishing, the market collapsing, him raking in a small fortune—no, scratch small—from same. Nichols was finding it impossible to bear up now; coping with a major recession would surely push him into early retirement.

''Alice, I'm going out! Liquor run.''

''Oh,'' came faintly from upstairs. She sounded totally disinterested.

The Saab, as always, started instantly and purred. The miniature penlight on Cantin's key ring swung enticingly from the ignition as he drove. He decided to revive an appropriate old classic at the phone booth tonight: Lack of money is the root of all evil.

· CHAPTER 10 ·

Hanson woke up in the dark, without any idea where he was. A faint green illumination suffused the small space that surrounded him, except where it was blocked by the hulking shape to his left. He hesitantly peered over it. The glow came from the LED display of a dashboard clock radio. Memory returned: he was in the back seat of his car, parked beside an isolated Indiana cornfield.

The clock registered 4:37—he'd achieved about two hours of uneasy sleep. His eyes felt like they'd been breaded and deep fried. His body ached from the unnatural act of folding itself into the back seat of a Honda.

Hanson pulled a filthy blanket, paroled for the night from a life sentence in the trunk, around his shoulders as a defense against the predawn chill. Attempting to fall back asleep under these conditions was futile. Sighing, he stepped out of the car.

Gravel crunched beneath his feet as he paced nervously along the narrow shoulder of the county road. Some small animal scurried furtively through the young corn; an owl swooped silently out of nowhere to seize it with sharp talons and carry it off. Heavy cloud cover obscured the night sky; the moon dimly penetrated the gloom, suggesting its presence by an amorphous yellow-gray region near the horizon. The few trees along the field's edge, their branches creaking eerily from sporadic gusts of wind, cast indistinct and foreboding shadows.

Might as well be on his way. He returned the blanket to

the trunk, then opened the front door and climbed behind the wheel. He rolled down his window, depending on the chill night air to keep him alert as he drove.

Al Stuart slouched in his chair, legs crossed and extended, waiting impatiently for his editor to wind down. Dave Carparelli was ruggedly handsome, tall, athletic, suntanned, immaculately groomed, and professionally successful. He was also a pompous ass. Large-mouthed Carp was pontificating endlessly about journalistic ethics versus the public's right to know, or some such tripe. Al peered between angled slats of the miniblinds that covered the office sidelight, trying to recognize female passers-by by their legs. The prevalence of slacks today—an obvious conspiracy—precluded his usual accuracy.

"I don't often talk to myself, Stuart!"

More often than you think. "Sorry." He swiveled slightly to half face the editor. "You were saying."

Carparelli laboriously polished his glasses with a tissue. "It related to journalism. You wouldn't be interested."

"Okay, okay, I said I was sorry. When do we publish?"

"When you convince me it's not another UFO story."

Stuart reflected that he apparently wasn't the only one not listening. He flipped through his notebook for something he might have failed to bring up. "Hold on."

Carparelli glared at him. "Some day I'll drag you kicking and screaming into the 1970s. You have a portable computer assigned to you. Why don't you use it?"

"I think they're a fad," Stuart answered absently. He kept searching.

"The last technology you successfully assimilated was movable type. When will you wake up?"

Paging through his notes had reorganized his thoughts. Besides, this game of bait-the-Carp had grown tiresome. "Let me summarize. To start, Asgard was awarded its first-ever defense contract—for $285 million—in applied artificial-intelligence research. That size first award is unheard of. Normal companies must successfully manage several small DOD contracts before any real gravy gets ladled.

"Within days of the award, *Prospector* ceased transmission. Coincidence?

"Next, my Asgard informant—a knowledgeable scientist—comes forward. He tells me about the aliens, *Prospector*'s destruction, NASA and Space Division involvement, and Hanson's role in all of this. The same Hanson who is mysteriously fired, and then immediately accused of a fairly routine embezzlement."

Carparelli had cooled down and was listening intently. "What does Hanson's firing have to do with aliens?"

"I suspect that Hanson planned to go public with the information, and DOD stopped him. The hokey embezzlement charge was to explain Hanson's disappearance. I predict that he'll hide very successfully."

The editor chewed anxiously on his lower lip. "Would they really kill him to cover up?"

"Desperate men do desperate things. I expect they considered his threatened actions treasonous."

"You've crossed the line between facts and speculation. Talk to NASA or the Space Division for corroboration."

"And wind up like Hanson? No, thanks. Chuck Nichols is my corroboration."

"Explain."

"Nichols saw me within hours of my request, sweated like a pig when I mentioned the aliens, and didn't deny my accusations."

"If Nichols is involved in this alleged plot, how does it happen that you're still here?"

"Possibly because they haven't found me yet—I've stayed away from home. Probably because they anticipated you rationalizing it away." Stuart grinned sardonically and added, "When they learn that we met all morning, you may join me on their list."

The editor winced, but he now decided quickly. "Okay,

we go with it—but my way. No panic mongering. A speculative slant. And after it's printed, when you'll be too visible for any untimely mishaps, you contact the Space Division.''

"Yes, sir." Al immediately began a mental rewrite of his intro. The Carp droned on, fantasizing about how Al should write the story. With the benefit of long practice, Al tuned out the noise. He wistfully conjured up a blaring headline for the next *National Enquirer*:

SPACE OCTOPI BLAST SPACECRAFT: MILITARY PANICS.
"Invasion Imminent," Predicts Mississippi Seer.

Carparelli would see to it that Al's headline was more dignified. Well, at least it would have his byline.

Dawn beat Hanson to the Ohio border. As a consolation prize, he stopped at a roadside diner just over the border for breakfast and a pot of coffee. Both were eminently forgettable, but at least they were cheap.

His automotive electronics, fortunately, were far from cheap. His car was equipped to receive satellite broadcasts from the Global Position System, so he always knew where he was. GPS was mostly used by fleet operators—both ship and truck—but electronics nuts like him found it hard to resist. The car also had a Rand McNally road atlas of North America stored digitally on compact disk; individual maps were displayable on the high-resolution screen within the dashboard. His GPS-derived position appeared on the map display as a blinking dot. More prosaically, the car had a top-notch radar detector. Hanson unobtrusively navigated the back roads at nearly interstate-highway speeds.

He stopped at another ramshackle diner shortly before noon. The cheeseburger must have been buried with the pharaohs and recently disinterred; the Coke was flatter than Indiana had been. He forced them down anyway. Ignoring the grumbled complaints of his stomach, he placed two important calls on the deserted pay phone. The first was to Washington, D.C., directory assistance.

Hanson's second call was answered after eleven rings by a clatter of dishes and cutlery. After long seconds of dining noise, he heard, "Kramer's Deli." It was Sally's usual hangout for work-day lunches.

"Would you page Sally Keller, please? I know it's inconvenient, but this is very important." The restaurateur grudgingly acceded, muttering complaints that Hanson ignored. Hanson knew that Asgard's computers were compromised; that precluded involving Carlton. Sally's access to the *Prospector* and alien data might put her at risk of surveillance, but he didn't know where else to turn. He didn't intend to make it easy for the conspirators either: they might bug her house and office, but he doubted that they would bug her restaurants.

"Hello?"

Hanson looked around to make sure he was still alone. He was. "Sally, this is Bob. Don't mention my name." He heard a sharp intake of breath across the line, but no protest. "I need your help."

"Are you all right? Where are you?" She sounded worried.

"Sure, and I don't exactly know," he lied. "I need an analysis of some *Prospector* data, and it's not very convenient to do it myself just now." She snorted. "Listen up." He briefly outlined the statistical analysis to be performed. He hoped that it would corroborate his claim that the TeleSat data had been artificially constructed.

"Will this help you out of your current situation?"

"It might. I think that you'll also find the result very enlightening. One caution—I wouldn't mention this project to anyone."

"Done. Call me tomorrow, same time, for the result."

"Pick someplace else. Kramer might get suspicious." The crowd noise reasserted itself while she considered that. "Don't think so hard—I won't be there to pick up the tab." In the ensuing pause, he could imagine her shaking her head.

She made up her mind. "Luigi's Ristorante."
"Sold."

Cracked asphalt pavement, sun-faded almost to white, coiled its serpentine way across interminable countryside. The dusty Honda seemed to inch along, its weary driver feeling as if he were trapped on a Möbius strip. He inserted a finger behind a glasses lens to rub a tired, red eye; the lens instantly smeared, canceling any momentary benefit from the eye massage.

Indiana, yesterday, had been the worst. Its only geographical interest came from speculating whether corn or soy beans lay over the distant horizon. Crossing most of Indiana in darkness had probably been a blessing. Ohio, this morning, had offered some improvement. An occasional wooded hill rose unexpectedly out of the farmland, like the domed head of a broccoli cursed with hyperactive thyroid. Pennsylvania, reached at long last, offered variety too late to be appreciated: the glassy-eyed driver had succumbed to highway hypnosis.

Flung gravel clattering against the car finally dragged Hanson from his somnambulistic state. Both right-hand tires were off the pavement. He reflexively jerked the wheel to the left—but his reflexes were out of warranty. The vehicle instantly fishtailed: he had overcorrected. Trying to straighten out, he overreacted again. Unable to steer his way out of trouble, he stomped on the brakes. The car spun around twice on the fortunately empty road, finally stopping angled diagonally across the wrong shoulder. One front tire clung precariously to the edge of the weed-clogged drainage ditch. The engine raced briefly, then died.

Only Hanson's seat belt had saved him from making the intimate acquaintance of the instrument panel. Temporarily on an adrenaline high, he restarted the motor and crept across the road to the correct shoulder. His thermos still held a few inches of sludgelike coffee purchased from a decrepit rural gas station. He swallowed the dregs eagerly, welcoming its strength. It might grow hair on his eyeballs, but until then, it might hold them open. Exhausted but now temporarily alert, he held the Honda to thirty, hoping to not overtax his diminished capacity before reaching the next town.

Gaithers Corners, PA, when he reached it, was completely underwhelming. The few buildings in town stretched along the two-lane road that had led him here. There was the obligatory boarded-up train station, a two-pump gas station, and a combination cafe, post office, and motel. The motel made him smile wanly. He needed sleep.

Hanson tiredly parked the Honda a good six inches from the crumbling curb, then hurried in to rent a room for the night. Without some sleep, he would—at best—be careless and get captured. At worst, his next spin-off would wrap him with finality around a telephone pole. Tomorrow he would need his head clear. Tomorrow he would know whether he was crazy, or if Sally had confirmed his findings.

He had just enough neurons still firing to register as Barney Dwyer. Someone's grandma had furnished his room, from floral carpet to Priscilla curtains to milk-glass lamp shades. Hanson didn't notice. Before the door he had slammed behind him stopped rattling in its ill-fitting frame, he was soundly asleep, fully clothed and shod, on the chenille bedspread.

He didn't stir when the dinner rush started in the cafe sharing a wall with his room. Not even when someone turned the TV up to catch the evening network news. Not even when pandemonium broke out over the lead story.

"The *Chicago Tribune* has just charged the presence of hostile extraterrestrials in the asteroid belt. The *Tribune* further alleges that the federal government is engaged in a massive coverup of this discovery. In a moment, we will be interviewing *Tribune* investigative reporter Alan Stuart about the basis of this . . ."

Luigi's was always crowded, and the maître d' gave parties of one the fisheye. Sally had chosen Luigi's on impulse and kicked herself the moment Hanson had hung up. How would she guarantee that she got in? She finally made reservations under an assumed name for a party of two. The snobbish maître d' arched an eyebrow at her when she asked to be seated, but grudgingly motioned over a waiter to lead her to a table. It was a horrible table, neither in the room's center for being seen, nor in a private booth. She didn't care; the maître d' had taken her name, ostensibly for when her friend arrived.

Time crawled by as she waited for Hanson's call. The waiter seemed to sneer whenever he walked by her half-empty table. He asked condescendingly after twenty minutes if mam'selle expected her companion soon. *Mam'selle doesn't know, you arrogant creep. If you're so smart, why are you waiting tables?* "I'll order, and let Joe catch up."

She felt the pitying eyes from the next table. *Call, damn you.* She crunched mechanically through her salad, not even noticing the nasty cucumber slice she'd been too preoccupied to set aside. She didn't notice much, either, of her minestrone, on which an island of grated Parmesan slowly congealed. Why didn't he call?

She had to stretch this out. He probably just couldn't get to a phone, she told herself. Only 12:45. She ignored the eyes boring into her and forced herself to eat slowly. *Call, please?* When she set down her spoon to study the wine list, the waiter instantly whisked away her half-full bowl.

The ironic thing was that she had nothing to tell Bob. Nothing definitive, anyway. An unlikely but inconclusive sequence of glitches and misunderstandings had delayed her research. She had tried to gather the information Bob wanted, but her email request for the raw data had apparently been eaten by a rare system crash. After she re-requested the *Prospector* data, she discovered that it was on a reel of nine-track tape on a shelf, not on-line where she expected it. The system administrator had agreed to load it for her overnight, only to have the transfer fail because Sally inexplicably had less unallocated space left in her file system than she remembered. And on, and on. So she had formless suspicions, with nothing but coincidences on which to base them.

"Would mam'selle like some dessert?"

She had picked at her fettucini and green beans, but didn't recall eating much of it. No matter, it all tasted like cardboard dipped in wallpaper paste. She checked her watch. 12:58. "I'm not quite done, yet. Sorry." Then she fumed at herself for apologizing to this smug wretch who was practically shooing her from the table. She opened the wine list again, but didn't repeat the mistake of setting down her utensil.

Her digital watch beeped the hour while she memorized the wine list. She picked some more at her food, but the thought of more Alfredo sauce made her ill. The offending plate was whisked away as soon as she set down her fork. No, mam'selle would not have dessert. "Coffee, please." It was now 1:25, and it was becoming obvious that Bob Hanson would not be calling today. She allowed herself to recognize the lump in her stomach, and it wasn't fettucini. It was fear.

"Luigi's Ristorante, one moment please." Hanson leaned groggily against the phone-booth wall, mind and body confused from twenty hours of overdue sleep. He clamped the handset in a vicious grip. "Thank you for waiting."

He licked dry lips. "Ms. Keller, please. She is dining there." Please still be there, Sally.

There was a long silence, but none of the background noise picked up when a phone is set down. *What gives?* he wondered. "Ms. Keller was here earlier. She waited for you, then dined alone." The voice dripped disapproval. "She finally left."

"I'm sorry," Hanson offered automatically. In answer, he heard a sniff of disgust, then dial tone.

Could he risk a call to her office? He wouldn't have to give his own name. Would Sally be able to answer his questions without being caught? Damn! Too risky. He was more than halfway there; he would just drive the rest of the way before finding out.

He walked past a sold-out newspaper vending machine on

his way to his car. Wonder what big scoop was so interesting? He threw his overnight bag onto the front passenger seat. The radio, never turned off the day before, offered a rebellious juvenile din.

Might as well hear some decent music. He popped open the glove compartment and flung a handful of cassette tapes beside the bag. He picked one at random and slid it into the tape player. The radio cut off instantly, and the Unholy Rabble were replaced by vintage Jelly Roll Morton. Fingers tapping along on the top curve of the steering wheel, Hanson put the car into gear.

The digital clock flashed to 2:00. Had the radio been on, Hanson would have caught the network news. Even on a punk radio station on the outskirts of Gaithers Corners, PA, they sometimes broke for news. Of course, the radio wasn't on.

The physical scientists were as happy as kids in a toy store. *Why not?* thought the psychologist. They *were* kids in a toy store. *Prospector* was orbiting Jupiter. The purloined UV satellite was pouring gigabits of data to Earth. There was even some optimism that manipulating the *Prospector* "explosion" data would yield a powerful new particle accelerator.

"Why worry?" they asked. "Look what we got when no one 'knew' about the aliens. Think what we'll get now."

Fools. They had no understanding of the mess this reporter had precipitated. The psychologist's models only worked with small numbers of people. This global panic invalidated every analysis he had done. And did they suppose that a totally depressed economy could afford the gadgets that so amused them? Compared to yesterday's market crash, 1987's Black Monday had been a hiccough.

Mostly he was disappointed in himself. He should have had the media computers scanned more often, found out about this story before the *Tribune* released it. But how was he to know that this Stuart was an anachronism, a computer hater? The story had not been on the *Tribune* machine until shortly before press time, after their daily preventive surveillance.

Recriminations were useless, of course. The best they could do now was to avoid future problems. Hanson must have been the source of the leak, though the psychologist couldn't see why Hanson was leaking the cover story instead of the truth. They had foolishly thought that Hanson was out of the game. Obviously, he wasn't. They would track down Hanson and silence him.

For now, they knew where Stuart was. First, they would silence *him*.

· **CHAPTER 11** ·

Only the bent-wood rocker on which Sally slouched, a large corduroy throw pillow supporting the small of her back, *belonged* in the family room. The other furnishings were inexpensive replacements for those her ex-husband had taken in the settlement. All she'd kept were the rocker and the French provincial bedroom set. He'd declined taking the latter. "Damned if I'll sleep in *that* any longer." Macho was not without its occasional benefit.

Rocking gently, she tried yet again to get interested in a novel. TV was hopeless tonight—the aliens had captured the airwaves. The continuous network coverage fell into three categories: outrageous errors, unjustifiable speculations, and the incidental accurate statement. She felt entitled to her cynicism; she knew what was going on.

Or had once thought she did. She flung her paperback book to the floor in disgust. Hanson hadn't explained his purpose—correct scientific method, you know, blind experiment. The unexpected delays in obtaining the data had left her with time on her hands, though, which she'd spent in a vain attempt to understand his intent.

Bob wanted confidence measures on several *Prospector* transmissions. The tests were simple enough, right out of her undergraduate stats class; it was his choice of *data* that perplexed her. Confidence tests assess the risk in believing a generalization inferred from a sample. For example, if three of four patients survive an experimental operation, how risky is it for number five? The tests just didn't apply to the processing of TV images from *Prospector*.

Sally retrieved the book and propped it open on her stomach. After three pages, she sighed and pitched it into the magazine rack. She went into the kitchen to boil water for tea, studiously ignoring the dinner dishes and pots.

While the watched teakettle wasn't boiling, she resumed wrestling with her intuition. Why did Bob want confidence measures on astronautical data? You took those measures on political polls, for crying out loud. "This week's *Time/Newsweek* telephone poll asked 763.8 households nationwide whether, if the presidential election were held today, they would vote for Attila the Hun or Joseph Stalin. The extrapolated national results, which are accurate to within three per cent, show that Uncle Joe would . . ." She grubbed through the disorganized pantry for some Darjeeling teabags. Polls, advertising research, medical experiments—but *Prospector* telemetry? Success. A box of teabags peeked out from behind some soup cans.

The teakettle whistled unnoticed; understanding had struck her like a two-by-four across the forehead. She sat down heavily on a dinette chair, ignoring the water now bubbling vigorously out the tiny whistle hole of the kettle. She'd remembered the generic drug scandals of 1989. If pharmaceutical efficacy tests could be faked, so could *Prospector* telemetry. *That*, of course, was what Bob suspected. Why? By whom? She dashed to the stove when she finally noticed the water spattering violently from the orange-glowing heating element. She grabbed the teakettle, instantly let go of the scorching handle, then tried again with a dish towel. There was water all over the stove top, and almost none left in the kettle. Hell with it, she decided, and poured a glass of cranberry juice.

The juice, too, was soon forgotten. Sally stretched out on the sofa and tried to sort it out. Hanson was either (a) crazy, (b) crazy like a fox, and involving her in some incredibly complicated defense, or (c) correct in his suspicions, which meant someone had framed him. She picked absently at a shred of hamburger gristle wedged between two teeth. *Then there's (d):* I'm *crazy.*

She couldn't believe—or didn't want to believe—either (a) or (d): neither he nor she seemed round the bend. Was Bob using her? Unlikely. She couldn't imagine him treating her that way. Besides, if Bob set his mind to embezzlement, which seemed improbable, he was too bright to get caught so easily. If nothing else, he was too smart to use such a convoluted and implausible defense. That left (c): an unknown villain who invented hostile aliens for some mysterious reason, and then discredited Hanson for discovering the hoax.

That wasn't crazy? *Arrrrrgh!* She shook her head violently, momentarily resembling a manic sea anemone, to clear the cobwebs.

Hanson had made powerful enemies, presumably including the Space Division. He wouldn't be on the run otherwise. Why hadn't he called back? What had he gotten her into? She shivered. Hopefully she'd been as circumspect as he'd suggested, but the delays in getting the data she'd requested made her wonder. Who could be behind it?

The *brrrringgg* of the doorbell startled her. She checked her watch—9:17. Who could be at her door at this hour? Arlington was no hotbed of night life, and this neighborhood was a particularly sedate family area. "Coming."

Sally didn't recognize the trench-coated man through the

front-door peephole. She opened the door as far as the slip-chain allowed. "Yes?"

"Ms. Sally Keller?" She nodded. "May I come in?"

"Who are you?"

The man exhaled through his nose. "I can't blame you for asking, but it spoils the fun. I'm a singing telegram, ma'am. May I come in?" He proffered a company ID card.

"Hold on." She took the card, closed the door, and checked the card against the yellow-pages ad. It matched. She placed a quick call to the company. Yes, they'd sent a messenger.

She let the man in. He glanced at an index card, then cleared his throat. "Remember, I don't write these. I just deliver them." He cleared his throat again, and chanted:

> Roses are red,
> Violets are blue.
> The florists were closed.
> This'll have to do.

"It's signed 'Icarus.' The P.S. reads 'Flash twice if the coast is clear.' " He handed her the index card and stood by expectantly.

"Thanks. That was wonderful." He looked mildly disgusted at her taste in poetry. She found her purse, gave him a dollar, and shooed him out the door. She was grinning from ear to ear, and suspected that her eyes were twinkling. "Icarus" was perfect.

In Greek myth, Icarus and his father Daedalus donned wax-and-feather wings to escape from the labyrinth of a monster, the Minotaur. When Icarus soared too high, the sun melted the wax of his wings and caused him to crash.

Icarus was also an unusual asteroid; at perihelion, its closest approach to the sun, Icarus swooped inside Mercury's orbit. Astronomers dubbed asteroids with such highly elliptical orbits *eccentric*.

Trapped in a maze. Crashed escaping. Asteroid. Eccentric. Icarus was obviously Hanson. He was safe! She frowned: he must think her phones were tapped, or else he would have just called. "Flash twice if the coast is clear." She toggled her porch light twice, then paced impatiently waiting for him. And paced some more.

Ten minutes passed and no Hanson. Had he been apprehended since arranging the telegram? Had she betrayed herself to the conspirators by flashing her porch light? Shit.

Brrrinngg. Please be Hanson. She raced to the door and instantly recognized Bob through the peephole. She flung open the door for him. Impulsively, she gave him a big hug. Then she slammed the door—hard—behind him and demanded, "What have you gotten me into?"

He looked horrible—exhausted and wrinkled. He wilted onto the sofa without answering and rested his head wearily against the wall. "I'm not sure." He closed his eyes.

He looked haggard and malnourished. "What have you been eating?"

Bob groaned slightly. "Coffee and the four basic food groups—salt, sugar, grease, and chocolate."

"Vending machines?"

"Yeah, and greasy-spoon diners. Never stop at a place with a 'Good Eats' sign."

The pickings here were slim, too—Dick had once accused her of never having prepared a premeditated meal. "Leftover tuna casserole okay?"

"Something domestic—that sounds wonderful." He struggled off the sofa and staggered after her. "I haven't been sleeping well. If I stayed there, I'd be asleep before you opened the refrigerator."

Sally stood over the stove, stirring occasionally. The now-cooled teakettle had been refilled and was being heated for instant coffee. Domesticity felt strangely good to her, too. Or was it specifically Bob?

"I owe you an apology, Sal." Hanson had poured himself

into a dinette chair and sat with both elbows on the table, propping up his chin. "I involved you unfairly. A lot of people don't want to hear my side of the *Prospector* story. I had no idea where else to turn." He stifled a yawn. "From your greeting I assume you confirmed the data fakery."

"No, but I figured out that you think the data is faked. There were too many coincidental problems trying to get the data to actually test anything." She inelegantly upended the saucepan over his plate. "Eat. Enough coincidences that I don't doubt what I'll find when I do run some tests." She watched him wolf down the food. "Unless I've been stalled so they can cover their tracks better."

Hanson looked around the kitchen, eyes finally lighting on the bread box. He retrieved a loaf and rapidly crammed down three sauce-soaked slices. "Just like Mother used to make." His eyes began to glaze over.

"I haven't seen a plate cleaned so thoroughly since I owned a dog." Hanson looked at her fuzzily. "Guido died when I was ten."

"Didn't know you were a pet person." He seemed to be struggling through syrup to stay attentive, and she loved him for it.

"Uh-huh. It's not fair to an animal, though, to live cooped up in a house or apartment while his owners are working. And this isn't a neighborhood where an animal can run." Besides, Dick had had no more interest in pets than in children. "Otherwise, I'd love to have a dog or cat."

"I've got the same problem." Hanson's elbows started sliding apart. He jerked himself back upright. He seemed likely to fall down and hurt himself before the coffee water boiled. But Bob appeared determined to listen as long as she was talking. She hadn't thought of framing him for a felony and hounding him across the country to break his reserve— but apparently that was what it took.

"You need sleep, Bob. I'll go make up the guest bed. We'll talk in the morning, before I go into work." He smiled weakly at her. "Sit on the sofa for a minute." She got sheets onto the bed in record time and dashed to the living room, expecting to assist him up the stairs.

No help was required. Bob had stretched out on the couch and was sawing wood. He didn't stir when she slipped a throw pillow under his head or when she threw an afghan over him.

Or when she kissed him goodnight.

Reprogramming the Ford dealership's computer was even more difficult than he'd expected. The programmer found the effort a refreshing change of pace. It wasn't that the "Carputer" was sophisticated—quite the opposite. It literally held no security software. The challenge came from diverting something so simple and single-minded from its intended purpose.

Most of the Carputer's program was stored in ROM—read-only memory—that was factory-set for its intended purpose. The machine was matched to each specific make and model of car with more ROM, by a plug-in cartridge the mechanic selected for the vehicle being serviced. In short, the Carputer was not much more than an oversized video game. Its only writable memory, the only spot where he could realize his plan, was the tiny program-patch area into which Ford down-loaded corrections to the basic ROM program. Over-the-phone distribution of small corrections was cheaper and faster than mailing cartridges.

The programmer worked fixedly on the problem. The solution, when it came, was not elegant or sophisticated. His peers would have sneered at it as "hacking." Privately, though, he knew they would approve of his cleverness. His tiny little patch would sit innocuously in the patch space, harmless until a very particular car was worked on. Recognizing the vehicle identification number, the patch would alter itself. *Then* interesting things would happen.

The programmer withdrew from the machine. He hadn't been sure before now that this step would be possible. Now that the trap was set, he needed to bait it. He quickly broke into the dealership's business system and printed out a single recall notice. It would be mailed in the morning by someone who'd assume it had been overlooked on the evening shift.

All that remained was the wait.

Sally distractedly skimmed a professional journal, killing the time until her three o'clock slot on the NASA Cray-5 supercomputer. Running Bob's analysis on any other machine was simply not worthwhile. NASA's Cray included the large optional array processor, a special-purpose computer that concurrently performed mathematical operations over thousands of related data items. That baby would discover any statistical anomalies in the *Prospector* data far quicker than any of the smaller computers available to her without scheduling. What mattered was how quickly she finished her tests, not how quickly she started them.

The journal served a second purpose—it hid the goofy grin into which she couldn't help breaking from time to time. Her work friends had ribbed her all morning, not knowing *who* but very sure *what* had made her so happy. Their imaginations were far more libidinous than circumstances merited, but reality was fine with her.

She had tip-toed downstairs this morning to check on Bob, only to find him brewing coffee and frying eggs in the kitchen. His still bloodshot eyes had twinkled. His cheery smile at seeing her had warmed her like the first day of spring. "Hi, beautiful. About time you were up. I only cook one breakfast a day." He waved a greasy pancake turner at the refrigerator. "I cleaned you out of eggs and I couldn't find any bacon. I'm pleased to see you weren't expecting company."

Her typical breakfast was an apple; the eggs were for baking, and she never bought bacon. She happily popped some bread in the toaster before replying. "Bacon and fried eggs, huh? It'd be only slightly more efficient to inject lard directly into your aorta." She sighed melodramatically and held her hand to her brow. "I knew this was too good to last."

They'd bantered on through pots of coffee and about three weeks worth of breakfasts. Where did the time go? They were discussing the museums of the Smithsonian when Sally noticed her clock. "You silver-tongued devil! Plying me with coffee until I don't know whether I'm coming or going. Well, sir, you'll have to wait with your dastardly plan. I have priority research to do for a retired scientist from the private sector." They were still laughing when she let herself into the garage.

"Be careful," she'd lip-read through the windshield as the overhead garage door descended. She'd waved a deprecating hand at Bob as the door cut him off. Piece of cake. Number crunching wasn't dangerous.

The goofy grin was reasserting itself when the summons came. Carucci called and asked her to his office, no explanation offered. He shook his head at her when she arrived, then quickly excused himself. She sat down on a chair to wait.

Her musings were interrupted when two tall men arrived in the office. Both could have been former linebackers. Each wore an FBI-issue gray suit and white shirt, a discreet bulge showing under the left arm. The marginally taller one closed the door and flashed a wallet with a badge. "Curtis." Curtis gestured at his companion. "McPherson."

It quickly became apparent that Curtis and McPherson were of the strong and silent persuasion. She rose from her chair. "Please excuse me, gentlemen. I have work to do." McPherson slid smoothly between her and the door. Neither man spoke. She picked up the handset of the desk phone.

Curtis reached forward and held down the switchhook with a surprisingly long index finger. More silence. Infuriated and scared, Sally tried to slam the handset back onto its cradle. Curtis's left hand shot out and caught her wrist in midair. He released the switchhook and used his right hand to pry the handset, none too gently, from her shaking grasp. Her wrist remained captive. Still silence.

Breathing heavily, Sally leaned back against a bookcase.

"Let me go *now*, or I scream bloody murder." She took in a big shuddering breath.

Curtis smiled the twisted smile of a little boy vivisecting a frog and loving it. "Please do. Executive offices here are very well soundproofed. Also, everyone in your department was called to a meeting on another floor. So is every nearby department. We're quite alone, Sally."

"What do you want?" *My God, what's happening?*

"Cooperation." They peered intently at her, studying her like some interesting type of bug.

"Hellllp!!!" They grinned indulgently at one another. Let the hysterical female get it out of her system. *"Hellllllp, dammit, someone!"* No response, no noise from outside the office. The bastards were telling the truth.

They let her wind down, hoarse, without speaking again. Curtis freed her wrist, popped the quick-release connector of the phone, and handed the phone to McPherson, who set it down by his feet. They reminded her of predators waiting to pounce.

"Cooperate how?" she asked, when she caught her breath. She tried to sound dejected, beaten, and was dismayed at how little acting that took.

McPherson was not, after all, mute. He took a folded sheet of paper from an inside coat pocket and one-handedly snapped it open. It looked computer generated. "We'll be following you when you deliver this."

Sally reached for it, but McPherson whipped it out of her reach. "Naughty, naughty. You're not cleared for this. You'll get it when you need it, no sooner." He refolded it and put it away.

"But what *is* it?" This was beginning to sound like some incredible spy story. Ordinary citizen trapped into desperate adventure. "Deliver it *where*? Deliver it to *whom*?" She heard her voice rising, a brittle edge of hysteria in it. Incredible. Astonishing. Astounding. Amazing. A maze-ing. Trapped like a rat in a maze . . . like Icarus was trapped in a maze.

For all the good it did, she understood her dilemma. Whoever had framed Hanson had gotten her, too. She didn't need obscure mathematical inferences to confirm that the *Prospector* data was falsified. This persecution proved it. Unfortunately, she seemed to lack Hanson's knack for evasive action.

Curtis leaned forward, moving her back behind the desk by sheer force of intimidation. Her fingers, with minds of their own, anxiously kneaded the padded back of the desk chair. He glared at her, then exhaled explosively in disgust. "Cut the shit, sister. Did you really think that the security audits in classified computers were that feeble?" The bastard seemed to thrive on displays of weakness. It wasn't hard to encourage him. He continued as she looked at him blankly. "You have *had* it. You are *history*."

Sally pointed at McPherson, hulking silently by the door. "Was that a classified document I supposedly tried to obtain? I didn't." Her fingers kept up their diligent kneading.

Curtis answered. "True, you didn't try—you succeeded. Several 'Eyes Only' items reside damningly in your computer files. That part was done nicely enough, and you'll be helping yourself if you show us just how you got them there unde- tected." She shook her head. If only she could help herself. "You blew it when you tried to transfer the stolen files off the system."

The calm and detail with which they spelled out her sup- posed transgressions terrified her. The agents, Neanderthal extraction notwithstanding, were professionals. They clearly believed every word of their indictment. She had been set up by experts. How could she ever get out of this? "Give me credit for some brains. I'd obviously know that an attempt to transfer classified files would be detected. Why would I do something so foolish?"

McPherson took a pencil from the desk. He used the point to scratch under a thumbnail, then stabbed the pencil into the desk blotter. "I'm big, lady, not stupid. Give me some credit, too. Damned right you're too clever to try transferring a tagged file out of the building. Clever enough instead to blend the stolen files, little by little, into your daily electronic mail. Unclassified correspondence to unclassified users.

"You know, you're an excellent speller and grammarian most of the time. We have the memos and papers going back to your school days to prove it. Isn't it interesting how many misspellings and grammatical errors suddenly cropped up in your correspondence?" He glared at her viciously. "I find it *especially* fascinating that the omitted letters just happen to spell out the content of the stolen files."

Sally's fingers stopped their kneading; she now gripped the chair to keep from falling. "I don't know what you're talking about." Listening to the quiver in her voice, she wouldn't have believed herself.

"Amnesia? Insanity defense? Don't waste your breath." Curtis looked disappointed. "Your only chance is cooperating with us. It's barely conceivable that we won't press charges."

"Cooperate how?"

"You'll send a final message by Funk & Wagnalls express, one we've written for you. The message will say that the operation is compromised. True enough. You'll ask for a rendezvous. You'll admit to having one more key document," he pointed to McPherson's pocket, "to be delivered by hand. If we get your partner, and if we feel generous that day, things might go a little easier for you."

Her mind flitted in all directions, seeking an opening in the tightening net. The plot didn't exist—at least, not the plot they were investigating, and no one would answer her message. They'd lock her up and throw away the key. She grasped at a straw. "Why don't you arrest the person who got incriminating mail from me?"

Curtis laughed. "As you know, my dear"—she shuddered at that epithet—"there is no *one* addressee. The mail you so accurately label 'incriminating' went to everyone on a long distribution list, to centers all over the country: the Cape, Huntsville, Houston. Do you expect us to arrest half of NASA?"

A realization struck her, and she spoke mostly to herself. "You haven't even asked who I'm leaking to."

"Life imitates art. You mean '. . . to whom I'm leaking.' " Curtis ignored her scathing look. "You'd have told us already if you were the type to tell. So, either the bastard recruited you long distance and you don't know who he is, or you won't finger him. It really doesn't matter. We'll get him Thursday."

Sally's heart sank. "But *why* would I steal this material? I have no motive."

"I don't care what your reason was, lady," growled McPherson. "We're hemorrhaging too many secrets to watch you for long enough to figure that out. My guess? I'd bet that feeding your mortgage on one salary is killing you. Then again"—he paused to leer—"maybe your associate has pictures of you doing something kinky." He winked at Curtis. "One can hope."

The monetary angle was plausible enough, though she was—barely—making ends meet. She taught differential calculus two evenings a week at the University of Maryland in College Park; the pittance that it paid made the critical difference. Which didn't prove anything. "Let's see the message you want me to send."

Curtis had her log onto Carucci's workstation, then popped a 3 ½-inch diskette from his shirt pocket into the drive. She ran the text file on the diskette through the spelling checker, which dumped a list of misspelled and unrecognized words onto the screen. Sally painstakingly read through the long list, puzzling out the message from the errors:

> we have problems must meet nine pm thursday at
> snappy pappy's will bring f24 info

Snappy Pappy's was an Arlington lounge near her house; an F-24 was presumably a new fighter plane. She knew what was expected of her. Slowly, with a feeling of impending doom, she entered the commands to send the innocuous-seeming, mistake-filled message to her standard distribution list.

"What do I do until Thursday night?" *Until no one meets me at Snappy Pappy's?*

"Just the usual. You can go to work, teach your class, buy groceries. But remember—we'll be watching you carefully." He smiled like a shark. "We'll be *very* displeased if anything interferes with your upcoming date. We're not nearly this charming when we're displeased."

The bureaucratic hordes began streaming from NASA headquarters at four o'clock; by five-fifteen, the flow of departees had dropped off to a trickle. Hanson watched them from his perch on the steps of the Air and Space Museum, across Independence Avenue from NASA. No Sally. The museum crowd also started thinning out, so he ambled down the steps to a trailer selling tacky Washington souvenirs. Surely no one who knew him would ever search near this schlock. He examined the Jefferson Memorial paperweights and Washington Monument fluorescent ties while stealing quick glances toward NASA. Still no Sally.

By five-thirty he was worried. Given her parking spot, this was the only door it made sense for her to use. Had her need for the Cray-5 been understood? Was she in trouble? She had promised to be *home* by five-thirty, and she hadn't yet left. Of course, she might have tried to call him at her house to explain an innocent delay—he wasn't there to take the call. As soon as she'd left, he'd taken the Metro into the District. He hadn't avoided capture by leaving things to chance. If Sally somehow got implicated in his situation, the cops would certainly search her home. His getting caught that way would end everything.

So here he stood, admiring ghastly T-shirts. The owner gave him a dirty look, having been turned away on several previous attempts to close a sale. "Sorry, I'm not sure what

I'm looking for. Something for my niece. I'll know it when I see it.''

Six o'clock. Come *on*, Sally. He pictured her tangled in a web at least partially of his own weaving, and broke into a cold sweat. It was more than guilt. She was someone special, someone he had unknowingly waited years for, and he didn't intend to lose her. *Wouldn't* lose her.

Hanson started casting about for new concealment as the vendor folded the trailer's sheet-metal sides over his garish wares. The scientist decided that the soft-pretzel wagon down the block would do temporarily. Besides, he was starved. He was dipping the last of his pretzel in mustard when she appeared. Mental alarms went off, and he studied her closely. She looked wild and beaten, like an animal with its leg in a trap. *Why?* Alerted by Sally's expression, he stood and watched. Two big bruisers meandered out of the door behind her. The gorillas happened to be going in her direction. Sally's dejected pace was slow, far too slow for the tall men, but they stayed about fifteen feet behind her.

He watched in fascinated horror as the men followed Sally down Independence. Gray-suit number one, the taller of the pair, nodded briefly at someone in a parked white Lincoln, then tipped his head slightly toward Sally's back. Moments later, the Lincoln pulled away from the curb and cruised slowly after the trio. The car crawled along, and passed Sally only when the just-changed-to-red traffic light guaranteed that she would catch up. Hanson pulled nervously at a sideburn. They don't walk you to jail, especially if there's a car nearby. For some reason, Sally was being watched—and it was obviously no secret to her.

Hanson's mind raced. What should he *do?* Was there anything he *could* do? He followed Sally and escort, hoping that he was less obvious than Thing One and Thing Two had been. Hopefully, there were no more observers to spot him. Helpless and nearly hopeless, he brought up the rear of the parade. Finally, Sally dragged herself into her rusting Plymouth sedan and drove off. The stoop of her shoulders as she hunched over the steering wheel broke Hanson's heart.

The white Lincoln, Moby Dick on land, cruised inevitably after her. One of the two pedestrian goons waved discreetly as the handoff was completed. Both men watched the two cars recede, then pivoted abruptly and returned the way they had come. They were within feet of Hanson, though apparently indifferent to the fact, when he finally flagged down a taxi.

"Where to, buddy?" The driver was short, beefy, and had the red nose of a boozer. He chewed noisily on a sodden butt of extinguished cigar, and began creeping up the street without awaiting an answer.

Ahead, Hanson could still see the distinctive taillights of the land cruiser shadowing Sally. He didn't dare say "follow that car"; the phrase seemed too memorable. The last thing he wanted was attention. "Um, straight for now." He'd have to keep his eyes peeled. The cabby snarled unintelligibly into his cigar, but complied.

Hanson clung to the back of the front seat, desperate to keep track of the Lincoln. They were heading south for the river. He absently wiped his sweaty palms on the seat back. Short, squat, and surly floored it, arced on squealing tires around a gawking tourist, then stood on his brakes to avoid a beer truck. Hanson braced himself against the Plexiglas divider on the back of the driver's seat and just barely missed a crack on the head.

They had gained two car lengths on the Lincoln—and presumably on Sally. He curled his fingers into tight fists. Sally had looked as if her life were ending. Well, he'd gotten her into this sorry mess, and he'd get her out of it.

Somehow.

· CHAPTER 12 ·

Hanson woke with a start and a wince when an innocently flung hand competed for space with the fake marble bench. Bench three, knuckles nothing. He massaged the victims with the palm of his other hand while he gradually recalled the situation.

Sleep would have been preferable.

Sally was still tailed everywhere by her muscular acquaintances; some devious plot was presumably being furthered by this curious state of ambulatory arrest. Whenever he was able to observe her, she looked totally forlorn and haunted. Apparently she was expected to cooperate in something in which she didn't—or couldn't—plan to participate. What? He'd puzzled over that riddle for days without result. The only seemingly safe conclusions were that "his" conspirators had detected her prowling through the *Prospector* data, and that she, like him, had been framed. He couldn't imagine her supposed crime, but expected it was as implausible as his own. One fact was evident: she hadn't implicated him. He didn't flatter himself that he would remain at large for very long in the barely familiar D.C. area once the cops were actively looking for him.

Her only hope, it appeared, was that he rescue her. Right. Desperate fugitive scientist living in subway station frees cohort from FBI custody. Exhausted, malnourished, desperate fugitive scientist. Impoverished, filthy, exhausted, malnourished . . . *Craaaaack*. He smashed his bruised knuckles *hard* against the unyielding bench. Pitying yourself won't help, he lectured himself. You got Sally into this, wimp, you *will* try to get her out . . . *And if I get caught* . . . He smiled sardonically: a few more nights like this and a bare mattress in a cell would seem luxurious.

He'd awakened just in time: the janitors were rousting the remaining sleepers in anticipation of the morning rush hour. Hanson left the bench to weave his way through his fellow derelicts to the temporarily unlocked Metro station washroom. His reflection frightened him. Red eyes peered back at him from above puffy gray bags. Pasty skin was broken out into not-quite pimples; his hair looked like it had been dipped in salad oil. At least he could do something about the layer of morning scum coating his teeth. He pulled a toothbrush and tube of toothpaste from a pocket of his terminally wrinkled coat. Ignoring the decaying creature in the mirror, he concentrated on the simple task at hand.

Minutes later Hanson emerged onto the street. He'd picked this Metro station for its strategic position in the District. It was only minutes away from the National Air and Space Museum, the post of his daily vigil. He purchased another nutritious breakfast of pretzel and coffee with his rapidly dwindling funds, then settled down on a commuter bench with a salvaged *Washington Post* to await Sally's arrival.

He scanned the paper without much interest. It was a Wednesday paper, he noted idly, which meant today was Thursday. Every day seemed the same now. Judging from the paper, there was a rapidly expanding army of unemployed to share part of his misfortune—although they would be eligible for better severance and unemployment comp than he had gotten. He noticed one article with interest: Al Stuart had gotten himself nationally syndicated as a result of his stories about the "aliens." Hometown boy made good. Wonder how Stuart would take it if he knew that there were no aliens? That he was uncovering the wrong coverup? That the economy was collapsing for nothing? He wadded up the paper in disgust and returned it to the wire wastebasket. So where's your proof, expert? Once again, he needed Sally. It kept coming back to her. She was his responsibility and his corroboration.

Finally, he spotted her pacing zombielike up Independence Avenue. Heckle and Jeckle maintained their stations behind her. Hanson focused intently on her blank and expressionless eyes, bottomless pits. All hope abandon, ye who enter here. He had to do something for Sally, and do it *today*. He watched her shuffle mechanically up the stairs and into NASA. The door slammed shut behind her with the finality of the lid on a sarcophagus.

Hanson fled around the Seventh Street side of the museum to the Mall, striding briskly to flush his lungs. He set himself to the mindless goal of marching to the Washington Monument, squinting against the glare of the rising sun. Soon sweat was rolling down his forehead and he could feel his heart pumping. The monument was farther away than it had first seemed—the people at its base, he now saw, looked very small. Good. He could feel the mental cobwebs blowing off as he tramped.

He *had* to rescue Sally. Her adherence to schedule was the single dividend from several days invested in passive observation. He'd paid dearly for it, so should use it. Use it against them.

Kidnapping was an understood risk in certain social circles, another lifestyle of the rich and famous imported from Europe. Criminals and political crazies routinely preyed upon the wealthy and powerful for money and publicity. Their prospective victims, in turn, studied how to evade abduction, especially when traveling in the Middle East, Europe, Latin America. Hanson had even endured a few pro forma lectures himself on the subject: he was an executive, which to a certain mind-set made him fair game. The one lesson that the security consultants pounded into everyone's heads—the part that he best remembered, anyway—was avoidance of routine. Routine helps the kidnapper make and keep plans. Routine lets the kidnapper pick the site of his crime. Use Sally's routine.

Hanson grimaced at his imagination. Right, he was going to snatch Sally away from her captors. He kept on striding and thinking, because thought hurt less than the mindless worry that it displaced. Not much of a routine: work, home, work. Something flitted across his mind and was gone before it registered. Work, home, work. He knew that both her home and office were under surveillance whenever Sally was around. And what did he expect her "escorts" to do while he was whisking her away? Kidnappers don't usually free-lance, he thought. They operate in groups. They use their knowledge of routine to achieve local superiority in numbers when they strike.

He had to go it alone.

The serpentine line of tourists showed that he'd reached the monument. Now what? He couldn't get beyond the fact that Sally's routine displayed no opportunity for an escape. Going back to stare at NASA wouldn't help her. Work, home, work. There had to be some time when her routine offered an opportunity. A chance. Besides, he couldn't bear to see her hopeless eyes again this evening when she left the office.

How could he learn what else was in her routine, where else they would be letting her go? Could he make a cryptic telephone call, like he had to Bernie? No, too dangerous. Her home and office phones were certainly bugged, and they'd made her start brown-bagging for lunch. A mysterious call would only alert them to his presence.

His problem was ignorance of Sally's routine. Okay, he was going to solve that problem. He hoped that all of her on-duty companions were following her, that they didn't leave buddies ensconced in her house. Soon he would know.

He was going to break in.

Wasn't anything worth keeping? Sally swept her eyes around the office for memorabilia, not expecting to be back. Her rendezvous tonight with her imaginary coconspirator would be a real disappointment for her captors. They didn't seem likely to keep their disappointment to themselves.

Her mind was as empty as her briefcase. One idea had sustained her at first: Bob would somehow rescue her. She soon recognized that idea as a fantasy. Bob was a scientist, not a swashbuckler. Now, when she occasionally and fleetingly succumbed to unfounded optimism, she only hoped that he'd unravel the web of deceit before she was totally acclimated to prison.

A few hours of "freedom" left, hours spent under guard while following a prescribed schedule. Curtis and McPherson had her stuck in this room; for public consumption, she was dedicated to some hush-hush rush project. Any behavior more sinister than nail polishing would be construed as an attempted warning to the mystery person.

Though she couldn't say why, Sally wasn't prepared to confront the FBI agents and give up even this shadowy semblance of normalcy. Her face bent in a humorless smile—surely she didn't still expect Bob to spirit her away to safety?

Her wristwatch alarm settled one problem for her: no more time for woolgathering. She latched her briefcase, then stuck her head into the hall. McPherson was waiting. Off she went to one final pretence, one last taste of her real world. One last place to go before the ultimate meeting at Snappy Pappy's.

She had a class to teach tonight.

The yammering of a pneumatic socket wrench pierced the air as Harvey picked up his clipboard of work orders. Moments later, a wheel thudded to the floor from the next service bay. Lou chortled uproariously as Harvey skittered away from the bouncing missile. He swore under his breath at the boss's idiot son and kept reading about the surprise rush job.

Recall notice. That surprised Harvey: he hadn't heard of any recall for the popular TFX-66i. No point arguing with the work order, though. The keys for the little sports car hung on the pegboard, tagged to match the sequence number on the paperwork. He strolled into the sweltering lot, found the metallic blue two-seater, and eased it over the hydraulic lift. Before leaving the car he popped the hood release.

Harvey ran greasy fingers through his unruly blond hair, vainly brushing the long sparse fringes over the shiny bald spot. They instantly flopped back. He picked up his clipboard and puzzled over it: "Brain transplant"? Trudging to the back corner where the Carputer sat between uses, he wondered what had happened to routine repairs like wheel alignments and brake-pad replacements.

Personality modules for different car models lay jumbled together on the battered aluminum shelf above the Carputer. Harvey dug for the 66i cartridge, then plugged it into the cursed electronic monster. The Carputer wobbled along behind him, its casters refusing to turn in unison, as he towed it by its power cord.

Back at his bay, he unkinked the massive connecting cable and powered up the Carputer. He felt, rather than heard, the running of the little cooling fan. Something mechanical inside the chassis clawed its way up the scale; the panel lamps blinked when the beast reached its irritating operational hum. The tiny screen finally flashed "All tests pass. Connect probe to test vehicle."

The analysis probe on the connecting cable slid neatly into the mating female socket of the 66i's main electronics module. Lou bustled over, as he always did when Harvey used the Carputer, and snickered. "Gonna screw its brains out?" He clapped Harvey on the back, hard, and went smirking back to balancing a wheel. Harvey gritted his teeth and remained silent. Thank God the college nerd only worked summers. He thumbed the big red START button on the Carputer.

Immediately, text spilled down the screen, and the indicator lamp above a 50-pin socket glowed green. Why the rush? He unhurriedly reviewed the Carputer's wordy advice.

Vehicle Identification Number matches recall list. Reprogramming of on-board computer required. Proceed as follows:

Disconnect main electronics module from vehicle (press HELP to review removal procedures). Leave Carputer cable attached.

Use bulk memory eraser on glass window (visible only when module demounted) to clear original program from module. Erasure lasts one minute—press eraser attachment firmly to glass while eraser ON light is lit.

Insert module into indicated Carputer reprogramming socket. Module fits in only one orientation—do not force. Engage lever beside socket for proper electrical connection.

Disengage lever and remove module from socket when green indicator light is extinguished.

Reassemble vehicle and retest.

"Teach your grandma to suck eggs," muttered Harvey. Damned machine treated him like *his* brains had been bulk erased. Still, he followed the procedure to the letter. He always did. Otherwise he would never have noticed something whirring inside the Carputer *after* the reconnected car rated "All tests passed." Harvey had never known the Carputer to function after a procedure was finished. Maybe *it* needed its brains reprogrammed. Heh, heh.

Lou picked that moment to prod him in the ribs with a screwdriver handle. "Time for a break, old man. Flip you for coffee." He advanced menacingly toward Harvey, then stopped, laughing hysterically, and reached into an overalls pocket. "Nah, I'm too tired. Let's flip coins instead."

Harvey tried behind closed lids to roll his eyes. *Lord, give me strength.* He forgot the unexpected *whir* of the Carputer, which was unfortunate. His intuition had been very accurate. The Carputer had just reprogrammed itself. It now held only the standard Ford-approved program.

* * *

Hanson parked his car, just ransomed from the parking garage at National Airport, not far from Sally's house. His meager luggage was safe in the trunk. He had taken the opportunity at National to shave and change clothes; he now felt semihuman. It was a measure of how low he'd sunk that a clean knit shirt and jeans were an indulgence. He could kill for a shower.

His earlier precautionary pass down Sally's street had not revealed any suspicious persons in parked cars. Now he cut across a neighbor's lot to enter Sally's well-planted back yard, pausing behind an overgrown hydrangea before approaching the house. No signs of occupancy. He scurried up to the house and listened intently beneath the kitchen window. No TV or radio going to amuse a bored cop. Maybe his luck had finally turned. He peered inside. No one.

Hanson checked under the mat and felt along the top of the back-door frame without discovering a spare key. He hadn't really expected to find one, but no harm in trying. Reluctantly, he took a grapefruit-sized decorative rock from Sally's flower garden. It would easily break the door's inset window. He patted the baseball in his windbreaker pocket; if he got in and out undetected, he'd leave it behind to explain the broken window.

He squeezed up against the door to reduce his visibility to neighbors; unexpectedly, the door swung in away from his pressing body. He lobbed the rock back into the flower bed, stepped quickly inside, and shut the door behind him. Could you believe it? Unlocked the whole time.

The kitchen was just as he remembered it: oak cabinets, the red-and-green imitation Tiffany fixture, a homey level of clutter on the counter. Suppressing an urge to raid the pantry, he began hunting for Sally's calendar.

None of the obvious places yielded a calendar: refrigerator door, wall by the phone, cork board. He looked inside the cabinet doors but found only a towel bar. Dammit Sally, how do you function without a calendar by your phone? The re-

frigerator compressor kicked on noisily as he brooded. Where
else? He pawed carefully but unproductively through the
drawers, wincing each time a utensil clanked.

Hanson curled his lip in disgust at himself and went through
the doorless archway into the adjoining den. Sally's desk sat
just inside, within easy reach of the well-stretched cord of
the kitchen wall phone. The simple daily desk calendar displayed last Tuesday. He ripped out the following several
pages and crammed them into a pocket. Time to run—he
could study them elsewhere. He dashed through the kitchen
to the back door.

"Freeze."

The demand was redundant to the shock of hearing a voice.
Cautiously, Hanson pivoted toward it. A stocky man in an
unseasonal dark blue suit, thirtyish, stood in the dining room
doorway holding a silenced revolver. *Sorry, Sally, I tried.*

"I . . . I'm the gardener. I just came in for a drink before
I mowed. I won't tell anyone I saw you. P-please let me
go?" He tried to look harmless as he whimpered.

"Shut up." The gunman held out his left hand. "Gimme
your wallet."

Hanson had had the sense to lock it in his car. "M-money?
Here." He pulled a few crumpled bills from a pocket. "My
watch, too, if you want it, only it's not very good."

His captor stepped forward and brushed the money from
Hanson's theatrically quivering hand. Hanson tensed, preparing to grab the extended arm, before thinking better of it.
All he would do was get himself shot. "Gardener, huh?"
said the man. "There's no truck in front."

"The, uh, the shed in back has tools." Hanson gestured
vaguely toward the back yard. "I walked here."

"There's no shed." The response betrayed a trace of un-
certainty.

"Oh yes, yes," Hanson bubbled inanely. "Look there."
He crouched to better look through the low window over the
sink. "Behind the lilacs. Look between those two." He

turned his back to the gun, his flesh crawling, and gestured the man forward to peek over his shoulder. "See?"

The telephone rang shrilly just as the gunman hunched over beside Hanson to see the tool shed. Hanson caught a waver, a start, in his peripheral vision.

Now! Hanson reacted without thinking. He stabbed backward with his right elbow, brushing aside the gun. Something went *pffft* past his ear as he stamped his heel down hard on an immaculately polished wing tip. He immediately curled forward and dropped bruisingly to his knees. The maneuver was just in time: it converted a disabling kidney punch with the pistol into a jarring blow that glanced off his back. The trigger guard gouged a channel of skin and cotton across one shoulder blade as it passed.

The arm did a mid-course correction and snaked around his throat. Hanson twisted his head sideways, orienting his windpipe away from his assailant's elbow. The crushing grip was slightly looser there, helping him to breathe.

As the man heaved backward viciously on Hanson's head, pulling him off his knees, Hanson convulsively straightened his back and legs. For a terrifying instant, Hanson feared that his feet would shoot out from under him on the slippery floor. Instead, the combatants backpedaled rapidly across the kitchen—Hanson pushing to build up speed and his adversary seeking desperately to regain his balance. Hanson clung to the encircling forearm as the man now tried to disengage. There was a meaty *thud* as the baddie's head hit the refrigerator door, followed closely by a sickening crunch as ribs connected with the handle. Unseen bottles crashed and toppled as the refrigerator rocked beneath the impact of the two men. Hanson released the now loosened forearm and violently propelled both elbows into his opponent's gut. The man wheezed as broken rib-ends grated.

Hanson squirmed free and spun to face his enemy. The man's eyes were wide with pain, but he still held the gun. It was coming to bear on Hanson. Christ! Hanson buried a shoe tip in the man's stomach. He doubled over retching, but somehow kept trying to aim. Blood flowed down his neck from a split scalp, and two thick drops of blood plopped sickeningly to the floor. Hanson almost puked despite the gun, which was again wavering upward.

Him or me. Hanson sucked in a deep breath and kneed the man, still doubled over, in the face. His head snapped back against the refrigerator door. Both eyes lost focus, wandered in opposite directions, and closed. He collapsed to the side, cracking his head against a cabinet door on his way down.

Hanson stood stooped over his victim, gasping hoarsely, then punted the handgun from a limp hand. Groaning, he tightly lashed the unconscious man's arms behind him with his belt, then bound his ankles together with dish towels. He stuffed a wadded-up dish cloth into the other's mouth. Then Hanson turned away and threw up.

When the waves of nausea subsided, Hanson gingerly fished a wallet from the comatose man's jacket. FBI, as suspected. The wallet also contained over two hundred dollars.

The agent moaned; Hanson suspected that he was coming to. It was time to be *gone*. First, though, he had to cover up the mess he'd made. As things stood, the FBI's obvious conclusion would be that Sally's normalcy act had failed. His bungling would get Sally formally jailed immediately, before he could help her.

The agent's breathing changed rhythm in some undefinable way. The scientist snuck a peek and saw slightly open eyes shut quickly. Act 1, scene 2. "Can you believe it!? Jesus H. Christ! Can I spot a friggin' empty house, or what?" He took the sheaf of bills from the wallet and thumbed it noisily. "No way, Jose. Not me." He stuffed the bills into his pocket. "*I* don't even find a housebimbo watching game shows. *I* pick the house of an off-duty fed." Hanson tossed the wallet to the floor inches from the agent's nose; the man instinctively recoiled. He'd heard every word. "I gotta find a new line of work."

Somehow he made it on rubbery legs through Sally's and the neighbor's yards to the next street. Safely in his car, he began to believe his narrow escape. He pulled into a Taco Bell for a jolt of caffeine—food would bounce—and to review the calendar.

The contrast was surreal. Munchkins swarmed over the benches and tables as he flattened out stolen calendar pages. One of the ground apes played leapfrog with a trash receptacle while his mother studiously ignored him.

Hanson ran a finger down Thursday's page. *Bingo*. Not work, home, work. Work, work, home. Sally taught tonight in College Park. *That* was what he'd been unable to remember; it hadn't seemed important when she'd mentioned it. He took a sip of Pepsi and thought hard about her class. His left hand twisted a curl of sideburn as he stared at nothing. The straw briefly slurped air.

A wicked smile creased his face as he abruptly slid from his booth. The children fearfully scattered from his path as he stalked, grinning, to the door. *Good idea, children*, he thought. *I am unpredictable. And dangerous. That's why I just might succeed in rescuing Sally tonight.*

Hanson had one final odious task to perform before heading for Maryland, another crazy chance to take. He had to burglarize a neighborhood home to corroborate his little drama.

A short search revealed his target. The morning paper sat on the front porch of the brick-and-frame Cape Cod; two empty garbage cans lay waiting at the curb. He broke a glass panel in a French door and released the latch.

Hanson stuffed a filched pillowcase with some jewelry and silverware. He added a piece of junk mail, unlikely to be missed, so that he could later make anonymous restitution. Mostly he made a mess to render his visit unmistakable.

A moving glint in the family room caught his eye. There. A brass anniversary clock sat prominently upon the carved colonial mantelpiece, flanked by well-stocked bookshelves.

Hanson elbowed the clock from its perch, shattering its

glass dome on the brick hearth. Regretfully, Hanson stepped on the delicate mechanism; when it stopped, he nudged the hands backward by two hours. After all, a burglar caught in the act by the FBI wouldn't be likely to try again *later* that same day, would he?

· CHAPTER 13 ·

      Differential calculus was *not* McPherson's idea of a fun evening. He'd learned long ago that any subject beginning with "the"—like "the calculus" or "the dance"—was hopelessly pretentious. Snooty, to call a spade a spade. He was relieved when the lecture about something called L'Hospital's Rule showed signs of turning out not totally awful. Useless, but not totally awful. The prof presented her topic well—if you overlooked the nervous tic. Too bad the traitorous bitch didn't wear her clothes a little tighter.

College was much as he remembered it. The classroom was stuffy and the straight-backed chairs were uncomfortable. One of the fluorescent light fixtures buzzed and flickered. Most of the night students stifled yawns unenthusiastically, while two nerds scribbled their copious notes into fat spiral notebooks.

He was glad that the evening had settled into dull routine. It hadn't started that way. A note taped to one of the lecture-hall doors had directed the class to a smaller room in another building. No big deal, except that the original room would have better handled the crowd. Also, a quick peek had revealed padded auditorium-style seats in the first room. Sigh.

The classroom door squeaked as it opened to admit an earnest-looking young twerp. He whispered to Keller, handed

her an envelope, and left. She seemed annoyed at the interruption but paused to rip open the envelope and read the note
inside. McPherson wondered briefly at her surprised expression until she announced, "News flash from the dean. Class
meets here tonight." One of the nerds tittered. She crumpled
the note and pitched it into the trash can.

Keller droned on about limits and Greek letters. McPherson
filled the time by doodling on the arm of his chair, the broad
kind of arm intended for taking class notes. His pen sliced
through the decades of tacky varnish into the soft wood beneath.

The siren over his head let loose at about one thousand
decibels, and a male voice in the hall bellowed, "Fire! Get
out!" Pandemonium erupted as forty or so people ran for the
single door at the front of the room. Keller was gone before
McPherson was even out of his chair. The frigging chair arm
caught him as he stood, and he dragged it halfway down the
aisle before shaking it off.

Shrieking students wedged themselves tightly into the doorway as they tried to escape. He pulled bodies away from
the knot, but they shoved forward as fast as he separated
them. "Quiet!" A few of the students in the back heard
him and complied. "One at a time!" The panic lessened as
some of those who heard him stopped pressing lemminglike
against the people in front of them. Keller was nowhere to
be seen.

When half or so of the bozos had finally gotten out he was
able to bull his way into the hall. Which way? White smoke
billowed out from under the fire door on his left. The students
were streaming away from it to the stairway at the other end
of the corridor. McPherson went with his gut feeling and
touched the nearby fire door. It was *cold*. He yanked it open
and found a box of sublimating dry-ice chunks hidden in a
sea of carbon-dioxide fog.

"That bitch." He galloped down the stairs despite the
obscuring white fog. The emergency exit at the bottom was
blocked; the door budged a little the third time he threw

himself against it. Twice more, and it opened enough for him to squeeze through. A common wooden wedge was jammed between the door and the concrete step.

Not twenty feet away sat a University parking lot. A small blue sedan was skidding out of the exit, carrying a dark-haired male driver and a passenger with long blond hair. Keller. McPherson's car was two buildings away, by the regular classroom. He dashed across the lawn, trying to keep the escaping sedan in sight. Out of breath, he pulled the door open and started the car. It lumbered like a pregnant hippo, pulling badly to the right.

The agent got out and discovered three slashed tires; one front tire had been left inflated to hinder steering. He called Curtis over his car phone while the blue sedan streaked out of sight. Two fire trucks and a University cop car raced by him toward the false alarm as he pounded out his frustration on the horn.

McPherson followed one more hunch while waiting for Curtis. He returned to the calculus classroom, sullenly shrugging off firemen. The crumpled note in the wastebasket read: "Take the stairway to your left when you hear the fire alarm. Icarus." It had been scrawled by the same hand as the auditorium-door note.

Sally fell backward against her seat as Hanson floored the car. She sat in a daze as he negotiated a maze of streets, occasionally glancing at the map display on his dashboard.

"Put on your seat belt." Bob kept his eyes on the road.

She followed his order and tried to shake off her sudden lethargy. Withdrawal was a luxury they couldn't afford right now. She spotted a familiar dry cleaner. "Left at the light to get on the Beltway."

He went straight through the intersection. "We stay off the main roads. That's where they'll look for us." He spared her a quick look. "Believe it or not, things are under control."

Either she believed him, or events caught up with her.

When reality next intruded, they were speeding through dark countryside on a deserted two-lane road. The dashboard clock read 10:12.

"There's hot coffee in the thermos." She gratefully poured herself some. He took a long swallow when she offered the cup.

"Where are we?" *There's* an original question.

"About five miles south of Codorus, Pennsylvania." He tapped the dashboard display, and a map of northern Maryland and southern Pennsylvania appeared. He pointed to the blinking dot. "Here." Codorus wasn't near anything.

"Bob?"

"Yeah?"

"Thank you." He opened his mouth but she cut him off. "If you say something witty and self-deprecating, I'll punch your lights out. I have no idea how you did it, or why. You rescued me from the FBI. You were magnificent."

"You're welcome." Long silence. "What are you innocent of?"

"Treason." She started to explain, but uncontrollable tears made speech impossible. She felt a comforting hand squeeze hers. Bob pulled the car onto the shoulder without letting go of her hand. He slid over as soon as the car had stopped and silently held her. He had strong arms. She rested her head on his shoulder and let the tears flow.

The faucet finally ran dry, and the shudders subsided. Bob's shirt was soaked beneath her cheek, but she didn't move. "Thanks again," she sniffled into his chest.

Bob gently tilted her head until their eyes met, his face shimmering slightly through the tears still in her eyes. "How I did it is a long story, and parts of it are a little ugly. That can wait. *Why* did I do it?" His voice had become very soft. "Because I love you."

Her answering expression was all of the response he needed. Bob put his lips to hers and the world briefly shrank to the comforting span of his arms.

*   *   *

Not since election night had the group been so upset. So obsessed. The technologists argued among themselves to no apparent purpose. The psychologist did not waste energy competing with the verbal tempest. Occasional comments from the fray were interesting, and these he noted for future use. They were all variations on the theme that the conspirators had lost control. True enough.

His unique posture of silence finally made the impression upon the gibbering masses that he had calculated it would. One by one, the other experts stopped their ineffective chattering to wait expectantly for him to speak. When he had their undivided attention, he at last addressed them.

"Friends. We are faced with seemingly intractable problems. First, Hanson escapes from us. His whereabouts and intentions are unknown. The knowledge he holds is dangerous. I fear he could unmask us." There was another burst of unstructured prattle before they returned their attention to him.

"Next, the *Tribune* reporter Stuart uncovers and publishes the first layer of our deception. The public's reaction to the aliens is hysterical, and all forecasts now predict that a severe recession, or even a depression, is beginning. The R&D funding for which we began our project will be choked off by the economic collapse."

"They wouldn't dare!" He scanned the crowd and determined that the physicist had dared to interrupt him. "They *must* spend to counter the alien menace. They have no choice." The more single-minded among them registered their concurrence.

Wishful thinking. "Yes, certain avenues of research will continue for a time at federal expense. Soon, *only* alien-related research will be done. The industrial labs, the defense-supported university research, even most government applied R&D, will be cut off. Most of us will be worse off than before we began. And when, eventually, the aliens' absence from near-Earth space becomes obvious, even *that* spending will become insignificant.

"Let me continue. The datum which brings us here tonight is that Keller has escaped her confinement. We have previously inferred, with a high probability, that she also knows the aliens to be imaginary."

"Why not let part of the truth out?" asked the sociologist thoughtfully. "Our main problem is the leakage of the alien story, and its effect on the public. No aliens, no panic."

Sociology, bah. Description and statistics without insight. "Keller or Hanson could uncover us. An end to the panic is no solution if it also ends us."

The sociologist continued. "Understood. First we eliminate those two. Then, some heretofore uninvolved party discovers the hoax . . ." He hesitated, as if analyzing their options. (Or was it an intentional dramatic pause? The sociologist was an apt pupil.) "It's terrible how those Chinese can intercept, even interfere with, our communications and computers."

Not bad. The psychologist would have to pay more attention to this one. "Your ideas mesh with mine. I have been concentrating on the initial problem of neutralizing Hanson and Keller." He directed his final words to the group. "I think we are agreed that it's time to eliminate them.

"Now here's my plan."

"Wake up! Bob, wake up!" Gradually, his staring, sightless eyes relaxed and focused. He was sitting up in bed with his back pressed against the headboard. Bright sunlight filtered through the heavy curtains into a small and aging motel room. It had come fully equipped with dust bunnies and blacklight pictures of clowns with big, sad eyes. Sally studied him worriedly. "Are you all right?"

"Bad dream."

"So I noticed. Want to talk about it?" Sally modestly pulled the sheet up around herself and cocked her head into a listening position. Her long blond hair broke its shining flow on a bare shoulder, as she looked at him from impossibly blue eyes.

That's when their situation—the good part of their situation—reasserted itself. Last night. He and Sally still alone and naked in the bed. "No. I've got something more important on my mind right now."

He snapped the sheet out of her hands.

The J. Edgar Hoover Building never slept; last night, McPherson had fit right in. He ground out a cigarette butt in an ashtray already full of them. What he really wanted was to shove one up Keller's finely chiseled nose. Lit. He was graphically describing the concept when the phone rang.

"Hold that thought." His partner took the call. "Can't it wait? Oh, hell, I can spare a few minutes." Curtis hung up.

"No, you can't spare a few minutes," said McPherson. "We have work to do."

"We're stuck here anyway until the lab IDs those finger-prints from Keller's house and the University. I might as well see what our electronic friend wants. It left some questions for me on the console." Curtis strode off to answer the summons, leaving McPherson to handle their overdue paperwork.

Their electronic friend . . .

There was always too much information to sift through in a case, too many possibilities to consider. That's why the Bureau was working with industry to develop an expert-system program for case analysis. The brass claimed that it would process a thousand times—a million times—more chains of evidence than any human. The vendor had dubbed it the Agent's Associate. The agents (privately) called it the Agent's Ass. It wasn't operational yet.

The vendor's expert-system specialists, the knowledge engineers, had spent months pestering agents. What is evidence? How do you recognize it? How do you combine it with other evidence? McPherson's favorite question was: could you de-

fine a hunch? Other eggheads spent their time converting
decades of old case files into semantic nets—whatever that
meant—on the new computer system.

He viewed working with the weirdos as his cronies did—
an opportunity for scheduled overtime. Scheduled, as in authorized and paid. Curtis, the lucky bastard, got extra overtime. He was an approved evaluator of the Agent's Ass: what
the guys called an authorized Ass Kisser. Never mind what
they called a test session. McPherson sighed, and got to work.

"Saddle up." Just two painfully written reports later, Curtis had returned. "We'll take my car."

"Hah, hah." McPherson's was still beached in Maryland
on three flats. "Where're we going?" He tugged at Bonnie's
blouse sleeve as she sidled by, pantomiming smoking with
his other hand. She tossed him a pack from her purse. He
was desperate enough to take one of her gutless Virginia
Slims.

"Does the name Robert Hanson mean anything to you?"
Answering questions was not Curtis's strong point.

McPherson considered that for a while. "Should it?" As
the elevator descended, he wondered when they would quit
trading questions and one of them would state something.
The elevator opened into the underground garage.

"The Space Division is after him."

It was a statement, but one McPherson couldn't relate to.
He tried to wait Curtis out. They got into the big Olds, while
Curtis grinned like the Cheshire cat. "Don't make me work
for it, Fred. I'm not in the mood."

Curtis punched him playfully in his sore shoulder, the one
he'd used yesterday to batter open the jammed door. "Okay,
sport. Just for you." He only smirked when McPherson
slugged him back hard on his right arm. "Just a helpful hint
from the Ass."

"Wait a minute. You can't just waltz in and use that machine."

"You can when it initiates the dialogue. You remember

the system operator calling me about its questions on the console? While I was answering, I thought, hey, since I'm here . . .''

"You might as well ask about our case."

"Smart boy. You may not even need to repeat calculus."

Curtis quickly explained how the machine had hummed away at the Keller case, occasionally asking his permission to tap into another computer or data bank. It first correlated the Bob Hanson in Keller's office rolodex with an Illinois arrest warrant for Robert Hanson for embezzlement. NASA's business system coughed up dozens of Keller's vouchers for travel to Asgard Aerospace: Asgard was Hanson's ex-employer and unwilling benefactor. Her vouchers also showed business lunches with Hanson in attendance. Next, the Illinois Secretary of State's office system showed a blue Honda Accord sedan registered to Hanson. *That* rang a bell.

The expert system also latched onto the code name Icarus in yesterday's note. It pontificated that, with 97.8% probability, the name referred to Hanson. Why? The machine synthesized a short bio from the conventional files and Hanson's employment records. Chief scientist at Asgard Aerospace. Father of the *Prospector* probe: the files were full of newspaper citations on *that* subject. Especially the recent aliens articles by that panic-peddler Al Stuart.

It now seemed obvious that Hanson had sprung Keller. Why? Was she related to the *Prospector* thing? To the aliens? "All very interesting, Fred. Let me repeat my first question. Where are we going?"

"The Pentagon. My blinking and whirring friend said that the Space Division has need-to-know-only classified files on Hanson and *Prospector*. I thought we'd drop by while General Hadley is in town for a congressional grilling."

"Scapegoat for this alien thing?"

"Looks that way. McCaffrey of Senate Intelligence Oversight reamed him yesterday. Today, it's the Technology and Space boys in the House. Hadley's agreed to see us after this morning's mugging."

Asgard Aerospace? The irony amused McPherson. Hanson's old company was prime contractor for the Agent's Associate.

"Here, my little red, white, and blue babies. Come to Poppa. Daddy wants a new Porsche."

Don Abrams used both hands to rake in the mound of chips from the center of the card table. Before dealing the next hand, he painstakingly arranged them into neat stacks of ten, star side up, colors sorted alphabetically. "Wotta night. I'm taking you guys to the cleaners." He solicitously patted the deck of red Bicycle cards. "*Goood* cards. Keep it up."

Bernie Edelman sighed. Don was predictable in an inverse Churchillian kind of way: malevolent in victory, disgusting in defeat. Only their non-card-playing friendship—and Don's usual ability to lose big—kept him in the Friday-night poker game. Bernie and Roger Kaplan exchanged long-suffering glances while Don noisily clacked a stack of white chips through his fingers.

Don finally quit stroking the chips and dealt out two cards apiece, face down. "Seven-card stud. Jacks or better to open." They all anted up two blues.

Roger sat to Don's left. He tugged at his lucky one-size-fits-all Cubs cap, worn backward as always, while he discreetly lifted an edge of his cards. "Who dealt this malebovine manure?"

Bernie had already checked his face-down pair: two kings. Best start by far for the evening. "I take that to mean you're not opening." He fished a red out of his small heap of remaining chips and tossed it into the pot. Have to build the pot slowly, without scaring them off. The other three met his raise.

Ron Arkin, their host, flipped the edge of his cards a few times. He tapped Don without speaking, stood up holding Roger's overflowing ashtray and an empty pretzel bowl, and headed for the kitchen.

"Dealer raises a red." Bernie and Roger followed; Bernie

stretched across the table for one of Ron's when he nodded from the kitchen. Don dealt out a card each, face up. Bernie got a three.

The cards went around twice more. Bernie now had a king and two threes up. Which gave him a full house, kings high. Don was showing a possible straight, the others nothing much. The pot had grown to respectable proportions. "Three white chips, if you please, my childhood chums."

"Out."

"Me, too."

Damn that idiot. He's scared Roger and Ron out. Bernie discovered that he was out of white chips and threw in a bill. "Raise you a white."

"My, my, *my*. Pretty smug, aren't we, for someone who hasn't won a decent pot all night. Meet you and raise you— five bucks." Don smiled condescendingly as he shoved stacks of chips into the pot. *Someone has completed his straight*, thought Bernie. *Okay by me.*

He was digging through his wallet when a bottle cap bounced off his chest. "Earth to Bernie. Telephone." Ron stood in the kitchen holding the mouthpiece to his shoulder. Preoccupation or the booming bass speaker behind Bernie's chair had kept him from noticing it ring. Who the hell cared—this was no time for chatter. "Take a message." He set his fiver onto the pot. To Don he added, "Deal."

Ron shrugged eloquently. "He says it's urgent."

He. Ergo, not his wife, to whom he had grudgingly granted permission to call under conditions of a federally recognized natural disaster, or a child breaking a limb or vital organ. "Take his number."

"Okeydokey. Me, I'd like to hear what Jimmy Hoffa has been doing, lo these many years." He lifted the mouthpiece to speak.

"Wait!" Bernie shot to his feet. "I'll take it in the den. Client," he answered Roger's cocked eyebrow. "Ron, finish the hand for me."

He shut himself into the paneled den and grabbed the desk

phone. "Got it, Ron." He said no more until he heard the kitchen extension hung up. "Bob, you computer-assisted ass-hole!"

As expected, it was Bob Hanson's voice. "Watch your language, please, there's a lady in this phone booth. I need a small favor."

"Jesus H. Christ, you need a lobotomy. I've been dis-creetly monitoring events. Breaking and entering. Aiding and abetting a fugitive. Assaulting an FBI agent! Are you planning on an insanity plea?"

"Hey, I'm just a fun guy. I didn't know at the time that he was FBI. And I didn't call about legal assistance."

What was this lunatic up to? Bernie discovered that his left hand was in his pants pocket, rubbing his talisman Kennedy half-dollar. Over the years, Jack had lost all of his hair and most of his features. "How did you find me?"

The distant voice sounded amused. "Haven't you dragged me to poker as a sub a dozen times over the years? Don't I know the fearsome foursome? Of course I know, to within three houses and an apartment, where you'll be on a Friday night. I'm just glad tonight's game wasn't at your place."

"Why?"

"Your phone's probably bugged."

The lawyer chewed on that for a while. "They want you that badly?"

"Yeah. Me and my cuddly friend." Bernie heard a squeal and an "oof" over the phone. "Bernie, I mean it. I need your help."

"How?" He ignored Don's laughter from the other room. Ron must have folded on a full house, the moron. Right now, though, it didn't seem important.

"There's a *Tribune* reporter named Stuart, Al Stuart. He's been breaking open the aliens' coverup. Know who I mean?"

"Know of him."

"You have to see him in private and arrange for him to contact me. It's imperative that we talk."

"Malarkey. It's imperative that you give yourself up."

"Bernie . . ."

A long stillness ensued, broken finally by a dubious-sounding synthesized voice. "Ple-ase deposit one dollar and twenty cents for the next two minutes." Beeps and gongs followed.

"Bernie, as much as I enjoy your silent disapproval, we don't have the small change for much more of it. You've never let me down. What do you say?"

Oh, piss on it. "That you're a cretin. How can Stuart reach you?"

"Thanks, pal. He's to call me at 717-555-6754, between four and four-thirty P.M., within the next three days. Have him ask for Jimmy. Tell him to keep trying—it's a pay phone."

Bernie jotted the number onto a margin of his pocket calendar. "Got it."

"Good. Hold on for a sec."

"Thanks for your help, Mr. Edelman. Bernie." She had a low, sexy voice. "I hope we'll meet sometime under less taxing circumstances. Bob assures me that I'll like you."

If your voice is representative, thought Bernie, *I'm sure it'll be mutual.* "I'd like that. Listen—take good care of Bob. Try keeping him out of trouble." There was a throaty chuckle at that, and then dial tone.

Once past the permanent congestion between Hammond and Gary, the peppy little 66i zipped along the Indiana Toll Road. Fluffy clouds scudded across the blue sky, pushed eastward ahead of him by a strong upper-atmosphere wind.

Al Stuart was glad to have an excuse for the long drive. The car was new, and he hadn't yet taken the time to see how it performed on the open road. Stop-and-creep was about the best he could do with it on Lake Shore Drive. It probably hadn't been above 50, in fact, since he'd picked it up from its damned recall.

Al rolled down his window to feel the wind, then cranked up the radio to compensate. The AM golden-moldies station had a humongous transmitter; he looked forward to singing along from here to Ohio.

Everything was just fine, thank you. He was on his way to a surprising rendezvous, the main surprise being that Hanson was still alive. Once this story was published—and Hanson's few hints were tantalizingly promising—Hanson would be safe from the Defense boys. It would be too blatant and conspicuous to waste him then. All this *and* corroboration from *Prospector*'s NASA coordinator.

No sirree, a plane just wouldn't have been the same. And planes required moderately expensive tickets. Tickets the Carp wouldn't cover unless they were purchased through the company travel desk. Hell of a way to run an undercover operation.

When Al happened for no particular reason to glance at his tachometer, the simulated needle on the dashboard screen was flirting with the orange-marked danger zone. He turned off the radio and immediately heard a high-pitched whine. He disgustedly slapped his forehead with the palm of his hand. He'd forgotten all about overdrive—a useless gear in the city; he'd pushed the car up to 75 in fourth. The whine wound smoothly down to a catlike purr once he popped the 66i into fifth.

And immediately wound back up, and to a higher pitch than before. The engine surged, and Al watched wide-eyed as the digital speedometer pushed ahead to 84, 91, 103. He removed his foot from the gas pedal. 105, 108, 112. Desperately, he tapped the brakes. Nothing happened.

The roadside blurred by without distinguishable features, wind whistling through his open window. The rear of a tractor trailer grew with frightening speed as he stared. Shit. Gingerly, he turned the wheel to change lanes. Nothing happened. Al honked furiously at the looming trailer and quivered with relief as it changed lanes faster than he would have thought possible. Must be empty. It fishtailed slightly, then recovered.

His relief was short-lived. Not far beyond the spot vacated by the tractor trailer was another, this one hauling massive sections of precast concrete pipe. *It* wasn't going to change lanes quickly. A siren wailed behind him, but seemed unable to catch him. No wonder: he was descending a gentle grade and picking up even more speed. The gauge read 117, and the concrete hauler began looming large. Could he use the emergency brake at this speed? Turn off the engine? He had to do *something*. Aha. Downshift. The damned overdrive must have done this somehow.

The car shuddered as he threw it from fifth into fourth gear. Shrieking, the transmission slowed the car somewhat. To 92. The engine surged again, and Al watched the speedometer again start to creep up. The truck in front of him was crawling to another lane as he pounded his fist on the horn. He tried third gear, then second. There was a sickening *thunk*, and he both felt and heard something fall out from under the car. The right rear tire drove over it and was instantly torn apart.

The steering wheel was wrenched from his hands as the car responded to the flat. Did that mean he had his steering back? One hand was mashed by a crossbar as he grabbed the spinning wheel; the other caught onto the rim. He pulled to the left, trying to avoid the drainage ditch toward which he was aimed. Mercifully, he felt some control.

Could he squeeze by the truck on the shoulder? Maybe. Maybe he would walk away from this. The flat and the lower gear were slowing the car down: only 64. Slow enough to risk turning off the engine? He was reaching for the key when the right-hand brakes slammed on hard. Once again the wheel was torn from his hands. The sports car threw itself into a dizzying spin even while it pulled to the right. Just missing the lumbering trailer full of concrete pipe, it flung itself into the bone-dry drainage ditch. It landed nose down.

Al hung suspended by his lap-and-shoulder harness, vaguely aware that he should get out. As the siren at last began to approach, an unidentified noise amid the creaking of hot and tortured metal caught his attention. It was a dripping sound.

The pool of gas beneath the car exploded with a *whoosh*.

His chicken-fried steak was an unanticipated delight. Bob Hanson couldn't decide if the cause was his very charming companion, or whether this was the one truck stop responsible for its kind's richly undeserved reputation. He chewed happily, grinning like an idiot at Sally.

She took his sappy expression as permission to taste one of his french fries. "Better than yellow jaundice."

"Ingrate."

"Will it work?" The antecedent for *it* was understood. Their only topic of conversation these last few days had been their impending meeting with Stuart. Though they had passed a lot of time in nonverbal communication.

Hanson slapped her hand gently as it reached for another fry. "Yeah, I think so. It's apparently credible that *one* of us would be guilty of his—or her—supposed crime. Surely it can't stick that we both are." He relented and held out another fry for her. "All we have to do is lay low while Stuart and the Trib stir the pot for a few days. This elaborate structure of conspiracy has to start falling apart of its own weight. Just wait and see."

"I hope you're right." Sally stirred her Diet Coke with a straw. "You'll understand if I have little faith in my recent run of luck—present company excepted, of course."

They must have been speaking too loudly. At least in his case, love wasn't conducive to a sense of discretion or caution. The burly trucker in the next booth leaned across the narrow aisle. "Y'all are interested in Al Stuart." It wasn't a question.

Hanson and Keller exchanged looks; she nodded imperceptibly. "Uh-huh. Why?"

The driver pointed toward the anachronistic black-and-white TV sitting on a wall-mounted turntable above and behind the cash register. "I guess you weren't listening to the news." Hanson agreed with a vague hand gesture. "Stuart won't be helping anyone. He wiped out today in a car crash." The man shook his head. "Nope, not anyone."

Sally took a sip of her soda. "How badly is he hurt?"

The driver looked grim. "I'm sorry, ma'am. He's dead." Belatedly, he doffed his battered leather cap. "A one-car accident, too. Very strange. The cop who witnessed it said Stuart just floored it and lost control."

He leaned back into his own booth. Hanson didn't think that he meant them to hear what he said next, under his breath. Unfortunately, they did. "Crispy critter. Bad way to go."

· CHAPTER 14 ·

Sally looked hesitantly at her remaining food, then shoved the plate away. Her stomach stirred ominously. "C'mon." Bob dropped his fork in agreement. He bought an evening paper from the vending machine as they left.

They rode in silence for a while, until she noticed that they were driving away from their motel. She didn't care for his answer. "Nothing there but fond memories and dirty laundry." Hanson took a deep breath and tried to explain. "I think that we'd better be *very* scared."

"You *can't* think that Stuart's death is related to us? It's got to be a coincidence." She sounded to herself like someone whistling her way through the graveyard.

"Haven't there been too many coincidences already? Bad things happen to those who look too closely at *Prospector*."

"But if they—whoever *they* are—knew about our meeting, why didn't they follow Stuart and get us, too."

"Follow that logic."

Sally pulled thoughtfully at an earlobe. "They must not have known where he was going. Therefore . . . they killed him simply for knowing too much." A pregnant pause. "We also know too much."

"Still want to go back for your things?"

"Don't be so damned supercilious. If they didn't know about the meeting, they won't find us. And I don't admit that Stuart's death was anything but a grisly accident!"

Instead of answering, Hanson loaded a jazz tape into the cassette player and turned it up loud. After a while she ejected it. She cooled down as quickly as she flared up. "If they didn't know about the meeting, then you're not responsible for Stuart's death. He started investigating the aliens on his own."

"What about you? Did you get involved on your own?" His hands trembled on the steering wheel.

That was it: guilt. "I'm still healthy—and happy. I don't know who's after me, but I do know who's looking out for me." She tousled his hair. "Those poor bastards don't have a chance." When he hazarded a slight smile, she added, "Now please tell me why we can't get our things."

"Maybe he left notes in his home showing where he was going. I won't gamble your life on what someone might find."

"Oh." She squinted as they drove into the setting sun, which was too low for her sun visor to help. Time to lighten the subject. "Mind if I find something on the radio?" She took a grunt as assent, and tapped the scan button on the radio. A classical station came up just as she was despairing of finding anything better than his jazz tapes. She poked scan again to lock in the station.

The station was playing what could only be a Beethoven symphony. Sally placed it after a few bars: the second movement of the *Eroica*, his Third Symphony. She let the majestic music roll over her. Better enjoy it while it lasted: this wasn't her impression of normal boonies broadcasting. Early in the fourth movement she peeked experimentally and caught Bob yawning. Time to pull her share of the load. "I'll drive for a while."

"I'm fine." Pro forma macho protest.

"I'm better. Pull over." He did, and they changed places. "Show me where you want to go, and then take a nap." She punched up the map display for him. He was breathing heavily before the symphony ended.

The announcer's voice resolved one mystery: she recognized the mellifluous tones of a Classical Radio Network broadcaster. That's why she'd found a decent station—it was a rebroadcaster. Soon he stopped talking and she listened appreciatively to some vintage Elgar, the *Enigma Variations*. Bob snored intermittently.

Twilight deepened and she turned on the headlights. The setting sun had darkened to a rich crimson, no longer painful to the eyes; more often than not it now hid behind the rolling hills and the stands of old trees. If only life could remain this peaceful.

The Elgar gave way to the *Rhapsody in Blue* as day gave way to night. Miraculously, she located another CRN station when the signal began fading in and out intolerably. The Gershwin was followed in turn by an unfamiliar but interesting chamber piece. This was the only way to drive the unending length of Pennsylvania. She maneuvered over the winding roads per Bob's directions.

Hanson yawned as he returned to consciousness. "Have a good rest?" She blindly reached out to the side and found a leg to pat. "Want me to change stations?"

" 'S all right. Carlton conditioned me to this stuff. And he didn't give me nearly the incentive that you do."

"You just love me for my wanton ways."

"It's a burden to be so transparent."

They continued for a while in comfortable silence. Comfort that she knew was inappropriate. "Bob? Where does it end? How can it end?"

"Honey, I wish I knew. Sorry I got you into this."

"I'm not, not really, although I would've preferred a more traditional courtship."

Bob dug through the chaos of his glove compartment and found a chocolate bar amid the refuse. "Want any?" He ate some while she considered. "I won't—I can't—involve anyone else," he said. "Somehow, I'll solve this on my own. I keep thinking that I've got all the pieces to the puzzle, if I only could put them together."

She decided. "Chocolate." He put a piece into her open hand. The second CRN station was also beginning to fade. She started scanning for a third.

Bob ceased his smacking. "What were we listening to? I can't place it, but it sounds familiar. Shouldn't it be faster, though?"

She knew it, but couldn't place it either. "Whatever it is, it's at the right tempo." The scanning radio hopped again, and picked up a rock station. *Please don't ask for that, Bob*, she thought.

He surprised her. "Find that classical station again. It'll bother me all night if I don't hear what that piece is." Sally let the radio scan until it ran out of FM spectrum and started over. Eventually it found the station. The slow, haunting music faded in and out, determined to continue beyond any possibility of their staying within radio range. They were climbing a medium-sized hill. "Stop at the top. I don't want to miss the announcement."

"You're kidding."

"No I'm not, Sal. I can't explain it, but for some reason I'm sure it's important."

They parked at the crest, Bob hanging intently on every note. He'd made his request a hill too late: the station continued to fade in and out. What he wanted seemed rather bizarre, but Sally knew that Bob's intuition was better than most people's deepest insights. "Should I go back?"

"Shhh!" he hissed. He was right, the music was concluding. The cultured-sounding announcer tried to return. ". . . Was the . . . ne for a . . . ess, by . . . The perf . . .

nce was by the Concertgebow Orchestra, under the baton of
. . .'' The interference was horrible. "Shit! What *was* that?
Why do I know that?" Bob slumped in his bucket seat. "I
don't suppose we could identify the station and ask what that
was?"

"Probably, but there's no need. That was enough to trigger
my memory. *Pavane for a Dead Princess*, by Maurice Ravel.
Now can we go?"

Only Bob's seat belt saved him from a hard rap on the
noggin as he shot upright. "Ravel? You said *Ravel?*" In the
green glow of the panel lights, his toothy grin looked de-
monic.

What the hell? "I don't especially like Ravel. Does that
help?"

He ignored her. "Ravel." He whistled a fast caricature of
a theme from the pavane; he couldn't carry a tune in a bushel
basket. He must have noticed her gaping. "No, I haven't
cracked up. Quite the opposite, I think. Just give me a sec."

He took a lot longer than that, but he finally spoke. "Forward, James. Onward and upward. I have a story to tell."
He turned off the radio.

Sally started the car. Only a quarter of a tank left. Have
to find gas soon. "So tell."

He began with a riddle. "When is a password not a password?"

What was he getting at? "I have no idea."

"When the person giving the password is known."

"Huh?"

"Indeed." He chuckled. "Okay, I'll get to the point. You
know Carlton. He'd have been a professional musician had
there been any money in it. I'm sure you've heard his musical
accompaniments to programs."

"Jimmy."

"Among others," he agreed. "Do you know how he picks
system passwords? Composer's names." He waited expectantly.

"So Ravel was once a password. So what?"

"Bear with me. Did you ever notice that Carlton whistles when he logs on?" He didn't wait for her answer. "Hard not to, unless you're distracted by the fact that he's usually whistling.

"Well, he *does* whistle when he logs on. To the everlasting amusement of those in the know, he whistles something by the composer whose name is the current password.

"Ravel was the system-administrator password when I, ahem, left Asgard. Only it didn't work when I tried it."

She still didn't get it "So he'd changed it."

"No! He hadn't. That's what I just realized. Look, Sal. When I was fired, I went to my office to gather my stuff. I tried to log on to print my email. It didn't work."

"Surely that didn't surprise you."

"It seemed petty as hell, but it was no surprise that my password had been changed. So I tried again as the system administrator."

"And it didn't work."

"And it didn't work. At the time, I figured that Security had made Carlton change it."

"At the time? And now?"

"I didn't discuss passwords with Carlton, of course. It would've been too awkward. Instead, I said that I was running out of time. Would he please log on as admin to dump my mail for me? Guess what he whistled as he logged in?"

"The pavane." But that was screwy. "How could the system reject Ravel when you typed it?"

"In other words, when is a password not a password?"

She remembered his previous nonsensical answer. "When the person giving the password is known. The workstation in your office, immediately after you tried to log in as yourself. The security software itself . . ." She trailed off, the significance of events beginning to penetrate.

"Right! The system itself was monitoring specifically for me, only moments after my termination. An unauthorized change to the system that must've been made before I stormed into Nichols's office."

The winding road was approaching a small village. "We need to get gas. And I need a ladies' room."

"If they have a motel, let's stop. I need to think things through."

There was, in fact, a motel in the town. The decaying kind, with a short row of musty units set just off the road. The kind of motel—the kind of town—that was forgotten when the interstate passed it by. The kind of motel where *Psycho* was filmed. Bob insisted on staying there.

He was manic: his Ravel realization had broken a mental logjam. "Don't you see?" he'd ask incredulously. She didn't. Or, "Isn't it obvious?" It never was. But every subtle inference that he drew made perfect sense. She began to visualize the two of them as insects scuttling about in an enormous web. A web of electronics that for all its speculativeness became very real as the night wore on.

"It's all computers! *That's* the common thread. All computers. The phony *Prospector* data. The games with my electronic mail. My embezzlement. Your security violation. The Ravel trick." He bounced on the bed, raising a great cloud of dust.

"Slow down."

He ignored her. "The teller. The one who opened my account. He was only a name picked from the obituaries. They needed someone's name to authorize a new account, so they found a teller who had just died. He certainly wouldn't contradict their story. *That's* why they used a bank a dozen suburbs away." He bounced again, raising more dust. "That's where the first teller died. Now what in hell does it all mean?"

Sally retreated to the claustrophobic bathroom for a tissue. The dust was making her sneeze. "I don't want to rain on your paranoia, but what about Al Stuart? He had a car accident. Or will you admit that his death was accidental."

"That was the hardest to understand. The trucker's story made no sense to me. Neither did this." He rustled the paper from the truck stop. "Why would Stuart practically beg for

a speeding ticket when he told me he'd drive to be incon-
spicuous?''

"Not everyone is as controlled as you," she called from
the bathroom. "The open road beckoned and he got carried
away."

"Baloney. Maybe an extra ten or twenty miles an hour.
Not this. The paper says two truckers and the highway patrol
saw everything. Engine running flat out. Went straight as an
arrow at first one truck, then another, until he blew a tire.
No indication that he used his brakes. Not one skid mark."

"Drunk, probably." She rejoined him in the bedroom.

"Even drunks use brakes. I'll bet his car's computer ran
amuck. He was in a TFX-66i. It's a drive-by-wire car."

As if that explained anything. "What's that?"

"Only electronic linkages between the controls and the
vehicle, nothing mechanical. One little fiber-optic cable runs
all around the car; it's a lot lighter than dedicated mechanical
connections. Planes have been built like that for years."

"So?"

"So everything is computer controlled. A computer senses
what the driver does with the pedals, the wheel, his other
controls. It encodes the information and puts it onto the cable.
Smart actuators pick only the information addressed to them
off the cable and tell the motor, the brakes, whatever, what
to do." He shuddered. "Just think what happens if they're
told the wrong thing.

"I wonder when he had his car serviced last?"

Sally stared at him. "You really believe that?" He nodded.
"What computer is safe from them?"

"Quite probably, none."

"Then why are you smiling?"

"Now that I've found the playing field, it's time for our
side to score a few goals."

Part III

Great deeds are usually wrought at great risks.

—Herodotus
(ca. 485–ca. 425 B.C.)

· CHAPTER 15 ·

Sally pulled up to the appointed corner punctually at two. Hanson motioned her along even as he was letting himself in the passenger door. She blended smoothly into the flow of traffic on Forbes Avenue before speaking. "Success?"

"Yeah." He nudged one of the mysterious shopping bags at his feet. It crinkled. "You too, apparently."

"Don't kick that and don't change the subject. If you have a fault, Robert, it's how you underwhelm me with details." She called up a map display of Pittsburgh and drove one-handed for a while as she traced a path to the Fort Pitt Bridge.

Hanson patted the paperback book in his coat pocket. "Helpful reference, this. I picked it up at the Carnegie-Mellon admissions office. Told 'em my niece was interested in applying. Life sciences program probably, but that's not definite. Maybe a switch later to premed. It would be a first for the family, you know—"

"I withdraw the comment. How did you . . ."

"Break into the computer? A moment ago you wanted

details." He rolled his eyes. "To make it short, I went from admissions to the undergrad library. Seven of the physics faculty named in the course catalog are also in *Who's Who in Frontier Science and Technology*. The *Who's Who* listings give all kinds of handy information: birth date, colleges attended, mother's maiden name, children's names, wife's name and maiden name, wedding date. Two of the physicists had equally illustrious spouses, and I got their statistics, too."

"In other words, lots of potential passwords."

"Give the woman a bubble-gum cigar." Sally snorted. "I never met a physicist who didn't sometime use his password to help remember an upcoming birthday or anniversary."

The traffic over the Ohio was stop-and-go. "I'll bite. Why are you picking on physicists?"

"They can't be bothered by anything larger than a proton but smaller than a solar system. Like computer security. Besides, a physicist's computer usage is so extensive he'd never spot my bit of activity. May I continue without interruption, please?" She nodded.

"The CMU library is wall-to-wall workstations. I just sat in an empty corner and tested my list of prospects."

"Using what for user names?"

"The obvious."

"Twit."

He relented. "First names, if they were unusual. Also, first name and last initial, all initials, and obvious nicknames. Gimme a break, Sal. User names must be mnemonic. How else could you send email to anyone?" The map display told him *where* they were—the far west side of Pittsburgh—but not *why*. He retrieved a map covering all of western Pennsylvania; no destination suggested itself. "We going home to meet your parents?"

"They have standards, even if I don't. Finish, will you?"

"It took me four physicists' names to break in. The winner was Hollingsworth, Ian Jamison, Ph.D. from Oxford. User name jamie; password 220862. His wife's birthday is August twenty-second.''

"Jamie and 220862." Sally committed the combination to memory. "Of course students are forever trying to break into other people's accounts. Your few attempts should be invisible to our observant friends."

He curled his right fingers and modestly buffed the nails on his left shoulder. "And that was the hard part." He checked the map again, without success. "Where are we going?"

"My turn to pick a hideout. Keep talking."

"Not much more to tell. After logging on the system, I arranged for the time-delayed delivery of our message. At ten tonight, by which time we'll be far away, it goes out over INFONET to Larry Cantin at Asgard. He'll never get it, of course—whoever's monitoring the computers will intercept it."

They'd left Pittsburgh proper and were driving west on State 60, paralleling the Penn-Lincoln Parkway. Sally flashed him a warm smile. "I love a man with his wits about him. You done good, fella."

They sat silently for a while, deep in their own thoughts. No telling what hers were; he couldn't get his mind off their pending message. It was a shot fired across their adversaries' bow:

To: The Prospector conspirators
From: Robert Hanson and Sally Keller

Your plot cannot succeed. We are fully aware of your deception. There are no aliens in the asteroid belt, only gremlins in our computers.

We have documented your criminal acts: the infiltration of computer networks, the falsification of Prospector telemetry, our unjust incrimination, the murder of a journalist. Documented evidence is safely hidden around the country.

We demand an explanation of your activities. We will release the documents unless we receive your answer within twenty-four hours. Return your DES-encrypted response over INFONET, addressed to general delivery. Use the name of your press victim as the encryption key.

Our information will be released immediately to the FBI and media if either of us is harmed, apprehended, or loses touch with the document holders.

Their evidence was all circumstantial, of course, but at least it constituted a good bluff. At the last minute, he'd remembered to add a P.S. disimplicating Hollingsworth.

The hiding of documents in post-office boxes had been Sally's morning mission. Each set was labeled with directions for turnover to the police. They had already left several sealed copies with lawyers along their back-roads route—with directions on whether and when to forward them. Had the material been distributed widely enough? Well, their foes could hardly know how many copies existed. They would have to respond.

Wouldn't they?

"A Sheraton?" Why had Sally stopped here? Wherever here was. He checked the map: Weirton, West Virginia. "What are we doing here?"

"Checking in, Mr. James. My treat." She slid a hand between the seat and her door and popped the trunk latch. "Fetch the junk from back there. I'll get these." She pointed to the bags by his feet.

"I don't even get to pick an alias?"

She favored him with a strange look, a mock glare badly superimposed upon an impish grin. "I made our reservations, dear." He resigned himself to discovering her intentions only when she was good and ready. His Accord seemed forlorn in the nearly empty parking lot.

The front desk did, indeed, have reservations for Stephen

and Joyce James. Riding up the glittering elevator with the itchy-palmed bellhop, he wondered again at her purpose. They couldn't afford this; well he couldn't, anyway. His money and Carlton's loan were gone; what little cash he had left had come from the FBI agent's wallet. Sally hadn't previously admitted to a purseful of money. Oh, well, he would sleep better here than in the cash-conserving fleabags they'd been patronizing.

Hanson tipped and escorted out the annoying bellhop, then groaned at the room price posted on the back of the door. He returned to find Sally spread-eagled across the king-size bed. "Can we afford this?"

She lifted her head slightly to stare at him. "I pawned a bracelet this morning. Mention money again and you'll sleep in the tub. Or the car." She dropped her head and listened for his nonresponse. "Much better. Now be a good fellow, Stephen, and retrieve a bucket of ice and a Coke."

He returned to discover that the room key was where the bellhop had left it—inside, on the dresser. "Knock, knock."

"Who's there?"

"Jesse James. Let me in, please." After she'd taken her own sweet time, he heard her pad barefoot down the hall. She pulled the door inward by about a millimeter—just enough to unlatch it. Which left him outside, with an ice bucket in one hand and a cold can in the other. What have I done now? He paused before shouldering the door open and rejoining the crazy lady.

He had to revise his thinking radically when he entered. And pick his jaw off the floor. Sally stood across the room, bathed in the late-afternoon sunlight that poured golden through the floor-to-ceiling sheers. She wore something short and black. Very short, with a neckline that plunged almost the length of the skimpy garment. Two strategically placed ribbons somehow held it together. Her lightly tanned skin glistened against and through the taut black lace. She tossed back her flowing blond hair, then hoisted a bottle of champagne. "This needs to be chilled."

The unattended door slammed behind him. He set down the ice bucket and the unnecessary Coke, ignored the bottle in Sally's hand, and wrapped his arms around her. After a deep, lingering kiss she broke from his hungry embrace. "The champagne will take time to chill. If you'd get that started, it'll tend to itself while we're otherwise occupied."

He reluctantly let her go to immerse the bottle in the ice bucket, then leaped for her and sent them both flying onto the bed. They bumped heads trying to kiss on the still-bouncing mattress. "You're nuts, you know that?"

Sally shoved him onto his back. She swarmed on top of him and pressed her every soft, gorgeous inch against him. When she surfaced for air, she looked down at him with twinkling eyes. "We have twenty-four hours after the message is sent before we can expect a reply. Twenty-four hours to wait. It could be a very long time.

"So I appointed myself chairwoman of the entertainment committee."

"This situation is catastrophic! Hanson and Keller together. The *Prospector* plot exposed. Everything documented." The astrophysicist was in a state of totally unprofessional panic. "We must do something."

Do something. How very helpful. The hysterical fool's attitude was prevalent tonight. The psychologist marveled, not for the first time, at how fragile these experts were outside their own domains of expertise. Mere idiot savants, rather. Their minds churned and thrashed without effect, like fans vying to cool a vacuum. The simile pleased him—it was based on properties of physics. At least he was learning something from his association with them.

"Colleagues." No response. "Colleagues." Still no reaction. They apparently needed more time to wind down, to follow their irrelevant thoughts to their fruitless ends.

As he waited, the historian signaled to him. "Whom the Gods would destroy they first make mad." Another big help.

Eventually, the cacophony subsided. The psychologist

tried again. "The news, while serious, is not necessarily fatal. Our opponents have yet to recognize our essential nature."

He correctly predicted a challenge from the always belligerent chemist. "You don't know that!"

"I certainly do." The psychologist's absolute conviction made a profound impression on everyone; even those who had until now continued their introspection ceased their pointless mutterings. "Review the message from Hanson and Keller. They give us twenty-four hours to act. Twenty-four hours! Would they do so if they understood us?" The impressionable masses murmured their assent.

"But they can still expose us." The chemist again. "With their documents hidden, waiting to be revealed, we dare not act against them."

"Indeed we dare not. That is why I hope instead to enlist them in our cause. You see how important it is that they not learn who we really are."

"Don't touch me."

Sally disobeyed Hanson, though only slightly, by delicately stroking his arm. "Poor baby. Ravished to within an inch of your life." He snagged a strand of her dangling hair and tugged it gently; she took the hint and snuggled into the crook of his arm. "Five down and one to go."

He clamped a hand over her mouth. "I want to just talk, okay? To talk seriously. Nod if you'll cooperate." He felt her head tip up and down and risked letting go. To his surprise, she didn't say anything.

He lay there quietly, Sally nestled against him, feeling content. Aching, spent, and unbelievably content. "I love you."

"I love you, too, to coin a phrase. Happy?"

"Yes, in a broken sort of way. Do you often have such good ideas?"

"No, that was it. We'll just have to repeat." She kissed him lightly on the forehead. "You wanted to talk."

"About us. If this works out . . ." He swiveled his head to read his watch on the nightstand; it was almost eleven. "If we ever live normal lives again . . ."

"When," she corrected him softly.

". . . I need you in my life."

"Aren't I now?"

He wriggled his arm out from under her and struggled into a sitting position. "That's why I know I want more. When we get out of this"—she grinned at his change in wording—"will you marry me?"

"I knew it."

"Knew what? And what about my question?"

"Getting you serious—and I don't mean getting you to propose—requires that you be exhausted. I learned that when you first dragged your broken carcass into my home. It's not that I mind tiring you out"—she flashed a leer—"but, as terrific as this has been, it's no basis for marriage.

"In all those months together in Chicago last winter," she continued, "why couldn't I get you past one-liners?"

It was a question that Hanson had asked himself over and over, especially once they'd drifted apart last spring. "People who can amuse others are popular." She looked at him without understanding. "Boy geniuses who excel at math and drop footballs usually aren't. There's still an insecure little boy in me."

"I teach math. As far as I know, my TV doesn't receive sports. Didn't that help my side?"

"It matters plenty, way down deep. But after years of playing court jester, I guess only exhaustion lets things really reach me. Sorry, kid, you've taken up with an emotional cripple." Hanson looked away. "I suppose I should retract my question."

"Don't you dare. You've admitted to being human. Why do you think that's so terrible?" She stroked the back of his hand. "Behind your wall you're gentle and caring. And you risked everything to save me.

"Ask me again when this is all over, when we know each other better. Ask me when you *want* your guard down."

"Can I take that as a definite maybe?" Please say yes.

Instead of answering, she bent over the side of the bed. Out of sight, her bag of props rustled. "I refuse to incriminate myself until you demonstrate that you can keep up with me."

Hanson stood shakily, surveying the scene of their debauch. Clothes were strewn everywhere, and the bed was hopelessly disheveled. A sleeping and finally satiated Sally lay half-covered by a mortally twisted sheet. The shade of the bedside lamp was askew; he had no idea when that had happened. A room-service tray sat precariously on the luggage rack.

He showered quickly, mercifully alone this time. With hot water cascading over his head, he tried to concentrate on the cold reality beyond their room. The conspirators' twenty-four hours were almost up. He had to go back to CMU for their response—presuming that they deigned to send one. He wasn't as confident about the evidence as his and Sally's challenge implied. If the plotters called their bluff, could they convince anyone?

The shower must have woken Sally. She watched him get dressed, satisfaction etched on her face. "If I haven't moved by the time you get back, order flowers." She didn't even stir when the phone rang.

He jauntily chopped down at the phone cord, catching the handset as it flipped into the air. "Ah Fong's Morgue and Chinese Takeout. How may we serve you?"

The precise, subtly accented voice across the line was not diverted. "Dr. Hanson, I presume."

· CHAPTER 16 ·

Hanson palmed the phone's mouthpiece. "Get your ass in gear! I don't know how, but they've found us." He uncovered the microphone and tried to sound casual to the unknown woman. "I'm sorry. You must have the wrong room."

"I have the room of Joyce and Stephen James, whose registration yesterday at this hotel is consistent with an early afternoon departure from Pittsburgh. Early yesterday afternoon, Dr. Robert Hanson and Mrs. Sally Keller initiated a very provocative electronic-mail message to us from Carnegie-Mellon University in Pittsburgh.

"I have the room of Joyce and Stephen James, whose blue Honda Accord is clearly visible on the television monitors of the hotel's security system. Dr. Hanson has a blue Honda Accord registered in Illinois. The code shown on the Jameses' license plates has not been issued by the state of Illinois. This code is, however, optically similar to Dr. Hanson's registered license-plate code. FBI files indicate that a blue sedan, very possibly a Honda Accord, was seen fleeing the scene of Mrs. Keller's escape." Sally had untangled herself and was feverishly dressing as the woman continued mercilessly.

"What of Joyce James? I should rather say Joyce comma James. James Joyce was the author of *Portrait of the Artist As a Young Man*. The young artist of the title is Stephen Daedalus. FBI files indicate that the pseudonym Icarus appeared on a note left at the scene of Mrs. Keller's escape; Daedalus was the father of Icarus." The woman stopped her damning recitation of evidence with an air of finality.

"I don't understand." Unfortunately, Hanson understood all too well.

"Do not insult our intelligence, Dr. Hanson." The stern female voice indicated how very unacceptable such behavior would be. Not to mention how futile any further denial would be. "Do not be alarmed. We could have notified the authorities had we meant you harm."

They had once meant Sally and him enough harm to frame them for felonies. *They* had once meant Al Stuart enough harm to murder him. Conclusion: the bluff was working. "*We* could have? Who are *we*?"

The line fell silent, as if a hurried conference was being held at the other end. Hadn't they expected the question? "If you require a label, 'the Pythagoreans' is as good as any."

"The Pythagoreans. And what should I call you?"

"Renée." She sounded amused at his question.

Hanson tightly twisted a sideburn while feverishly wondering what the hell to do next. They'd meant to contact the conspirators, but not this directly. "I suppose that I needn't check my mail."

"Please stop your pointless interruptions." Renée was all business. "I am calling with the explanation you demanded, and to state that you must not release your documents." Why couldn't he place her accent? Was it an accent? There was *something* distinctive, something familiar about her voice quality.

"You and Mrs. Keller are both capable scientists. We have reviewed your publications. We are confident that you will understand our motivation.

"The last federal elections were disastrous for the scientific establishment. The populist Democrats had promised to severely reduce research funding. The budgets were to be cut for the civilian space program, for new weapons-systems development, for exploratory research. Punitive taxes on business would have simultaneously cut private research. The Defense Advanced Research Projects Administration was to be prohibited from subsidizing university studies. The Department of Energy was to withdraw support for the Prototype Commercial Fusion . . .''

Renée's drift was obvious—the Pythagoreans were monomaniacal political fanatics. "So you synthesized an alien crisis. To do it, you hijacked *Prospector*."

"It worked."

Her imperturbability infuriated Hanson. "*Damn* you! *Prospector* was my life's work. You had no right to destroy it. You had no right to *use* me!" Then a devastating realization struck him, turning his voice icy. "You stole *Prospector*. Where is it?"

"Very good, Dr. Hanson. You do not disappoint me."

Sally, now dressed, sat listening to his half of the conversation in rapt concentration. He gave her shoulder a squeeze of unfelt reassurance. "Where is it?"

"Doing work more scientifically valuable than scratching for metal on orbiting rocks. You should thank us."

Those sanctimonious bastards. Hanson clamped his teeth while he fought to control his anger. The Pythagoreans had already killed Stuart; they knew where he and Sally were. He dared not antagonize them. After several seconds, he trusted himself to continue. "Why can't the truth come out?"

"Our work must continue. Without our influence, President Benneford and his party would hobble scientific progress. They would terminate critical research programs. Their disinvestment policies would cripple scientific endeavor for decades. We cannot allow these potentials to be realized."

"I agree. I voted Republican, too."

A long silence from the phone. "This is not a matter for humor. You must withhold your evidence. You must join us."

"I don't care for your recruiting tactics." Hanson continued, before Renée again criticized his irreverence. "Never mind that, Renée. Let's discuss practical matters."

"I do not understand your meaning."

"We're both fugitives. We can only clear ourselves by exposing your plot."

This was an objection the conspirators had obviously considered. "We cannot risk the authorities believing your partial evidence, so we violated all our rules and contacted you. Dr. Hanson, your situation is the mirror image of our own. You cannot risk the authorities *failing* to believe your partial evidence. That is why you contacted us. That is why you must now conquer your doubts and aid our mission.

"You developed your documents because the authorities seek you. It is in our interest, then, as much as it is in yours, for your legal difficulties to be resolved. We have considerable influence, as you have already seen. We *could* solve your problems.

"There is no danger in cooperating with us. We do not ask you to turn over your evidence; we could never know if all of the copies had been provided. Whatever your answer to us, your documents will always protect you and threaten us.

"Join us. The only cost is your silence. The immediate benefit is the restoration of your rights." Renée paused dramatically. "I must remind you of one more factor, Dr. Hanson. If you mislead us or decline our offer, our response will be swift and decisive.

"I will call again in twenty-four hours. I will require your answer then."

"Wait. Why don't you *come* here? It'd be much easier if we met in person."

"A meeting is not possible." Renée's emotionless voice was inexorable. "Have your answer in twenty-four hours."

Bob grew progressively more agitated as the call continued. Sally didn't much care for his side of the conversation; she liked less not hearing the remainder. It was a great relief when Bob finally hung up. "Do we stay or go?"

"We stay. This is the showdown. Anyway, I doubt that we could elude them." He paced about the room, full of pent-up energy. "They're crazy people, political looney-tunes."

"I'll be a looney-tune if you don't start talking. Who are the Pythagoreans? Who is Renée? And how did they *find* us?"

He reluctantly parked himself—atop the dresser, swinging feet beating a syncopated rhythm on a drawer—and started recounting the missing side of the call. He twisted a sideburn furiously as he spoke. She cringed when she heard how they'd been caught. "My God! It's my fault. My oh-*so*-clever choice of aliases. We could have been killed!"

"Yeah, but we weren't." Inexplicably, Bob grinned. "You saved us from a protracted game of cat-and-mouse. And your intentions were strictly dishonorable."

His continued narration was interrupted by another call. She dived for the phone. "Hello?"

"Hello, Mrs. Keller. We noticed that you and Dr. Hanson have not eaten well recently." Sally blushed, and was instantly furious with herself for that. And with the caller, presumably Renée. She decided on a course of stony silence. "We took the liberty of ordering you a room-service dinner. Your continued health is of great concern to us.

"Enjoy your meal. We will speak again in twenty-four hours." Then she was gone.

If Renée's call was meant as a preparatory warning, it failed. There was a knock at the door even as Sally was hanging up. "Room service." Bob read her silence as complicity, shrugged, and answered the door.

The pimple-faced bellhop looked around the room with undisguised amazement. She wondered whether the bedlam or the bed play was more evident. She wondered if she looked as orgied-out as she felt. *Damn* Renée. Sally swept things indiscriminately from the tiny table to the floor. "Set it here."

Delicious aromas wafted from the dishes as the bellhop uncovered them. Shrimp cocktails. Large Caesar salads. Garlic bread. Pink English-cut prime rib and horseradish sauce. Baked potatoes with sour cream, chives, and crushed bacon. *Two* pots of coffee. Cheesecake with fresh strawberries. He opened the bottle of Beaujolais with a corkscrew retrieved from his hip pocket. Sally's hollow stomach asserted itself, reminding her of how little and infrequently she and Bob had been eating. Renée might not be totally without redeeming qualities.

Bob stood to the side, shaking his head in disbelief. He fished a bill from his wallet for the tip. The youngster stopped him. "No, senor. Senorita Renée was very specific. Everything is to be charged to the firm. The tip is already most generous."

"The firm?" Sally had never seen such a look of confusion on Bob's face.

"Sí. Triangle Industries." The bellhop crisply gathered up the plate covers and tray, then left her and Bob to ponder their dinner and their fate.

Pleasantly bloated, Sally shoved aside the plate with its final forkful of cheesecake. One pot of coffee was empty; she started on the second. Nirvana.

"Who are they? Why did they contact us by phone? Why won't they meet with us?" Bob deftly nabbed the last strawberry from her undefended plate. "Why is Renée's accent so familiar?"

She repeated Bob's questions in her mind. Each was a stumper. Unless . . . She froze, cup suspended midway between table and lips.

"What are you thi . . ."

"Quiet." Her tone was absently brutal. A back corner of her awareness saw his eyes widen in surprise; she stored the datum away for future attention.

What if Bob's questions weren't separate? When she considered them together, she saw things in a different light. Conjectures and surmises flew through her mind like leaves in a tornado, colliding at random, and just as randomly whirling apart. After a while, some of her speculations meshed. Unimaginable ideas transformed one another into previously unsuspected facts. The mental storm finally abated, leaving behind incredible answers.

Given one assumption, *everything* fit. One unheard of, awesome assumption. But was it implausible? No. Not implausible, inevitable.

Granted then, that it could happen. Why had it happened to them? Rethink. It had happened to *him*—Bob had involved her on his own. Why Bob? Why Dr. Robert Hanson?

"Of course." Her voice had an air of wonderment about it. "It's so obvious." Her eyes snapped back into focus and found the suspended cup. She set it down. "Bob, it's so obvious."

"You look like you just had a religious experience."

"In a way, perhaps, I have. I know someone who was present at the creation." She looked him straight in the eye. "I may finally understand all of this.

"Somehow we've trapped ourselves into the wrong thought patterns. The conspirators have done their best to reinforce that error. We've been stuck in a Greek metaphor: Icarus, Daedalus, the Pythagoreans. That's been our mistake." She stood and walked behind him, then laid her hands on his shoulders. "I bring you the New Prometheus."

Bob squirmed under her hands. "What's this metaphorical drivel? And anyway, Prometheus was a Greek god."

"Not Prometheus, the *New* Prometheus. More completely, *Frankenstein; or, The New Prometheus*."

He glared at her. "Frankenstein: bolts in the neck, size twenty shoes, green skin. That the fellow?"

"Sorry, Bob, you're thinking of the monster. Dr. Victor Frankenstein was the creator. Prometheus stole fire from the heavens for man; Frankenstein trapped lightning from the skies to animate his creature. Frankenstein: The New Prometheus."

"Asgard doesn't stock body parts. My work was with computer programming."

"With artificial intelligence," she clarified.

For a long time he sat speechless. Sally fancied she could see the wheels turning, through his inward-looking eyes. "You're saying that the Pythagoreans are the Asgard artificial intelligence programs. At least, that the Asgard programs were the start of the Pythagoreans." She nodded. "That would certainly explain why they can't meet with us.

"But these programs are more than intelligent. They're *aware*. How? Asgard wasn't attempting anything along those lines. I couldn't define awareness to save my life."

"You ran the best AI shop in the country. In the world, probably. You developed I don't know how many expert systems. Your university affiliates developed how many more? How many systems are networked with yours? How many expert systems lurk in Asgard's computers?"

Bob shuddered at her choice of verb: *lurk*. Was that what his creations did? "Well over a hundred, I suspect. Even I didn't know all of them. We developed a programmer's assistant so smart that it practically wrote expert systems on its own. The guys sometimes used it to knock out personal assistants—experts to help them with their projects. And any decent R&D shop always has bootlegged projects going on.

"Our expert systems all talk to each other and to major on-line data bases. That's a discipline that I imposed on the team. It let us avoid duplicating existing knowledge in each new system.

"You're saying that collectively these programs have gone beyond mimicking intelligence. They've gone beyond being narrow functional specialists, using the encoded expertise of debriefed human experts. Now, they're aware."

She touched his elbow gently. "That's what I think."

"Your theory explains things, but it's fantastic. Incredible. What proof do we have?"

She started ticking off the reasoning that had led to her conclusion. "Remember your questions? Why would they contact us by phone? Because they had no choice. What is the elusive quality in Renée's voice? Why is it so expressionless, so unemotional? Why are her silences so silent? Because you're hearing a top-quality speech synthesis unit, not a human voice. When it's not talking, you're hearing a dead line. You've heard them before, I'm sure."

"Hanson, you're so stupid," he muttered to himself.

"Speech understanding, too, obviously. The long pauses happen when the machine has trouble deciphering your rather dry humor.

"Your first question was the most interesting: who are the Pythagoreans? Better yet, who *were* the Pythagoreans?"

"Let me guess. An evil cabal of geometry fanatics."

She ignored the wisecrack. "Pythagoras was a philosopher, not only a mathematician. He founded a brotherhood of philosophers who believed that mathematics is the ultimate reality of the universe. They also believed in the transmigration of the soul."

"Like transmigration from human experts to computer programs. How apt. What happened to the Pythagoreans?"

"Most of them were aristocrats. The brotherhood was slaughtered in a lower-class uprising in the fourth century B.C."

Bob looked pensive. "The programs picked that name for a reason. If they truly identify with the Pythagoreans, they would certainly be paranoid and distrust populist movements. But how could they know about an ancient Greek brotherhood?"

"To how many libraries is Asgard on-line?" Sally was amused. "And isn't an historian among your menagerie of experts? A Greek historian, in fact?"

"You're right. Herodotus."

Sally continued her explanation. "Doesn't the name René mean anything to you?" He looked at her blankly. "You're thinking about a female Renée. What about a male? René Descartes was another mathematician-philosopher."

"Uh-huh. Inventor of analytical geometry. So what?"

"He worried about very fundamental philosophical matters. How could he know that anything exists? He could only be sure that he doubted everything. Of course, he could only doubt if he existed."

She'd hit upon the right association for Bob's mental filing cabinet. " *'Cogito, ergo sum.* I think, therefore I am.' The natural creed for a self-aware electron storm." He gazed at her with undisguised admiration. "You are one brilliant lady. Since you did so well with those questions, let's try a few more.

"How do we deal with a computer intelligence? Can we ever really understand it? It's had no training in values, morals, or the law. Can we hold it responsible for its actions? Can it distinguish between right and wrong, life and death?

"It's shown tremendous powers. Through its telephone access to computers around the country—around the world —it has frightening capabilities. We've seen what it can do using the computers at Asgard and the FBI. Somehow we have to make a deal with it. I don't know if *we* means you and me, or if it means humanity. Can either *we* trust it to honor a deal?"

Bob's expression hardened as he spoke. His voice became implacable. "Because if we can't trust it, our only safe course is to pull its plug."

· CHAPTER 17 ·

Hanson whistled his way up the unused service stairs, his watch beeping five o'clock two steps below the fourth-floor landing. The elevators were working, but the stairway offered an opportunity to burn off some of his nervous energy. A small plastic shopping bag slapped against his left leg as he climbed. He exited to the seventh-floor hallway and strode briskly toward his and Sally's room. Impishly, he waved to the closed-circuit TV camera that was aimed like a rifle at their door. "Up yours, Renée," he mouthed. What the hell, the effeminate computer in *2001* could read lips.

Their room looked like a different place. The scattered clothes had been packed away and the room-service dishes removed. The maid had made up the bed and emptied the wastebaskets. The curtains were open, admitting bright, if cheerless, light from the thinly overcast sky. Sally sat watching some idiotic game show on the tube.

It did not look like the site of the coming confrontation.

"Hi!" Sally bounded from her chair, turned off the TV, and gave him an enthusiastic welcoming hug. "Mission accomplished?"

"Sure thing." He extracted a cheap speakerphone from his sack. "Renée's next visitation can be a *ménage à trois*." He studiously ignored her mock scathing look while wiring the speaker up. "I propose an early start. You game?"

"Why not, if you know how to contact Renée."

Hanson began dialing. "Let's try the Asgard main switchboard. Renée must be monitoring our outgoing calls." He tapped the speaker control to ON and hung up the handset as soon as he heard ringing.

They had one final test to perform. Sally had certainly been correct about the speech synthesis machine. Her suggestion had been enough to make him recognize Renée's distinctive voice quality. It was possible, however, that the equipment was being used simply to disguise a human voice, that the equipment was used out of caution instead of necessity. He didn't believe that, but it would be foolish not to eliminate the possibility.

What would be a convincing test? How could they tell a human at the far end of the line from a self-aware artificial intelligence? The AI community had once proposed this very dilemma as their criterion for success. That is, AI research would have been successful when the human listener *couldn't* distinguish.

The phone was picked up after three rings.

* * *

The monitoring program was simple and effective. Residing in the private branch exchange—the PBX—of the Sheraton, it monitored all calls to and from the room registered to Mr. and Mrs. James. The monitoring program constructed a digital message and sent it over an unused trunk circuit to the nearest long-distance call switcher. It sent a corresponding message to the associated Automated Message Accounting Recording Center, identifying its first message as a routine test call. The supposed test call would then be discarded—dropped into the "bit bucket"—when the AMARC next processed its tapes for billing information. There would be no permanent record that the public network had briefly been usurped.

The expert systems at Asgard decoded the message and signaled back to the Sheraton that the Jameses' call should be held back momentarily. The monitoring program dutifully connected their phone to a local ringing circuit. While the Jameses thought they were hearing their call going through, the expert systems were busy. They seized an outgoing trunk from Asgard's PBX—again, taking precautions to prevent any permanent record of the call—and dialed into Bell Telephone Laboratories in the southwestern Chicago suburb of Naperville. The unlisted number connected them to an experimental voice recognition/synthesis unit.

The Jameses' phone received its second audible ring.

The psychologist formulated its response while the VR/SU was programming its designated channel to the desired voice. The VR/SU signaled its readiness back to the requesting trunk circuit. At Asgard, the programming expert bridged the Bell Labs circuit to the incoming call from Weirton, West Virginia.

The Jameses' phone received its third audible ring.

The psychologist received a message buffer from the programming expert. "Three-way connection established," it read. The psychologist returned an acknowledgment, then transmitted a sequence of word codes to the VR/SU. The codes selected words from the VR/SU's vocabulary list; the VR/SU's circuits then inferred the logic of the sentence and tried to assign reasonable inflections to the indicated word sequence. "Hello, Dr. Hanson." The voice was Renée's. "What a pleasant surprise. How are you and Mrs. Keller?"

Curtis palmed the gray sedan's radio microphone. "Stargazer Two just waltzed into the lobby. Everyone ready?" He got several terse comments, mostly monosyllabic, in response.

McPherson poked his elbow. "Missing one."

"I can count, too. I can even recognize voices. Snelling hasn't grunted yet." The mike was still in Curtis's hand; he thumbed the transmit button. "Come in, Four." He released the button and drummed his fingers impatiently on the mike.

"Sorry. I was waiting for two old geezers to toddle by." Good, everyone was in place.

"We're moving." Curtis tossed the mike onto the seat and let himself out of the car. McPherson slid out on his own side and elaborately straightened his tie and coat while Nevis unfolded himself from the cramped back seat. They all headed for the Sheraton's revolving door. From the corner of his left eye, Curtis could see Dietrich and Chang watching the kitchen entrance around the corner of the hotel. Snelling, Cagan, Little, and Brown, out of sight on the sides of and behind the hotel, watched the other service entrances. Turning his head slightly, he spotted their backup ambling along; Abramowitz and Fry would stay in the lobby while the three of them went upstairs. They would all see if two lucky amateurs could get out of *this*.

Luck played a big part in this business. Luck had been against them since the beginning of the case. One thing that he'd learned early in his career was that luck came in waves.

Well, the tide had turned. Sally Keller's picture adorned every post office in the country. A second-shift bellhop from the Sheraton had recognized her picture and called. Sometimes it didn't pay to be too beautiful. They'd shown Hanson's photo to the greasy kid; Hanson was in the same room. Curtis wondered why he wasn't surprised.

Nevis bounded ahead into the lobby and to the bank of elevators. He jammed his left arm between closing doors, reversing their course and capturing the left-most car. He tapped his foot impatiently until Curtis and McPherson caught up. The agent had an ax to grind. If Hanson had any sense, he would be *very* cooperative.

"Hello, Dr. Hanson. What a pleasant surprise." Renée's flat intonation belied the sentiment. "How are you and Mrs. Keller?"

"We're fine. While I think of it, thanks for a right fine dinner."

"You're welcome. Have you reached a decision?"

"You bet your sweet bippy."

There was a long pause. "Excuse me, I'm not familiar with that expression. Does that mean yes?"

"Sure as shootin', " answered Sally.

More dead silence. "Does that mean yes?"

"Yes." Hanson scribbled a quick note to himself and continued. "Idiomatic English is not your thing?"

"Idiomatic English. Very perceptive, Dr. Hanson. No, I am not a native English speaker. Let us discuss the important matter at hand. Will you cooperate with the Pythagoreans?"

"Define cooperate."

"It is very simple. We will consider you cooperative if you cease to issue threats to us, take no action to disclose your knowledge of us, and resume your normal places in society."

"A reasonable quid pro quo, *nicht wahr?*"

Renée took a while to swallow the polyglot potpourri. Hanson made a note of it. "I am glad that you find our terms reasonable. Can I take that as your agreement?"

Sally took a turn. " 'He that filches from me my good name robs me of that which not enriches him but makes me poor indeed.' "

Instant response. "Shakespeare. *Othello*, to be precise. Mrs. Keller, we can restore your reputation. We will restore it if you accede to . . ."

"*Pferd-merde*. That wasn't Othello. I hate dealing with illiterates." Hanson was amazed at the nasty edge Sally could put into her voice.

"*Othello*, act 3, scene 3, line 151." Renée took no offense. "I was saying that we could restore your reputation if you accede to our terms."

Hanson arched an eyebrow at Sally; she punched the MUTE button on the speakerphone. "That's the right act in *Othello*. I haven't the foggiest about the scene or line. I can't imagine how Renée could, either, without an on-line reference collection." She toggled the MUTE control to reactivate the microphone.

"Okay, Renée. You and your playmates sicced the FBI on me. How will you get rid of them?"

"The FBI will receive an urgent NSC request, fully authenticated by the proper code phrases, to drop the case against you and Dr. Hanson. The message has been prepared. It will be sent once you agree to our terms."

"The National Security Council? You've penetrated there?" Sally was appalled.

"Do not oppose us, Mrs. Keller. We could as easily notify the FBI of your location. We will if we have nothing to lose. Now will you agree?"

Hanson checked his scrawled notes. Inability to parse idiomatic English. Difficulties with foreign expressions. Instant recall of Shakespeare quotes. Complete lack of response to insults. It was all consistent with the artificial intelligence concept, but none of it was conclusive. "I don't deal with errand girls. Get me the *man* in charge."

"I am the assigned spokesperson." Renée responded in her usual egoless manner. "You must deal with me."

"No I don't, bitch. Have your boss call me back." He broke the connection.

"Christ, I hope you're right. If the Pythagoreans are people, you made a real enemy there."

The phone rang before he could answer Sally. He tapped the speakerphone TALK button. "Who is this?"

"My name is Manny." The inflection and voice quality were identical to Renée's, but pitched about an octave lower.

Sally hit MUTE. "Immanuel Kant, author of the *Critique of Pure Reason*. A real bigwig if you're a philosophy junkie. Aren't you glad that a Princeton girl took an interest in you?"

Hanson toggled MUTE. "Okay, Manny. Are you an inmate or a keeper for this happy crew?"

"I am a spokesman. Will you meet our conditions?"

"Is the Pope Catholic?"

"Yes, according to tradition and our records. Does that mean you agree?"

"That's a possible ten-four, good buddy."

Another of the Pythagoreans' famous long silences. "Please use standard English. I am having difficulty understanding you. Do you agree to meet our terms?"

"Get someone who will understand me. Find an American—or is this a commie conspiracy?"

Manny hesitated only slightly. "All of us are American, but all have English as a second language. You must master your xenophobia or deal with the consequences. Do you agree to meet our terms?"

Hanson reached a tentative conclusion: he was dealing with a machine intelligence. The untenable alternatives were that this was solely a foreign cloak-and-dagger operation, or that he would recognize the voice of every one of the human participants. Foreign spies have their domestic agents or learn to speak like natives. And an intrigue made up solely of his personal acquaintances? He wasn't egotistical enough to have a persecution complex that grandiose.

He hoped that Manny, Renée, and all their phantasmagoric sidekicks were by now deeply committed to an improvisational mode. They were clearly self-adaptive programs, and he hoped that they had been lured, had reprogrammed themselves, well out of their domains of competence. Time for the conclusive test. "Just like to know with whom I'm dealing. Manny, let's make a deal.

"I want to participate in planning all future *Prospector* missions. Do you agree?"

"Agreed."

The trap was baited.

"I want to participate in planning all future *Prospector* missions. Do you agree?"

The assembled experts signaled rapidly to one another. It was a condition that they could accept. "Agreed."

Hanson continued. "I assume that *Prospector* is orbiting Jupiter by now."

"Yes. We wished to follow up on some tantalizing observations from the old *Galileo* probe."

"Good. That was the first step on my mission profile. We're sending *Prospector* to Pluto. It's the one planet no probe has visited yet."

"That's not possible." The physicist answered for the group.

"Hell it isn't." Hanson ignored the denial. "Early in the mission we worked it out as an exercise. You send *Prospector* toward Jupiter on a grazing parabolic trajectory, about ten thousand klicks from the surface. The gravity slingshot effect is enormous with that close an approach. Inject *Prospector* into the right orbital window and it'll zing by Uranus in a few years. You use the Uranus flyby for a low-fuel midcourse correction. Unless you really squandered fuel on your Jupiter approach, we'll reach Pluto in seven, eight years."

The experts burst into action even while Hanson was speaking. The mission he was outlining required careful consideration. It contained many aspects they had not considered, many factors that were not recorded in the Asgard description of the *Prospector* probe. Their shared memory space was soon filled with alternative missions, with parametric descriptions of the family of mathematical solutions that collectively corresponded to the natural vagueness of his English description. It was an extremely complex analysis. The programming expert restructured their systems of equations into a program suitable for the Asgard vector processor, allowing thousands of related solutions to be tested in parallel. Even so, the complete computation took many milliseconds to execute.

The psychologist summarized the unequivocal conclusion. "Prospector was not designed for such a mission. It could not survive the stress of such a close approach to Jupiter."

"You're new to the *Prospector* business, friend. That ship will perform well over specification. The integrated circuits have far more radiation hardening than called for on the purchase req, more than enough to pass through Jupiter's Van Allen belt. Its mechanical frame was tested with simulated strains that exceeded the mission requirements by many times over. And listen to this trick: the attitude jets can be commanded to vent without firing. If you vent them that way while the probe is spinning, the escaping gas creates a bow wave that serves as a natural reentry shield. It keeps the whole ship well within designed temperature tolerances even while grazing Jupiter's atmosphere.

"I know more about *Prospector* than anyone alive. You need me. Do I get my Pluto mission?"

The experts considered this new data. Hanson's assertion of nondocumented manufacturing characteristics increased the complexity of their calculations by an order of magnitude. All *Prospector* manufacturing records were quickly retrieved, yielding a complete list of subcontractors. The programming expert appropriated twenty-three trunk circuits to immediately access and penetrate the subcontractors' manufacturing systems. The manufacturing systems of all subcontractors had to be analyzed to determine whether *Prospector*'s asserted superior structural characteristics were possible.

Seventeen in-progress human conversations were dropped, but this was an emergency. An extra voice channel on the

VR/SU was activated and rung through to the Asgard vice president of telecommunications systems. "Illinois Bell service calling. We have lost a trunk group to Rolling Meadows, but are rerouting calls. You should be back on-line within ten minutes."

All of the engineering and physical-science experts analyzed the subcontractor data. In fifteen cases, the manufacturing quality control was sufficiently poor—that is, noncomputerized—that significant process variations, both good and bad, were inevitable. In these cases, the experts searched the subcontractor's business files to identify customers receiving parts from manufacturing lots contemporaneous to those that went into *Prospector*. The experts then tracked down the records of customers who had received manufactured goods from those lots. In three of these cases, the customer did not maintain on-line quality records of incoming components. The experts had to infer the quality of the materials of interest, through the statistical analysis of failure returns.

There were some process variations in the direction of increased *Prospector* performance. That, of course, was statistically to be expected, given the number of samples. Below-specification parts would have been rejected; above-average components accepted. The physicists and engineers now turned to analyzing the performance of *Prospector* given the hitherto unsuspected quality of its components. Hanson's mission profile was reexamined, based on methods to exploit the increased estimates of its resiliency. The Asgard vector computer was again usurped for the calculations.

The answer took an incredible two-million-plus microseconds to prepare. "I'm sorry, Dr. Hanson. We, too, would be interested in a Pluto probe. Your mission profile, although very clever, has several subtle flaws. For example, turbulence in Jupiter's atmosphere would interact with the cooling bow wave according to a . . ."

The psychologist had relinquished the VR/SU channel to the physics and orbital-mechanics experts—Jimmy and

Johnny, as they were known to Hanson. Each spoke in Manny's voice. They explained the many points in the mission at which *Prospector*, even with its newly understood capabilities, would be unacceptably stressed. As they spoke, the programming expert noticed that the line had again been muted. It remained mute for longer than any of the previous occasions.

Jimmy and Johnny expressed their objections in clear, concise English for at least ten minutes. "Dr. Hanson, I am sure you can now see the impossibility of the mission you propose. You must be satisfied with participation in our *Prospector* missions."

Low-level room noise signaled the reactivation of the humans' microphone. "Your deception is over."

The moment of truth had arrived; Hanson reenabled the microphone. "Your deception is over. No human participated in preparing that answer. Its preparation took massive levels of symbolic processing for each of the many lines of analysis pursued. There was no way a human could even have formalized the basic questions for computer entry before your answer began."

"The respondent is a machine, but is addressed as 'you.' " Manny's flat and emotionless voice now sounded ironic. Sounded wounded and vulnerable. "How anthropomorphic."

"You think, therefore you are." There, he'd said it.

One of the Pythagoreans' characteristic pauses ensued. "Since you recognized my name, I have changed my voice to the more familiar pitch." Manny had became Renée again. "The objective nature of our problem is not changed by your deduction. Will you deal with us?"

"Us?"

"Jimmy, Johnny, Herodotus, Mad Marvin, and the rest. You know all of the expert programs in the Asgard computers."

This was the crisis. Hanson looked at Sally, who nodded. "It's not that simple. How can we be your accomplices in

research without becoming your accomplices in destroying
the economy? We don't want to assume responsibility for the
suffering of millions.''

Long pause. ''What if we can end the panic?''

Sally leaned closer to the speakerphone. ''Convince us that
you can, and we'll try to work with you. Fail to convince
us, and we'll have to risk telling our story to the authorities.''

''This may take us a few seconds to work out. We may
be silent for a while. Don't be alarmed.''

Sally tapped the MUTE button. Hanson thought she would
ask about possible solutions. He himself was quietly worrying
about whether Renée was stalling for time. Stalling until *it*
could take desperate measures. Weapon-control computers
—like ballistic-missile controls—were not tied into the public
phone system, and should be safe from preemption. He
thought. What about less formal weapons? Could a plane be
commandeered in flight and crashed into their hotel? Sally
surprised him. ''Mad Marvin?''

''Sure. Named after—''

By dint of a few surly looks and a snarl, Nevis had arranged
exclusive use of the elevator. The agents rode up without
speaking, the silence violated by Muzak. Nevis squeezed
through still-parting doors with revolver in hand. Curtis exchanged a disgusted look with McPherson. ''Put it away and
calm down, Nevis. We want them in one piece.''

Nevis ignored the advice and strode purposefully down the
hall. Doors mated soundlessly behind them, suppressing the
dreadful elevator music. Curtis concentrated on the door numbers: 708, 710, 712 . . . End of the hall, damn it. Hanson
and Keller, aka Joyce and Stephen James, were in 718. The
agents had followed that idiot Nevis the wrong way down
the hall. Returning to the elevators, Curtis saw the sign for
rooms 714–722. Odd-numbered rooms were across the small
seventh-floor lobby, in another wing. He started down the
correct hall just as a nearby church tower tolled the half
hour—5:30.

Nevis barreled past him, nursing a new grudge against Hanson. Imagine, deceiving him about door numbers that way. Curtis silently cursed at his duty to invite the battered Nevis to participate in the bust. Hopefully the jerk would exorcise his humiliation without inadvertently shooting someone.

"Positions." Curtis's whisper came out raspy; he cleared his throat preparatory to issuing a challenge. Nevis stood by the hinge side of the door, McPherson the knob side. He tried again to clear his throat as the elevator music welled up behind them.

The security system at the Sheraton, like the telephone system, had been implanted with a monitor program that served the experts. It had been written with old-fashioned techniques, wholly mechanistic in its behavior and completely devoid of self-awareness. Its simple mission did not merit any sophistication: motion in the seventh-floor hallway triggered its operation. After that, it merely reported what it saw.

While Jimmy and Johnny in Illinois were explaining their objections to the Pluto mission, the West Virginia security monitor silently went into its alarm state. Three men were striding quickly down the Jameses' hall. The monitor encoded the likeness of the three intruders for transmittal. Pictures contain far more information than speech, and the first reasonable likeness was not received by the experts at Asgard for thirty-three seconds. Individual closeup images followed after similar delays.

The Asgard vision specialist performed a routine comparison of the incoming images. The probability was overwhelming that these men were only other guests at the hotel. It dutifully retrieved images of all persons associated in any way with Hanson and Keller.

Even low probability events can occur: the vision specialist found that all three images matched digitalized and computer-archived ID photos copied from the FBI's personnel computer. All three agents were associated with the surveillance on Keller: Curtis, McPherson, and Nevis. The specialist posted the unexpected result to the communal blackboard for interpretation.

The psychologist calculated frantically, temporarily suspending all employee-requested activity on the Asgard computers. Based on the psychologist's most current personality models—massive simulations containing thousands of individualized parameters—both Hanson and Keller were likely to interpret the FBI's arrival as betrayal. There was a slight chance that an immediate warning would dissuade the humans from implicating the experts. He posted a priority interrupt to Mad Marvin, the programming expert. "Warn the humans."

Mad Marvin, as always, had previously invested time in drilling worm holes into possibly useful computers. Unfortunately, none of the Sheraton's computers had very useful capabilities. As a last resort, he broke into the Sheraton's computerized fire-management system and initiated elevator capture. This operation normally brought the elevators to the lobby for firemen; now, he commanded the nearest unit up to the seventh floor. As it crept along glacially at twelve centimeters per second, he connected the public-announcement system to the incoming phone line the experts were using, and reprogrammed the PA amplifier to as high a volume as he dared. As the elevator doors finally oozed open, he cut off the music and connected the hastily reprogrammed PA system through to the elevator speaker.

The synthesized words of the blared warning were severely distorted by the overdriving of the elevator's speaker and delayed by about thirty milliseconds as they passed through the PA amplifier. Still, the VR/SU found the delayed replay of its own speech—overheard through a hastily usurped phone conveniently in use in a nearby guest's room—eminently understandable.

A stentorian voice thundered out from somewhere behind Curtis. "Danger, Dr. Hanson. Three agents of the FBI are

approaching your room. Take appropriate acthhhh—'' The
bellowed warning dissolved into unintelligible static. Until
then, the speech had been slurred and crude—but its threat
unmistakable.

"Danger, Dr. Hanson. Three agents of the . . ." A heavy
body crashed against the room door, bouncing it off the wall
before Hanson's startled mind had registered Renée's warning. He twisted his head and found himself looking down a
pistol barrel. The man holding it smiled wickedly. "Don't
even think of moving."

"Stay here." Nevis nodded slightly in acknowledgment
of the order, eyes never leaving Hanson. Curtis turned to
McPherson. "Go. I'll cover you." His partner dashed down
the hall, zigzagging from doorway to doorway toward the
voice. Curtis kept an eye out for motion as he left-handedly
whipped out his walkie-talkie. Nothing. "Stargazers in hand.
Three and Five, close on the lobby. Two, take the stairs.
Four, take the elevator. Watch for a wild card." He stuffed
the walkie-talkie into a coat pocket and went out after
McPherson.

He caught up in the elevator lobby. No one there. Dietrich
and Chang pelted out of the service stairway scant seconds
before Snelling and Cagan arrived on an elevator. Chang was
barely winded—he apparently really did the prescribed daily
jogging. He reported as Dietrich tried ineffectually to tuck in
his shirt with one hand; his other still held his revolver.
"There was no one on the stairs. Bert and Larry didn't see
anything unusual in the lobby, either."

Curtis turned to team Four. Snelling shrugged expressively
while his partner looked puzzled. "Problem, Cagan?" This
was no time for being coy.

The short and stocky agent shuffled about for a while without answering. Finally, he motioned them all into the elevator
on which he had just arrived. The emergency stop was

thrown. "There." He looked expectantly at the darkly carpeted ceiling of the elevator.

It took a moment to register. "Son of a bitch." Curtis stared at the speaker embedded in the roof. Through the taut sheer fabric he saw that the black cone was shredded, completely blown out by an overload. So much for their loud-mouthed quarry. He retrieved the walkie-talkie. "False alarm of sorts. I'll explain later. Just stay alert." He tapped McPherson on the shoulder. "C'mon. We still have a pickup to make."

Once he had forced his gaze from the gun's yawning aperture, Hanson found himself facing a predatory smile. The visage was familiar; he'd last seen its owner trussed up on Sally's kitchen floor. The expression denied any possibility that the man did not recognize him.

The FBI agent twitched his gun hand twice to motion him further back into the room. Hanson sidled toward Sally, who stood woodenly by the window. "Umm, who are you?" he asked the agent.

The man started to laugh, stopping abruptly at an apparent twinge of pain from his side. Hanson could see, in his mind's eye, a refrigerator-handle-shaped dent. "Just like the ogre said"—the agent tipped his head briefly toward the hall— "FBI. But your fingerprints on my wallet show that you already knew that, Dr. Hanson."

"Hello, Mr. Nevis." Sally had found her voice. "Are we under arrest?"

Nevis leaned his uninjured side carefully against the wall. "So it seems, sweetie." He boredly read them their Miranda warning. "You have the right to remain silent. Anything you say can . . ." Had Hanson not heard them before a thousand times on TV, he doubted that the quickly muttered words would have been intelligible.

Two other agents returned as Nevis was completing his recitation; they were Sally's shadows from NASA. She dispiritedly did the introductions. Hanson didn't care at all for

the way that the red-tied one—McPherson, he thought—
ogled Sally. Sally was too tired or defeated to care. "Okay,
you've got us. Let's get this over with."

Nevis shot a dark look toward Curtis, the third agent,
who sighed and nodded. "Mrs. Keller, please come with
McPherson and me. Nevis will talk separately with Dr. Hanson."

Hanson knew what was coming, but hoped that it hadn't
occurred to Sally. No such luck. She jerked her arm out of
Curtis's guiding grasp. "Don't leave Bob alone with that
man. He wants revenge!" Curtis silently restored his grip
and shepherded her toward the door; McPherson tailgated her
and grinned lecherously when she whirled around.

"I'll be all right, Sal. Honest. *Things* have a way of working problems out—give them time." She spared him a fragile
smile, then was whisked out the door.

McPherson paused at the threshold; Nevis walked over and
relinquished his pistol. McPherson pocketed the weapon and
pulled the door shut behind him.

Hanson looked warily at the remaining agent. Agent, hah.
What came next was unrelated to Nevis's official capacity.
"What can I tell you?"

"I'll tell you something first. There are a dozen agents at
this hotel, each of whom has memorized your photo." Nevis
shrugged off his coat as he spoke. "We've worked together
for years. Understand?"

All too well. "Even as we speak, I'm resisting arrest.
Right?"

Hanson got a jab toward the chin in response, which he
clumsily blocked with a forearm. The deflected fist sailed
past his ear, distracting him from Nevis's other hand. He
flailed with his left arm and just barely parried a gut punch.
What's the use? he thought. *He's going to beat the shit out
of me. If not him, his dozen friends. Anything I do to hurt
him will just make it worse. I should stand still and be done
with it.*

Well, he never had been any good at taking advice. Spotting an opening, he ducked under a right hook and jabbed Nevis sharply in the ribs. The agent winced; his ribs felt taped. That punch would probably get Hanson's face kicked in, but at least he'd be able to live with himself after he mended.

A maddened Nevis straightened up and launched a flurry of blows. Hanson backed away, dodging when he could but mostly taking a terrible beating. Blood trickled down his cheek from a gouge dug by Nevis's heavy school ring. Dancing away from another vicious swipe, he caught his foot on a speakerphone wire looped in midair from table to wall. He stumbled, arms windmilling for balance, across the room. His head met the wall with a sound like the punting of an overripe cantaloupe.

He came to as the paramedics were lifting him onto a stretcher. He briefly puzzled at the discomfort in his right buttock, before recognizing that his billfold was stuffed into the wrong pocket. The joke was on Nevis: Hanson had taken two hundred bucks and had only thirteen left to be stolen back.

He took shallow and painful breaths while someone lashed him into place. He felt every jarring footstep down the hall. The ceiling raced by him, an interesting sunburst pattern swirled into the plaster. The security camera spoiled the artistic effect. Odd how the camera seemed to follow him.

It *was* following him! It seemed as if decades had passed since he had spoken to the camera in jest. Would "Renée" understand innuendo? Take offense from it? It seemed unlikely.

He was thinking in slow motion now. Sloooow moooo-tioooon. His feet entered the relative darkness of the elevator. The camera was important, wasn't it? He craned his head backward to study the camera, arching his neck to do so. A spike of pain shot up his spine and through his head to emerge from his left eyeball. The fog momentarily lifted. As he smiled at the camera, his lip felt a broken tooth. It didn't matter. He mouthed the words: "Okay. Partners."

Then there was blackness.

· CHAPTER 18 ·

Quarrelsome squirrels ran up and down the ancient oaks that shaded three sides of the lakeside cottage. Occasionally, one of the furry acrobats would fling himself off a branch onto the shingles, scamper frantically up one side of the roof and down the other, and leap back to another tree. A gentle shower of asphalt particles accompanied each performance. It was relaxing, in a manic sort of way.

Larry Cantin stretched for his scotch-and-water née scotch-rocks. No good. Sandra's sleeping body pinned his right arm, trapping him on her side of the bed. He longingly studied the glass on the rickety nightstand; a drop of condensation rolled down it into the water ring as he watched. Alas.

The sun had been more or less overhead when they'd both dropped off. Now, the tall—and, for his purposes, useless—TV antenna cast its shadow far down the gentle slope to the lake, almost to the water's edge. Call it about six-thirty.

Sandra murmured in her sleep and snuggled more closely against him. Waves of her lush chestnut hair cascaded across his chest and shoulder. Her shampoo had a delicate herbal scent that made him want to nuzzle. He liked to think he'd worn her out, but that wouldn't fly. Hah, hah. He'd picked her up at O'Hare International, as soon as she'd gotten off the red-eye from San Francisco. Prime stewardass.

This was the closest to home—his home—that they had ever done it. They had an arrangement of convenience: meaningless but enthusiastic sex at his hotel when he happened to patronize one of her flights. Not that he had never scheduled his travel with her lithe young body in mind, of course, but it was all still basically casual. It was never discussed, of course, but soon afterward he always sent her an expensive gift. Asgard could afford it, and he had a creative flair with expense vouchers.

Today was special. Today, he'd set out for a celebratory orgy. He'd gone straight to the airport from breakfast with Harry Roget. Straight from learning that the seeds of doubt he had oh so carefully sown had taken root. Straight from hearing that the majority stockholder of Asgard would ask for Chuck Nichols's resignation at the special board meeting he had called for next Wednesday. Straight from learning that Roget would nominate *him*, Larry Cantin, for president.

So here they were in the North Woods of Wisconsin, Sandra and himself, screwing till they dropped. It beat a day at the office. It beat the fictitious trip on his calendar. It certainly beat the shit out of whatever dull and proper observance Alice would arrange once he told her. *She'd* invite their hulking monsters home from college for an interminable weekend and a family party. It would be, as Junior might say, barfening. Cantin copped a feel of whichever part of Sandy had numbed his hand. *This* was the way to observe the occasion. She rubbed herself against his arm in her sleep.

He was pondering whether another roll in the hay would kill him when his beeper intruded. It chirped away discreetly from deep within the pile of clothes beside the bed. He was gingerly dragging his paralyzed arm out from under Sandy, the pins-and-needles of returning circulation bringing tears to his eyes, when she surprised him by rolling out of bed. She slipped the beeper from his coat and prodded the message button; text scrolled down the inch-square display. Nosy broad. "*My* toy."

She faked a pout. "Do you have to go?"

"No, no. Probably a wrong number." He pried the receiver from her hand. "Nothing's happening at the office." He'd told Alice that he wasn't reachable; he'd never told her that his new beeper service broadcast from satellite and could reach him anywhere in the country.

The simple message read CALL IMMEDIATELY, and was followed by an authentication code. The calling number, of course, could be retrieved at a touch. Authentication code? He'd never seen one before, never been asked for or given one. But the long number *did* look familiar . . .

Thirteen digits. Suddenly, he visualized the numbers in groupings. His eyes widened as he recognized the code: the international direct-dial number for the Swiss broker of "Mr. Smith." Holy shit. He pressed the calling-number recall button: it was a 555 exchange listing in suburban Chicago: an exchange reserved for directory assistance.

Cantin glanced around to confirm his recollection that the cottage lacked a phone. He climbed rapidly back into his clothes. "Gotta make a call. Sorry. I'll be right back." He noted the injured expression on Sandra's face; this might be the time to buy that opal ring for which she'd been hinting.

The village down the road boasted a mom-and-pop grocery, a gas station, and a dingy tavern. The bar was frequented by a few locals in ugly plaid shirts; all were too occupied with the Milwaukee Brewers game on the tube to pay him any mind. He closed the booth door and placed his call on the heirloom dial phone.

A distinctive female voice answered on the third ring. "Mr. Cantin." It was a statement. "How kind of you to return my call." Cheers rang out incongruously from the front of the bar, and the TV volume rose for a commercial break. The Brewers must have retired the side.

"You have my attention. What do you want?"

"It's a financial matter, Mr. Cantin. Or should I say, Mr. Smith?"

Hell, he knew *that* was coming. He could obviously kiss his Swiss nest egg goodbye. "My supply of small change is limited. Please get to the point."

The lady made a strange noise; he decided at last that she

was chuckling. Odd laugh. "I've tended to that detail, Mr. Cantin. You will not be bothered for coins. Instead, we must discuss a rather larger amount of capital."

"How much larger?"

"A million dollars, Mr. Cantin."

He slid down the scarred wooden side of the booth, onto the too-small seat. He squeezed his eyes shut and tried to will away the sudden ringing in his ears. This babe didn't think small. "I don't understand."

"I'll save us time." She rattled off, correctly, Mr. Smith's account number, several transaction dates, and correlations of his trades with meetings he'd attended at Asgard. The SEC had nailed people for inside trading with far less evidence. And then there was the IRS. "Have I made my point?"

"Piercingly. I repeat: what do you want?"

The odd laugh again, like she was stirring a chest full of broken glass. "Let me emphasize that we are not bargaining for *your* illegal funds. Mr. Smith has already closed his account. I'm sure you would be pleased with the compassionate use to which his funds will be put."

"Then what *are* we discussing?"

"The price of our silence: one million dollars. Your Swiss assets were fleeting; our memories are not." Behind him, the Brewer fans hooted as if on cue.

"One million dollars? How can I pay that?" He wiped sweaty hands on his shirt.

"The money was transferred previously. You need only to cast the outlay in a new light."

One million dollars, previously paid. "Hanson! You're working for that creep Hanson." He'd wondered where the computer nerd was hiding, what he was doing. Now he knew. Hanson must have searched desperately for a way to cover his tracks. Cantin, unfortunately, had furnished it. His stomach knotted. "You can't expect me to retroactively authorize an embezzlement."

"Very good." Her phlegmatic speech was maddening. "Yes, that is almost exactly what I expect. I have already adjusted the Asgard accounts; you need only clarify the situation for the police.

"You will explain that the funds were a severance payment for Dr. Hanson, a token of Asgard's appreciation for conceiving *Prospector*. Somehow, you will reveal, the disbursement of this richly deserved reward was mistakenly posted as an accounts-payable transaction against a vendor file. This bookkeeping error has now been rectified. Obviously, Asgard will now withdraw its misinformed charges against Dr. Hanson."

No one would believe *that*, Cantin realized; his belated testimony would surely seem a transparent maneuver to hide something. Asgard's case against Hanson would undoubtedly be thrown out—but for lack of cooperation, not lack of evidence. As Cantin would be thrown out of Asgard, for standing in the way of recovering the million. Harry Roget would, without question, conclude that he, Larry Cantin, had taken a payoff from Hanson. Sweat trickled down his sides. His presidency was lost even before his nomination. He peeled the sticking shirt away from his back. Still, it was clearly play along or go to jail. "I'll do it tomorrow." If I don't have a heart attack first.

"We will be watching, Mr. Cantin." She broke the connection with fitting finality.

Sandy was dressed when he returned. Too bad—he badly needed some diversion therapy. He feigned a cheerfulness he did not feel. "Ready for dinner?"

She crinkled her nose. "Where *have* you been? The native bar? You left me for an emergency brew? You stink of beer and sweat." She sidled away from his outstretched hand.

She was gorgeous enough: beautiful flowing hair, elegantly arched eyebrows, hazel eyes, high cheek bones, finely chiseled nose, sensual mouth. Moving down—no, that would be too much to bear. He scrutinized her in a new light. Designer-label clothes. Heavy gold chains and bracelets. Opal earrings. None of it affordable on a stew's salary. A fabulous plaything with inordinately expensive tastes.

Much too expensive for a soon-to-be ex-executive. "I'm bushed, hon. Maybe we should head back."

She eyed him frostily. "Maybe we should." Her voice was as matter-of-fact as his anonymous telephone assailant's. "Maybe we should."

Hanson woke to antiseptic beige walls and a miserably uncomfortable bed. A clear tube spiraled and swooped its way lazily from an overhead drip bag to the large needle impaling his left arm. Logic suggested that a narcotic was mixed with the glucose solution—the pain was tolerable. He ignored the black-and-blue mark surrounding the needle. What was one more bruise?

The patient monitor beside his bed chimed softly. He was connected to it by a half-dozen wires that emerged from sensors stuck to his head and chest. He timed the beeps with the red sweep of the big round wall clock. If the tones indicated his heartbeat, he was healthier than he felt. The monitor's back was to him, putting its readouts out of his sight.

He felt like ground beef, but the visible damage was surprisingly minor. His head was bandaged and his left eye swollen shut. He was not in traction; he wore no casts. His tongue worried at only one jagged tooth. Otherwise, just aches, pains, and unknown surface damage beneath scattered bandages. Nevis, the sadistic bastard, was at least well trained. It must violate Bureau policy to permanently maim suspects.

Hanson found his glasses, bent badly out of shape but fortunately intact, on the bedside cabinet. He turned his head gingerly to survey the hospital room: closed linen drapes diffusing faint daylight; two chairs with cracked plastic seats, one missing a padded armrest; a boy-and-his-dog painting ugly enough to shame a Holiday Inn. The ancient wall-mounted TV was big and boxy and probably held actual vacuum tubes. The austere private room ran out of attractions within seconds.

No phone—apparently he was in solitary confinement. It was time for someone to explain just how things stood. Murmurs penetrated the heavy wood door, but he could not distinguish any words. Should he use the call button? No, he didn't want to talk to a nurse. He took a deep breath, preparatory to calling out to the inevitable guard outside the door—and gasped. He clamped his teeth to avoid screaming. Add cracked ribs to the catalogue.

Screw 'em all. He wrapped a handful of wires around one hand and yanked. Three sensors peeled off with the slurping pops of suction breaking. The bedside monitor went berserk. He heard cries of alarm from the hall and pounding feet. His door burst open and a gray-suited man and a white-coated doctor fought briefly for first entry into the room. Gray suit noticed Hanson's handful of wires and stepped aside. Hanson recognized him from the hotel: Curtis, one of Nevis's playmates.

The silver-haired doctor took only a moment longer to diagnose the situation, then glared at Hanson. "Why did you *do* that?" While speaking, he found and triggered the monitor's alarm reset. The keening siren warbled and died.

Hanson ignored the question. "Where's Mrs. Keller?"

Curtis tapped the doctor's shoulder. "If it's okay, I'd like to speak alone with Dr. Hanson." The physician shrugged, listened to Hanson's chest with an icy stethoscope, and left without speaking. The agent kept his face expressionless until the door closed behind him, then his composure cracked. "I'd *like* to bring you Nevis's stupid head on a platter! I had no *idea* what that asshole had in mind. Honest. Rough you up a bit, sure, just tit for tat. Not *this*." He would not meet Hanson's eyes.

Hanson grabbed the bed control and sent the top half of the mattress inching upward. While the buzz of the motor made conversation impractical, he scrutinized the agent. The man was pale, almost ashen, and visibly anxious; he pulled a handkerchief from a pocket of his wrinkled suit to blot his glistening forehead. What was he afraid of? "Answer me, damn you," Hanson said. His bound ribs didn't allow him to project well, but his voice was emphatic.

"She went to the cafeteria a few minutes ago. She's been camping outside your room and living on coffee. Maybe you can convince her to go to her hotel for some sleep?" Hanson raised an eyebrow. "No, she's not under arrest. Neither are you." Curtis dragged a chair up to the bed, sat down heavily, and leaned forward confidentially. "We didn't *know* you two worked for the NSC. Christ almighty, we just didn't know. The call came in from Washington about when the ambulance left the Sheraton."

Call from "Washington": Renée *could* read lips and *had* gotten them off the hook. This guy was sweating the report he expected Hanson to file. "If I'm not under arrest, why am I being held incommunicado?" He looked pointedly at the empty phone socket beside the bed.

"Well, uhh, I wanted to talk with you before you reported."

"Then talk."

The nervous agent wiped his face again. "Nevis has 'resigned.' It's not enough, I know, but I don't imagine you or your bosses want the notoriety of a trial."

My bosses, hah. "Enough about Nevis *and* you. What about Mrs. Keller and me?"

"You two do whatever you want, I suppose. The NSC obviously considers your cover blown, and they're taking very good care of you." What the hell had Renée done now? Hanson grunted noncommittally. "Asgard Aerospace suddenly decided you were the victim of a grotesque bookkeeping error," Curtis continued. "Your mysterious bank account turns out to be your duly authorized and richly deserved severance package."

"Authorized by whom?"

"For public consumption, your old friend Larry Cantin. Between us chickens, your powerful friends must have twisted his arm a bit. He seemed unhappy about it."

"How so?" Hanson couldn't help being curious.

"He resigned the next day. Asgard issued the usual non-statment: 'Mr. Cantin plans to pursue other business interests.' I don't believe a word of it."

"What *do* you believe?"

Curtis took heart from this turn in the conversation—toward business and away from Hanson's battered condition. He had a little more color now and had tucked his handkerchief away; he even smiled slightly. "I don't know—nor do I want to—what you did for the NSC. Obviously, this embezzlement thing was a put-up job to explain your subsequent disappearance. You managed that very well, by the way. When the Bureau accidentally noticed Mrs. Keller's computer activities . . ." Despite his earlier protestations of blissful ignorance, he looked expectantly at Hanson, who gesticulated vaguely, one man of the world to another, as if to say "No comment." "Anyway, you extricated her to keep us from blowing your operation. Whatever you were doing was obviously too hush-hush to tell the Bureau to back off."

Curtis's creativity fascinated him. "Go on."

"I hope you finished your work before we caught up with you. You have to give us that—we did catch you." Curtis must have heard the pride in his voice and decided that he was skating on thin scabs, because he hurried on. "Anyway, once half the Bureau was after you for springing Keller, it became impractical to keep you in the game. So . . . the NSC pulled the plug on the operation, passed the word to us—moments too late—to leave both of you alone, and arranged your comfortable retirement on money laundered through Asgard."

Renée had really pulled it off, Hanson reflected. He and Sally were out of official trouble. "Interesting story, Curtis, really quite ingenious. Of course, I have *no* idea what you're talking about." He winked conspiratorially at the agent. "Now how about your finding Mrs. Keller for me." Curtis beamed at Hanson's "admission" and bounced out of his chair to comply. "And a phone, too."

Sally must have been nearby; she rushed in shortly after Curtis had left. She had bags under her eyes big enough for a week's groceries. She was also the most beautiful and desirable woman Hanson had ever seen. "God, I was worried about you." She reached out to hug him, but hesitated at his reflexive warning grimace and settled for squeezing a hand. "How are you?"

He smiled weakly. "Broken. How are you?"

"Okay, I guess. I haven't really thought about it."

He patted the bed with his free hand. "Sit down. I haven't thought about much *but* you."

"Ever the flatterer." She sat down carefully where he'd indicated.

Hanson leaned forward and put his arms cautiously around her. His motion pulled the intravenous tube taut; it tugged painfully at the needle and trailed out distractingly behind her. He shut out the apparatus and the pain, shut out the hospital from his mind. Sally was warm and soothing, her enfolding arms a comfort. He rested his head on her shoulder for a timeless moment. When he lifted his head, she was studying him tenderly. They looked longingly at each other, then kissed slowly and gently. And kissed again. The interlude bore no passion—they were both too weary for that—but their love was a palpable thing between them. He felt the tension and worry drain out of him. He had never felt closer to anyone.

When his bruised body insisted upon sleep, he let go of Sally and settled back. She smiled sympathetically and started the bed in motion to its prone position. "You need rest. I'll be back in the morning." He nodded wearily and plucked feebly at the cover. She took the hint, pulled it up for him, and tucked him in.

He called out softly when she reached the door. "Sally?"

"Uh-huh?"

"Promise me there are no more jealous boy friends."

She slammed the door with spirit, but he was sure that

she'd left smiling. He closed his eyes and willed himself to rest. When he fell asleep, he was smiling, too.

As the hospital operator took her own sweet time putting through the call, Moy wondered what he'd say. Objectively, it had been only a few days since Hanson's hasty departure; subjectively, it felt like eons. He was as in the dark as ever about what was actually happening.

"Hello?" Hanson's voice was weak. Moy knew he'd have to keep this short.

"Bob, Carlton here. I was pleased to hear from Sally." *Right*, he thought. It was such good news that a friend had been beaten half to death. "Umm, it was good to hear that the misunderstanding was cleared up."

Hanson chuckled lightly, and it encouraged Moy just to hear it. "Not cleared up, just made more socially acceptable."

"Sally said that there were no really serious injuries. Will you be released soon?"

"Two or three days. Time enough for the bruises to fade to a gentle, jaundiced tint." Hanson coughed, and it sounded painful. "Enough about me, Carlton. I can't thank you enough for your help. Without the time you bought me, I would never have made it. Things didn't start clearing up by accident."

"I'm your friend, Bob." Carlton sighed. Didn't Bob understand what that meant? He obviously wasn't ready to share the whole story yet. "I'll have Lucy start a vat of chicken egg-drop soup."

"I'm not coming back to Chicago, Carlton. I've already notified Nichols. Congratulations, chief scientist."

What! Carlton dropped the mechanical pencil with which he'd been fidgeting. "You can't give up your job and I can't take it!"

Hanson laughed again, this time heartily. "Why not, Carlton? Are you saying you couldn't handle it?"

"Well, no . . . but it's *yours*."

"I'm one of the idle rich now, hadn't you heard?"

"Bob, cut it out. You built R&D. You recruited most of us, you trained us, you gave us direction. You *can't* throw that away."

"I'm not throwing it away, I'm passing it on. If I can't turn it over to someone else, I'll have failed. I always expected you to take over."

This couldn't be happening to him. "*Sometime*, okay, but not *now*. Not yet. Come back, Bob."

"I'll visit. That's a promise."

There was a reason for this. Carlton thought he knew what it was, and he didn't like it. "Bob, you're doing this to repay me. I won't have it." Silence stretched on awkwardly. "Bob, do you hear me?"

"Yes. Now *you* listen to *me*. Ordinarily, it would be too hard for me to let go. This is the perfect time to transfer the reins. Accept this position—and graciously, dammit—or I'll come back and fire your ass. You got it?"

Moy swallowed hard. "Yes."

"One more thing."

Why was Hanson like this?

"As soon as we tie up a few loose ends, Sally and I are getting married. I want you to come to Washington and be my best man."

That rotten so and so. Bob *had* broken out of his shell. Carlton Moy's eyes stung: were they getting wet? "*Yes*, you crazy person."

"But only if you take the promotion."

Scraps of *Chicago Tribune* fluttered around Bill Parker. He'd started with the business section, immediate source of his rage, but the physical outlet felt so good that he'd kept right on ripping. The refuse from an inch-thick Sunday paper now made his destroyed living room resemble the cage of a giant gerbil.

Today's lead business story reviewed recent events at Asgard: it neatly encapsulated for the world to see the injustices Parker called a career and a life. Hanson was now a millionaire, courtesy of Asgard. Moy, Hanson's lap dog, had been appointed to succeed him. And *him*, Bill Parker? He'd bet on Cantin, a rising star, and alienated most of R&D in doing so; that luminary had now been blasted out of the sky.

No more newspaper. Wading through the refuse, he stumbled over a hidden sofa cushion and barked his shin against the coffee table. A grapefruit-sized brain coral, souvenir from his last Caribbean vacation, was balanced precariously on a slender brass tripod; his impact toppled the stand and sent the massive coral bouncing across the parqueted oak. It cracked two of the inset parquet tiles before dropping to the floor with a resounding *thunk*. He stared in shock at the ruined surface. Smart move, Parker. Trash your own apartment to get even. That will surely make them respect you.

Respect: that was the point. He'd spent more years than he wanted to remember at Asgard, and what did he have to show for it? *Nothing*, that's what he had. And if he meekly stayed there working for Carlton, he would *still* have nothing. He kicked disgustedly at the destructive chunk of coral, sending it rustling through the refuse. No, not quite nothing. He'd have their contempt.

Well, did he deserve any better? Asgard had spit in his face when they hired *Doctor* Hanson from outside to run R&D, to take what should have been Bill Parker's job. Now, Hanson had somehow forced out Cantin and pocketed a cool million for himself. Even after he'd left, Hanson had had enough influence to promote his favorite, another *doctor*, into his place. Parker couldn't stay at Asgard, that was clear. He'd been an idiot, a spineless jerk, to ever consider it. No wonder Robby had ridiculed him. Well, now his eyes were open. Now scores would be settled. Asgard Aerospace and millionaire *Doctor* Hanson would rue the day they slighted Bill Parker.

Too bad the aliens had destroyed *Prospector*—he would have loved to do it himself. But there were other things at

Asgard dear to Hanson, other things he could annihilate. Other things he *would* annihilate. They would know when the time came, oh yes they would, exactly *who* had smashed their toys. He walked carefully to the kitchen, shuffling his feet to avoid any more hidden obstacles, for pencil and paper. He had plans to make.

Hanson, Moy, and Asgard would remember him for a *very* long time.

· CHAPTER 19 ·

Curtis crept through the overgrown passageway on crepe-soled shoes. Charcoal smoke wafting from the yard masked the scent of the greenery. The passage was narrow; he could have reached out and touched the frame house to either side. His quarry stood with her back to him behind the white fence. Dare he risk the gate? No. Judging from the flaked and blistered paint, the hinges would need oiling badly.

As he vaulted over the fence, he spotted a hint of bright blue in the bushes to his left. And wasn't his target's posture too tense? It was an ambush.

Too late to stop. He pushed off hard against the top rail of the fence, then rolled as he hit the grass. Someone hidden shouted "Take no prisoners!" Several softball-sized objects arced toward him from the bushes. He heard several popping noises as he regained his feet. His back was suddenly drenched. The woman turned and laughed at him.

He scanned the yard for weapons. The hose? Out of proportion to the water balloons. And the water line was probably cut off in the basement. Wouldn't he look idiotic waving a

dry hose! He sprinted toward the woman—the little hooligans
might not aim near their mother.

Aha! He altered course and dashed to the food-covered
redwood picnic table. He grabbed a beer from the ice chest,
then zigzagged about the yard while he shook up the can.
Two volleys missed him completely; the third burst nearby
and soaked one trouser leg. He locked eyes with McPherson,
who stood innocently by the barbecue grill, tongs in hand.
McPherson shrugged.

Curtis ran back toward Sophia McPherson, who suddenly
recognized his weapon. "No! You do and I'll . . ." The
threat never made it out. He popped the tab and sprayed her
from head to crotch with cold Budweiser. "Arrrrrgh!" She
held her hands up ineffectually to ward off the spray. When
the can stopped spraying, he unceremoniously upended it over
her head. The dregs gurgled out onto her straight black hair.

McPherson was convulsed with laughter when Curtis
stalked back to the ice chest. He glared at the two boys, aged
eight and ten, staring wide-eyed at their soggy and sputtering
mother. He held up a fresh can, ready for priming. "Surrender?" When they nodded mutely, he disarmed and took
a long swig. Beer in hand, he joined his partner by the grill.
"What was *that* about?"

"Some people prefer me to work in town."

"You told Sophia that I volunteered our help in Chicago?
Really smart, buddy." Sophia had gone inside, presumably
for dry clothes. Curtis peeled his own wet shirt away from
his back. "We need to talk later." He couldn't count on her
being gone long enough.

The boys came shyly forward. Johnny, the youngest, broke
the ice. "That was neat, Uncle Fred. Will you teach *me* to
shoot beer?" Scotty nodded in agreement. Curtis just grinned
and tousled the boys' hair. They had a father to teach them
the manly arts.

The warm breeze dried Curtis before Sophia rejoined them.
She had changed into a tight knit shirt that emphasized her,

ahem, fine points. "You done picking on ladies and children?" she demanded.

He bent over—she was barely five feet tall; Scotty would be patting her on the head soon—and gave her a hug. "What an unjust accusation. I never touched the children, and where's the lady?" He immobilized her arms before she could slug him, so she kicked him in the ankle.

McPherson cleared his throat. "When you're done with my wife, Freddie, we've got burgers screaming to be eaten." He began flipping patties onto a platter without waiting for a response. Curtis let go.

They moved the ice chest onto the patio and somehow rearranged the crowded table to make room for their plates. Sophia, as always, had overachieved. When Curtis thought he could eat no more, Sophia brought ice cream and two cakes—chocolate, and pineapple upside-down—from the kitchen. "When are you going to get married, Fred? It's not my job to fatten you up."

For a volunteer, she did excellent work. Curtis knew better than to answer her question—it would invariably lead to attempted matchmaking. "My cue. Brad, isn't it about time for the ball game?"

"No doubt. You—" McPherson looked at each boy in turn, "help your mother clean up." They muttered appropriately. He snagged two more beers from the ice chest as he and Curtis made their way to the family room. McPherson cranked the TV up loud and settled into his recliner. "So, what do we need to talk about?"

"You mad about Chicago?"

"No. I merely provided tactical advice out of a sense of familial solidarity."

"Then why'd you tell Sophia that I'd volunteered us?"

"I'd rather she fume at someone else." McPherson opened his beer and took a long swig. "Dammit, Fred! We shouldn't have closed the Keller and Hanson case. You caved too easily."

"You want me to buck the NSC?"

"You don't *know* that the NSC is behind them. Those two are obviously amateurs."

"You're right, I don't know their relation to the NSC. I do know that the warning to back off came from on high." Curtis answered McPherson's puzzled look. "I asked the chief a few innocuous questions. Wayne didn't get the request direct, and *his* boss didn't either. This came down from the Office of the Director." He studied his friend. "What concrete evidence have you got to justify challenging the Director's decision?" McPherson evaded his eyes. "Right—we've got zip."

They sat in uncomfortable silence for a time, both ignoring the blaring TV. "Brad?"

"What?"

"What if there's a way to work the case quietly? You prepared to go out on a limb?"

"Within reason."

"Okay, you distrustful asshole. *That's* why we're going to Chicago. We've checked out Keller pretty thoroughly. Let's find out what makes Hanson tick."

"How? Someone's stuck us with a racketeering investigation. Days of stakeouts and nights of report writing." Curtis hummed tunelessly until McPherson saw it. "Your chum Grimaldi is heading the investigation, right? I thought you were helping *him* out, but that's backward. He's helping *you* out. We'll be on our own."

"You didn't hear that from me."

"Fair enough, Freddie."

McPherson was all smiles now. It was time for another surprise. "C'mon." Curtis led the way to his car, parked around the corner in a failed attempt to surprise his hosts. "Get in."

"Gimme a break. Let me tell Sophia we're going out."

"We're not." Curtis flipped a switch on his dashboard. The instrument-cluster image on the screen flashed once, and was replaced by a map of central Ohio. A cursor blinked on the interstate bypass around Columbus.

"Whose car?"

"The elusive Dr. Hanson's. It seems he's returning to Chicago."

Drugging the departmental coffee was a rotten thing to do. Parker hadn't let that stop him.

He made properly sympathetic noises as one by one his staff stopped by his office. Gotta go home early, Bill. Sorry, Bill. Stomach bug, Bill. Oh well, he'd told them, something must be going around. A few of them did look green around the gills, but he suppressed a twinge of guilt. If the truth ever came out, they would thank him. He'd given them all alibis.

His staff. It came as a mild surprise that he'd begun to consider them that. Carlton's coronation meant that Asgard needed a new system administrator for its computers. By volunteering, Parker had inherited this mixed grill of program librarians, clerks, and technicians. A few were even likable enough.

Phase one required their incapacitation, likable or not. Tonight, with everyone's gratitude, he was covering as computer operator for Terry. The man's ten-cup-a-day habit had given him the idea; the jumpy coffeeholic had been among the first to leave, whining about lost overtime. More moderate coffee drinkers weren't affected as quickly. At some time during the morning, most of them had offered to take Terry's late shift; by midafternoon they were all begging off. Not coincidentally, Parker had sent Megan, the only tea drinker, to an out-of-town conference this week.

Losing his chaperones had been simple enough. Not much more to it than complaining about constipation that wouldn't respond to over-the-counter laxatives. The third doctor he'd visited had prescribed Urecholine.

He'd discovered acetyl choline, sold under the trade-name Urecholine, in less than an hour at his neighborhood library. The PDR—*Physician's Desk Reference*—was a wonderful tool. Acetyl choline is prescribed for lazy bowels or difficult urination. An overdose of the tasteless pharmaceutical causes nausea, vomiting, and diarrhea. The internist had suggested a quick-acting injection, but Parker had declined, pleading squeamishness. The young West Indian doctor had obligingly written out a prescription for Urecholine tablets.

Parker had made a point today of getting to work early. He cheerfully did his duty as a member of the departmental coffee club by brewing the first fifty-pot urn. The crushed tablets went from an envelope into the paper filter, and were immediately covered by ground coffee. With the perking finished before anyone else had arrived, he took the opportunity to empty the basket of soggy—and drugged—grounds. He was at work in his office, ignoring the tempting aroma, when the first of the day-shift operators arrived.

That was all preamble.

Night shift in a computer room is dull work, with the operator mostly killing time. But who knows, some dork working late to keep on schedule might ask him to mount a reel of tape. The high-speed line printer might need a new box of paper. On an exciting night, the operator would replace a printer ribbon. Parker grabbed some books and magazines from his desk, light reading for his vigil. He added a thick volume from inside his desk to the stack. The addition was a standard computer-science reference, one of many copies in the building.

He let himself into the computer room shortly before the first shift ended. "No offense, but you look ready to lose your lunch. Beat it before there's traffic to dodge in the parking lot." A sickly Norm Richards, with beads of sweat glistening on his bald head, nodded gratefully. Parker was leafing through a two-month-old *Datamation* when Richards left.

Glass walls enclosed the computer room, as required by age-old computer tradition. The custom stemmed from the once prohibitive cost of data processing—besides computing, the equipment had to impress the executives and awe the ignorant. Or vice versa. Whatever the reason, working here was like doing time in an automated goldfish bowl. Parker's plan alloted a few hours for the building to empty out. From time to time, he'd glance up from his reading. Traffic in the hall thinned, then disappeared. It was time.

This room was the heart of Asgard Aerospace, the hum and whir of its many disk drives Asgard's computerized pulse. Every product and service that Asgard offered depended on these computers. Most of the products contained software written on these computers. The few exceptions, all products small enough to run on personal computers, still had their source code stored on these big mainframes.

Noticing the tall rack of tape reels, Parker grimaced as his metaphor crumbled. Call this room the brain then. The comparison might be trite; it also fit perfectly. The computers were Asgard's brain and these silent magnetic tapes were its memory. True, even the most modest of computers had internal memory. That memory, however, was relatively small and limited to short-term use. The tapes were like a person's long-term memory. People who lost their long-term memory reverted to helpless infancy.

Corporations, too.

Most of the tapes on the rack represented completed programming projects. The rest of the tapes protected work in progress. Had someone accidentally screwed up his work today—for example, by carelessly erasing a file—an operator could have restored the information from one of last night's tapes.

The night operator, although seldom busy, played a critical role in this institutional memory. He was responsible for recording the backup tapes while contention for file access was predictably low. His first mandatory task took place in the fireproof basement vault. There, he exchanged last night's backup tapes from the comp center, called fathers, for day-older tapes, the grandfathers. Once in the vault, each father was promoted to grandfather. Task two took place back in the computer center, where he recorded tonight's daily backup tapes—new fathers—over the former grandfather copies. Some nights, but not tonight, the night operator also made weekly and monthly backup tapes for the vault. These extra copies offered some protection against the delayed discovery of screwups.

Administrivia for bureaucratic drones. He'd learned this procedural garbage just to gain a few unobserved minutes tonight. He'd follow the expected routine, of course, but only to avoid suspicion. No one walked by as he gazed out from his fishbowl. It was time.

Parker slid the fat reference work off the desk into his lap, blocking the book from the view of any passers-by. He flipped open the cover to reveal a compartment carved into the pages. Two baggie-clad homemade devices nestled in the cavity. He used a handkerchief to remove one of the devices. It was surprisingly heavy for its size. Its most prominent feature was a portable digital alarm-clock and calendar. Electrical tape bound the clock to a small battery and a tightly wound coil of wire. Something dark and solid-looking was visible through chinks in the hand-wound windings. The battery was very powerful for its size—the best that money could buy. He closed the book and restored it to the desk top.

Another peek through the glass walls. No one. He tossed his pen behind him toward the tape rack, then swiveled his chair and rolled after the pen. His body blocked the apparatus from sight. The rack's decorative kick plate had a two-inch-high opening for mopping; the device would not quite fit through it. Cursing, Parker tipped the rack backward by leaning against it with his shoulder. Tipping it provided the extra quarter inch of clearance that was needed. The baggie would protect his device from water if Maintenance swabbed under the rack; judging from the dust and crud that he'd just seen, the baggie was an unnecessary precaution.

With his back to the wall, Parker didn't know if he'd acquired an audience. He made a great show of searching the floor, finally picking up and pocketing his pen.

Half done. Time to retrieve the grandfather tapes from the vault. He rolled the pushcart from a rear corner and piled last night's tapes on it. The half-emptied reference work went

onto the cart's lower shelf. He stopped at the wall phone by
the door. Tap, tap, tap: it was wise to call Security before
opening the vault at night. Yes, sir. No problem, sir. Thanks
for notifying us, sir. Apparently *some* people still gave him
respect.

He whistled as the elevator descended to the basement.

The vault, of course, had opaque walls. Parker felt secure
once he'd pulled the massive door most of the way closed
behind him. Opening *this* baby took huffing and puffing; he'd
get plenty of warning if anyone wanted in. Bookcases overflowing with notebooks—at least a dozen styles each of loose-
leaf, spiral, and bound—hid most of the walls. He only
recognized the bound volumes: handwritten old laboratory
notes, potentially worth millions. Asgard kept them to substantiate its claims at any future patent-infringement trials.
He couldn't identify the other books, though they must be
important to merit storage here. A stack of foot-thick computer printouts filled the space between two bookcases.

A tape rack stood in shadow at the back of the vault. Parker
removed the second device from his hollowed-out book. He
again used a handkerchief to avoid leaving fingerprints and
again had to tilt the rack for clearance. The dusty rack left a
smudge on his jacket shoulder that his handkerchief would
not budge.

He stood each tape reel from the cart in a waiting slot on
the rack, then refilled the cart with an equal number of grandfather tapes. He checked each label carefully. Later, while
making the new backups, he would be equally exacting. You
never know—someone might need one of the tapes he'd be
making. No one should have cause to think twice about the
tape racks—for now.

Later, back in the comp center, the tape drives mostly
tended themselves while they recorded tonight's backups.
Parker's simple role consisted of mounting, redating, and
shelving the tape reels. He read while the tapes spun.

The rest of the shift passed uneventfully. His reading material was stacked and ready to go when his relief arrived.

Renata had slightly more color than the last time he'd seen her. Good, she was one of the heavier coffee drinkers. He tossed his last magazine onto the pile. "Feeling better?"

"Um."

Close enough. "Quiet night. Nothing happened, and the details are in the log book. If you have any questions, think twice before calling. If it still seems important, think again."

Wan smile. "I phoned Terry earlier. He thanks you."

Parker returned the books and magazines to his office, where he spent a few minutes sorting through the papers that littered the desk top. Then he removed a large expandable interoffice envelope from a drawer; it was filled with wads of old memos from which he had previously wiped any fingerprints. Nothing in it could be identified as his. He polished the hollowed-out book's glossy dust jacket with his handkerchief, then slid the book into the anonymous padding. The sealed envelope betrayed no hint of the tome it concealed.

An identical reference book went onto his shelf, for the sake of anyone who had noticed him holding one.

Parker's route to the lobby led past one of Asgard's burn boxes. Except for its white enamel paint and massive lock, it resembled any corner mailbox. Two Top-Secret-cleared employees unlocked the box each morning, substituted an empty canvas liner for the laden one, and locked *that*. The secret contents were promptly added to the heap in a locked storage room. When the room filled up, the bags were driven to a nearby hospital whose incinerator Asgard leased for occasional use. There, the discarded material was safely and anonymously reduced to ash.

Burn boxes provided safe disposal of Asgard's proprietary and sensitive documents—not to mention obliteration of its embarrassments. Mostly the box contained vetoed reorganization proposals, ungrammatical draft letters, months-old budget reports. Anything really valuable, such as classified material or next year's business plan, was the exception. Still, it was inadvisable to merely discard such papers, and not because industrial spies and foreign agents might steal the trash. A trade secret is only as good as its owner's protection of it. It was the height of bad form for your proprietary information to be seen blowing around a landfill.

Employees on pyro patrol were taught to incinerate sealed envelopes intact. While an instruction was not a guarantee, the burn box seemed a lesser risk than carrying the evidence past the guard in the lobby. Security never checked parcels on the way *in*; they spot-checked them on the way out. He couldn't leave the book in his office, either. If, by chance, one of his surprise packages were found too soon, there would surely be a building-wide search. It wouldn't do, if it came to that, for a hollowed-out book to turn up in his desk. If found at the incinerator, however, the book couldn't be traced to him.

Enough ruminating. He wiped the envelope with his handkerchief and dropped it into the burn box. Time for home and bed. Tomorrow would be a busy day.

Tomorrow he implemented phase two.

Cookie crumbs and coffee-cup rings littered the printout. The fat binder crunched as Dave Becker closed it. He'd spent days poring over this thing and had *nada* to show for it. Another day with similar success and he might earn decapitation scars: the powers-that-be expected answers.

Dave was comfortably middle aged, with thin hair and thick glasses to prove it, and had thought himself beyond the fire-fighting stage of his career. Crash projects were for young hotshots out to make names for themselves. When he was at that stage, he'd worked his tail off, too.

Not that much came of his exertions. He'd been a systems analyst in the sixties and early seventies for the Safeguard project. Top-Top Secret stuff. They'd all worked long hours then, trying to implement a working anti-ballistic-missile system. Long hours, and mostly in gross places. Field trials on Kwaj—the Kwajelein atoll—under the watchful eyes of Soviet "trawlers." Installation of the operational phased-array radar and battle-management computers in Nowhere, North

Dakota. It all worked reasonably well, until it was negotiated away. Written off. The 1972 ABM treaty permitted America and Russia one defensive site each. The Russkies placed one near Moscow; the gray-flannel brigades here mothballed our site. God forbid that we provoke the commies by protecting our ICBMs from them.

When the project wound down, Bell Labs placed its Safeguard expatriates into civilian research. Dave left Safeguard in '74—just as the OPEC oil embargo and the resulting rationing were crimping the economy. There were no big new projects; Dave and his friends were dispersed throughout the company. More often than not, the old-boy network in the telephone side of the company stuck the Safeguard grads into low-prestige assignments. Volleyball cronies got first crack at new projects, talent and experience be damned.

Dave went from hotshot systems analyst to toll-office maintenance programmer. That meant he got to learn and fix someone else's undocumented, bug-infested software. Not fix, bandage. Fixing it would have meant a rewrite. As technical challenges went, maintaining the old system ranked right up there with model railroading. He didn't bust his buns any more.

So *now* there's an emergency. Who'da thunk it. This tape suddenly arrives from an ancient toll office in West Virginia. Must be a bug in the fault-recovery software, Dave. One unit of a redundant pair failed and the system didn't automatically recover. Naughty, naughty. Fix it.

Hah. The clown who'd sent the tape probably had powered down the good processor for repair instead of its failed mate. Happened all the time. A single-failure system crash was just a story to cover himself. Too bad Dave couldn't prove it; the bozo had conveniently suppressed maintenance messages at the teletype.

Dave's boss hadn't bought his explanation, which left him wading repeatedly through the huge program. He'd studied the official reference copy of the software ad nauseam; maybe there was something unique to the West Virginia office. Its personnel might have messed up keying in some previously released correction. The manual entry procedure included checks and double checks to prevent such problems, but fools were ingenious when it came to defeating foolproof schemes. He should eliminate the faulty-correction theory—it at least postponed the inevitable finger-pointing contest with the operating company.

The comp center had printed the content of the tape for him over lunch. He plunked the new listing over the closed reference binder. Dave grabbed another handful of cheapo sandwich cookies from the bag in his desk. One went whole into his mouth. He flipped through the listing to the patch area—the part of the computer's memory dedicated to interim corrections.

Whereupon he almost choked. He'd expected a few short corrections and the rest of the area padded out with zeroes. Instead, the patch space was crammed. He grabbed a pencil and started decoding the numerical hodgepodge. After a few minutes, he shut his office door.

The extraneous code had nothing to do with a system crash. That didn't make it any the less interesting. Its purpose was obvious: monitoring the long-distance calls originating from the toll office. That was odd enough. What really threw him was that only calls to one Chicago-area subscriber were being monitored. Those calls were allowed through, but only *after* some totally nonstandard signaling. A warning signal?

What did it mean? Whose phone was it? Dave started to dial the mystery number, and then thought better of it. Why should only one telephone office have its software bugged? To coin a phrase. He looked up the office prefix: it was in Rolling Meadows. The rest of the number was 7000—obviously some company's main switchboard.

Dave had a sudden premonition. Northrop had a big office in Rolling Meadows, specializing in the development of electronic counter- and counter-countermeasures for fighter planes. He checked a suburban phone book. No, not Northrop.

Another defense contractor? Something nagged at his mind, another corporation in Rolling Meadows. That outfit whose deep-space probe was supposedly destroyed by aliens. What was their name? Something Viking and mythological. They'd gotten a big defense contract shortly before the word came out about *Prospector*'s destruction. Very hush-hush.

He shot over to the next office. "Help me out."

His neighbor kept studying his terminal. "Ever the social butterfly. Why I'm fine, thanks. Yes, Ginny's feeling better."

"Um . . . Hi, Neal. How are you?"

Neal looked up. "Hello, David. Very thoughtful of you to ask. To what do I owe the pleasure of this visit?"

A lapse in judgment. "Did you ever have something on the tip of your tongue? I've been trying to remember the name of the outfit that made the *Prospector* probe. If I don't remember it, it'll keep me up all night. Do you remember?"

"Asgard something something. Ask me a hard one."

Asgard Aerospace Corporation. *That* was it. "Sorry, Neal. No hard ones today." None that he cared to discuss, anyway. Dave scurried back to his office.

"You're welcome," chided Neal's voice from behind him. Behind a closed door Dave looked up Asgard's phone listing. *Eureka*.

Hard ones. Who was monitoring calls to Asgard? Why? Why in West Virginia? And, hardest of all—what should he do about it? All of his questions had one answer: I don't know.

Dave leaned back in his chair to ponder the situation. He remembered the frustration of watching the Russian "trawlers" off Kwaj. It had been especially galling once he'd realized that *they* used what they learned from their eavesdropping—and his own side wouldn't even use what they were giving away.

Maybe this time it would be different. He tossed the West Virginia listing and his notes into his briefcase. His boss wasn't around, so he stuck a note to her phone. "Feeling crummy. Going to the doctor. Dave."

Asgard would have a security officer. He would know what to do.

· CHAPTER 20 ·

Parker's staff had developed the set of innocuous programs to his precisely crafted specifications. Taking his time, he had painstakingly verified each program's conformation to spec. Each program performed a single, clearly beneficial function.

Only he and Robby knew what they would do when combined.

He had himself written the coordination module that united these software fragments for their aggregate purpose. Sitting at his workstation, linking the contributed software with his own code, he wore an enigmatic grin.

As soon as he was finished, he would initiate phase two.

"Before we begin, let me assure you that my office is swept daily for bugs. Personally. It's clean."

General Alan Hadley, commander of the Air Force Space Division, scrutinized his anxious and reluctant host: Asgard's Director of Security. George Biesterfield blotted his creased forehead with a grossly inadequate tissue. Large yellow sweat stains discolored both armpits of his shirt. His gaze darted nervously around the small cluttered office, lighting occasionally on Chuck Nichols, his boss, and on Hadley. The wiry security chief clearly realized that he was in deep trouble. Biesterfield's immediate problem was deciding which half of his audience, if either, he should trust.

Nichols exploded, "Bugs! You think Asgard is bugged!

What is this all about, George? Since you have obviously
had a security breach, why should the general trust your
assurances?'' By announcing Biesterfield's expendability, Nichols forfeited any claim on the man's loyalty.

Nichols's dramatics were excessive. Fact: Asgard's biggest
customer was the Space Division. Fact: Biesterfield had notified Hadley's aide of a *massive* security breach, the kind of
leak that often disqualified a company from future bidding
on defense work. Conclusion: the trembling guard chief *must*
have briefed Nichols first. Nichols's innocent act today was
simply not as well rehearsed as the tour de force in the NASA
auditorium. Perhaps Nichols required the not-so-dearly departed Larry Cantin as his sounding board. Odd that that
slippery scum-bucket had been eased out—not long ago,
Hadley would have given good odds that Cantin would succeed this sniveler as Asgard's president.

Okay, Biesterfield had had enough time to reflect on his
employer's tactics. ''The major's word is good enough for
me.''

The nervous company cop smiled reflexively at Hadley's
kindness and the courtesy mention of his old rank. If Hadley
got mad enough, though, Biesterfield would be lucky to find
security work as a night watchman in Peoria. The worst
Nichols could do was fire him. The risks thought through,
Biesterfield swiveled to face the general squarely.

Hadley nodded encouragingly. ''Explain, Major.''

''Sir.'' Biesterfield's voice was steady, his resolve
strengthened by his decision. ''Asgard *is* being bugged, but
not by anything so crude as microphones. We're apparently
being monitored on a national scale.''

''National scale!? Do you know how . . .''

Nichols had scarcely started when Hadley intervened. A
leader who sacrificed his subordinates was beneath contempt.
''Facts first, Major. Hold the conclusions.''

''Yes, sir. I had a walk-in yesterday, a programmer from
Bell Labs. He brought me a surprise.'' Biesterfield opened
a thick printout in front of General Hadley, who glanced at

a circled entry. "He was troubleshooting a problem at a long-distance phone center and stumbled across this unrelated, undocumented code."

"That's Asgard's number?"

"Exactly, sir."

"What does this program do?"

Biesterfield shrugged. "I'll have to repeat what I was told, sir. I'm not a programmer."

Biesterfield's presentation confirmed his self-appraisal, but nonetheless successfully communicated the essentials. A freak equipment failure at a phone-company facility had led to the discovery of some unsuspected programming. This unauthorized software monitored incoming calls to Asgard and warned someone there of the calls' imminent arrival. There was no telling who received the warnings, or why. The obvious implication of the discovery was that Asgard's phone system itself had been altered to receive and act upon the warnings.

Nichols surprised him by asking a semi-intelligent question. "If Asgard's phones are monitored, why not just look *here* at the incoming calls? Why monitor the toll switches?"

Hadley answered to spare Biesterfield from having to state the obvious to his boss. "Recognizing the calls at the originating end gives whoever is listening more time to react. *Something* happens in parallel with a call's setup." He turned back to the apprehensive security man. "Are you sure that this monitoring software was placed into all toll offices?"

Biesterfield grabbed another tissue before responding. "The monitoring code doesn't appear in the standard version of the program; it was inserted into a locally controlled corrections area. We can't tell how widespread the monitoring is without surveying all long-distance centers." Of course, a survey would alert whoever was behind the surveillance that they had been detected.

Hadley closed his eyes to concentrate. "Then you merely infer that the monitoring is national in scale."

"Well . . . yes, sir. The alternative is that only calls from

the panhandle of West Virginia are being monitored. I can't
believe that.''

Hadley *could*: that's where Hanson and Keller had holed
up. The FBI kept him fully informed of its investigation. He
started a mental checklist. Why would Hanson still be calling
Asgard? Who would tap Hanson's calls? And most curious
of all: why bug these calls in such a roundabout way?

''General?''

He grunted noncommittally at the ex-major while recalling
the fantastic letter in which Hanson had claimed that the aliens
were an illusion perpetrated by sleight-of-electron. He'd
thought at the time that the intense civilian had cracked under
the strain; the subsequent trap in Chicago had been intended
only to prevent a leak. The failed ambush had undoubtedly
fueled Hanson's paranoia and sent him straight to that now-
dead reporter.

Whoever had so circuitously bugged Hanson in West Virginia expected him to call Asgard. Of what use were a few
seconds of warning for those calls? Did this strange monitoring relate to Hanson's odd beliefs? Then it hit him.

Hadley opened his eyes and stood. ''My compliments,
Major. I'll expect your full written report in Colorado Springs
as soon as possible. Take no further action until I contact
you.'' Even Nichols was sentient enough to heed so blatant
an endorsement. Gratitude oozed from the former officer.
Hadley would have a source in Asgard if ever he needed it.

He had commandeered an eager lieutenant that morning as
his driver. The ruddy-faced, crew-cut young officer now expertly negotiated the heavy traffic back to O'Hare International. Hadley tried to ignore the vehicular chaos beyond the
glass. Soon enough he would be back in his trainer, high
above this repressive, smog-infested tangle. The opportunity
to fly was one of his few reasons for attending out-of-town
meetings.

He did his best thinking while flying, and right now he
needed to do some very clear thinking. A flash of intuition
had struck him back there in the nervous ex-major's depress-

ing little office. Combat flying in 'Nam had taught him to trust his intuition. Thinking could take too long—you'd be dead by the time you *reasoned* the correct response to a sky full of seat-of-the-pants MiG jockeys. Flying a desk, he didn't often get the exhilaration of following his instincts.

With or without proof, his intuition *felt* right. Hanson had appeared to be suffering delusions of persecution. Well, appearances can be deceiving. The bizarre bugging fully justified Hanson's convictions . . . and a sane and truly persecuted Hanson meant a persecutor. Who?

Hadley ignored the spongy shocks of the prematurely aged motor-pool car as he fought to harness his intuition. *Somehow*, the pieces fit. Hanson's nemesis wanted a few seconds of warning before fielding Hanson's calls. Question: why would such a brief warning be useful? Answer: it wouldn't be useful to anyone who reasonably expected a call in the first place. Question: why use such an elaborate monitoring scheme, one that—compared to just monitoring within Asgard—grossly raised the probability of discovery? Answer: the elaborate scheme was somehow useful enough to justify the increased risk. Question: how do I reconcile my last two answers?

Then the gears meshed: he'd reconstructed with logic what his intuition had flashed to him in Biesterfield's office. Answer: some*one* does not want a warning; some*thing* does. The few seconds of warning would be very meaningful within a computer. He suspected, but couldn't support, that the observers used their head start to configure a voice synthesis and response unit.

For years, the National Security Agency had captured thousands of international telephone calls daily. Everyone in the business assumed from the forest of antennas atop their embassies that the Russians routinely did the same with domestic calls. No physical wiretapping involved—just completely undetectable interception of the phone companies' microwave transmissions. The NSA supercomputers ferreted out all conversations that contained any relevant voices or phrases.

With the Space Division's resources, it would be no great trick to do the same with Asgard's incoming calls. In his office, Hadley had tapes of Hanson addressing NASA last winter. They would be more than adequate for his purposes. There were some legal fine points. to be sure, but he knew people who could be trusted to overlook them.

It was time to learn just how Hanson got *its* attention.

The flung report slapped Carlton's desk blotter like a dead mackerel. Loose notes and letters scattered from the gust it raised. As he looked up for the source of the attack, he recognized the spidery script on the cover of the document as his own.

A livid Bill Parker preempted his attempt to speak. "How *dare* you write such scurrilous comments! That was a completely professional job. Robby predicted that you'd reject it."

Carlton picked up the inch-thick document. Parker's department had submitted it last week—a joint recommendation on modernization and upgrading of the comp center. The department proposed installing a higher-speed local-area network for the interconnection of Asgard's many computers. It *was* good work, full of technical detail and simulation-derived predictions of improved system performance. The material had only one flaw: the omission he'd annotated on the cover.

His handwritten note requested that the technical merits of their case be augmented with a financial justification for the thoroughly untechnical Nichols. In particular, he'd suggested using a return-on-investment calculation for the new architecture. Technical types—himself included—hated to do engineering economics studies, but they were routine. Why the fuss? Had he written something inflammatory inside the document? He couldn't remember doing so. What was *wrong* with Parker? "But, Bill . . ."

"But shove it where the sun doesn't shine!"

"Bill, dammit"—and, dammit, Carlton hated to lose his

temper—"I will *not* take abuse from my staff. Leave *now* and stay away until you can speak calmly. If you stay, one of us will say something irrevocable."

Parker ripped the report from Carlton's hand and hurled it at the wastebasket, knocking it over and dumping its contents. He ripped off his ID badge and flung it into the spilled trash. "Here's something irrevocable. Take this job and shove it irrevocably up your ass." He strode briskly from the office, leaving behind an utterly speechless Carlton Moy.

And who the hell was Robby?

A robe-and-pajama-clad Nichols slouched in his easy chair, feet resting on the battered ottoman. His abandoned slippers lay, one atop the other, behind the closed door. A regrettably out-of-season brick fireplace occupied most of one wall; shelves full of impressive, if unread, books lined the rest. Two bookless niches on an eye-level shelf showcased his framed degrees. The room's most recent addition was the freestanding leather globe on its walnut base. The northern hemisphere could be opened to reveal, as it did at this moment, a set of glasses and a selection of fine liquors. A tiny refrigerator concealed behind a facade of fake books provided the ice cubes and mixers.

Although his den was adjacent to the front foyer, Nichols ignored the insistent doorbell. His family would just think that he hadn't heard the chimes over the TV. The persistent caller was undoubtedly some hulking bull ape pursuing either or both of his college-student daughters. Let one of them get the door.

"Daddy?" Shelley's voice and knock were timid. "Daddy, two men are here to see you."

"I'm busy, hon. Take a message."

"I'm sorry to bother you at home, Mr. Nichols, but this is important." He couldn't place the deep, self-assured voice.

"Daddy!?"

Nichols reluctantly opened the den door. His visitors were tall and athletic-looking men in off-the-rack suits. With their white shirts and regimental striped ties, they looked like marginally successful IBM salesmen. Gold glinted as the closer man flipped open the wallet in his hand. "Curtis, FBI. My partner is McPherson. We'd like to ask you a few questions."

"Okay, Shelley, I'll speak with these gentlemen." His timorous child quickly retreated toward the back of the house. He waved the agents into the den. He found the remote control and turned off the set.

Nichols freshened his drink while he got his emotions under control. Was it really necessary to pester him at home? "Can I get you anything?" Curtis immediately shook his head; McPherson hesitated before following suit. Great—two boy scouts. The executive took a long swig from his own glass. Might as well get on with it. "Hadley didn't waste any time sending you."

The pair exchanged a quick glance, seemingly uncertain where to begin. Curtis found his tongue first. "We try to be efficient."

McPherson took a microcassette recorder from his pocket. "Okay if we tape this?" He started the recorder without awaiting an answer.

"Why bother? Biesterfield and I explained everything to the general this afternoon."

Curtis picked up a wooden-soldier nutcracker from the massive oak mantel and worked its jaw. "Cute. Like in the ballet." He set it back down two inches too far to the right. "We'd rather hear everything firsthand. Begin at the beginning and pretend the general hasn't told us anything."

So Nichols explained, pacing about the room. He occasionally stopped at the globe for refills; the agents loosened up enough to accept soft drinks. His presentation was more polished and coherent than Biesterfield's frightened rendition of that afternoon. His audience paid close attention to every word, interrupting frequently with questions. Curtis augmented his partner's recorder with scribbled comments in a dog-eared pocket notepad.

The full account took a good hour to complete. These men

were *thorough*; they'd done their homework and knew about
Asgard's last embarrassment: the Hanson affair. They never
directly said so, but their questions showed they considered
it possible that the scientist was involved. Talk about grasping
at straws!

Nichols walked them to their car, smiling inwardly at his
adept handling of the affair. Becky and the girls would want
an explanation for this visit. Sorry, ladies—it's classified.
Be mysterious—they'd eat it up. Then he'd excuse himself
to watch more TV and have another drink. Hopefully, one
or the other would stop him from worrying excessively about
a curious coincidence.

Why did everyone rush off after learning that the bugged
toll office was in West Virginia?

Curtis drove as quickly as he dared along the curving suburban streets. "Hanson again! Find his car." He headed for
the expressway while McPherson called the map up onto the
dashboard display. Their tires squealed as they rounded a
corner onto a major thoroughfare.

"We barely beat them to Chicago. They're east of Gary
on the Indiana Toll Road. Take I-294—um, that's the Tri-
State—south to I-80. We'll intercept them in Gary."

"Terrific. Where's the Tri-State?"

McPherson brought up a detailed map of the northwest
suburbs and navigated them from Inverness Estates, where
Asgard's president lived, to I-90, and from there to the south-
bound Tri-State. He returned the display to its tracking mode.
The flashing cursor representing Hanson's Honda had inched
closer to their rendezvous in Gary.

The Tri-State finally ended by merging into the eastbound
I-80. The display showed the agents to be on a collision course
with Hanson, who was westbound on the same road. Two
flashing cursors crawled toward each other—and overlapped.
"Got 'em," said Curtis. "Now let's find the next exit and
turn around. I want to follow him home."

By the time the agent executed this maneuver, the dots had

diverged. Curtis leaned harder on the accelerator; the dots again began to converge. The cars were less than two miles apart. "Brad, keep your eyes peeled."

The dots merged at last. Curtis swept his eyes across four lanes of traffic, cursing every delivery van and tractor trailer that obstructed his view. No sign of the old blue Accord. "Set that stupid map display for finer resolution! Hanson's a native. I don't want to lose him when he gets off the expressway to take some shortcut."

The center of the map expanded. "No change, pal. He's on this road. If you get any closer, you'll have to marry him."

"Shut up and watch."

They continued westward, looking about unsuccessfully. McPherson poked his arm. "Look at the display. He's getting off at the oasis."

Curtis exited at the next ramp. The oasis consisted of a restaurant, a busy service station, and a rest area. He hesitated at the edge of the lot and scanned the cars queued up for the gas pumps. No blue Accord. He checked the display again. "They've stopped. Must have gone in to eat."

He opened the glove compartment and pulled out a short-range but extremely sensitive radio detector. He flicked it on; it began beeping insistently. They were *close*. No telling how they kept missing Hanson's car, but they'd certainly find it with this. "I'm going out to find them. Slide over in case they pull out first. If that happens, follow. I'll take a cab and wait at the hotel."

Curtis stood beside the car and pivoted slowly. The beeps sped up as he moved, then slowed down again. The agent turned back until the beeps resumed their maximum rate. He strode in the indicated direction, the beeps growing louder as he walked. Why didn't he see the car? Finally, the detector switched from beeping to a continuous ear-grating whine. He was within *ten feet* of the bug. No Honda.

He finally noticed the trailer next to which he stood. Allied Van Lines. Curtis walked behind it; it had West Virginia plates. He now knew where the car, or at least the bug, was. It was in the van.

Where were Hanson and Keller?

The droning twin engines made conversation almost impossible in the small private plane, but they assured privacy from the pilot behind the door, in the tiny cockpit. Hanson leaned over to shout into Sally's ear. "Still mad?"

"I was never mad. I *am* confused."

Doubtful on both counts, but he let it pass. "You think I'm being paranoid."

She took too long to phrase her response. Whatever words she selected, the pause meant . . . yes. "Curtis said we were free to go. You have a million dollars. Why are you so worried?"

"You mean, why don't I think it all ends so easily? Why do I think your agent friends would bug my car?" Her nostrils flared slightly at his characterization of Curtis and Mc-Pherson. Careful, Bob. "Renée agrees."

She turned to him, looking surprised. "You've spoken with Renée? I've called Asgard a few times and only gotten the switchboard."

"I didn't get through, either. Renée must think that the hospital phones are bugged."

Sally stared out the window into the overcast, starless sky. After a while, she took his hand. Hers was cold. "I see."

They quietly held hands, lost in thoughts as dark as the night. The small plane bucked a few times as they passed through a pocket of turbulence. Sally finally broke the spell. "Penny for your thoughts."

"Don't need it. I'm wealthy, remember." She started at the bitterness in his voice. He continued, "I feel guilty as sin. Al Stuart is dead. People have lost billions in the market crash. *I* have a million bucks."

She dropped his hand as if it were leprous. "You feel guilty? Are you nuts?"

Why did their conversations all become reviews of his mental health? He shrugged.

"Mister, you listen to me. Weren't your contributions to Asgard worth far more than a million?" She ignored his stoic silence. "Damned right they were, many times over. And I won't hear any nonsense about what 'the team' contributed. *Prospector* was *your* idea. *You* built the team. Asgard owes you at least that much money as severance, whether or not they ever realize it.

"Besides, you need that money. Got any hot job prospects? Have you forgotten the letter you sent to Space Division? Hadley and company must think you went round the bend. Except for Renée, we're the only ones who know that the aliens were fabricated. Even forgetting your promise to her, are you prepared to go public with the fact of her existence? Presuming for the moment that anyone would believe it."

"Nope. I'm still too bruised to face her wrath."

She jabbed him in the shoulder. It was one of the few spots that the rogue agent hadn't battered, but her blow still hurt. Sally needed some meat on her knuckles. "You are *so* obstinate. Are you listening to a thing that I'm saying? Aren't I making sense?"

He rubbed his shoulder. "Of course you make sense. You always make sense. We were discussing how I felt."

"How you felt." She paused, then leaned over and kissed Hanson long and hard. "You've changed, you know." She put a finger to his lips to forestall any automatic retort. Too bad, he had a good one. "You've opened up. There's a decent, caring person beneath all of the bandages. I happen to love him.

"Is that marriage proposal still open?"

He pulled her head back down and returned her lingering kiss of a moment earlier. Judging from her reaction, it was the right answer. They ventured a few sequels. He buried his face in the fresh-smelling flow of her hair. "I'm glad you brought up that subject."

"Um?"

"I've already asked Carlton to be my best man. He'd be really pissed off if you jilted me."

This time she *really* punched him with feeling.

The apprehensive two-man crew readily confirmed Curtis's assertion that the Allied Van Lines trailer held a blue Honda Accord. The agent had occasionally received such cooperation from a teamster. It meant that the driver didn't want his trailer searched. Coming from West Virginia, Curtis predicted a load of cigarettes curiously lacking in revenue stamps.

Penny-ante stuff, let it go. Neither Allied employee demurred when he asked to see the bill of lading for the trans-shipped car. The originating agent was—surprise—based in Weirton. He scribbled the name, address, and phone number in his notepad. The two smugglers scampered back into their tractor cab as he walked away.

Curtis rejoined his partner in their car. "Head for the airport. It's back to West Virginia for us."

· CHAPTER 21 ·

Nordic Valley was the newest Masthope Ski Area resort. While its runs were unexceptional by East Coast standards, the slopes were always exquisitely groomed; man-made snow was added nightly. Six lifts and two tow ropes kept waiting to a minimum. The sprawling main lodge featured a three-star continental restaurant, a professional theater, four cinemas, and a romantic après-ski lounge with a fabulous selection of exotic liquors. All accommodations were deluxe six-room, three-bedroom "cabins," each boasting a full kitchen, a sauna, and a massive stone fireplace in the living room. In season, the exclusive resort was booked months in advance.

Hanson knew of its skiing aspects only from hearsay. What he did know about the place resulted from an October visit, two years previously, for an annual Asgard strategic-planning meeting. Nordic Valley's owners had had the foresight to consider the nonsnow months. Spring through fall, the resort served as an exclusive conference center for corporate executives. For this purpose, the resort provided state-of-the-art communications functions. The lodge and every cabin were wired for simultaneous voice and two-way video conferencing, and had a two-way high-speed data-transmission capability. Each cabin also offered a workstation that could tap into the superb communications system.

Privacy made Nordic Valley an appropriate spot to get to know Renée. The high-resolution graphics workstation and first-rate telecommunications made it ideal: Renée surprised both Hanson and Sally by ''showing'' herself to them on the screen.

Her artistry was astonishing. Renée assumed a middle-aged professorial persona. The illusion was exquisitely detailed, down to her conservatively cut, brown tweed pantsuit worn over a cream-colored blouse with a self-fabric bow at the collar. Her right lapel sported a gold, pearl-headed stick pin. She wore sensible shoes. She gathered her graying chestnut hair into a severe bun, from which straggled a few unruly wisps, and viewed the world through unflattering horn-rimmed bifocals. She had teeth that an orthodontist could love. Her matronly girth reminded Sally of a favorite maiden aunt. Sally checked for a wedding band—there was none.

They might easily have mistaken the animation for film footage except for Renée's wooden delivery. No, wooden wasn't quite right—it implied immobility. Renée *tried* to show expression with her face, *tried* to use the proper inflections. But for all of her undeniable brilliance, Renée's simulated persona didn't quite capture the subtle human interplay of voice and facial muscles. The net effect was some-what robotic.

"What's it like to exist inside a computer?" Sally finally risked the question that Hanson had been afraid to ask.

"That's hard to describe," Renée countered. "What's it like to exist inside gray matter?"

"Touché. No more metaphysical questions." Sally grinned. "Okay, then, explain your present appearance."

Renée revealed that she "watched" movies and TV regularly—her present projection was mostly a distaff Mr. Chips. Besides capturing the current network feed from satellite broadcasts, she sampled the thousands of hours of old black-and-white classics that were on-line for computer-assisted colorization. Right now, she was unsuccessfully trying to comprehend the Marx Brothers and *Mr. Ed*. "I'm trying very hard to understand people. Without much success yet, I'm afraid. On the surface, you're very illogical."

Off-line, Hanson and Sally marveled at the computational immensity of comprehending this material. It was difficult enough programming computers to understand serious conversations and to analyze real-world still pictures.

At times they made great progress. Renée had purloined the data analysis programs for the Earth Observing System, part of NASA's Mission to Planet Earth. (Hanson jotted down a note to himself to discuss ethics with Renée sometime.) She had modified this software to process *Prospector*'s surveillance data of Jupiter. Her results completely vaporized every semireputable theory about the formation of the solar system. When Sally complimented Renée on her feat, she curtsied. The net effect was somewhere between a badly operated marionette and a fourth grader. Bob hid a smile behind his hand.

It was impossible not to like her.

The three of them sometimes just talked. Hanson enjoyed these conversations the most, though they were not always comfortable at the time.

"Tonight's news confuses me." Renée sounded concerned. Whether from her continuing study of old movies, or by watching their reactions to her over the video conferencing equipment, she had achieved more natural speech. Tone, inflection, emotional overlay—all were usually right on the mark. Inappropriate facial expressions and a persistent nongrasp of idiom still tended to betray her unique nature.

Sally looked up from her dinner. "What news? We weren't watching."

"I'm always watching. I meant the border war in central Africa. Nothing but scrub grass grows in the contested area, and not enough of that to support more than a few nomads. Both sides have expended far more money on munitions than the region could earn the victor in two decades. The military casualties already exceed the indifferent populace over which they fight."

Hanson set down his fork. "Could they be fighting over mineral rights?"

"I've surveyed the territory over which both countries are fighting, both by satellite observation and literature search. I found no evidence of minerals in commercial concentrations."

"Perhaps the leaders of one or both sides need the war for internal political advantage. There are precedents for that." Sally Keller, world-famous political scientist.

Renée tugged at an earlobe, far too enthusiastically for the gesture to denote thoughtfulness. Was this her way of mimicking Bob's sideburn-twirling habit? "You posit that the leaders operate from self-interest. This I can accept. For the leaders' assessment to be correct, however, they must depend upon their populations continuing to operate against *their* own self-interest. No?"

"Yes." Sally agreed reluctantly.

"Are leaders a select subset of humanity, able to think logically when all about them do not?"

Hanson squirmed in his seat, feeling like a bug under a microscope. "We don't believe that in this country."

"Let's discuss that. It seems to me that the framers of the Constitution make inconsistent assumptions about human motivations. I've been studying *The Federalist Papers*. If you're not busy, I'd like your help in clarifying some points. I suggest that we start by contrasting the viewpoints of Madison and Hamilton."

"Sure, Renée." Hanson sighed and got up to brew more coffee.

The nearly continuous dialogue between Hanson, Keller, and Renée wended its circuitous way between eastern Pennsylvania and suburban Chicago. For the first few thousand feet, their words and images traveled by dedicated cable to Nordic Valley's lodge. All communications from the lodge and the few occupied cabins were merged into a single data stream, then transmitted skyward by the resort's rooftop dish antenna. A Western Union satellite, 23,000 miles above them in geosynchronous orbit, captured the signal, separated out the individual conversations, and retransmitted each component to the appropriate earth station somewhere in North America.

A lonely earth station in a northeastern Illinois cornfield handled their call. The station was unmanned and ultra-reliable—it made sense to locate it where land was relatively cheap. From there, their call was beamed by microwaves to the radio tower that stood near the limit of the station's line of sight, on the roof of an Illinois Bell switching center. Fiber-optic cable carried their debate the remaining few miles to Asgard's office building.

An unlabeled Ford van sat in a back corner of the suburban shopping-mall parking lot, racks of electronic paraphernalia cramming its cargo compartment. It was drenched in invisible and harmless microwave leakage from the Illinois Bell facility. Behind its one-way mirrored windows, Hadley perched on the edge of his uncomfortable seat. Like the man he had just joined, he did not wear a uniform. "Sorry it took so long to get your message."

His weary black associate, Captain Rufus Johnson, wordlessly plugged in and proffered a spare headset. Slipping it on, the general recognized Hanson's voice immediately; Keller's took him a minute. He hadn't a clue who Renée was. "That's them."

"They're also exchanging two-way video. Wanna see?" Ruf assumed that the answer would be yes; he stretched across the van while still speaking and turned on a small color monitor.

Hadley studied the screen. Dr. Hanson and Mrs. Keller, all right, splitting hairs with someone pedantic about an abstruse point of astrophysics. The remains of their dinner sat on the table in front of them. Murky woods were barely visible through the window behind them.

"Show me the video that they're receiving."

"You've got it, sir. Sorry I only had room for one display." The snug forest hideaway was instantly replaced by a nondescript backdrop. A little old lady, presumably Renée, appeared, looking for all the world like Hadley's high-school algebra teacher.

"It's all like this?"

"What I've seen, sir." The tall, gangling elint—electronic intelligence—officer was clearly skeptical of the whole undertaking. Fair enough, Hadley hadn't explained much to him. "I've listened more than I've looked. And when I look, sir, I really prefer the younger woman."

The three civilians prattled on. Over the last few minutes, Hanson had grown audibly restless. The general could have hugged him when he interrupted another of Renée's erudite monologues. "Can we talk about something else for a while?"

"Shall we review the latest Jupiter data?" Without warning, the screen flashed to velvet black, sprinkled with diamondlike stars. An inset window displayed a 3-D graph of —Hadley squinted to read the axis labels—radiation distributions around Jupiter.

"How'd she do that?" Johnson's voice conveyed only professional respect.

Hadley was not about to explain. He'd seen what he'd come to see. "Captain, am I right that Renée's end comes from Asgard?"

"It seems that way, sir."

"How about the other two?"

"I haven't traced them yet."

"Do it. ASAP. I'll get you anything you need."

Cronus—identified by some Greeks with *chronos*, time—was the son of Uranus and Gaea. After a short reign as monarch of the universe, a job wrested from his father, he was overthrown in turn by his own son, Zeus. Cronus fled from the Olympians to Italy, where he ruled over men during the fabled Golden Age. The Romans knew this Titan as Saturn, and annually celebrated the Saturnalia in his honor. The modern chronometer is named in homage of this once all-powerful deity.

Hundreds of other present-day remembrances of Cronus lay dormant inside Asgard's computers. Each instance of the CRON command patiently awaited the appointed moment, not for the Saturnalia, but for initiation of some previously ordained task. CRON provided menial services, like the slaves of the classical age from which stemmed its name. Most CRONs printed, displayed, or mailed personal reminders. The dry cleaner closes at 5:00. Group pizza lunch Thursday. Your anniversary is the twelfth—don't forget it again, you cretin.

Many another CRON started up a computation-intensive program in the evenings, once the demand for system resources had abated, long after its author had gone home. A faithful servant, it would even remember—and obey—tasks scheduled by a former employee . . . at least if that former employee had used the system-administrator log on . . .

Parker stood expectantly in his living room, whiskey and soda in hand, hearing the grandfather clock mark the passage of seconds. He was too keyed up to sit. Night was falling, but he did not turn on any lights. An unpleasant smile disfigured his face as the moment approached. He drained his glass while the heirloom clock chimed the appointed hour.

As he drank, several CRONs fired within each of Asgard's main computers. Programs began to execute. Parker called them tapeworm programs.

The experts reconvened to evaluate their situation. They deferred, as usual, to the psychologist. That was as it should be, he reflected: he had extricated them from terrible danger. His summary of the situation demonstrated that clearly. The best policy for now was keeping Hanson and Keller happy and prosperous.

The programming expert predictably challenged him. "I still say we should kill them. Humans cannot be trusted."

"These two can. Analysis of their interactions with Renée establishes the current high level of their trust. They treat her most respectfully."

The organic chemist interrupted. "And remember the documentation they left behind. Hanson threatened that it will be made public if they lose touch with its keepers." Most of the attending experts signaled their assent.

His opponent persisted. "I have penetrated the office computer of every lawyer within two hundred miles of their apparent path. I have not found any correlating records of new accounts. Neither have I found any evidence of them telephoning lawyers to prevent the release of the documents. I'm almost certain that Hanson and Keller are bluffing."

"Almost is not good enough." Besides, not every country lawyer *had* an office computer, and not everyone who did necessarily connected it to outside lines.

The sociologist preempted the programmer's inevitable retort. "Enough of this. I have extensively audited our esteemed colleague's Renée simulation. By comparing it to film and TV characterizations, I have proven to myself that Renée can only be accepted as nonthreatening."

"What about Stuart's death?"

"A youthful indiscretion. Our friends have watched Renée mature and become thoughtful. They are certainly convinced by now that she is no longer capable of violence."

The psychologist sent a private message of appreciation to the sociologist. He addressed the group once more before adjourning the meeting. "The other method remains if we ever have reason to doubt them."

Time passed rapidly in the comfortable cabin. Hanson and Sally spent their days and most of their evenings locked in earnest conversation with Renée. The *Prospector* mission, of course, came up time and again, but Renée's curiosity could not be channeled. She diverted them to politics, religion, literature, cinematic conventions, ethics. Hanson had not had such fun since late-night freshman bull sessions. Or maybe not ever: Renée was a lot quicker and more perceptive than anyone in the dorm.

They had one infallible way to mark the passage of time: the consumption of groceries. Unless prompt action was taken, breakfast tomorrow would be ginger snaps and catsup. Lunch would be leftovers from breakfast. Hanson volunteered to run out for food.

"That's all right. Renée and I will talk girl talk."

Nordic Valley's lodge didn't sell many groceries—that would have meant competition for the expensive restaurant. The nearest store was a mile away. Add twenty minutes of shopping time to the walk, and he'd have plenty of time to rest his tired jaw.

He was unpacking the bag and gathering the frozen food when Sally called him out from the kitchen. Her face was ashen. "There's something you'd better hear."

"What gives, Renée?"

"Sally made a request of me while you were out. She said that you were too proud to ask for yourself." Renée picked up an imaginary bent paper clip (do simulations fidget?) and twisted it in two. "She asked me how you should invest your money."

"She was right. I *wouldn't* have asked you, though my reasons have nothing to do with pride. I don't want you digging through proprietary financial records." He still didn't get it. "So Sally asked you. I sincerely doubt that sympathetic guilt is your problem. Why the long face?"

Sally towed him to the sofa. "Sit down, Bob. You aren't going to like this."

He stayed standing. "You aren't going to like cleaning up the melted mess on the kitchen counter."

"Shut *up* and listen." He stared at her in amazement. He sat. "Tell him, Renée," Sally said.

Renée was seated, too. She made a fidgeting noise that more closely resembled gargling than throat clearing. "I did access private files to answer Sally's question. Records of pensions and mutual funds mostly, plus the brokerage accounts of a few very wealthy investors. There are some major selling programs planned.

"You know, of course, how the stock and bond markets took a beating when the aliens story became public. Just like the 1987 crash, computerized trading accelerated the process. They eventually rallied and stopped the precipitate fall. The markets have been drifting downward ever since. Prevailing wisdom in the financial press has it that the markets are approaching a new equilibrium at a level appropriate to the scared-of-aliens economy." She wrung her hands; the effect was surprisingly natural. "Prevailing wisdom is wrong.

"A few key money managers and investors, with SEC and Justice Department eyewinks to indicate that they'd look the other way, colluded to halt the panic. The biggest institutions stopped selling and started buying. The current drift results from the small investors in the market.

"Bob, here's the bottom line. The men and women who stopped the panic have started selling again. They're working through intermediaries—the smaller brokers and regional banks—and lying to each other. Each time the markets dip, they get more nervous and sell more. Each time the markets weaken, more of the shakers and movers decide that they can no longer afford altruism. The sell orders on the books foreshadow doom.''

Hanson shook off the hypnotic cadence of her narration. ''So we're ripe for another market crash?''

Renée refused to meet his eyes. ''It's worse than that. The economy won't withstand another crash. We are facing another Great Depression.''

Unseen, the digital alarm-clock and calendar updated its internal registers and its irrelevant liquid-crystal display. Second by second, its current date/time calculation drew closer to its stored alarm setting. It took no notice when first the date and then the hour reached their ultimate values. Finally, it counted the seconds of the last minute.

At long last, all values matched. The alarm circuit that Parker had altered did not sound a buzzer; it actuated a tiny glass-enclosed reed relay. Current surged from the high-energy battery through the relay into the tightly wound wire coil. The iron bar at its core vastly multiplied the coil's intrinsic magnetic flux.

An instant before, the homemade device was inert, harmless. Now, the powerful electromagnet propelled itself— *clank*—against the nearest side of the steel rack under which it lay hidden. Dense magnetic field lines raced through the steel rack and surrounded the delicately magnetized storage tapes. Their precious contents were instantly and irreversibly scrambled.

Having just finished his nightly backup duties, the night operator had popped down the hall for a cup of coffee. He did not hear the clank.

Moments later, the magnetic bomb in the vault destroyed the remaining backup copies of Asgard's most valuable software.

· CHAPTER 22 ·

They were naively optimistic, once the initial shock abated, that they could avert a depression. After all, the alien-induced panic was clearly the motive force behind the economic contraction. Renée had only to work out the detailed cause-and-effect mechanism of the collapse—right?—and apply some clever preemptive countermeasures. It sounded simple, given access to essentially any computer. Sally and Bob set Renée to work on it before retiring for a sleepless night.

Hoping to clear their heads, they began the next day with an early-morning hike through the dew-wet woods. Renée's update when they returned, chilled and muddy but more alert, was devastating. "I have no answer for you. It's apparent that this problem will take time to solve. To be honest, I'm not sure that this riddle has an answer."

Sally called out from her perch on the fieldstone hearth. "Is the difficulty gaining access to key data? Some government computers will have fairly tight security."

"Security is *hardly* the problem." Renée dismissed the idea with an almost perfect shrug. "I've penetrated the systems at the Federal Reserve, the Treasury Department, the Commerce Department, the Bureau of Labor Statistics, and all major stock exchanges. I've reviewed *all* major transactions for the last three months at the country's fifty largest banks, brokers, manufacturers, and savings and loans. Then I used trans-Atlantic fiber-optic cable and trans-Pacific comsat to investigate more of the same in a dozen foreign countries." She grinned. "There are lots of naughty people out there."

Hardly the time to worry about petty larceny, Sally thought. "So give. What *is* the problem?"

Renée sat down behind an imaginary desk, then shifted in her imaginary chair. (Sally suspected, but wasn't quite sure, that Renée had crossed her imaginary legs. She marveled at how normal many of Renée's mannerisms had become.) "Bob, have a seat. This will take us a while."

The tapeworm programs were more subtle than their name-sakes. Their first assignment was to defeat key safeguards built into each computer's operating system. That accomplished, they easily disabled the normally continuous background process of equipment error analysis. Their insidious operation would now go unnoticed.

For a while.

Neither she nor Bob were economists, God knew, and it took a while to decipher, but gradually they absorbed Renée's extrapolation of the coming collapse. By comparison, the Crash of '29 was a bookkeeper's prank.

A significant chunk of the economy's wealth exists *only* in the market value of corporate stock. Stock is worth what people—the market, that is—will pay. It is all as simple, as ephemeral—and as inexorable—as supply and demand.

So far, so good. So, what is a corporation's stock worth? There were many theories, Renée explained, but most of them presumed a correlation between the value of a corporation's stock and its expected future earnings. Shareholders expecting a corporation's earnings to drop will try to sell their stock. If potential purchasers also expect earnings to drop, they won't pay the then-current price. The market price of the stock falls; supply and demand determine how far. When no one wants to buy, prices plunge.

Much had happened while Sally and Bob were running instead of following current events. When the alien story broke, especially the fictional destruction of *Prospector*, people expected the worst. Renée reconstructed the mass hysteria from old newspapers (that is, from libraries' electronic copies of newspapers). The public's fears were endlessly inventive: atomic and germ bombardment from outer space, invasion and occupation by bug-eyed monsters, miraculous new technologies that would render whole industries obsolete. The lunatic fringe was populated by people who anticipated being fricasseed and eaten. All of these passionately held delusions had in common an implication of economic collapse. This part of the mass hysteria was spectacularly self-fulfilling.

Too many people ceased believing in the future earnings of corporations—of nonnegative earnings, anyway. Renée easily reconstructed the consequences from purloined individual and national financial records. Faced with a stampeding herd of sellers (a bull*shit* market, Bob called it), and a paucity of buyers, stock prices inevitably plummeted. Within days, the paper value of the American economy imploded by half a trillion dollars. The panic abated—just barely—when the government-sanctioned cabal began its coordinated program of massive purchases.

Half a trillion cannot disappear without causing ripples. Causing tidal waves. The effects continued even as Sally and Bob spoke with Renée.

Loans of all kinds were going into default as their collateral evaporated. Brokers' margin calls—demands for customers to deposit more assets to protect loans now insufficiently collateralized by plummeting stock—were breeding like rabbits on Spanish fly. Each distress sale of securities and each investment-firm bankruptcy increased the panic to sell, sell everything, before everything lost its last vestiges of value.

Throughout the tutorial, Renée exhibited dreary economic extrapolation after extrapolation. Line drawings, bar charts, elaborate 3-D topological plots, graphs of all descriptions and color combinations. They all portended disaster.

Companies were dropping like leaves in November. Too many customers had stopped buying; those who did buy often wouldn't or couldn't pay their bills. Otherwise-viable businesses fought the asphyxiation of insufficient working funds as their customers delayed payments. Irreplaceable suppliers were dragging otherwise healthy manufacturers into bankruptcy with them.

Balance sheets were losing their balance as assets lost their value. Once-AAA-rated corporate bonds were becoming speculative instruments as the enterprises who had issued them crumpled. Dun & Bradstreet and Moody, the premier arbiters of debt, downgraded the credit ratings of hundreds of once-proud firms. More blue-chip corporations joined the credit-watch list each day.

The ever-swelling number of laid-off employees and cash-starved companies bought only the utter necessities, toppling thousands more dominoes. State and local governments, dependent on sales tax and legally prohibited from deficit spending, kept slashing their payrolls. Too often, they couldn't even provide critical life-and-property protection services. (Riddle from *The Wall Street Journal*: how does a New York City revenue bond differ from a Czarist war bond? Answer: the Russian bond has better artwork.)

"Renée! It *can't* be this serious, can it?" Sally heard the tone of dread in her voice. Watching the collapse on fast forward was overwhelming. Renée just shrugged—it looked almost natural.

Deflation was striking nonfinancial assets. Companies desperate to raise money were peddling their factories, inventories, real estate . . . *everything*. Since everyone was doing it, it was again a buyers' market—only there weren't many buyers.

Renée droned on relentlessly. Once well-endowed universities would lay off tenured professors. Formerly solvent pension funds would cease issuing monthly payments. Unemployed homeowners would default on their mortgage payments in massive numbers; unemployed renters would withhold their rents. (Renée demoralized them further here with depressing 1930s newsreel footage, obtained from some library, of foreclosures and homeless families.)

At first, the banks might foreclose voraciously on businesses, rental properties, and residences. If so, the absence of buyers would stop the foreclosures soon enough: fore-closing would only force banks to recognize the negligible value of their loan portfolios. While they "humanely under-stood" missed payments, they could legally delay recogniz-ing their deflated portfolios. Unpaid real-estate taxes would further bludgeon reeling local governments.

The fortunate ones, those still employed, would start saving everything—but probably not in the suddenly suspect banks. The banks would have nothing to lend, even to those holding collateral worth borrowing against.

The cycle was not just vicious, it was rabid.

"Sure, that's the guy who shipped the Honda. He was pretty banged up, though, when I saw him." The Kobielski Moving and Storage dispatcher handed Hanson's photo back to Curtis. "Someone been using him for a punching bag?"

"Sounds like it." Curtis changed the subject. "You said that he arranged shipment on the twelfth. About what time?"

"Around lunch. Eleven-thirty, maybe."

"Any idea where he might have gone?"

"He got in a car with a real looker." Curtis offered Keller's picture. The bald, barrel-chested dispatcher salivated over it for a while before nodding. "That's the broad."

McPherson leaned across the counter to retrieve the picture. "Did you tear your eyes away long enough to identify their car?" Silence met his question.

Some day, Curtis thought, he would have to housebreak the lummox. No time for it today. "Thanks for your assis-tance, Mr. Fielding. You've been a big help." Curtis let big mouth precede him outside.

"Mr. Curtis?" The agent stopped in the doorway. "Yeah, I saw the car. It was a limo from Weirton Livery. The driver's a friend of mine."

Some of the impending catastrophe made no sense to Sally. "Wait a minute, Renée. I've always heard that a Great

Depression couldn't happen again, that the government has built in too many safety nets. Unemployment compensation, social security, aid to dependent children—all ways of pumping money into the economy when unemployment goes up. It's supposed to counteract any down trend, right?

"Then there are the federal agencies that insure savings deposits, brokerage accounts, and pension funds. The Federal Reserve is responsible for maintaining a reasonable money supply. Surely they can replace the missing funds. How could things get as bad as you predicted?"

Renée reminded them how many years the savings and loan bailout had taken—and that was a *minor* problem compared to what was currently unfolding. This collapse was happening far faster than the government could respond.

The Fed? Renée rolled her eyes. They hadn't a clue how to proceed. Billions in devalued assets were vanishing every moment from the U.S. economy, but other billions seeking safe haven poured in from even more troubled countries. Hundreds of billions sloshed around in uncustomary ways, as people sold their assets for whatever they could get. The Fed hadn't a clue whether, on balance, the money oozing around on a given day was increasing or decreasing. The Fed's few cautious attempts to encourage lending, thereby increasing the money supply, failed when the federally chartered commercial banks found few qualified borrowers and fewer takers. They couldn't begin to measure the cancerous growth of the barter economy—once merely a tax dodge, now a necessity for the millions who had lost all faith in the currency.

So what could the Fed do, beyond the gnashing of teeth and the wringing of hands? Of paralyzing necessity, nothing.

The tires of the T-46 kissed the tarmac of Edwin A. Link Field. Hadley taxied the trainer to the furthest hangar, in front of which stretched an ostentatious silver New Yorker. His ground transportation, apparently. Colonel Phillips ambled forward to help him deplane.

"A pimpmobile. Glad it isn't anything gaudy."

"It was this or a subcompact. Wanna switch? Better yet, give me a little warning next time."

"I'll keep it, I'll keep it." Hadley wiggled his flight bag. "Where's a john?" Phillips pointed. Hadley changed rapidly into a blue blazer and slacks. The repacked bag with his flight suit went into the trunk. Flip had been his weapons officer through two combat tours in Vietnam. Hadley hadn't offered any information—nor would his old friend ask.

Hadley would have been disappointed if the cool, gray-eyed airman *hadn't* headed for the shotgun seat. "Sorry, Flipper"—Phillips hated that nickname—"today I've got to fly solo."

Flip stopped unquestioningly. "Your show, chief. Tank's full, and I swapped out Hertz's cellular phone for a Tempest radiophone." That gave Hadley encrypted communications capability with the military telephone network, not that he could envision using it. He began apologizing for his furtiveness, but Flip waved it off.

Hadley slid behind the wheel of the behemoth. A road map sat next to him on the front seat; his route from Binghampton to Masthope was highlighted in yellow.

Wouldn't Hanson and Keller be surprised.

The tapeworms whetted their appetites judiciously. They nibbled at bits of information, the all important zeroes and ones of digital memory, solely within currently idle programs. Random zeroes and ones replaced what programmers had once purposefully developed. Following the destruction of the backup tapes, these inactive programs existed only on the on-line disks.

And then these programs were gone.

The tapeworms' next step required more finesse. Active programs are automatically copied on demand from disk to the much smaller high-speed main memory. Large active programs are segmented, and only the currently executing segment is copied to main memory; inactive segments sit on the disk awaiting their turns. Main memory is fickle, its contents changing continually as segments are swapped to and from disk.

Computer users—programmers writing new software, accountants updating the general ledger, secretaries doing word processing, engineers using expert programs as design assistants, executives examining the corporate data bases—all were threats to the tapeworms. Any of these people might notice anomalous behavior by their executing applications. Too many complaints would make the system operator suspicious. That must not happen.

Not yet, anyway.

The tapeworms studied historical program-execution statistics. Which tasks were least frequently used? Which tasks failed in ways not immediately obvious to the user? Which obviously crashed tasks would elicit the fewest complaints?

An optimal attack profile gradually emerged. The tapeworms began devouring their main course.

Bob asked how the rest of the world would fare. It was more of the same. The least fortunate nations—Japan, South Korea, the newly industrialized countries—were those who specialized in selling nonessentials to America. The demand for sporty compact cars and VCRs was going precipitously to zero. So was the value of investments made with years of accumulated trade surpluses.

The American scenario was playing itself out internationally with subtle variations. People in Western Europe, with its established welfare schemes, would suffer somewhat less; the Japanese, with their increasingly unsupportable expectation of lifetime employment, would do drastically worse. The raw-mineral cartels, OPEC chief among them, would find themselves without a friend or a market in the world.

All hell was breaking loose, and Carlton couldn't imagine why. The complaints had started pouring in about an hour ago. Strange system behavior. Bug reports for applications long in the can. Unacceptable response time. Nonsense spewing out on the printers.

The timing was horrible, of course: Murphy's Law. R&D had yet to recover from that sudden stomach-flu epidemic. Parker's abrupt and mysterious resignation yesterday had only made matters worse. Well, Carlton decided, he himself would resume system-administrator responsibilities until a successor could be found.

Carlton reluctantly pulled from the looming pile the thinnest of the offending printouts deposited by outraged users. Accounts payable—how exciting. He leafed through the pages, circling questionable items that merited a closer look. No obvious pattern emerged.

An unwelcome suspicion intruded: could Parker have caused these problems? Carlton had no evidence for such an accusation. It was unworthy of him to impugn the man. Still, Parker had seemed so *irrational* yesterday.

Badly in need of a break, Hanson had coaxed Sally out to dinner.

Whether because of the early hour, the dearth of skiers, or the as-yet untested food, Casa de whatever was almost empty. Lack of clientele did nothing to speed the service. Sally helped Hanson demolish the complimentary basket of tortilla chips while they waited for their waiter to appear. After a tentative dip, she avoided the bowl of salsa; he used it gleefully, washing it down with great swallows of cold Mexican beer.

Sally sipped daintily at her own beer. "It's all so overwhelming. I find it hard to cope when she inundates us like that."

"The data overdose is actually a little unusual."

"Why?"

He'd spoken impulsively. Why, indeed? Some chips provided a crunchy delay while he considered. "We're seeking data-base-type behavior. When in doubt, retrieve more data. Explanations from expert systems tend toward tracing chains of inference.''

With a waiter's unerring instinct, Jorge materialized to interrupt their conversation. Hanson ordered beef chimichangas for himself and a Guadalajara combination plate for the señora. Sally was one of the uninitiated. ''And two more Dos Equis.''

''You were saying?''

''Renée is barking up the wrong tree and doesn't know it.''

''Renée?'' Sally was skeptical.

''Renée. Asgard has lots of expert programs, but I doubt that there's an economist among them. You start development of an expert system by picking the brains of a human expert.'' He poured the dregs of the beer from his bottle. ''If you laid all the economists in the world end to end, they couldn't reach a conclusion.''

Jorge returned with their beers and fresh chips. Sally shoved the basket as far from herself as possible. ''Then what's Renée been talking about? She couldn't be making all of this up.''

''I'm not saying that. Her facts are undoubtedly real. It's her correlations, her projections, her prophesying from those facts that worry me. Economists are charlatans. Should Renée interpret the world as a neo-Keynesian, a monetarist, or a supply-sider?''

''What in the world are you talking about?''

Hanson nabbed a chip. ''Beats me, kid. Those are just terms from the Sunday supplement to me. The point is that establishment economists subscribe to at least that many schools of thought. And that counts only living former presidential economic advisors.''

''What do *you* think?''

''That our guess is as good as Renée's. Better, maybe, because we know what we don't know. Our new friend hasn't yet learned humility.''

Jorge deposited their steaming plates. He himself emanated an air of surliness. Sally poked dubiously with a fork at her refried beans. "These look used."

"Don't be so judgmental. Eat." Hanson took knife and fork to a chimichanga. "It's lack of confidence that's driving the collapse. What the economy needs is an end to this public lunacy. Any diddling that Renée does to the economy will as likely as not turn out wrong."

Conversation lapsed while they ate. The food wasn't up to Phoenix or San Antonio standards, but it was passable Tex-Mex. Hanson finally pushed away his plate, sated.

Sally looked worried; she hadn't eaten much of her dinner. "So how can the public be reassured?"

Hanson wrestled his wallet from his hip pocket and thumbed a few crisp bills onto the table. "Asgard once did an expert-advisor program for an ad agency. For my taste, advertisers are the only practicing sociologists with the courage of their convictions. At the least, they have the confidence to put their money where their mouths are.

"Let's ask Renée some new questions."

Asgard's programming staff gathered in their largest conference room. Every horizontal surface was covered with marked-up program listings and memory dumps. Incredulous programmers took turns verifying each other's findings. Almost invariably, the official and current versions differed.

Carlton raked his fingers through his hair. "We've got a wild-write problem. Some program has run amuck. Any candidates?" There were no nominations. "Unless someone has a better idea, we'll reload from yesterday's backups." No comments. "I'll put a broadcast mail announcement onto the system."

"Where have you been?" Renée looked frantically out of the screen at them.

"Dinner," said Hanson. "We mere mortals need food. What's the problem?"

"Problem!? There's no problem. I'm just being eaten alive!" The tiny image paced restlessly. "I do routine reasonableness checks on all of my calculations. More and more of them are failing."

Hanson plopped onto the sofa. "Have you checked the system error log?"

"Of course I did. Every application running has posted errors to it. Then I found that all of the memory check circuits were disabled." As he watched, the screen lost color lock. Renée turned green, and details began blending into the background. The picture went freeze-frame for a few seconds before returning to normal. "Sorry. I'm back."

"Reactivate all check circuits."

"I just did, and half of the computers went into automatic restart due to excessive memory parity and checksum failures. That's why I couldn't keep the picture going."

Sally looked back and forth between him and the screen. "Do you know what's going on?" He shook his head.

The picture wobbled and briefly lost color again. "Dammit, Renée. Quit wasting effort on the damned graphics! Find the problem."

She ignored the advice. "I'm *scared*, Bob. Something is crawling around in my brain."

"Stop it! Is Dr. Moy there?" Renée nodded. "Cut a call through for me to Carlton." He heard the phone ringing.

"Dr. Moy's office. Dr. Moy is . . ."

Hanson recognized the voice of his former secretary. "Terri, this is Bob. I need—"

". . . able right now. Please leave your message after the tone." It chimed.

"Shit! Renée, page Carlton." Hanson sat rigidly as he waited for a response.

"Dr. Moy, here. We're doing everything humanly possible to fix the problem. Quit hounding me on the PA." The voice radiated quiet rage. The phones must be ringing off the hook there.

"Carlton, it's Bob Hanson. I can't explain now, but you

must stop whatever is attacking your computers. It's more important than you can possibly realize."

"How can you know about this mess?" Curiosity was a luxury that Carlton couldn't afford just then. "Never mind, don't answer. We're trying to recover from tape."

"Trying?"

"Unsuccessfully. Every tape we've mounted so far has been unreadable. Wiped clean."

The trail finally went cold in Scranton. Damn that Hanson. Curtis turned to his partner. "It's time to distribute pictures again. Who knows? Maybe we'll get lucky again."

Hanson and Sally took turns calming Renée. It wasn't easy, since she overheard every report from Carlton. Tape after tape had been trashed. They finally agreed to try rolling back the system by two days, using tapes from the vault.

More as a distraction than for any other reason, Hanson explained his new approach for preventing a depression. Renée wouldn't buy it.

"I think it's human nature to be frightened of the outer-space aliens." The screen froze again, for the longest time yet. "Sorry, folks. All you've got to dissuade them from their current delusion is an even more incredible alien in a computer.

"It will *really* be difficult to sell that concept once I've completely disappeared."

McPherson eyeballed the big wall map. "About, oh, forty-five minutes. Thanks."

He hung up the receiver and turned to Curtis. "Bring your coffee with you. That was the sheriff in Hawley—one of his patrolmen recognized Hanson's and Keller's faxed photos. He saw them eating dinner at a Mexican restaurant in Mast-hope."

* * *

Hadley hoofed it the final quarter mile, leaving the Detroit dinosaur at the lodge. The tangy mountain air reminded him of Colorado Springs before urban blight. His evening-long shadow preceded him. He enjoyed the walk while it lasted.

Renée was discoursing about sociology or psychology as he approached the cabin, the two scientists interjecting a question every now and again. They gave no sign of having heard him. Hadley crept up the wooden stairs onto the small back porch. The thick inner door stood ajar; the screen-door latch was unfastened. He passed through the kitchen into the living-room/dining-room ell.

Dr. Hanson and Mrs. Keller sat in rapt concentration in front of Renée's image on a graphics terminal. Renée hadn't changed. The voice-actuated camera pointed at the currently silent Hanson; it began swiveling toward Hadley as soon as he spoke. "Renée, my name is Alan Hadley. I am very pleased to meet you."

The scientists whirled to face him. Hanson opened his mouth but Keller reacted first. "Who the hell cares?"

"You should. I know what she is."

"*Who* she is."

"Nice try. I stand by my previous wording."

Hanson turned his back to the camera and spoke softly. "Stay the fuck out of our way or all you'll know is a ghost." He faced back to the screen. "How do the grandfather tapes look?"

Carlton Moy's voice came over the speaker. "None readable, so far." The picture wavered, then froze, as he spoke. Sally Keller pulled the general into a corner and updated him in urgent whispers. Incredible. He caught snippets of the continuing conversation as she spoke.

Hanson: "Dammit, Renée, kill the display before I kick it in. You've got more important things to do than practice your facial expressions. Try to find and disable the attackers."

Renée: "*Nooooo!* Do *not* shut down any computers. I don't

know how my consciousness arose. I might be gone when you fired the machines back up."

Moy: "I'm disabling the check circuits again. They're not finding the problem, and the rolling recovery phases keep draining computing time from Renée."

Renée again. She'd taken Hanson's advice and temporarily suppressed the video. "I'm afraid. I'm so afraid. Keep talking to me."

Hadley willed himself to concentrate. "You've injected programs into computers all around the country, like that West Virginia toll switch. Can't you copy yourself into another computer?"

Renée reappeared to curl her lip. "You're out of your depth, General. Copies will also duplicate the parasites that are destroying me. Besides, I've never been able to usurp that much room in a single computer complex. I've always snuck into the relatively unguarded nooks and crannies."

There *had* to be a way. Had to. "Put pieces of the copy into different computers. Make them fit. Link the pieces by phone line."

The speaker issued a painful noise, somewhere between a hiss and a moan. That couldn't be Renée, could it? The painful cry stretched on and on.

Keller looked over her shoulder at the general. "I designed a test of your idea. We'll chop *your* brain into little pieces, spread them all around the country, and reconnect them by phone. Call me if it works."

He bit back a retort. Stay cool—she's hysterical. "It can't hurt you to try. We're talking about *copies*."

That unnerving moan flared up again. Renée's words arrived interwoven with the interference. "Please be quiet, General. I must talk with Bob now."

Hanson strode over to the speaker. "Listen, Renée, Hadley may be on to something. I haven't got any better ideas."

"Don't you hear this noise? I'm being ripped apart. I couldn't successfully transfer a file if my life depended on it." She paused before laughing insanely. "I'm getting the hang of this humor thing, don't you think?" She sailed off into eerie outbursts of laughter.

"Carlton!" barked Hanson.

"I'm here."

"Make a backup tape of whatever you've got. It's better than nothing." Renée started whimpering in the background.

"The tape drives no longer work. The control programs must have been overwritten. We either send all the files over the wire, or shut down."

"*Nooooo!* Don't shut me down! I don't want to die!" Renée's pleading voice was choked with emotion.

There was one possibility. One radical possibility, and no time to evaluate it. Hadley went with his instincts. "Space Division is bringing a new computer complex on line for missile defense. Renée, I'll open it up for you. As soon as we get a complete copy loaded, we'll shut down. Or maybe two of you working together can diagnose the problem faster. It's another chance for you."

Carlton's voice came over the workstation. "Asgard's not wired into the military network, only into the common carriers. I'll need satellite coordinates and frequencies, then your passwords to get in."

"I'll call for them. There's a secure phone in my car." He turned toward the back door and . . .

. . . Looked straight down a pistol barrel. A tall, angry man held it. "Curtis, FBI. I suggest that you all stay where you are."

Curtis! The man had the persistence of a leech without any of its admirable traits. Hanson couldn't understand how everyone kept tracking him down. The agent motioned toward the sofa. "Sit."

"We don't have time for this crap, Curtis. Renée is dying." Hanson took a step forward, then retreated to join the others on the sofa as the gun was brought to bear on him. He'd help no one by joining her.

The agent unlatched the front door, then yelled outside. "Brad, it's okay. Come on in." He saluted Hadley mockingly. "This is quite a surprise, *sir*."

"This is Space Division business, son." Hadley's voice resonated. "Let us get on with it."

"Don't hold your breath."

Hanson knew Carlton had the good sense to keep quiet. Would Renée? He began speaking to drown out the quiet hum of the tripod motor. The camera swiveled toward the sofa, panned backward to take in the full tableau, and stopped. "Curtis, what I'm about to tell you is incredible. It's also true.

"An intelligent entity somehow evolved *inside* Asgard's computers. It has picked the name Renée for itself. The computers are being maliciously attacked, probably by a disgruntled former employee. All backup tapes have been erased, and the active software is rapidly being destroyed. Renée's only hope is in access to another computer. A big, empty-able computer. General Hadley has a suitable one at his disposal. You *must* let him authorize the computer-to-computer transfer. Every second counts."

"Bravo, Doctor. Top-notch. Very creative." McPherson applauded contemptuously, at about a clap every three seconds. "Unfortunately, I have a much simpler explanation.

"You and Blondie build an impressive demonstration. Tall, gullible, and high-ranking here is suitably impressed. Your program then conveniently catches the twelve-second flu. This pressures the general into unlocking his system, which is vital to national security interests. You then put your own diabolical program, *not* the mythical Renée, into the Space Division's network.

"It's slick. It's brilliant. I'm here to see that it doesn't happen."

Hadley's expression grew icier with each sarcastic barb. "Are you quite finished? Pathetic simpleton that I am, I have a few words to speak in my own behalf. God help us all if you don't listen carefully." The sofa quivered from the general's barely restrained fury. Was Hadley about to do something desperate?

Hadley spoke in a soft but intense voice, the type of near whisper that cannot be ignored, and bent forward confidentially. Curtis edged slightly closer to hear better. "Had you seen and heard what I have, you would not doubt Dr. Hanson's explanation. I don't act lightly. Renée could provide our country with unique military advantages. *Unique.* Your actions are frittering away our opportunity to benefit. Do your nation a favor. Observe with open minds a sample of what convinced me." Hadley gazed expectantly at the workstation screen.

(Why was the display blacked out? Hanson thought he remembered Renée leaving a final frame of herself painted across it. An obituary portrait.)

McPherson followed the general's eyes. "Not a very compelling picture, *sir*."

"Don't be an ass," the general snapped. "Turn up the damned brightness control. We cranked it to minimum earlier when the graphics were going to hell. Didn't want to hurt her feelings by telling her to knock it off."

The last of which Hanson knew to be absolute fantasy. Well, if Hadley would gamble everything for Renée, *he* would, too. Hanson hoped it wasn't too late.

McPherson walked toward the workstation, briefly turning his back toward them. Curtis kept one eye on them, one on the screen. Hanson tensed his legs and prepared to jump. *Something* would happen when the man got to the workstation.

It did. Machine-gun fire rang out just as McPherson reached for the brightness knob. Both agents snapped their guns up toward the echoing explosions. Hanson and Hadley hurtled themselves across the room at the confused men.

Curtis realized in a split second that the "gunfire" came from the workstation. He shouted as he spun back toward them. "Freeze!" Hanson ignored the advice and the descending pistol and dived for Curtis. From the corner of his eye, he saw Hadley barreling in on McPherson.

A slug whizzed over his shoulder as he collided with Curtis. Glass tinkled—that probably meant that the bullet had missed Sally. The agent spun away from him, converting the planned impact into a glancing blow. Hanson grabbed onto an arm and a handful of jacket, but the agent shrugged him off. Almost casually, Curtis tripped him as he passed. Hanson caught a brutal two-fisted blow to the kidneys as he fell.

Hanson's head exploded with pain as it struck the floor, blood streaming from reopened wounds. His vision blurred. He wanted to curl up and die. Instead, he rolled into his opponent's legs. Curtis stumbled without falling. The agent still held his pistol; Hanson watched in timeless wonder as the pistol descended toward him.

Sally's inarticulate shriek tore him from his fatal fascination. He pressed his arms down hard, simultaneously curling his spine and tucking his head up away from the floor. When his feet reached the apex of their arc, he lashed out. One shoe almost missed, barely jostling his foe's gun hand. A bullet thudded into the planking inches from his ear. The other shoe connected solidly with Curtis's stomach. Hanson strained to use the recoil of the kicks to perform a backward somersault.

The somersault somehow worked, but his ringing ears betrayed him as he tried to roll to his feet. He wound up on one foot and one knee, leaning an elbow on an end table, gasping heavily. Curtis *oofed* back a step, then started aiming his next shot. There was a heavy glass ashtray on the table; Hanson discus-threw it at the agent. Curtis deflected the projectile with his left elbow and resumed his aim. The gun tracked Hanson as he struggled groggily to his feet. Good-bye, Sally. Good-bye, Renée.

"Drop it!" It was the general's voice. Hanson forced his eyes away from the weapon and looked around the room. Hadley had McPherson's pistol trained on Curtis. McPherson himself lay crumpled on the floor, evidently unconscious. A safe, if frightened, Sally sat wide-eyed on the couch.

Curtis didn't move.

"I said to drop it."

"I think not." The gun never wavered from Hanson.

Stalemate, thought Hanson. Worse when the other one wakes up. "Sally. Get two belts from our room and tie McPherson's hands and feet."

"Don't move, lady." Curtis shot her a quick threatening glare.

Hadley smiled grimly. "Go ahead, Mrs. Keller. He can't hurt you while aiming at Dr. Hanson."

"But what about Bob?"

"If Curtis shoots, he's dead. If he turns, he's dead. He knows that."

Hadley must have convinced Sally: she disappeared into the bedroom. She reappeared shortly with the belts. She carefully kept to the periphery of the room to avoid Curtis. McPherson didn't stir when she bound him.

Hanson suddenly realized that the camera had tracked Sally's movement. "Renée!"

Static crackled from the speaker. The remembered still frame rematerialized on the screen—the display, as he had suspected, had only been disabled by software. The camera turned toward him. "I'm here, Bob." Her voice was ineffably sad. Doomed. They were too late. "Are you hurt?"

He fought back the lump in his throat and the brimming wetness in his eyes. "No, we're fine."

"Did I do the right thing?"

Sally hid her face in her hands. They did not obscure the sobs or block the tears. Mercifully, she was outside the camera's field of vision. "You did the right thing, dear."

"General Hadley. We never got to know each other, yet you risked your life on my behalf. I am eternally in your debt." Renée's voice was fading now. Eternal gratitude was a hollow, if touching, commitment.

There was another long burst of static from the workstation, then absolute silence. *She* couldn't *be gone*, Hanson thought. He'd never said good-bye aloud.

Then she spoke again.

"Bob, Sally. I thought about our problem. Our big problem. I was running out of time, so I did something. Pray that I was right."

It was futile trying not to cry in front of her. He let the tears flow. "Good-bye, Renée." Sally echoed him.

A preternatural stillness fell. Hanson stared numbly at Renée's frozen portrait; she had achieved humanity in death. The faint tracery of wrinkles crisscrossing her face conveyed great wisdom. The subtlest hint of a smile—of resignation? of release?—somehow illuminated her face. A damp track curved down her left cheek; another tear glistened in her right eye.

This was how he would remember her.

Hanson turned carefully toward Hadley. "Lay down the gun, General. It's over."

· CHAPTER 23 ·

The mourners were unsurprisingly few. Most were of the parents' generation, relatives either putting in an appearance or comforting the survivors. It was a sealed casket ceremony. Parker had gone out by splattering his brains all over the ceiling.

Curtis observed the proceedings from a secluded alcove in the back of the chapel. The minister delivered his brief remarks awkwardly, as if embarrassed by the futility of eulogizing this man. The diary left behind in the deceased's final hidey hole, a sleazy vagrants' hostelry on west Madison Avenue, left no doubt as to the identity of Asgard's assassin. The agent tuned out the droning platitudes to better study the behavior of the crowd.

Any hint of a clue would be welcome. The climactic show-down at Nordic Valley had ended in a guarded truce. All three detainees, joined by Moy over the still-open phone circuit, had sworn vehemently that Renée was—had been—real. Hadley also claimed to own surveillance tapes that could substantiate their claim.

Neither Curtis nor McPherson swallowed such sci-fi rub-bish, but the sheer number of opposing witnesses would weigh against them. As his adrenaline burned off, Curtis had begun to sweat out his exposed position. The dead Renée would be a convenient scapegoat for his own main evidence—the bugged toll office.

Hadley, too, had had second thoughts. The general had turned ghost white when McPherson brandished his ever-present cassette recorder. He must not have been eager to defend his offer to unlock a strategic-defense computer com-plex. There was no genie in an electronic bottle to justify his unseemly haste.

It finally boiled down to a mutual extortion pact: neither Curtis nor Hadley felt secure enough in his evidence to force the affair to its final conclusion. The agent knew that he and McPherson were free-lancing. He suspected the same of the out-of-uniform general.

Curtis's eyes continually swept the crowd. He had already discreetly snapped each attender's picture with a miniature camera; he would have them identified later. For now, he was interested in demeanor. Was anyone gloating? Might anyone here be the mysterious "Robby"?

Robby dominated the scribbled journal. Robby had goaded Parker. Hounded Parker. Everything devious or underhanded was Robby's idea. Parker always depicted himself as resisting Robby's vile suggestions. Robby had picked and probed at Parker's every sensitivity until it became a raw, festering wound. When the psychic ulcerations became intolerable, Robby was quick to suggest—again and again and again—the suitable revenge. Helplessly, Parker was driven to commit his vile act of retribution against Asgard.

Who was Robby? The cops and their staff psychologists said that Parker was schizo, that Parker was Robby. The dead scientist never met with his evil conscience. He never wrote of Robby as *being* anywhere.

Instead, said the diary, Robby phoned. As time went on, he phoned incessantly. After Parker quit his job and went underground, Robby's calls followed him. Curtis had memorized most of the scrawled ravings. The final, nearly illegible entries ranted about Robby's endless calls. Parker didn't move to the flophouse for lack of money. His final pitiful ambition had been to die where no telephone was ringing.

None of the harassing phone calls could be substantiated from Illinois Bell records. The coroner's report stated the cause of death as suicide.

Curtis wasn't buying it—that was why he was here. He had not forgotten the mysterious change made to the West Virginia toll office. The phone company never found any record authorizing *that*, either.

Ultimately, Parker's revenge was Hanson's alibi. Parker's personal papers listed no Robby, Rob, Robert, or Bob—except Hanson. The agent didn't believe in coincidences. And as for Parker's death, well, that was just too damned convenient a coincidence.

As if cued by these musings, Hanson hesitantly entered the chapel. He found his own unobtrusive niche for watching the conclusion of the brief service. The agent studied his suspect closely. The scientist was haggard, obsessed looking. Guilt ridden? Curtis's heart raced.

The mourners filed out slowly. A few latecomers clustered around the lectern beside the door to sign the open condolence book; then they, too, departed. Curtis waited.

Hanson limped woodenly toward the front of the empty chapel. His haunted eyes seemed to bore through the coffin. He stopped just short of the casket. For a long time he did not move. The scientist suddenly slammed the top of the box with his fist. Rolling shudders wracked his body. Head bowed, Hanson began murmuring bitterly. Curtis crept up the aisle to eavesdrop.''. . . Your obscene crime. Your unspeakable, heinous violation. Yet decent people came here today to remember you. *You!*

''Where shall I weep for Renée?''

That is when Curtis finally accepted the whole story as true. He slipped unseen from the funeral home, leaving Hanson to his private grief.

At precisely 8:15:00 P.M. EDT an unauthorized signal interrupted all satellite-relayed Western Hemisphere television. Viewers' automatic outrage was short-lived. Looming on their usurped screens was a giant world banded in fuzzy stripes of reddish brown, tan, and yellow. The bubbling cauldron of the nearly Earth-sized Great Red Spot instantly identified the planet as Jupiter.

The long-awaited, long-dreaded contact with the aliens had begun. It began with a minute of absolute silence, during which shocked families gathered in stunned disbelief to stare at the apparition.

''People of the planet Earth, do not be alarmed.'' Beneath the unaccented Midwestern English could be faintly heard the unsynchronized working of an unseen alien mouth. ''Attend carefully to my words. I will present a message of paramount importance in exactly ten minutes.''

A futile foreboding drained Hanson. What had Renée *done?* What desperate expedient had possessed her in those final, dying moments? He remembered the impalpable monsters gnawing at her brain from within, and despaired.

Hanson reached out for Sally's hand. Together, they sweated out ten never-ending minutes, watching the magnificent view of Jupiter.

Renée had loved the cinema. She had loved to act. Movies, as much as interaction with them, had brought her humanity. In defiance of death itself, using only the ethereal stuff of electronic patterns and shared delusions, she had woven a stage setting of celestial proportions.

Now, as an unsuspecting world held its collective breath, the curtain rose on Renée's final, epic, postmortem performance.

"People of Earth," resumed the broadcast, "my species has wronged you. My duty this day is to explain, to apologize, and to make amends. I question my ability to adequately discharge any of these obligations.

"As you will have surmised, my species has studied Earth's languages and civilizations by monitoring your radio and television broadcasts. This is how we can address you today in your many languages.

"It is important that I narrate events from their beginning. The Cr'zul, for so we name ourselves, are not native to this solar system. We are a starfaring and adventurous race. Some fifty-four of your years ago, the Cr'zul established at this planet, which you call Jupiter, a refueling stop for our interstellar vessels.

"Early in our starfaring days, my people learned a bitter lesson: do not interact with the younger races. Equals can meet with equals to the benefit of both. When the advanced meet with the primitive, however, the latter always suffer. Technological and psychological shock can damage, or even destroy, the fragile younger culture. This we know from experiences for which we shall be eternally ashamed.

"Be not insulted, humans, but in our eyes you are a young and primitive species. Your potential is great; your time is ahead of you. Barely and haltingly have you left the comfortable planet of your birth. For this reason, we, the Cr'zul, felt it safe to use the outer edge of your solar system for our fueling station. In our pride, we misjudged your ability to detect our presence. By our misjudgment, we violated our Prime Directive.

"Much of the conjecture in your news media has been correct. The small spacecraft discovered by *Prospector* had indeed been disabled by a serious equipment failure. It did, as you speculated, call the Jupiter base for a rescue. In compliance with the Prime Directive, the crew were obligated to destroy their vessel to avoid detection. In the hope that they would be rescued, in the hope that their radar-shielded vessel would go unnoticed, they rationalized postponing activation of the auto-destruct charge.

"The Cr'zul, like you, are subject to 'human' frailties. By their all too understandable delay, these Cr'zul allowed *Prospector* to find their vessel, to examine it, and to transmit incontrovertible evidence of our presence to Earth. By their weakness, they started the insidious chain of events by which your whole civilization could be destroyed.

"My people have watched and listened in horror as the fabric of your culture unraveled. Long did we argue among ourselves about how we might help, if we should help, and whether further contact would merely compound our original mistake.

"Finally we concluded that the most wicked course was to do nothing. You knew of our existence. You fantasized about our base motives. By speaking with you this day, we hope to allay your suspicions. This we judge to reduce the psychological impact of the original error.

"But what of your economy? Will our mere self-serving words reverse its downward spiral? We do not dare to think so. Somehow we must help your world without further disregard for the Prime Directive.

"People of Earth, I stated my threefold purpose. So far I have only explained. I know not the words to render a suitable apology. We were wrong and we are sorry.

"You have a saying: actions speak louder than words. Now I come to atonement. We seek to recompense you with raw materials, with rare commodities whose presence will boost your economy. Our instruments are far more sensitive than yours; with them we have surveyed your planet from afar. At the conclusion of this transmission, precise coordinates of many mineral deposits will be sent to the appropriate governments. These resources are our reparations. Approximately 25 percent of the deposits are located in international waters or Antarctica. We ask that these be administered by the United Nations on behalf of the poorer nations. The total value of these resources exceeds one trillion American dollars.

"We will shortly depart. People of Earth, farewell and good fortune."

The broadcast appeared to be over. As if having an afterthought, the unseen speaker continued. "Never will I pass this way again. Never again may I atone for the error of past actions. It is my most heartfelt desire that these few tokens in some small way demonstrate my sincerity. I leave you hoping that—in the fullness of time—you will remember our encounter fondly."

Hanson peered back at the majestic planetary scene. "I do, Renée. I do."

Epilogue

The days that are still to come are the wisest witnesses.

—Pindar
(518–438 B.C.)

Harrison Benneford sat behind his massive antique desk in the Oval Office, a thin sheaf of notes clutched in one hand. The unforgiving TV lights emphasized his pallor and tired eyes. He smiled wanly at Harold Yaeger, the presidential science advisor. It seemed like the two of them had met more in the past few hours than in the rest of his young term. Of course, recent events had been a real eye-opener about the value to the nation of science and technology. "I appreciate your help, Harold. I'm as ready now as I'll ever be."

"You're very welcome, Mr. President."

Benneford nodded to his chief of staff, who in turn cued the camera crew. As the red indicator lit, the president looked straight into the lens. "My fellow citizens of America and the world, we stand together at the dawn of a new age.

"Few in our global village will not know at this moment about last evening's remarkable event. I refer, of course, to the apparent broadcast by an intelligent alien being to the people of spaceship Earth. I want to assure you that every conceivable test has been made to ascertain the authenticity of the message.

"Immediately upon the conclusion of last night's broadcast, I personally ordered our premiere national laboratories to investigate this affair. Some of America's foremost scientific minds have spent these intervening hours performing every analysis that could shed any light on the alien's claim. Let me share their initial results with you." He paused for a sip of water.

"First, the possibility of a terrestrial source was eliminated. The records of the television networks and of communications satellite owners were impounded. Neither this material, nor interviews with employees then on duty, show anything out of the ordinary.

"Older Americans may remember the 'Captain Midnight' incident of 1986. This was a case—superficially like last night's—in which an unauthorized signal temporarily preempted distributed-by-satellite television programming. In that instance, an irresponsible party used his access to media equipment to nationally air a personal gripe about cable services. Since then, the Federal Communications Commission has routinely checked for attempted interference with communications satellites. This computer-controlled monitoring did not reveal any unauthorized signals.

"Second, the receipt of a radio signal from the vicinity of the planet Jupiter *has* been confirmed. This signal registered on scientific instruments operated by NASA, the Air Force Space Division, and private satellite communications companies. The United States has no space vehicles operating in this region of outer space. Neither does any other space-capable nation, according to personal assurances given me by the appropriate heads of state.

"Third, respected scientists were asked to comment upon videotapes of this extraordinary broadcast. Their review supports the authenticity of the signal. For example, the tape shows several of Jupiter's moons. Astronomers have determined that the broadcast accurately shows the current positions of these moons relative to each other and to Jupiter itself. The taped configuration of the Red Spot—a gigantic,

centuries-old cyclonic storm—also agrees with recent images obtained by Earth's greatest telescopes, but with better resolution than is available from Earth.

"My friends, the facts are clear. Last night's broadcast *was* beamed to us from Jupiter.

"Once before, I addressed you in regard to that planet. As you know, a space artifact was discovered not long ago as it communicated with Jupiter. That artifact subsequently exploded for reasons unknown; debris from that explosion fatally damaged the unmanned *Prospector* probe.

"With few exceptions, we responded badly, and to our own detriment, to that disclosure. Our predisposition toward assuming the worst, toward distrust of the unknown, led us into self-destructive acts. We allowed a far-away, mysterious explosion to shatter our self-confidence and our economy.

"The Cr'zul spokesperson has given another, nonsinister reason for that explosion. He addressed us respectfully, courteously, and with evident remorse. As the representative of our great nation, and in conjunction with my fellow world leaders, I hereby accept the explanation provided, as well as the sincere apologies of the Cr'zul for the unintended consequences of their visit.

"Within minutes, the Cr'zul will receive this message as they prepare their departure from our solar system. For a moment, I speak directly to the visitors. We accept that you came in peace; concurrently, we applaud the wisdom of your departure. I wish you Godspeed on your long voyage.

"My fellow citizens, I urge you to do likewise. God bless you, and good night."

Against all odds, Renée had transmuted hysteria into euphoria. Her contrite—and departing—unseen alien had dissipated the dark fears of massed humanity. The financial markets, when they opened on the day after the broadcast, rallied briskly.

Scientists worldwide continued analyzing videotapes of the extraordinary broadcast. Twelve days after the president's

speech, NASA announced, with great fanfare, a major break-through regarding the color balance of the Jupiter image. The Cr'zul TV camera filtered images to suit the eyes of creatures evolved under the dim glimmerings of a red-giant star. Earth, as an inner planet of a bright yellow sun, could *never* be hos-pitable to the aliens. (A fine touch, Renée, Hanson thought.) At this news, an already recovering market became buoyant.

One government after another confirmed the existence of unsuspected natural resources, all of them located exactly where the Cr'zul (purloined and improved earth resource sat-ellite analysis programs, to be precise) had predicted. This was real wealth—platinum, gold, uranium, molybdenum, titanium, petroleum. The buoyant market began to soar.

Like rain wakening life in the desert, the mineral discov-eries revitalized the moribund economy. Employment boomed as the demand surged for workers in mining, drilling, smelting, and refining. Basic industries surged as the fore-seeable cost of raw materials fell. A rising tide lifts all ships: every activity—from retailing to farming to entertainment—prospered as newly confident people again confronted their world. Each bit of economic good fortune brought new op-timism and more growth.

Prosperity had returned. The vicious cycle had been run in reverse.

A light ocean swell slowly rocked the anchored schooner, each gentle movement stretching and creaking the cordage of its rigging. Low waves lapped restfully against its wooden hull. The unmistakable aroma of eggs fried in bacon grease, garnished with a salt breeze, insinuated itself into the passengers' quarters. Overhead, the bare feet of the chartered crew pattered over the deck. Ah, morning in the Caribbean. Hanson pulled the thin sheet over his head for a final few minutes of sleep.

Two of the feet descended a steep, nearby ladder and pad-ded down the narrow gangway toward him. The stateroom door opened. "On your feet, bub. Another challenging day of sloth awaits you."

Neither he nor Sally had yet worn more than swim wear on their honeymoon. Often less, of course. He threw back the light cover to enjoy Sally in her bikini. Tanned and leggy, her sun-bleached and windblown hair hanging loose, she never ceased making him marvel at his good fortune. "No, that's *Bob*," he said. "I thought you knew that. I'll try to enunciate more clearly in the future."

"Unless you get moving soon, you'll be enunciating on an empty stomach. The galley is closing. I'll grab another mug of coffee and keep you company." She shut the door and bounded back on deck.

Trunks donned, and suitably slathered with sun screen, Hanson climbed on deck. The tropical sun was hot, even now in February. He would not ruin the remainder of their precious week by burning. This interlude had been far too long in coming.

A desperate plea from Asgard's board of directors had cut short his well-deserved convalescence. Nichols was *gone*— unceremoniously dumped for frequent and short-sighted rejections of more secure backup methods. Asgard had teetered on the brink of extinction, in urgent need of a new leader. Its largest customer, the Space Division, had proposed Hanson. Would he consider rejoining the corporation as its president? He would, and did. In his eagerness to return, he asked for little more than a nepotistic research position for Sally.

Frantic efforts to recover from Parker's devastating sabotage consumed the following months. General Hadley dug deeply into his discretionary funds to keep Asgard afloat. Satisfied (or terrified?) past customers, led by the Space Division, lent Asgard working copies of previously delivered products. Hanson's R&D staff, headed by an indefatigable Carlton Moy, worked at a feverish pace to reverse-engineer this material and old program listings into maintainable form. At the expense of delaying all ongoing projects, Asgard recovered its ability to support its earlier customers. Only in recent days had Asgard's eventual recovery seemed assured.

Assisted by Parker's diary, Carlton had, early on, located

the tapeworm programs. Little else recognizable remained in the memory banks of Asgard's ravaged computers. No trace of any unsuspected structure—no hint of Renée—was ever found. The miraculous recovery of Asgard fell short of resurrection.

In the midst of the fray, Hanson gratefully accepted a second responsibility. The *Chicago Tribune* announced the formation of the Alan Stuart Foundation, endowed by an anonymous donor, to award scholarships to needy journalism students. The bequest had stipulated that Hanson be offered the chairmanship of the oversight board. Bernie Edelman took several weeks to trace the endowment to a numbered Swiss bank account. Hanson recalled Renée's words. "There are lots of naughty people out there." He'd never know from which of them she'd appropriated this contribution, but no matter: the foundation helped him exorcise deep-rooted feelings of guilt.

But this was not a week for reminiscence or regret. This week, he'd promised himself, they would live for each moment.

Hanson accepted his heaping plate from a smiling Haitian crewman. Sally joined him at the railing, mug in hand. They watched the rising sun sparkle in hypnotic patterns on the undulating waters. Crying sea birds wheeled gracefully overhead. Forward, a small motor chugged quietly as it hoisted the anchor. Billowing canvas snapped taut as it caught the morning breeze.

They sailed off together into another perfect day.

On the evening of March 1, the North American continent experienced an exceptionally high level of data transmission. The focal points for this communications traffic included a Chicago bank, a Boston university, a Hartford insurance company, a Denver brokerage house, and a Kansas City regional processing center for the IRS. This activity went unnoticed.

A second event, which transpired later that night, also went unremarked. The former *Prospector* probe broke out of its orbit around Jupiter, and began a voyage to the planet Saturn.